JASON WRENCH

GOALIE &
THE
Geek

Goalie and the Geek
Jason Wrench

Pink Sloth Books

Contents

constant /ˈkänstənt/ • **noun**

1. A quantity or parameter that does not change throughout the execution of a program; a fixed value in a varying equation.

2. The control group against which all other variables are measured. The only element that remains true when the rest of the world is in flux.

entanglement /enˈtaNGɡəlmənt/ • **noun**

1. (Physics) A phenomenon in which a pair of particles interact such that the quantum state of each particle cannot be described independently of the state of the other, even when separated by a large distance.

2. The condition where two variables become inextricably linked; the proof that distance does not result in disconnection.

iterate /ˈitəˌrāt/ • **verb**

To perform a function repeatedly, where the output of one cycle becomes the input for the next. To build upon a previous version, flawed as it may be, to create something stronger.

singular /ˈsiNGɡyələr/ • **adjective**

1. Denoting or referring to just one person or thing; separate; individual.

2. (Mathematics) A matrix that cannot be inverted; a point where a function is not well-behaved.

3. Exception to the rule. Not the state of being alone, but the state of being without equal.

Chapter 1
Home Ice
Advantage

LUKE

Five days into preseason and I was already exhausted. I shouldered my goalie bag and pushed through the propped-open doors of Stony Creek Hall, the August humidity clinging to my post-practice sweat. The lobby, which had been empty for the last week while I got settled, was now a war zone on a Thursday afternoon. Parents maneuvered flatbed carts like battering rams, and the air smelled like floor wax, cardboard, and the frantic stress of a thousand goodbyes.

I dodged a dad carrying a futon and headed for the elevator. Move-in day. The one day I'd been dreading since I picked up my key a week ago.

I'd spent the last week in a quiet rhythm: wake up, two-a-days at the rink, lift, eat, sleep. Room 317 had been my sanctuary. I was guaranteed a single, one of the last on campus. That was the deal Coach Harper had swung for the transfer. Get in, steady the crease, keep the grades serviceable, and prove I could be the starter when the season kicked off in October. And so far, I'd been living up to my end of the bargain in practice. Admittedly, it was just the first week, but the team was good. Their previous goalie graduated, and I'd been recruited from a lower-division college the previous spring.

The elevator lurched open. Two first-years squeezed in with me, one holding a tower of plastic storage bins, the other juggling a mini-fridge. They stared at the massive goalie pad sticking out of my duffel, then at the Frost Demons logo on my dry-fit shirt.

"You guys start already?" Mini-Fridge asked.

"Preseason," I said, pressing the button for the third floor. "Been on the ice a week."

"Nice." He shifted the fridge, grimacing. "Heard the Demons needed a miracle in net this year."

I lifted my eyebrows but let the comment slide. People talked; I stopped caring about unverified opinions two teams ago. The doors opened on three, and I nudged the bag out into a hallway of buzzing fluorescent light and mismatched carpeting.

I headed for 317, anticipating the silence waiting for me. The rest of my day included a shower, a protein shake, and zero human interaction. I reached for my key, ready to unlock my fortress of solitude—and stopped.

The door was unlocked.

Actually, it was cracked open an inch.

My grip tightened on my bag strap. *I swear I locked it.* Routine was the only thing keeping me sane, and locking the door was step one. I pushed it open with my shoulder, ready to tell whoever was confused about their room number to get out.

But the room wasn't occupied; it had been colonized.

A guy my age stood by the far wall—average height, lean in that effortless way runners always looked, with brown hair that probably argued with a comb every morning. He wore a faded Harbor Commons T-shirt and shorts, and he was placing a stack of books onto a second desk that hadn't been there this morning.

Behind him, the room had transformed. My bed was still on the left, but a second bed had been jammed against the right wall. Two dressers. Two desks. One... roommate.

I dropped by gear bag on the ground. The thud made him jump. "Who are you?" I asked.

He turned, holding a mechanical pencil like a dart. His eyes scanned the goalie gear, then my face. "I'm guessing you're Luke." He looked at me, took a couple of steps toward me, and extended his hand, "Austen Lovell."

I didn't take it and watched as he lowered it looking at the scowl crossing my face.

"Yeah, I was guaranteed a single, which is what I've had for the last week. By myself." I gestured around the cramped space. "What is all this?"

"Furniture, mostly." He was annoyingly calm compared to my rising panic. "Housing sent me over about an hour ago. Apparently, the 'single' on your housing contract was a clerical error."

"A clerical error," I repeated flatly.

"That's what they called it when I showed up, and they didn't have a room for me in the system." He pointed to the new bed, which sat about three feet from mine. "I filed for a single too, if it makes you feel better. Neither of us won that lottery."

"But they told me there'd be space."

"And yet, here we are." He looked at me with a scowl that matched my own. "Trust me, this isn't my idea of a good time either."

Heat crawled up my neck. I'd planned for late dorm noise, forced fire drills, the weird smell common rooms developed after midnight. Not this. This was the equivalent to a breakaway before the puck even dropped.

I moved my gear bag by the unclaimed dresser. "Housing must've screwed up. I'll straighten it out."

Austen hummed noncommittally. "If you get a miracle out of them, tell me how you did it. I'll buy you dinner."

The words were casual, but his shoulders stayed tight. He flopped down on his bed, picked up a notebook, and started scribbling away. He was leaving space, letting me set the tone. Fine. Tone would be composed. Controlled.

I pulled my phone, thumbed to the contact sheet they'd emailed earlier, and found the number for housing services. I stepped into the hallway for privacy, closing the door enough to muffle my conversation but not enough to feel like retreating.

Four rings. "Northern Ridge Housing, this is Trish."

"Hi, this is Luke Carter. I checked into Stony Creek Hall, Room 317. I was assigned a single. And I got back from practice to find my room had been invaded along with new furniture."

A keyboard clacked. "Hmm. One moment."

I waited, eyes tracing the cinderblock wall, patches of tape peeled where old decorations had come off. Someone down the hall laughed too loud; a door slammed.

Trish came back. "Looks like the database still shows that room as designated for double occupancy because of fall semester overflow."

"But I was guaranteed a single. My coach guaranteed me a single. I'm on the hockey roster." I hated how that sounded—name-dropping the program—but eligibility had been the reason they'd rush-processed my housing application. Athletic department had pulled strings; that's what Coach Harper told me.

"I understand," Trish said pleasantly. "Unfortunately, we're beyond full capacity. The new dorm construction is behind schedule, so we converted several singles."

"Maybe a different dorm? There's gotta be somewhere on campus."

"Sorry. Right now, we're rearranging some rooms for three occupants and even housing a few first-year students in a local hotel until we iron out campus housing."

"So, what, I just—" I forced my shoulders down. Yelling at staff never helped. "Could you put me on a list? First open single, call me?"

"I'll add your name to the list," she said. "Earliest reassessment date is four to six weeks. Until then, university policy is shared space."

We'd be starting the season by then. Four to six weeks might as well be forever.

"Okay," I said because the alternative was nothing. "Thanks."

I slid the phone into my pocket and rested my head against the wall for a count of three. Plan B. Adapt. That's what goalies do when the play breaks down—square up, track the puck, trust the angle.

Back in the room, Austen hadn't moved. Still sat cross-legged on his bed, holding the mechanical pencil and writing in his notebook. He looked up, expression neutral. "Any luck?"

"I was put on a list, four to six weeks minimum before housing can do anything about this."

He nodded as if he'd anticipated this outcome. I exhaled through my nose and rubbed the crease between my eyebrows.

"Look," he said, without staring up, "I'm not trying to invade your space. This happened fast."

"Pretty sure it's happening to both of us." My tone wasn't sarcastic, more observational.

"I took the empty closet." I glanced at his side. Sweatshirts ordered from dark to light, shoes lined under the bed.

The one where I'd been storing my gear bag, which alone could eat half the floor. "I'll stack my duffel on my desk, for now." I picked it up and placed on the empty desk on my side of the room.

He tapped the pencil against the notebook twice. "Fair enough."

A bang erupted from the wall—metallic pipes protesting like they did every evening around this time. Austen flinched.

"AC unit," I said. "Maintenance hasn't fixed it. Clanks around two a.m. So, if you're a light sleeper—"

"Eight hours of partial differential equations tends to induce coma-level sleep." He shrugged. "I'll adapt."

"Math major?" He nodded. I thought of the intro sequence I'd dodged by choosing business. "Sounds intense."

"Let me guess. Business major?" A flicker of humor—almost a smile—crossed his mouth.

I didn't love how easily he'd clocked me. "That obvious?"

"Hockey player, business degree. It's a statistically reliable pairing." He said it without malice, just observation. "You're clearly not a first-year student, so I take it you transferred here to play hockey?"

"Yeah." I shoved the folder deeper, pretend casual. "Needed the right system."

He nodded like that translated. Maybe it did; I was told hockey in Cold Harbor was local currency.

"One more thing," I said. "The guy next door likes to play EDM at midnight. Thump the wall twice. He'll kill the bass. Still haven't seen him, so have no idea why he moved into the hall early. He's always gone before I am in the morning and comes home much later than I do at night."

"Midnight EDM, two thumps." He mimed knocking. "Noted."

I checked my watch—fifteen past five. Tomorrow's practice started at six sharp, meaning a 4:45 alarm if I wanted pre-ice stretch and coffee. A week ago this room had felt like a sanctuary. Now it felt like a penalty box built for two.

Austen stood, pocketed his phone. "I saw the fridge. Top shelf yours?"

"Yeah. Bottom's free." I'd already claimed my territory—protein shakes lined up beside the peas I used for icing.

"Got it." He grabbed a jacket from the hook he'd commandeered. "I've got a study group at eight. I'm out most nights till eleven, if you want private time."

"Study group? School hasn't even started."

He cocked his head. "You've been here for a week playing hockey and school hasn't started."

"Yeah, but that's practice. We're gearing up for the season."

"And we're gearing up for the school year." He reached for the doorknob, then paused. "Luke?"

"Yeah?"

"I don't mind sharing space. Just communicate, and we'll be fine."

"Copy that," I said, hand lifting in a small salute.

He disappeared into the hallway, footsteps fading. The latch clicked, and the room felt different—smaller, somehow, even with him gone. I sat on the edge of the mattress and braced my elbows on my knees.

Four weeks. I can do anything for four weeks. I closed my eyes, picturing the crease—painted blue, edges sharp. You don't control the team, the refs, the crowd, or the rink. You control the crease. This was the same. Control what's closet-sized and let the rest be noise.

A single had been the plan. Dad always said a plan kept you from sliding. He had plenty of plans, once, until the knee ligament shredded and he slid anyway. I shook off the thought, reached for my phone, and pulled up tomorrow's checklist: 4:45 alarm, medical clearance documentation, team physical at 5:30, dynamic stretch routine, on ice 6:00–8:15.

I set the alarm, resisted the urge to set three backups, then stood. Most of my stuff was already in place—had been for a week. The dresser drawers I'd organized on day one. The toiletries claiming half the narrow sink shelf. All of it now sharing airspace with someone else's things.

The AC rattled again, pipes banging like someone dropping pucks down the wall. I'd gotten used to the sound over the past week. Wondered how long it would take Austen.

I shot a quick text to Ryan O'Connell—left-wing enforcer, one of the few guys who'd reached out after the transfer.

Me: *Housing screwed me. Got a roommate now.*

Ryan: *Welcome to Cold Harbor luxury suites. Who'd they stick you with?*

Me: *Math major. Seems quiet.*

Ryan: *Could be worse. Could be Javier. He snores during video review.*

Me: *Good to know.*

I tossed the phone onto the pillow and surveyed Austen's side. His stuff was neat. Almost too neat. I mean, who arranges their sweatshirts arranged dark to light? I stared at his desk. Even his books were stacked by size. The precision should have been reassuring. Instead, it felt like someone had moved furniture in my head without asking.

Dinner. I should go eat. I grabbed my wallet, checked the knob out of habit—it still stuck sometimes, but I'd learned the trick—and stepped into the hallway.

The floor hummed with early-semester energy: doors open, people laughing, somebody blasting Mario Kart music. I'd at least avoided the move-in chaos by arriving a week early. I'd already found my footing. Devon, the RA, had given me the welcome packet and the sympathetic grin about the AC. Now, I was just another face in the crowd.

Outside, dusk had settled. Cold Harbor's campus lights glowed soft gold, and across the lawn, the science complex flickered with late-night labs. Ridgeway Hall, the math and science building, stood off to the right—windows lit sporadically. I imagined Austen sitting in a room of friends doing math problems on a whiteboard.

A gentle breeze took the sting off the summer evening. I jammed my hands into my shorts pockets and set off toward North Point Dining Hall.

Inside North Point, the grill line was short. I loaded a tray—chicken, rice, and whatever vegetable wasn't dripping butter—and claimed a table near the windows. Students buzzed around me, laughter bouncing off cinderblock walls. Groups formed and re-formed, tables claimed, inside jokes flying. The kind of chemistry teams tried to manufacture in locker rooms.

I ate methodically, fueling more than tasting. Between bites, I opened my planner: class list, rink schedule, workouts. Every block accounted for. The plan. Except now it had an asterisk—room shared, privacy compromised, mental space unknown.

Halfway through dinner, a text popped from Coach Harper: *Reminder—medical clearance forms due at 0530 tomorrow or you're off the ice.*

I replied: *Form signed, see you at five.*

Coach Harper wasn't big on emojis. Good. Neither was I.

I finished eating, bused the tray, and ignored the surrounding chatter about upcoming ski trips and fall singles mixers. Back outside, the air felt sharper. I retraced steps to Stony Creek Hall.

The lobby was quieter now, lights dimmed. Third floor was quieter too, though EDM bass thumped faintly behind my neighbor's door. I tapped twice, testing my own advice. The bass cut off mid-drop. At least that still worked.

Inside 317, the AC unit sputtered but hadn't started its percussion solo. Austen's bed was empty, desk lamp off. The clock on my phone read 7:43. Plenty of time before he came back.

I toed off shoes, left them by the door—same spot as always—and changed into sleep shorts and a T-shirt. Then, because routine mattered, I unrolled the yoga mat between the beds. Tighter squeeze now, but it still fit. Ten minutes of hip mobility drills, pausing for a second only when the floor creaked in the hallway and I thought my new roommate was coming home. But the door remained locked. Stretching ended with me on my back, lying on the yoga mat and doing goalie-specific visualizations my high school coach had taught me—crease, angles, shooter patterns. The exercises usually cleared my head. Tonight, they only underlined that I was practicing recovery breathing six feet from a stranger's pillow.

I stood, rolled the mat tight, and slid it under the bed. Considered reviewing the team's playbook again, but rejected the idea. Brain done. Instead, I turned off the overhead light, climbed under the covers, checked the alarm on my phone, and stared at the ceiling. The hairline crack spidering across cinderblock looked vaguely like a face—I'd named it Gary on night three. I blinked until it became patternless again.

Footsteps approached. Austen's key scraped the lock at 10:56. I checked without meaning to. The door opened; he slipped inside, closed it softly.

"Hey," he whispered, seeing me awake.

"Hey." My voice came out rougher than intended. "How was your study group?"

"Good." He hung his jacket on the hook—his hook now, I supposed. He went to his set of drawers and pulled out a pair of sweatpants and a T-shirt. The room was dark, but my eyes had already adjusted. I should have looked away. I didn't.

He slid out of his shirt first. Lean shoulders, the kind of definition that came from movement rather than weights. A runner's build, maybe, or someone who biked everywhere. His spine curved as he reached for the sweatpants, and I caught the shadow of muscle shifting across his back before he stepped out of his jeans.

I stared at the ceiling. Forced myself to count the cracks.

The rustle of fabric said he'd finished. I heard him grab something from the desk—toiletry bag, maybe—and the door opened again, light slicing across the floor.

"Bathroom," he said, half-whispered.

I nodded, not trusting my voice.

The door clicked shut. I exhaled slowly, rubbing a hand over my face. *What the hell was that?* I'd seen guys change in locker rooms a thousand times. This was no different.

Except I hadn't looked away.

A minute later, footsteps returned. The door opened, closed again softly. Darkness settled back over the room. Only the glow of my phone remained.

He pointed at the screen. "Alarm early?"

"Four forty-five."

"Got it." He fished wireless earbuds from the desk drawer. "I'll keep quiet."

He didn't need to; his presence barely registered sound. Mattress springs sighed as he lay down, and for a minute only the hum of the AC filled the room. Then—bang—metal pipes clanged like an unwelcome drum solo.

Austen chuckled under his breath. "Showtime, I assume?"

"You'll sleep through it by Wednesday." I flipped onto my side, facing the wall. "Took me till Thursday."

"Noted." Rustle of sheets. "Goodnight, Luke."

My brain cataloged practice drills: T pushes, butterfly recoveries, rebound smothers. Anything but the fact that my room had become our room, my silence had become shared silence, my sanctuary now came with a witness. The AC settled into a steady hum. Austen's breathing evened out, quiet and rhythmic.

Four weeks, I reminded myself. *Control what's yours.*

I closed my eyes. The mattress felt the same, but everything else had shifted. Somewhere between pipe hiss and dorm quiet, sleep dragged me under.

Alarm. 4:45. Phone vibrated against the nightstand—barely a nightstand; more like a plank screwed to the wall. I slapped the screen, silencing the buzz before it could wake Austen, then swung my legs over the edge. The AC ticked in post-performance cooldown, otherwise silent.

I dressed in low light—compression gear, hoodie, track pants—breathing through each motion. *"Tomorrow's routine starts with today's discipline."* Dad's voice, years old, still coaching. I tied my laces, shoulders rolling loose. I grabbed my gear bag and tried to be quiet, but the heavy plastic pieces clanged against each other.

A rustle behind me. I looked over to see Austen rolling onto his side. I slipped out of the room as quietly as possible, angling my body to block the hallway's light from pouring into the room. I inhaled the cold dorm air mixed with stale pizza. One day in and my perfect fall plan had cracks, but the ice waited.

I jogged down the stairwell, bag over my shoulder, and stepped into the predawn dark.

Chapter 2
Ground Rules

AUSTEN

I woke to the drone-rattle of the AC and the absence of Luke's alarm. 6:42 a.m. Monday. First day of classes. I had seventy-eight minutes before Complex Variables. Luke had slipped out hours ago—4:45, if the pattern held. Three days of cohabitation, and I'd learned his schedule without trying: early alarm, soft footsteps, door click, silence. By the time I surfaced, the only proof he existed was the dent in his pillow and the faint smell of peppermint soap lingering in the air.

Ships passing. Fine by me. Four weeks would fly if we kept this up.

I rolled out of bed, toes landing on the narrow rug I'd measured to avoid the cracked linoleum seam. A quick shower and two pushes of the French press, three measured scoops, kettle to boil and my morning routine seemed to steady the room.

Luke's side had settled into a state I'd classify as "organized chaos"—water bottle on the floor, stickhandling ball under the desk, notebook open to a drill diagram I could only interpret as circles and angry arrows. We'd exchanged maybe forty words since Friday. Pleasantries. Logistics. The verbal equivalent of nodding across a crowded hallway.

I kept my gaze on the coffee bloom instead. Numbers made sense; curves on a sheet of ice did not.

At 7:08, mug in hand, I locked the door behind me and headed for Ridgeway.

Ridgeway Hall smelled like whiteboard cleaner and over-brewed tea. I slid into the second row of Dr. Renner's lecture a minute before the bell. Proofs flowed, Hagoromo Fulltouch chalk flew across the board, my pen keeping tempo.

An hour later I claimed a carrel on the top floor. The desk light flickered until I smacked the switch—three times for consistency—then settled into homework. Because Dr. Renner had assigned a stack of problems for us to complete by the next class period. Outside the window, a warm drizzle drifted sideways across the quad, slicking the early autumn leaves. Somewhere under that gray sky, Luke was blocking pucks and pretending the humidity didn't matter.

My phone buzzed.

Maya: *lunch? 12:15, Blue Mug.*

I typed with one hand, the other scribbling a boundary condition.

Me: *Can do. Need ten quiet minutes first.*

Maya: *define quiet.*

Me: *Quiet = no hockey gear, no AC drone, no people levitating a mini-fridge down the hallway.*

Maya: *so...library steps?*

Me: *Deal.*

I finished the problem set, checked it thrice, and jogged downstairs.

Maya waited on the wide stone steps, baseball cap pulled low, glasses perched on her head. She handed me a to-go cup before I said a word.

"Iced white chocolate mocha," she declared. "Because you look like you slept in Ridgeway Hall and it's eighty degrees out."

"You know me, took a nap and dreamed in LaTeX," I admitted.

She grimaced sympathy. "So, roommate?"

I exhaled, taking the cold cup. "Exists. Tall, hockey, polite. Also takes up space that should be mine."

"Luke Carter." She dug in her pocket for lip balm. "Saw the team's Insta earlier. They were filming goalie drills at dawn. He's kinda hunky. If you like someone who is..." She dug out her phone and opened the school's Instagram account and started reading, "'Six-foot-two, 220 pounds of solid muscle from what I can tell. Short brown hair and brown eyes," she said as she zoomed in on his face.

"Is that his athletic profile or are you looking at his dating app?"

"Oh, is he on Grindr?" she asked

"I wouldn't know," I said rolling my eyes. "And I doubt he's gay. And even if he was, I doubt he'd go for someone like me. We're very different. Anyway, changing topics, housing promised Luke four weeks, then they can move people around and—fingers crossed—get us our singles back."

"You file for a move?"

"No. I let the jock do it." I nudged a pebble off the step with my sneaker. "Transfer paperwork comes up, scholarship office notices, and I'm the cost-intensive kid complaining about freebies."

"Scholarship is housing-inclusive. You're entitled."

"Entitled is a loaded word when you don't pay full freight."

She squinted at me. "Translation: you'd rather recalibrate than risk notice."

I lifted a shoulder. Confirmation enough.

We walked toward Blue Mug, shoes scuffing on the pavement. Maya matched my pace, deliberate and steady.

"You like him?" she asked.

"I've collected approximately twenty minutes of data. He labels fridge shelves."

"That's bordering on soulmate territory for you."

I elbowed her, gentle. "Funny."

We ducked inside the café's air-conditioned blur of espresso and indie guitar. Lines moved fast; campus noon rush. I grabbed a turkey wrap, Maya a lentil soup. No seats open, so we claimed a standing counter by the window.

She blew on her spoon. "So, what's the actual problem with him as a roomie? Space? Noise? Or that he's an unknown variable?"

"Unknown variable," I echoed. "My room was fixed; now it's fuzzy logic."

"From what I remember of calculus, variables can become constants," she said, eyes grinning over the rim of her cup.

I broke the wrap in half, less hungry than restless. "Constants take time. Also, he smells like hockey pads."

"He showers eventually. Or should I explain to him the necessity of soap and water?"

"Sure thing, Dr. Chen." A laugh escaped before I could stop it. Relief tasted like oregano and too much student-loan caution. I swallowed. "I'll adapt."

"From your mouth to Sun Wukong's ears."

"Really, the monkey king? From what I remember, he's a trickster god."

"More mischievous than trickster. I think he's just misunderstood. Like someone else I know," she opened her eyes widely, creased her brow, and tilted her head in my direction.

"I'm not misunderstood. I'm perfectly understood by those who possess more logic than a testosterone-fueled meathead."

"Have you actually talked to him? Beyond 'your shelf, my shelf, goodnight'?"

"We've exchanged enough information for cohabitation purposes."

"Austen." She set down her spoon. "That's not talking. That's a terms-of-service agreement."

"I wasn't aware roommates required emotional bandwidth."

"They don't. But you're already cataloging his sleep schedule and shower habits." She raised an eyebrow. "That's more attention than you gave your last three lab partners combined."

"Survival metrics. Entirely practical."

"Mmm hmm." The sound carried an entire thesis of skepticism. "Just promise me you'll say more than ten words to him before the semester ends."

"I'll consider twelve if he stops leaving his stickhandling ball in the middle of the floor."

She saluted with the soup spoon. "Text me updates. Especially if he offers a private stickhandling lesson."

I beat Luke back to the room.

The chill hit first—someone had set the window unit at arctic blast. I spun the dial down to low, then faced the room. His gear bag was open on top of his desk, gloves drying over a vent. A faint rubber-sweat mix hung in the air, familiar from every gym corridor on campus.

I stepped around the stickhandling ball in the middle of the floor, "accidentally" toe-poking it until it rolled under his bed.

Then, I turned to my desk.

It was too cluttered. The messiness was making my skin itch. I rearranged immediately: office supplies on the left, laptop centered, calculators on the right,—aligned parallel to the edge—and all of my writing utensils nicely stored in a metal pencil holder—writing tips pointed down.

The act slowed my heart to its usual cadence.

It was an old reflex, a hangover from the system. When you grow up sleeping in bedrooms that belong to other people's kids, or in group homes where privacy is a theoretical concept, you learn to keep your perimeter tight. If your things are scattered, they're vulnerable. If they are aligned, cataloged, and locked down, they are yours.

I ran a finger along the edge of the stapler. Perfect alignment.

For tonight, at least, I controlled this variable.

Then came the heavy artillery. I pulled a massive hardbound book from my bag and dropped it onto the wood surface with a thud that made the bedsprings vibrate. *Advanced Topology*. Dr. Aris Thorne had warned us that her thesis requirements would make grown men weep. I intended to be the exception.

The door latch clicked. Luke walked in, hair damp from a shower. I refused to look at his naked torso, but I stole a glimpse, anyway.

"Hey," he said.

I raised a hand. "You survived practice and your first day of class."

"Barely. Harper skated us after scrimmage. The ice felt soft with this humidity." He toed off sneakers, noticing the glove on the vent. "Sorry about the smell. Needs to dry or it rots."

"It's fine." I nudged my chair under the desk. "Vent's communal property."

He grinned as if that was a joke, though I'd meant it literally. "I'll crack the window a minute. Let some real air in."

The sash squealed open the whole six inches we were able to open the windows. Warm, damp air slashed in; the glove fluttered. Luke braced a textbook against the sill to keep it from slamming shut.

I pressed save on my code file, realized I'd done no work since entering. "Got class in twenty. Mind if I change?"

"Do your thing." He grabbed a protein shake from the fridge and drank half without breathing. Then he glanced at my polo shirt and dress pants—slate gray, low on style, high on function. "You presenting?"

"TA session. They expect us to dress professionally." I smoothed the collar.

"Looks sharp." He said it casually, like stating the hallway color. Compliment or observation? Hard to tell. Either way it unsettled.

I buried my nose in my textbook, gripping the edges like a steering wheel. Behind me, the wardrobe door creaked. The soft *whump* of a damp towel hitting the floor followed.

I didn't turn around. I stared at a complex derivative, willing the numbers to make sense, but my brain was entirely focused on the acoustic data behind me: denim sliding over skin, the click of a belt buckle, the snap of a fresh T-shirt being shaken out. Finally, I heard the creaking sound of his box springs as he sat back on his bed. I let out a breath I hadn't realized I'd been holding.

Cardiovascular beats pulsed from his earbuds, faint but insistent. Luke bounced a rubber ball off the wall—*tap, catch, tap*—keeping rhythm with the track. My eye twitched at the disruption, or maybe just the proximity, but he stopped after three and pocketed the ball.

"Too loud?" he asked.

"Rhythmic. Unexpected. Reminds me of a metronome." I gathered my stuff and stood to head back out.

He nodded, then zipped the ball into a small cloth pouch and set it inside his skate. Contained.

"Headed to lecture?" he asked.

"Calc II. The professor has a pop-quiz today to see what the students remember from last semester. I'll be grading quizzes." I slung my backpack. "You?"

"Film study." He was massaging his foot. He saw me looking and added, "My toes are still numb from the ice bath." He made a face. "If they fall off, you get the bigger closet."

"Generous trade." I opened the door.

As I left, he called, "Austen—thanks for being chill."

I paused in the threshold. *Chill.* I gave a short nod and let the hallway swallow me.

TA duty ended at five sharp. Thankfully, most of the students remembered at least a fraction of what they'd been taught in the previous semester. A few, well, they had forgotten simple addition over the summer. I detoured by Blue Mug and ordered two iced coffees—one extra large. I didn't examine the purchase until I was halfway back to Stony Creek, cups sweating through cardboard sleeves.

Our door stood ajar. Voices drifted: Luke's low rumble and another, lighter—female? I nudged the door wider.

Luke sat cross-legged on his bed, laptop open to game footage. The visitor stood beside him, ponytail flipping as she turned toward me. Blonde, North Ridge letterman jacket.

"Hey," she said brightly. "You must be Austen."

"Depends. Who's asking?"

"Devon's girlfriend," Luke clarified. "Kayla. She's borrowing my psych notes."

I held up the cups. "Coffee run. That one's yours if you want."

Luke's brows climbed. "Serious? Lifesaver." He hopped up, took the large, and sipped. "Perfect."

"Personally, I'm caffeine-cutting," Kayla said. She tucked a USB into her pocket. "Thanks, Luke."

She exited with an easy wave.

Luke set the coffee on his desk, dragging in the rich scent. "I owe you."

"My friend Maya said I needed to be nicer to you. Call it my version of a grand gesture."

He laughed, surprised. "Fair." He closed the laptop. "You good with company popping in? I should've texted."

"It's your room too." I flipped my notebook open, uncapped a pen. "But if you give notice, I'll steer clear. I can always hang out in Ridgeway Hall or the library... if you need privacy."

"Deal." He stretched, shoulders cracked. "But privacy? I seriously doubt I'll need privacy. I don't have time for that in my life. I'm meeting the guys for dinner at six. You hanging out in the room?"

"Probably." I gestured at the stack of graded quizzes. "Still need to log these into Canvas for the professor."

"Cool. I'll grab my stuff." He grabbed his wallet and phone before throwing on a baseball cap. Then he hesitated at the door. "You need anything from the dining hall? Cookies? Those weird energy bars?"

"Blueberry oat if they're stocked."

He gave a mock salute and disappeared.

The room fell quiet enough for my pulse to surface. I pressed two fingers to my wrist, counting. Even. Good.

I sorted quizzes. Midway through the pile, I paused at a shaky derivative, red-penciled a B minus, then wrote, *check sign on chain rule.* My handwriting shrank toward the margin, habit from years of making comments fit where space allowed.

The chain rule always felt like foster care forms—carry what matters forward, drop the rest. I recapped the pen.

A floorboard creaked. I looked up. Empty room, of course. I pulled my planner from the desk shelf.

If I wasn't getting a new room, we needed a few boundaries:

1. Quiet hours: 11 p.m.–7 a.m.

2. Window cracked only when necessary.

3. Advance notice of guests.

4. AC objective temperature 70°F.

I underlined each twice. Order against entropy.

Pens tapped downstairs; someone shouted "shotgun" followed by laughter. I shook off the noise and refocused.

At 7:03, Luke returned, carrying a to-go box.

He nudged the door with his hip. "Got your bar."

I accepted the package. "Thanks."

Then he spotted the list taped above my desk.

He read silently. "Rules?"

"Guidelines." My ears warmed. "Negotiable, but clear."

"Looks reasonable." He pointed. "Advance notice of guests—minimum lead time?"

"Text five minutes before arrival?"

He scrolled through his phone. A chime sounded on mine. Notification: *Luke: 'Kayla @ 4:40 was minus five.'* Followed by a laughing emoji.

I snorted. "Future events only."

He grinned, took a swig of his diluted sports drink, and flopped into the desk chair backward, knees draped over the armrests. "What are you working on?"

"Eigenvalue proofs."

"Sounds lethal."

"To non-math majors, yes." I opened the bar wrapper. "How was practice today?"

"Javier landed three top-corner shots on my glove side in six minutes. My ego's limping." He massaged his left shoulder, winced. "Icepack calling."

He rummaged in the freezer and pulled out his bag of peas. He pressed the pack against his shoulder, hissing. "You ever stare at numbers so long they rearrange themselves?"

"Daily."

He whistled low. "We're not so different, then. I track shooters, you track numbers."

I held his gaze a second longer than intended. Something in the way he said "we" nudged that carefully parked unknown variable closer. I broke eye contact, pretending the wrapper demanded immediate recycling.

He shifted the pack, easing a sigh. "Tomorrow's practice ends at nine. After that, I'm free until weights at four. If you need uninterrupted crunch time, claim it."

"I might."

"Consider it booked." He rose, rotated his arm. He gave a quick salute and crossed to his bed, stretching calves against the frame. Every move economical. I recognized the instinct.

The AC compressor shuddered on, right on schedule. Luke snapped his fingers in rhythm—a plastic-on-metal rattle—and mumbled the melody of some song. I capped my pen.

"Let the record show," I said, "the AC makes better percussion than your rubber ball."

He laughed, bright and unguarded, and for three seconds the noise didn't feel invasive.

By ten, silence reclaimed the room.

Luke lay flat on his stomach, sports medicine book propped against pillows, highlighter uncapped. I finished the last grade entry, closed my laptop, and stretched until vertebrae popped.

"Lights?" he offered.

"Give me one minute." I printed the guidelines in smaller font, laminated with packing tape, and smoothed them on the mini-fridge door: roommate constitution, version 1.0.

Luke watched, amused. "Should I sign?"

"Optional."

He reached for the dry-erase marker, scrawled *L. Carter 09/09*, then drew a tiny goalie glove next to his name.

The gesture shouldn't have mattered, but the validation settled something in my chest. I flipped off the desk lamp.

Darkness, except the streetlight halo bleeding through blinds. I climbed into bed, listening to Luke shuffle pages.

"Austen?" he whispered.

"Yeah?"

"Window's closed, but if the room ever smells bad, say something."

"I will."

"Night."

"Night," I echoed.

I rolled onto my side, facing the wall. The AC droned, dissolving into white noise.

Chapter 3
Screening the Goalie

LUKE

Two weeks into the semester, and I already felt like I was barely keeping my head above water. Still no word on the single, but that was the least of my worries. Between hockey and financial accounting, I regretted life choices.

Ryan didn't knock. He pounded on the door of 317 with a rhythm that sounded like the drum intro to a Metallica song.

"Carter! Lovell! Suit up. We're rolling in ten."

I looked up from my desk, where I was pretending to organize my syllabus binders for the third time. "Rolling where?"

"The Barn," Ryan announced, pushing the door open. He was dressed for a Saturday night in a flannel shirt that cost more than my textbooks and jeans that fit a little too well. "Rookie initiation party. Well, 'initiation' is a strong word. It's mostly cheap keg beer and Javier trying to DJ."

I tightened my grip on the binder. "We have a six a.m. skate tomorrow."

"Which is why you'll be drinking club soda and leaving by midnight. But you have to *show*, Monk. It's optics. Team bonding." He pointed at Austen, who was frozen halfway to the mini-fridge, holding a carton of oat milk like a shield. "And you're coming too, Math."

Austen blinked, looking at Ryan like he was a variable that refused to solve. "I am statistically unlikely to attend a hockey party."

"Maya's already there," Ryan countered, grinning. "She texted me. Said to bring the 'hermit crab' or she's telling everyone you listen to polka when you code."

Austen's jaw went tight. "It's not polka. It's symphonic metal. There's a vast difference."

"Whatever. Ten minutes. Wear something that can survive spilled lager."

Ryan slapped the doorframe and vanished down the hall, humming something that was not symphonic metal.

The silence that followed was heavy. I looked at Austen; he looked at his laptop screen like he was considering climbing inside it.

"You don't have to go," I said. "Ryan's bark is worse than his bite. Usually."

"Maya doesn't bluff," Austen replied, closing the laptop with grim finality. He walked to his closet. "And if I stay here, the EDM guy next door will vibrate my fillings loose. A different bass line might be an improvement."

He pulled out a navy hoodie—clean, simple, zero team logos. He held it up, inspecting it.

"You?" he asked.

I sighed, tossing the binder onto my bed. "Ryan's right. Optics. If the new guy doesn't show up to the first mixer, the locker room assumes he thinks he's too good for them."

"Or that you value sleep hygiene," Austen muttered, pulling the hoodie on.

"Hockey culture doesn't believe in hygiene of any kind," I said, grabbing my keys. "Let's get this over with."

The Barn was exactly what it sounded like—a dilapidated off-campus rental in the middle of nowhere that housed five seniors and, at the moment, half the student body of Northern Ridge.

The bass hit my sternum before we cleared the mudroom. The air inside was a tropical storm of body heat, Axe body spray, and the copper tang of cheap beer.

Control, I told myself. *Read the room like a zone entry.*

"Stick close," I yelled to Austen over the noise.

He didn't answer. A group of volleyball players cut through our lane, separating us. By the time I shouldered through the gap, Austen was gone—swept toward the kitchen by the current of bodies.

"Carter!" Javier Morales loomed out of the fog, shoving a red Solo cup at my chest. "Hydrate or die."

"I'm driving," I shouted back, taking the cup but not drinking. I sniffed it. Vodka tonic. Not water.

"Boring!" Javier slapped my good shoulder—hard. I flinched, teeth gritting, but forced a smile. "Relax, newbie. Goalie corner is out back."

I navigated the living room, dodging elbows and spills. My brain tracked threats automatically: drink sloshing at three o'clock, flailing dancer at nine. Exhausting. I wasn't wired for chaos I couldn't block.

The "Goalie Corner" was a sagging couch on the back porch, but it was currently occupied by the starters from the women's team. I said hello. I did a lap, scanning for Ryan or an exit. You see, I'm a people-person when we're one-on-one or in a small group, but enormous masses of swarming bodies, not my thing.

Then I saw him.

Austen was pinned against the sliding glass door in the dining room. A massive defensive lineman from the football team—I think his name was Tank—had one hand on the wall above Austen's head, leaning in, drunk and explaining something with wet, spraying enthusiasm.

Austen stood stiff as a goalpost, arms crossed tight against his chest, eyes fixed on a point near the ceiling. He looked like he was calculating the structural load of the drywall to keep from screaming.

I edged closer, gauging whether he needed rescue or was holding his own.

"—and the thing about raw yolks," Tank was shouting, "is the bioavailability. You cook the egg, you kill the enzymes. It's science, bro."

"It's salmonella," Austen corrected, voice tight but audible. "The thermal denaturation of proteins is necessary for safe consumption."

Tank blinked, swaying. "De-nature-what? No, man. It's about the primal fuel source. Rocky did it."

"Rocky is a fictional character," Austen said. "And he likely suffered from significant gastrointestinal distress off-camera."

Tank laughed, slapping the wall. Plaster dust drifted down onto Austen's shoulder. "You're funny! I like you. You should try it. Tomorrow morning. Six eggs. Raw."

Austen looked like he was about to vomit. "I will not be doing that."

Tank leaned closer. "Come on, bro. Don't be soft."

"Hey," I said, pitching my voice low but hard.

The lineman blinked, turning sluggishly. "Who're you?"

"Luke. Hockey." I nodded at Austen. "And I need my roommate. Burst pipe in the dorm. Emergency."

A terrible lie. The lineman frowned, processing speed slowed by cheap tequila. "Pipe?"

"Everywhere," I said. "Water damage. RAs are freaking out." I grabbed Austen's sleeve. "Let's go."

Austen didn't hesitate. He phased through the space I created, ducking under the lineman's arm. We didn't stop moving until we hit the back door, shoved it open, and spilled out onto the rotting wooden deck.

The cool night air hit like relief. Quiet here—just the muffled thump of bass and wind in the trees.

Austen leaned against the railing, exhaling a long, shaky breath. He pulled his sleeves down over his hands.

"Burst pipe?" he asked, voice flat.

"I panicked. First disaster I could think of." I dumped the vodka tonic into an overgrown flowerbed.

"That guy was explaining the nutritional benefits of raw egg yolks for twenty minutes. I was plotting a way to jump through the glass."

"Defenestration is a valid exit strategy."

Austen looked at me, surprised. "You know the word defenestration?"

"I do crosswords on the bus," I said. "Goalies have a lot of downtime."

He almost smiled. Small, a twitch of the lips, but in the dim light of the porch bulb, it looked like a victory.

"Thanks," he said, "for saving me back there."

"Blocker side was open," I said. "Easy read."

"I have no idea what you just said," Austen admitted. He turned to face the yard, shadows cutting across his face. "I hate this. The variables are too random. The noise-to-signal ratio is zero."

"Yeah, I have no idea what you just said." I chuckled, leaning back against the siding. "I guess we both have things to learn from each other. Me, I spend my whole life trying to control angles."

I squared my shoulders, demonstrating. "It's about depth. You step out, you cut the line of sight. You make the net disappear behind you so the shooter has nothing to aim at."

I dropped my hands.

"But here? I can't square up to this. This place is ricochets everywhere."

We stood there for a minute, shoulder to shoulder in the cooling air. The first time since I'd moved in that the silence between us didn't feel like a standoff. It felt like a bunker.

The sliding door rattled. Ryan stuck his head out, spotting us.

"There you are! We're doing a keg stand competition. Carter, you're up against the freshman d-man."

My stomach turned. Not the alcohol—the performance. The eyes.

I looked at Austen. He was shrinking into his hoodie, bracing for impact.

"Actually," I said, loud enough for Ryan to hear, "Lovell's not feeling great. Something with the... pipe situation."

Austen caught on instantly. He put a hand to his stomach and offered a grimace that was truly Oscar-worthy. "Bad eggs," he whispered.

Ryan looked between us, disappointed but not suspicious. "Weak sauce, Math. Fine. Carter, get him home. But you owe me a round next week."

"Deal," I lied.

Ryan ducked back inside. I looked at Austen.

"Bad eggs?" I asked.

"Callbacks are the foundation of good improv," he deadpanned.

"Come on." I nodded toward the side gate, bypassing the house entirely.

We walked to the car in silence, dry leaves crunching under our boots. When we got inside the truck, the engine groaned to life, blasting stale air before the climate control kicked in.

Austen buckled his seatbelt with a decisive snap, staring straight ahead. "I never located Maya."

"Your friend?" I asked, checking the mirrors.

"Yep. I was supposed to rendezvous with her." He rubbed his temples.

"If she's inside that house, she's probably fine," I offered, shifting into reverse. "Or at least too distracted to notice we left. That crowd seemed... occupied."

"Probability high," Austen agreed, though he didn't look convinced. He leaned his head back against the seat, eyes closing.

I merged onto the dark road. The silence felt heavy again, but not in a bad way. It felt like the air leaving a balloon.

I reached for the radio dial, instinct taking over.

"Luke?"

"Yeah?"

"Please don't turn on the radio."

I paused, hand hovering over the volume knob. "Why? You hate Top 40?"

"I hate unpredictability," he murmured, eyes still shut tight behind his glasses. "DJs talk too much. The songs change tempo without warning. I need a constant. I need the sine wave to flatten out."

"So... silence?"

"Silence is predictable."

I withdrew my hand. "For a guy who lectures me about symphonic metal, you're surprisingly sensitive to noise."

"Metal has structure," he said, cracking one eye open to look at me. "It's mathematical. It follows a progression. Complexity doesn't equal chaos, Luke. Radio is chaos."

"Fair point." I kept my hand on the gearshift, letting the engine idle at the stoplight. "Quiet hours start now?"

"Quiet hours start now."

I pulled out onto the main road, keeping the radio off. The only sound was the hum of tires on asphalt and the fan pushing warmth into the cab.

It wasn't the dorm. It wasn't a single room. But for the first time in a week, the roommate situation felt manageable.

Chapter 4
Provisional Start

LUKE

The puck cannoned off my blocker and ricocheted to the near-side corner, exactly where Coach Harper wanted it. Whistle. She pointed her stick down the ice.

"Reset, Carter. Five-puck sequence. Same shooters."

I shuffled back across the crease, edges biting through the frost-fogged blue paint. Breath crystallized inside the cage of my mask; sweat soaked the neck of my base layer. Six hours ago I'd been in a dorm room the size of a parking spot, taping a "roommate constitution" to a mini-fridge. Even though we were three weeks into the semester, twenty pairs of eyes waited to see if the transfer kid could keep the net.

Javier Morales circled at the top of the left dot, puck on his tape, visor clouded with condensation. He didn't talk trash; he stared glove side, daring me to flinch. Ryan lined up beside him, stick blade flat, humming something off-key that sounded like early-2000s pop punk.

Harper's whistle shrieked.

Javier snapped first—low blocker. I kicked it wide.

Second puck: Ryan, quick release, looking five-hole. I closed the pads, smothered, popped it out for the manager collecting rebounds.

Third: Javier again, this time high glove. He'd beaten me there yesterday in film, and he knew I knew it. I pushed forward, cut the angle, felt the sting in my palm as the puck slammed leather but stayed out.

Fourth and fifth blurred—shoulder save, then a desperation toe on a deflection. Harper blew the drill dead.

"Better," she called. "Still leaving snow up the middle on your recoveries. Clean it or get used to chasing loose change."

"Yes, Coach." I sucked air through the cage, heart hammering.

She didn't nod, didn't smile—flicked her whistle toward the boards. "Water. Three minutes."

I glided backward, tapping blocker to post before turning. Habit. Post-check, angle, rhythm. Control what's crease-sized.

Ryan coasted beside me as we headed for the bench. "Nice robbery, Carter. Javier's starting to pout."

"Morales doesn't pout," I said, popping the helmet strap and chugging water. "He recalculates trajectories."

Ryan snorted. "Nerd."

I wiped sweat off my brow with the back of a soaked glove. "You skate with the math major, you pick up vocabulary."

"Roomie treating you okay?"

"Taped a rules list to the fridge," I said. "Color-coded. Even signed by yours truly."

"That's either adorable or serial-killer stuff. Jury's out."

Javier slid to a stop in front of us, spraying a sheet of ice at our skates. "Glove looked sharp," he said, voice even. "But you're still late on push-outs when I shade right." He shoved his mouth guard between teeth and skated away before I could answer.

Ryan lifted his brows. "Translation: You're earning respect."

"Or I'm a science project."

"Science projects don't dress for Friday's home opener." He nudged my elbow. "Relax."

Easy advice when you weren't the newest transfer wearing borrowed expectations like a too-tight chest protector.

Harper whistled again. "Full-ice scrimmage. Two fifteen-minute run-time periods. Carter and Decker split."

Decker—last semester's backup—tapped my pads as he passed. "You start?"

"Coach hasn't said." But every cell in my body prayed for it.

We took positions. First unit against first unit. Crowd noise would be triple Friday, but right now the rink was quiet except for the Zamboni exhaust lingering from the morning cut and the smack of sticks on ice.

Faceoff. Puck dropped. The rush built quick—Morales scooping possession, cutting inside our rookie defenseman, flipping to Ryan streaking down the wing. Ryan ripped a snapshot glove side. I snared it clean. Play whistled dead.

I tossed the puck to the ref stand-in, heart rate steadying. Felt good. Felt right.

Next shift, Javier deked our captain, toe-dragged forehand, and fired low blocker. I read it, dropped, paddle down. Rebound kicked out too far. He shoveled it upstairs before I could recover.

Ping. Water bottle off.

Harper's whistle. "Keep the rebound inside the blue paint!"

My chest burned. I'd let anger torpedo games before; couldn't now. Dad's voice hissed somewhere beneath the mask—*"don't let them see weakness, kid"*—but I ignored it, dialed in.

When the first period ended 2–1 red squad, Harper waved me over. She didn't raise her voice; she never had to.

"Carter, you're tracking well, but your weight transfer is slow when you reset after a high shot. Less pop-up, more edge-load. Got it?"

"Got it."

"Show me."

Second period: I focused on staying loaded, shoulder down, nose on puck. Javier kept testing glove high, but I met him every time. Ryan scored on Decker at the other end, cackling loud enough to echo. The horn sounded—scrimmage tied 3–3.

Harper blew her final whistle. "Bag skate tomorrow morning; film this afternoon. Weights at sixteen-hundred. Hit the showers."

Players scattered. I crouched, tapping both posts again before sliding out. My shoulder throbbed where yesterday's scrimmage had clipped me, but adrenaline masked most of it.

Inside the tunnel, fluorescent lights hummed. The gear smell thickened—wet tape, rubber, ammonia crystals from sweat-soaked pads. Voices bounced off concrete. Ryan threw an arm over my helmet, steering me toward the stalls.

"Friday's our house opener against Caribou State," he said. "Stands'll be packed, student section liquored up by warm-ups. You ready?"

"If Coach calls my name, yeah."

"That glove side looked ready." He bumped fists, then ducked into his stall.

I peeled off gloves, chest pad, jersey—steam curling off fabric. Equipment clanged into my locker. When the last strap cleared, I sat on the bench, elbows on knees. The pressure opened like a valve I'd been clamping shut since Harper first called my transfer meeting.

Dad's career highlight reel flashed in my head—rookie year hat trick, then the slow fade after the ACL tear, beer cans on the coffee table. He never said it, but I knew: keep playing well, or life starts playing you.

I ground the heel of my palm into the ache in my shoulder.

"Carter." Harper's voice cut through the clatter. I jerked upright; she stood outside the trainers' room, arms crossed over a down vest.

"Need a word," she said.

I grabbed a towel, wiped sweat from my face, and followed.

The trainers' room smelled like antiseptic and menthol. Harper leaned against a treatment table, studying something on her tablet. She thumbed the screen off before speaking.

"Good adjustment in the second period," she said. "Still rough edges, but"—she exhaled through her nose—"you've earned the start Friday."

Heat hit the back of my neck. "Thank you, Coach."

"It's provisional." She fixed me with that x-ray stare coaches perfected. "Keep numbers tight in film and don't dog weights, or Decker suits up."

"Yes, ma'am."

"Team needs stability in the crease. Think you can give it to them?"

"I can."

She nodded once, pushing off the table. "Grab lunch, hydrate, see Dalton if that shoulder nags."

"It's fine."

Her expression said she heard the lie. "Athletic training opens at eleven. Use them. That's not a suggestion."

"Yes, Coach."

She left. I stood alone, the word *starter* pulsing behind my ribs like a second heartbeat—equal parts relief and threat. Opportunity and warning, same coin.

I returned to the locker room as Ryan—already out of the shower—was putting on deodorant. "You look like you got called to the principal's office," he said.

"Harper named me provisional starter."

"Hell yeah." He slapped my damp shoulder pad—hard. I winced.

He saw it. "Injury?"

"Bruise. I'll get ice."

"Hit Dalton for stim. Harper loves her data, but she loves healthy goalies more."

"Noted." I untangled the rest of my base layer and stepped into the showers.

Hot water hammered the knots in my back. I closed my eyes, letting the roar drown everything: Harper's warning, Dad's ghost stories, the mental whiteboard where I tracked save percentage.

When I came out, towel around hips, Javier sat lacing shoes. He glanced up.

"Good battle," he said. That was it—no smile, no critique. Respect in two words.

"Thanks," I said, and meant it.

He finished tying his shoes, then straightened. "Caribou's first line loves back-door seams. Stick lifts, no whistles. Heads up."

"Appreciate the scouting."

He tipped an invisible cap and walked out.

I dressed quickly—compression leggings under faded jeans, team hoodie over a plain tee—and loaded gear into my stall to air. The shoulder throbbed as the adrenaline faded. I flagged down Dalton, the team trainer, as he moved down the aisle. He tossed me a heavy flex-pack of crushed ice.

"Twenty minutes," he ordered. "Don't freeze the nerve. I'll see you on my table in twenty."

I wedged the pack under my hoodie, hissing as the cold hit the bruise.

Ryan noticed the crinkle of plastic. "Cryotherapy already? We haven't even hit the highway."

"Dalton's orders." I adjusted the fit against my skin. "Said he doesn't want me locking up before we get back to campus."

"You know you're a legend already, right?"

"Because of ice?"

"Because you're the only guy here who walks in day one and posts a .920 against Morales."

"It was practice."

"Practice with Coach Harper filming every angle. Relax, Carter. Enjoy the dub."

I didn't correct him—because it wasn't a win yet. Friday would decide that.

We headed up to the players' lounge. Fluorescent lights flickered against trophy cases; smell of day-old coffee hovered. Ryan raided the snack shelf, tossing me a protein bar.

"You ditching afternoon weights to cry in an ice bath?" he asked.

"Wouldn't dream of it."

He peeled open his bar. "You got time before film. Wanna grab real food at Buckman Grill?"

"Need to hit Dalton first."

"Cool. Meet you after?"

"Yeah." I checked my phone—8:57 a.m. Two missed texts, both from Dad. I didn't open them.

"Everything good?" Ryan asked, nodding at the screen.

"Fine." I shoved the device into my pocket. "See you in thirty."

He eyed me but didn't press, strolled off humming that same off-key pop punk.

The training room was half full—cross-country guys foam-rolling, a volleyball hitter ankle-deep in an ice bucket, our freshman defenseman getting his wrist taped. Dalton, the senior trainer, waved me to a table.

"Left shoulder still?" he said, digging an ultrasound wand out of a drawer.

"Impact bruise."

"Shirt off." He flicked the machine on. "New program's been rough on you?"

"Finding angles."

He spread gel across my deltoid, pressed the probe. "Just inflammation. You'll be fine once the tissue stops yelling."

I stared at the ceiling tiles, counting rivets. Dad's texts burned in my pocket—probably congratulating me for making it here, probably reminding me what happens if I fall short. He'd been supportive in his own way since I left Glen Rock, but the subtext never changed: *Don't repeat my mistakes.*

Dalton finished, wiped gel with a towel. "Stim for fifteen. You know the drill."

I lay back, electrodes buzzing. I focused on the minor electric pulses instead of the unseen messages waiting on my phone.

A notification buzzed—different tone.

Austen: *When are you going to be in the room? I'm in class till noon.*

Practical, efficient. Also weirdly grounding. I thumbed a reply with my free hand.

Luke: *Film ends at 12:30. Then weight training. I'll run by and say hi after that.*

I tossed the phone aside before I could overthink why typing that made my chest unclench.

Film review at 11:30 sharp. We crowded the small theater—rows of fold-down seats that smelled like old popcorn and hockey tape. Harper stood beside the screen, laser pointer in hand.

Every freeze-frame that featured me came with commentary.

"See your torso angle?" she said, highlighting my clinched stance on a two-on-one. "If you stay compact there, rebound slides into the slot. Open up, and you direct it into the pads. Simple physics."

I nodded, scribbling notes. *Glove tight, chest square, edges loaded.* Ryan drew a cartoon goalie on his page, labeling me "Wall-E." Childish and perfect.

Harper finished with a clip from last year's Caribou game—our ex-starter beaten five-hole. "They disguise shot angles. Read the hands, not the eyes."

She clicked the projector off. Lights stung. "Rosters posting outside my office at fourteen-hundred," she said. "Starters marked in red. Practice tomorrow at six. Weights in one hour. Questions?"

Silence.

"Good. Hydrate."

The room emptied. Ryan elbowed me. "Starters in red. Must be your color."

"We'll see."

"You act chill, but your gear bag's already vibrating."

I tried to laugh. It snagged halfway up my throat. "Tell that to my shoulder."

He slapped my good side. "Weights, then lunch. Come on."

"Need to check one thing first." I pointed at the hallway that led past Harper's office. "Meet you in the gym."

"Don't keep me from leg day glory," he said over his shoulder.

Coach's door was cracked. The roster sat taped outside—white sheet, names typed, positions. I scanned.

GOALTENDERS Carter – starter (red) Decker – backup

Red text, bold. My name lit like a warning flare.

Provisional starter or not, it was real enough to print.

I exhaled. The breath steamed the roster for half a second. I touched the paper—brushed it, like proof—and walked away before anyone saw.

Weights at sixteen-hundred hurt worse than any drill. Harper watched from the balcony while our strength coach barked sets. Ryan cursed through goblet squats; I counted reps by multiples of five, math trick to keep rhythm. Shoulders held. Core held.

Afterward, I showered fast, pulled on sweats, and jogged across campus. The sun barely cleared the library roof—shadows stretched long.

Austen sat at his desk, laptop open, earbuds in. He looked up as I shouldered my gearless backpack onto my desk.

"Hey," he said, tugging one bud free. "Practice?"

"Over." I toed off sneakers. "Coach named the starter for Friday."

He angled his chair. "And?"

I held up an imaginary red marker. "Provisional, but mine."

A smile threatened the corner of his mouth. "Congrats."

"Thanks." I unzipped the hoodie, tossed it on my bed, then remembered gear etiquette. "Stuff doesn't smell today. No need to open the window."

"Appreciated." He saved whatever code glowed on screen. "Dinner?"

"I've got team meal at six-thirty." I checked the time—5:12. "You?"

"TA session ends at nine. I'll grab something to go." He paused. "Should I evacuate while you nap?"

I shook my head. "Not sleeping. Brain's loud."

He considered that, then closed the laptop. "Chess?"

"What?"

He pulled a magnet board from a desk drawer—hand-sized, tiny pieces in a zip bag. "Keeps numbers busy."

I laughed, genuine. "I'm garbage at chess."

"I'm mediocre. Perfect match."

We set up on the floor between beds, the AC behind us like a metronome. Austen moved a knight; I mirrored. He explained en passant; I told a story about my first shutout. We didn't talk about rosters or families—pieces, angles, and why bishops felt like wingers who never back-checked.

When he checkmated me in twelve moves, I blamed the sore shoulder. He looked skeptical.

I lay back, arms folded under my head, staring at the ceiling crack that resembled a goalie mask. "Friday's going to be loud," I said.

"Crowds are math," he replied, kneeling to sweep pieces into the bag. "Sum of individual vectors. Ignore amplitude; focus on trajectory."

"That's... strangely helpful."

"Put it on your headboard if it tests well in practice."

I chuckled. The ceiling crack blurred—maybe exhaustion, maybe relief. If this wasn't temporary, I decided, it could still be stable.

Phone vibrated—Dad again. Grimacing, I silenced it.

"You good?" Austen asked, eyebrow flicking toward the device.

"Family check-in."

He nodded like that explained everything. Maybe it did.

AC clanged, right on schedule. We both looked at it, then at each other, then laughed—short, overlapping.

At 6:20 I grabbed my hoodie, ready for team meal. I slid Austen a blueberry oat bar across the desk without comment. He nodded.

At the door, I hesitated. "Thanks for the game," I said.

"Anytime," he answered, already typing calculus into existence.

I left the room lighter than I'd entered.

Chapter 5
Observation Deck

AUSTEN

"Focus." Maya tapped her pen against my notebook, right next to a line of derivatives. "You dropped a negative sign here. You're hemorrhaging value."

"I wrote what the caffeine told me to write." I flipped the page, unwilling to erase the mess. My brain felt like it was floating in formaldehyde; the chalkboard smell of Ridgeway wasn't helping.

Outside the seminar room, Friday afternoon energy vibrated through the hall—zippers zipping, voices pitched high. Game day static. Every scrap of conversation drifting through the door ended with "Caribou" or "Frost Demons."

Maya's phone buzzed on the table, vibrating against a stack of anatomy flashcards. A push alert lit up the screen: **CARTER TO START IN NET TONIGHT.**

She angled it toward me, eyebrows raised. "Well. It's official. Your roommate just went viral."

"It's a starting lineup, Maya. Not a pandemic."

"Tell that to the campus," she said, gesturing toward the noisy hallway with her highlighter. "Symptoms include face paint and screaming. You ready for the exposure?"

"I'm ready to finish this problem set," I lied, recapping my pen with a precise click. "The rest is just noise."

"You're going." Not a question. A decree.

"I don't care about hockey. Not my scene."

"You also never share a dorm with the starting goalie."

"Correlation is not causation."

She grinned. "Cop-out. Game starts at seven-thirty. That gives you"—she checked her watch—"three hours to finish math and decide which side of the rink you like."

"North side," I said automatically, then cursed internal muscle memory. My foster placement in eighth grade took me to three local games; the foster dad always sat north end because tickets were cheaper. Data point lodged deep.

Maya heard the slip and let it hang without comment. Instead, she packed her laptop. "Dinner?"

I nodded, stacking the corrected quizzes. "Food that isn't vending-machine biscotti would be an upgrade."

We pushed through Ridgeway's double doors. Cold Harbor's sky had the flat, dishwater gray that turned every outdoor sound brittle. Students hurried past dressed in school merchandise. North Point sat across the quad, windows lit like a convection oven.

Halfway there, a trio of freshmen jogged by chanting, "Let's go Demons!" One wore face paint.

Maya smiled. "Entire campus is vibrating."

"Just campus?" I flexed my left hand; the fingers tingled, leftover adrenaline from grading under a time crunch. "My window at seven will be rattling in sympathy."

"You'll be inside the arena, so it won't matter."

"I—" I started, then shut up because my rebuttal sounded flimsy even to me.

North Point's heat flushed my glasses. We joined the queue, trays clattering ahead. The display boards had swapped the usual slideshow for hype videos: saves from last season, slow-mo glove snags, students losing their minds in the stands.

I stepped forward, tray vibrating in my hands.

Maya selected chickpea curry. "You okay?"

"Noticed they updated the garnish on the salad bar."

"Such drama."

I shoveled rice onto my plate, then added two slices of pizza because carbs felt correct. We found a table near the back, mostly deserted except for a philosophy grad student—I knew peripherally—asleep over handouts.

Maya unwrapped her spoon. "So. Why the resistance? Why don't you want to go to the game?"

"Crowds." I poked at the slice. "Noise. Potentially freezing my butt off."

"You look nervous," Maya said.

"I'm not the one facing pucks at ninety miles an hour."

"Ahh, that's sweet. You're worried about your roommate. It's kind of cute."

"I'm not worried about my roommate. I'm worried about what would happen to me if something happens to him."

Maya paused, her fork hovering over her salad. "Clarify."

"Blast radius," I said. "He is a high-pressure system. If he crashes and burns out there, the debris field hits our dorm room. I finally have the environment stabilized. I don't need a sullen, defeated athlete destroying the equilibrium. It introduces chaos into my living space."

"So, you're worried about collateral damage?" she asked, amused. "You think if he misses a puck, your side of the room explodes?"

"I think emotions are contagious variables," I countered. "And I have a weak immunity to drama."

"Yet, you are being a drama queen. Get over yourself. You're going to go watch some hockey, clap politely, support your roommate, and go home."

"And if he implodes? The entire town will talk about it for a week."

"And if he stands on his head, the town will talk about that." She leveled the spoon at me. "Either way, Luke survives. You, walking in or out of the arena, doesn't change his save percentage."

"I know." The pizza sauce tasted like ketchup. "But I still feel exposed."

"Because you're invested." She waited a beat. "You know that isn't a crime, right?"

I exhaled through my nose. "I bought the man coffee. I didn't adopt a puppy."

"Sometimes coffee is the puppy."

I snorted. "Is that Plato or Kant?"

"Maya Chen." She speared a chickpea. "Philosopher of unspoken feelings."

My phone buzzed. A text from Luke: *Team departs for rink at 5:45. If AC unit achieves liftoff, call the tower.*

I typed back: *Holding steady at 70°. Runway clear. Good luck.*

He answered immediately: *Bring earplugs if you come. Student section rowdy.*

No assumption, no pressure. Data. My thumb hesitated above the keyboard before replying: *Noted.*

Maya tilted her head, reading the exchange reflected in my glasses. "You're halfway through the door."

"Quarter." I pocketed the phone. "Maybe an eighth."

She grinned. "Better than zero. Finish eating."

We demolished the food in companionable silence broken only by North Point's distant dishwasher roar. I checked my watch—5:12.

I looked at my empty plate. Well, almost empty, the rice I'd put on there still sat in pile. Why I thought rice went with pizza was beyond me. Maya was right. Sitting in my room worrying about the blast radius wasn't going to prevent the explosion. It just meant I wouldn't see the fuse get lit.

"I have recitation homework to prep," I said, stacking my napkins with unnecessary precision. "It'll take me forty-five minutes to clear the queue."

Maya tilted her head, sensing the shift. "And after that?"

I sighed, defeated by my own curiosity. "After that... I suppose I should collect some empirical data. The sample size is currently zero."

Maya grinned. "I knew you'd cave."

"I am not caving. I am conducting field research." I stood up, grabbing my tray. "Meet me at the dorm?"

"6:15," she said, pointing a fry at me like a baton. "Sharp. If I miss the anthem, I'm charging you for emotional damages."

"6:15," I confirmed. "Don't be late."

She touched my sleeve—a short, approving squeeze—and let go.

Back in Ridgeway, the corridor lights flickered under motion sensors. I claimed the small copier room because it had a door that closed and, crucially, no loud AC. The hum of the machine replaced the buzz in my head while I printed blank quiz templates. Seventy copies spat out, warm stacks soothing the chill in my fingers.

Staple, align, repeat.

On the forty-fifth packet, my mind drifted: Luke's bag slung over his shoulder, shoulder taped beneath jersey, helmet perched high during warm-ups. I saw the crease through his eyes—the sliced ice, the painted lines, the impossible angles.

I shook myself. Packet forty-six.

At packet sixty, the copier jammed. I popped the cartridge door, tugged free a crumpled sheet, and remembered Luke untangling his headphone cord with the same frown of practical focus.

Five twenty-two. Copier reset. Quizzes finished. I marked my checklist for class finished, which made me think about the tidy checklist taped to the fridge back in the dorm: Quiet Hours, Guest Notice, AC 68°. Simple rules we'd signed together. I imagined a new bullet—*Arena attendance variable.*

Ridiculous.

I sat. The bench felt cold despite the crowd heat.

"Penny for your thoughts?"

I looked up. Maya stood in the aisle, clutching two soft pretzels wrapped in foil. She grinned, dropped into the empty seat beside me, and offered a pretzel.

"I'm still glad you came," she said. "And I bet your new BFF hottie goalie will be glad you showed up to."

"He won't even notice I'm here. Besides, I am observing," I corrected, taking the pretzel. "Distinct difference. They're like fish swimming around in a bowl, and I'm on the outside watching them."

"Ah yes, a boy aquarium. Uh-huh. Keep telling yourself that."

Down below, the players flooded onto the ice for warm-up. The noise level spiked to a roar. Luke skated last: controlled V-push to the crease, one, two, distinct tap of the left post with his glove, tap of the right post with his stick.

I knew the pattern from chipped AC nights.

Maya chewed a piece of salt. "He always does that. Tap, tap. Sports superstition is wild."

"It's not superstition," I said, leaning forward. "It's proprioception."

Maya blinked. "Bless you?"

"Proprioception," I repeated, pointing at the ice. "The body's ability to sense its location in space without visual input. Luke can't see the net behind him. He's touching the iron to calibrate his internal map."

Luke dropped into a butterfly, popped up, and tapped the posts again.

"He's establishing his coordinate system," I explained, watching Luke's movements track with the imaginary lines in my head. "Defining zero on the X and Y axes so he never has to look back to know where the center is. It's not magic. It's geometry."

"Dear God, you can turn anything into math."

"It's the universal constant. Besides, even Dr. Thorne would lose her mind over this. It's a perfect closed loop. High efficiency. Zero waste."

"Your scary professor?" Maya asked, taking a bite of her pretzel.

"She's not scary," I said, tracking Luke as he stretched. "But, she will ruin my GPA if I don't come up with a senior thesis topic soon."

Maya looked from me to Luke, then back to me, a slow smile spreading across her face.

"You have got to be kidding me," she laughed. "You're turning hockey into homework."

"I'm turning it into something solvable."

Down on the ice, Luke squared to the first shooter. Pads clicked; puck ricocheted. Routine.

Crowd noise washed over us, but the vectors behaved. Like he'd said, constants kept you honest. He was the constant right now, bright blue paint framing a problem set he solved in real time.

My pulse ticked a half-beat faster. I leaned forward, elbows on knees. I could see the mathematical proof developing in front of me.

Chapter 6
Signal Noise

AUSTEN

Silence in a double-occupancy dorm room is a statistical anomaly. It usually indicates one of two things: vacancy or tension. At 4:15 p.m. on a Tuesday in early October, our room was heavy with the latter.

I sat at my desk grading a stack of Linear Algebra quizzes that suggested the first-year students believed numbers were decorative. The room was quiet, but not peaceful.

Luke was pacing.

He'd come back from the athletic center twenty minutes early, skipping the post-lift meal he usually treated like a religious rite. He hadn't greeted me. He hadn't lined his shoes up. He'd dropped his bag and started pacing the six feet of floor between our beds.

Step, step, pivot. Step, step, pivot.

I kept my eyes on the red pen in my hand, but my peripheral vision tracked him. He was vibrating. Not the usual post-practice adrenaline, but something jagged. He kept checking his phone, screen lighting up, thumb hovering, then screen dark again.

I considered putting my headphones in. Noise-canceling technology was my primary defense mechanism against the chaos of shared living. But curiosity—or maybe a survival instinct that wanted to know when the explosion was coming—kept them on the desk.

Then his phone rang.

Not a ringtone; a jarring, standard-issue buzzer. Luke stopped mid-pivot. He stared at the screen for exactly one second, his posture snapping from agitated to rigid. He looked like a soldier called to attention.

He swiped answer.

"Yes, sir," he said.

The "sir" scraped against the air. Not respectful; fearful.

I capped my red pen. I shouldn't listen. The roommate social contract demanded I pretend to be deaf, or at least deeply absorbed in vector spaces. I turned a page, staring at a student's illegible proof, but the room was too small.

"I know the stats," Luke said. His voice was tight, stripped of the easy confidence he wore. "I'm on the depth chart. Harper said—"

He stopped. Cut off.

I couldn't hear the words coming from the other end, but I could hear the cadence. Staccato rhythm. Sharp. Loud enough that tinny distortion leaked from the speaker.

Luke flinched. Physically flinched, his shoulders curled inward.

"I am focused," he said. "I'm at the rink six days a week. My grades are…" He swallowed, throat bobbing visibly. "My grades are fine. I'm handling it."

More tinny shouting. I caught a word this time. *Investment.*

Then another. *Waste.*

My stomach twisted. I knew this tone. I'd heard it from three different foster dads and one caseworker too burned out to care who heard her screaming in the kitchen. The sound of a stakeholder managing a failing asset.

Luke wasn't having a conversation with a parent. He was undergoing a performance review where the penalty for failure was total liquidation.

"I won't," Luke whispered. He turned away from me, facing the corner, pressing the phone so hard against his ear his knuckles turned white. "I won't blow the knee out again. It's strong. I'm… I'm the starter, Dad. I promise."

Dad. The word sounded like a plea bargain.

The voice on the other end delivered one final, quick burst of static. Luke didn't say goodbye. He lowered the phone slowly, like it weighed fifty pounds.

The silence that rushed back in was deafening.

I waited for the release. I expected him to throw the phone, kick the bedframe, yell—something to discharge the kinetic energy the call had loaded into him.

He didn't.

Luke sank. He didn't sit; he let gravity take him, sliding down the wall until he hit the floor. He pulled his knees to his chest and buried his head in his arms. His breath hitched—a ragged, wet sound that he tried to choke back immediately.

He was shaking.

I sat frozen, pen hovering over a quiz. This was data I wasn't supposed to have.

If I acknowledged it, I shamed him. Luke Carter—Division I goalie, campus celebrity, guy who didn't color-code his closet—was hyperventilating on the rug because his father treated him like a broken racehorse. If I looked at him now, I'd be breaking the only rule that mattered: don't see the weakness.

But ignoring it felt like leaving a crash victim on the side of the road because you didn't want to get blood on your upholstery.

Calculate, I told myself. Variable X is Luke's dignity. Variable Y is Luke's current respiratory distress. Solve for equilibrium.

I needed a third variable. A distraction.

My eyes landed on the radiator. The antique cast-iron beast that Facilities had turned on yesterday. We'd traded the drone of the AC—which sounded like a jet engine during takeoff—for a heating system that clanged like a ghost dragging chains through the pipes.

I moved. Deliberate. Noisy.

I scraped my chair back against the linoleum—a harsh *screech*. Luke's head jerked up, but he didn't look at me. He wiped his face aggressively with his sleeve.

I stood, grabbed the small steel wrench I kept on the windowsill, and marched over to the radiator. I crouched down, turning my back to him, granting him the illusion of privacy.

Clang.

I hit the pipe with the wrench. Hard.

"Stupid valve," I muttered, loud enough to cover the sound of him sniffing.

Clang.

Clang.

"First the AC sounds like a Boeing 747, now this thing thinks it's a percussion section." I rattled the metal cover. "Can't concentrate."

I gave the valve a meaningless twist and banged it one more time for good measure. The noise was abrasive, filling the room, drowning out the jagged rhythm of his breathing.

I stayed there for a full minute, crouching by the heater, staring at the peeling paint, giving him time to reassemble his face.

When I stood up and turned around, Luke was off the floor.

He was sitting on the edge of his bed, back rigid. His eyes were red-rimmed, his face pale, but the mask was back in place. A fragile reconstruction, taped together, but there.

"Radiator acting up?" he asked. His voice was wrecked—hoarse and raw.

"Yep," I said, not looking at his face. Instead, I turned to the fridge. "I'm getting a seltzer. You want one?"

He hesitated. "I'm okay."

"Lime or plain?" I asked, ignoring the refusal.

"...Lime."

I opened the fridge, light spilling out. I grabbed two cans before walking over and setting one next to him.

I stood there for a second. The air between us felt different now. The membrane had thinned.

"My foster dad in eighth grade," I said, keeping my eyes on the seltzer tab as I cracked it open. *Click-hiss.* "He used to call me into the kitchen to review the grocery bill. Would circle every item I ate in red marker. Tell me what my ROI was for the month."

I took a sip. The bubbles burned pleasantly.

"Some people," I said, looking at the wall, "don't want kids. They want portfolios."

I risked a glance at him then.

Luke was staring at me. Shocked, exposed, and—slowly—relieved. The tension in his shoulders dropped an inch.

He reached out, his hand shaking a little, and cracked his own seltzer.

"Portfolios," he repeated. The word sounded heavy in his mouth.

"Bad investment strategy," I said. "High volatility."

Luke let out a breath that was almost a laugh, though it sounded painful. "Yeah. High volatility."

He took a drink. He didn't say anything else about the call. He didn't have to.

I went back to my desk and picked up my red pen. I didn't look at him again, but I could feel him there. Sitting.

I graded a quiz. I marked a question wrong, then hesitated, and drew a small smiley face next to the correction.

We sat in the quiet, drinking lime seltzer, listening to the radiator tick.

Chapter 7
The Shutout

LUKE

The puck dropped for the third-period draw and vanished in a mess of sticks. I tracked the blur long enough to see it squirt back to Caribou's right-defense. Shot probability from there: medium. Crowd volume: stupid.

I tuned both out, set my angle, and let muscle memory finish the math.

Clack. The slapper ricocheted off our captain's shin pad, bounced into the slot, and died in a puddle of snow nobody expected. Their center lunged. I slid, sealed the ice, and felt rubber thud into my ribs. No rebound. Whistle.

Seventeen thousand bodies erupted. Or maybe seven thousand; hard to count noise.

I skated a lazy arc while the ref fished the puck out of my gear. The student section hammered on the glass—painted faces, foam horns, a banner that read *CARTER = COLD FRONT.* Nice. I forced slow breaths, eyes up to the Jumbotron so I wouldn't stare at the clock.

Instead, my gaze snagged on the north-end stands. Mid-tier, two sections left of center, somebody sat stone-still amid the chaos. Gray hoodie, elbows on knees, spine straight like a geometry proof. Hair a little too neat for a Friday night rink.

Austen.

He wasn't cheering, didn't have a foam finger. Watching, as if the whole sheet of ice were another chalkboard and he planned to grade it.

The ref tapped my pad. "Ready, goalie."

I nodded and shuffled back into the crease, pulse louder than the drums.

We led 3–0 with thirty-nine seconds left when their coach yanked the goalie. Six skaters swarmed. Caribou won the draw, swung it to the far point, quick D-to-D, then a low snap pass to the back door like the film warned. I launched across, right pad flat. The shooter tried to roof it; puck clipped my mask cage and ricocheted into the corner.

The horn chased the rebound, and helmets slammed my shoulders—Ryan, Javier, and a couple guys whose names I hadn't pinned yet. The bench emptied. I stayed upright long enough to tap both posts, then let myself believe the scoreboard.

FINAL: NRU 3 – CSU 0.

The building shook. Through the mess of gloves and blockers, I glanced north again. Austen was on his feet now, still silent, hands in his pockets. He turned to the woman next to him, said something, and was already moving toward the exit.

The locker room was a riot.

It smelled of victory, which mostly meant champagne (cheap stuff Ryan had smuggled in), sweat, and someone's Axe body spray. Someone needed to put a stop to that nonsense... fast. Had to be a freshman. No adult would wear that stuff unless their goal was to repel the opposite sex.

Someone cranked the stereo to a level that vibrated my fillings. The bass line of a hip-hop track thudded against the metal lockers.

Ryan stood on a bench, shirtless, whipping a towel around his head like a helicopter rotor.

"That's how we do it in our house!" he screamed, his voice cracking. "That's how we do it! Whose house?!"

"OUR HOUSE!" the team roared back, twenty voices merging into one primal shout.

I put the catcher and blocker on the bench before peeling off my mask, hair plastered to my forehead. My ears were ringing.

Javier Morales slammed into me, wrapping me in a headlock.

"You stone-cold bastard!" Javier yelled into my ear. "That glove save? Are you kidding me? You're a freak!"

"Let go, Javi," I wheezed, laughing despite myself. "I need oxygen."

He released me, slapping my chest protector hard enough to make a hollow *thud*. "First star, Carter. First star. You earned the shower beer."

He tossed a can of cheap light lager at me. I caught it, fumbled it slightly before gripping the cold aluminum.

"Drink! Drink! Drink!" the guys chanted, pounding their sticks on the rubber floor.

I cracked the tab. Foam spilled over my jersey. I took a swig—warm and tasted like horse piss, but in that moment, the best thing I'd ever tasted.

I looked around the room. Chaos. Loud. Everything I was supposed to want.

But my head was pounding. The adrenaline was crashing, leaving behind a jagged edge of exhaustion.

Coach Harper stepped onto the rubber flooring. Conversations clipped instantly. The music didn't stop, but someone turned the volume down to a dull roar. And the guys hid the alcohol and Coach pretended not to notice.

"Solid work," she said, voice carrying. "Glove transition still late on high cycles—fix it before Tuesday. Once you're showered and changed, I'll need O'Connell and Morales for press."

Then, she turned and looked at me. "Good start, Carter. I won't make you step in front of the press tonight, but I can guarantee you'll receive a few emails to your student email account. Just politely forward any of them to the Athletic Department's media account. Don't respond directly. We don't want to encourage that behavior." She turned to leave. Without looking behind she said, "And make sure you take any evidence of the alcohol with you. You know you can't have that stuff on school grounds."

She retreated. Chaos resumed—music back up, yelling, towels snapped like whips.

I showered fast, let scalding water hit the bruise on my shoulder, then dressed in jeans and a fresh team hoodie. My phone lit up with celebratory pings; the screen showed three missed calls from Dad, one unread text from Mom-figure #4 in New Jersey, and a group chat exploding with demon emojis.

I responded to none of it.

Ryan clipped my shoulder. "Buckman Grill in an hour? Burgers on me. We're shutting the place down."

"Later," I said, shoving my gear into my bag. "Need air."

"Suit yourself, legend." He headed out, still chirping at a rookie.

I walked out the side door, away from the fans, away from the noise.

Campus looked dipped in liquid silver, a very light snow reflected off arena lights. Fans spilled toward bars, dorms, anywhere warm. A young woman in a beanie yelled, "Carter, you beauty!" before dissolving into a giggling fit with her friends. Sure, we weren't allowed to have alcohol back in the locker room, but that didn't stop the concession stands from serving the crowd. I lifted a hand, kept walking. Halfway to Stony Creek, the adrenaline crash arrived—hands shaking, vision grainy at the edges. I exhaled through a four-count the way a previous sport psychologist had taught me. *In two, three, four, and out two, three, four.* I ran through a couple of cycles, bent over with my hands on my knees.

"Is that dude about to throw up?" I heard someone ask. I lifted a hand with a thumb in the air, showing I was fine. With my back to the unknown person, no one knew who I was.

Austen had been there. I grinned at the thought. I recounted my breaths until the quiver eased.

When I got back to the room, I found Austen sitting cross-legged on his bed, laptop balanced on his thighs, earbuds in. He looked up, paused whatever glowed on the screen, and pulled the buds free.

"I felt more invested. Normally, when I watch sports, I don't care who wins or loses. And people yelling at the players or referees like their single loud voice is going to change anything is beyond me. And even more absurd when I observe people yelling at a television screen."

He looked at me, and I gestured for him to continue as I sat down, kicking off my sneakers. Austen's eyes tracked them immediately as they tumbled onto the rug. I caught the look. Without a word, I leaned down, grabbed the shoes, and lined them up neatly under the bed frame.

"It's statistically insignificant," he continued, leaning back in his chair. "Inputting energy into a system that cannot receive the signal. But tonight... the variable had a name. It wasn't just 'the goalie.' It was the person who sleeps with me. It changes the equation when you know the person inside the mask isn't just a data point."

Sleeps with me? I wanted to crack a joke, but I held back. "So, you yelled?" I asked, amused.

"I... observed with high intensity," he corrected.

I shrugged out of my coat. "Crowd was louder than the pipes tonight."

"I noticed." He set his mug down. "Nice glove on the back-door play."

I froze, one arm halfway out of my sleeve. I stared at him. "You know what a back-door play is?"

"I do now." Austen adjusted his glasses, looking slightly defensive. "I didn't know the terminology at the time. I just saw the geometry of it—the cross-ice pass, the calculated open space. I had to consult a secondary source to acquire the correct nomenclature."

He tapped a key and swiveled his desk chair, turning the laptop screen toward me.

The glow from the monitor lit up his face. It was a YouTube window, paused on a post-game media scrum. Ryan stood in the center, grinning, a cluster of microphones in his face.

"Your defenseman seems to enjoy talking to the press," Austen said. "He broke down the sequence in the second period. He called it 'robbery.'"

My cheeks went hot—ridiculous after surviving Caribou's top line. "You saw that?"

"North-end view caught the whole angle."

Silence stretched, not awkward, just full. I smelled peppermint from his mug, the lingering sweat from my underlayer, and the faint, clean detergent scent from his blanket.

I cleared my throat. "So. Did the chaos behave?"

Austen took a slow sip from his mug. "It was... loud. At first. Too many variables."

"But?"

He picked up his mug and took a sip. He licked his top lip when he pulled it away. *Wonder what that tastes like? Down boy!* I said to my hormones as I felt them rising. Post-game always made me a little on edge, sexually. *Austen's probably not even gay. He seems more... asexual, if anything.*

"But then I stopped watching the people and started watching the math." Hearing his voice brought me back to the present. He set the mug down, his hand tracing a line in the air. "Force vectors. Every player is just a mass moving at a specific velocity.

The puck is a projectile on a decaying trajectory. Once I started calculating the angles of incidence—where the lines were going to intersect—instead of listening to the screaming, it settled down."

He looked at me, eyes scanning me like I was still a diagram. "You have excellent spatial intuition, by the way. You put yourself at the convergence point of every vector. It was... satisfying to watch."

"I'll take that as a compliment," I said, suppressing a smile.

"It is. But the acoustic data was overwhelming," he said, rubbing his temple. "How do you maintain focus in the crease with all that noise?"

"I cheat," I confessed. "I wear custom-molded earplugs under the mask. They cut the volume by half. Otherwise, I'd lose my mind."

Austen's face lit up—a genuine, surprised look. He tapped his own jeans pocket.

"Convergent evolution," he said. "I admit that I put mine in during your warmups. Even with the noise-blocking technology, it was still very loud."

The grin cracked loose before I could hide it. I crossed to the fridge, grabbed a can of lime seltzer. I held it out to Austen, "Want one? I need to stay hydrated."

"Sure"

He accepted. Our fingers brushed against the cold aluminum; static zipped up my arm, sharper than usual.

Click. We both opened the cans, took the same first swig.

"I do have one technical inquiry regarding the pre-game kinetics," Austen said, staring at his can.

"Yeah?"

"The synchronized maneuver where the entire roster lies prone and... grinds their hips against the frozen surface like frogs." He looked up, expression blank. "Is that biome-chanically necessary, or were you all just trying to conceive a puck?"

I choked. Lime seltzer went down the wrong pipe, up my nose, and sprayed across my duvet. I hacked, thumping my chest, eyes watering as I stared at him.

"Are you—" I wheezed. "Are you serious?"

Austen didn't blink. "It looked very intimate. I wasn't sure if I should avert my eyes."

Then, the corner of his mouth twitched. Just a fraction.

"You're joking," I rasped, wiping my chin. "You're actually making a joke."

"Humor is a coping mechanism for trauma," he said, taking a sip. "And watching twenty men hump the ice was traumatic." Austen took a swig of his soda. "Congrats on the win."

"Team effort."

"Stats disagree. Thirty-three saves." He nudged his laptop, angling the screen so I could see the box score window. "I ran the numbers while the people behind me were chanting. Your save percentage is two standard deviations above the league average."

"Of course, you calculated that."

His eyes flicked up, amusement quiet but bright. "Data calms the crowd, Luke. Or at least, it calms me."

I sank onto my mattress opposite him. Muscles complained immediately; I rolled my left shoulder and winced.

"Still bad?" he asked.

"Impact bruise. Dalton's on it."

Without comment, Austen angled off the bed, rummaged in the freezer, and produced the bag of peas. He tossed it underhand. I caught, pressed it to the spot.

"Thanks."

"Roommate constitution, article four: frozen produce used for injury management shall be rotated and refrozen." He climbed back onto his bed.

"Didn't know we'd updated articles."

"Version 1.2 pending approval."

I laughed, then let the quiet settle. Streetlight glow bled through blinds, striping the floor between us. The radiator ticked, tame.

"I saw you," I said.

Austen's forehead creased. "Obviously."

"No, I mean—I saw you. North-end, mid-row, gray hoodie. Right after the whistle with seventeen-something left. Everyone else was standing and screaming, and you were just... you."

He didn't blink for a moment. Then he capped the laptop and set it aside. "Does that bother you?"

"Opposite." I adjusted the peas. "Made the rink smaller. Easier to track lanes."

His gaze dropped, unreadable. "Good. Because the north-end seat was optimal for exit vectors. I might reuse it."

Warmth prickled under my collar. "I'd like that."

A slow nod. Nothing more.

We both finished the seltzers. He collected the empties, crushed them enough to fit the recycling bin, then sat again, legs dangling this time, nearer. Three feet of checkerboard rug separated our knees.

He unfolded a granola bar from his desk drawer—blueberry oat. "Energy replacement," he said, offering half.

I broke it clean, passed the bigger portion back. "Macro ratio matters."

He didn't argue, just ate.

Words felt too clumsy to cram into the space that existed now, so I let them be. Instead, I peeled the game puck from my hoodie pocket—equipment manager had tossed it at me during cleanup—and rolled it between fingers.

Austen watched, expression curious.

I extended it. "Souvenir."

He hesitated. "Shouldn't that go on your shelf?"

"Already got shelves. I need constants." I nudged the puck closer. "Consider it article five."

After a beat, he accepted. His thumb traced the scuffed paint where NRU logo had chipped. "It's heavy."

"Density of vulcanized rubber, roughly 1.5 grams per cubic centimeter." The stat spilled out before I caught it.

He huffed a laugh. "I guess I won't need to Google that fact." He placed the puck on his desk, exactly centered between stapler and pens.

The clock on his nightstand clicked to 12:04 a.m. Game day officially over.

Austen stood, flicked the main light off, leaving only the desk lamp beside the puck. "Quiet hours," he reminded softly.

I slid under covers, peas balanced on my shoulder. He shut his laptop, toed off shoes, and moved around the small room with efficient hush. Mattress springs sighed as he lay down.

Dark, but not empty. The radiator's gentle hiss, hallway muffled laughs, my pulse decelerating. And Austen, eight feet away, constant as posts.

His voice drifted through shadows. "You did good work tonight, Luke."

It hit deeper than any chant. "Couldn't have done it without north-side logistics."

"Correlation," he murmured, "occasionally is causation."

I smiled into the pillow.

Silence followed, not awkward, just suspended—like the rink before puck drop, all potential.

I let my eyes close, peas cooling the bruise, muscles unknotting by degrees. One last thought surfaced, uninvited and absolute:

I want him there next game.

The radiator ticked in agreement, and sleep took the rest.

Chapter 8
The Assist

AUSTEN

The check engine light was the first variable to fail. The steering column was the second.

I was somewhere on Route 9, a stretch of asphalt that felt less like a road and more like a river of gray slush. The rain wasn't falling; it was being driven sideways by a vindictive October wind.

My 2014 Camry shuddered. The dashboard flickered—green, amber, dead—then the engine cut out completely.

Momentum carried me to the shoulder. I wrestled the wheel, tires crunching onto gravel, and came to a stop on the side of the road.

Silence.

No hum of the heater. No NPR. The sound of rain hammering the roof like a thousand tiny fists.

"No," I whispered, gripping the wheel. "No, no, no."

I turned the key. The starter clicked—a dry, hollow sound. *Click. Click.*

Battery? Alternator. Definitely alternator.

I rested my forehead against the cold steering wheel. I ran the numbers. My bank account balance was $842.15. The tow truck would be $150 minimum. The diagnostic fee $90. The part $200. Labor $120 per hour.

$842.15 minus approximately $600.

That left $242.15 to survive until the end of the semester. I'd hoped to stretch my summer earnings across the finish line, but the car gods had demanded a sacrifice in the form of a new alternator. That buffer was gone. I didn't want the distraction, but I didn't have a choice. I was going to have to pick up tutoring shifts again.

Panic, cold and sharp, spiked in my chest. I had a plan. My safety net. And now it was scrap metal.

I pulled out my phone to call a tow truck. And I had no bars. *Of course, my car would die in a dead zone.* I leaned forward and hit my head against the steering wheel.

I got out of the car. The wind hit instantly, soaking my hoodie in seconds. I knew where a garage was nearby, so I braced myself against the weather and started hiking.

Forty minutes later, the verdict was in. The shop was closed. The tow truck was "delayed due to weather."

I had two options.

> 1. Wait two hours for the bus, walk a mile in the sleet to campus, and leave the car to get towed/impounded.

> 2. Call someone.

I didn't have "someone." I had colleagues. I had professors. I had Maya, but her Mini Cooper was in the shop, and she was terrified of driving in rain, anyway.

I pulled out my phone. My thumb hovered over *Roommate (Luke)*.

Asking for help violated the primary rule of the system: *Minimize debt.* In foster care, favors were currency. If you gave someone a ride, they owned you. If they bought you food, they expected compliance. Debt was dangerous.

But my options were limited.

I hit call.

"Hey. You, okay?"

Luke's voice was deep, warm, and startlingly alert for a Tuesday night.

"I," I started, then my voice cracked. I hated it; hated sounding small. "I need a favor. A logistic assist."

"Name it."

I heard the jingle of keys on his end. He wasn't asking what it was. He was mobilizing.

"My car died," I said, listing the symptoms and the location. I tried to keep it clinical. Facts. "I was going to walk to the bus stop, but the weather is... suboptimal. And the bus runs once an hour."

"Where are you?" he asked. I gave him directions.

"Stay there," Luke said. The command was absolute. "I'm leaving now. Ten minutes."

"Luke, you don't have to—"

"I'm walking out the door. Stay inside where it's warm."

The line went dead.

I stared at the phone. He didn't ask for gas money. He didn't ask why I was stupid enough to drive in this weather. He calculated the vector and launched.

Ten minutes later, I was huddled next to the shop under an overhang when Luke's massive black truck pulled up to the curb.

Luke got out. He wasn't wearing a coat, just a gray thermal henley that clung to his shoulders. The rain didn't seem to touch him. He moved with that goalie efficiency—no wasted steps.

"Come on," he gestured for me to get in. Held opened the passenger door.

I threw my bag over my shoulder and ran for the opened door and scaled the truck to get inside.

"Heat's on max," Luke said, getting back into his side before putting the car in gear.

I nodded, unable to speak. My jaw was locked up from the shivering. I pulled my hood down, water dripping onto my nose.

"Thank you," I managed. "I hope I didn't pull you away from anything important."

"I was throwing a tennis ball at a wall," Luke said, merging into traffic. "You saved me from terminal boredom." He turned and gave me a sideways glance. "Dude, you're shivering."

My teeth chattered in response. I gave him a weak smile and wrapped my arms around myself tighter. "At least you have heated seats."

He drove differently than I did. I drove defensively, calculating risk. Luke drove like he owned the physics of the road. His hand rested lazily at the top of the wheel, his eyes tracking threats before they happened.

"Is the car dead-dead?" he asked. "Or just sick?"

"Expensive-dead," I murmured. "My best guess is four hundred for the alternator and labor. That's..." I trailed off. The math was suffocating me. "That's a problem."

I glanced at him. He wasn't judging. He was acknowledging the variable.

"We can probably find someone else to look at it," Luke said. "Ryan's uncle owns a shop in town. Might give a discount."

"It's not just the repair." I wiped my glasses on my shirt, though it was wet too. "It's the liquidity. My scholarship covers tuition and housing. It doesn't cover alternators."

The silence stretched. I felt exposed. Luke Carter, with his expensive Division I gear and his seemingly endless meal points, probably didn't understand what it meant to have your entire future jeopardized by a car part.

"You hungry?" he asked abruptly.

I blinked. "I missed dinner."

"Good. Because I'm starving and I'm not eating North Point rubber chicken tonight. There's a diner up the road. My treat."

"Luke, I can't—"

"My gas, my rules," he said, voice firm. "Consider it payment for the radiator fix."

I opened my mouth to argue the inequity of that exchange—manual labor on a valve versus gasoline and chauffeur services—but he pulled into the Galaxy Diner before I could formulate the equation.

The diner was a sensory overload of neon and grease. We slid into a booth.

I ordered a grilled cheese and tomato soup—the cheapest warm thing on the menu. Luke ordered a burger the size of a human head.

When the waitress left, I wrapped my hands around the mug of tea, trying to leach the last of the cold from my fingers.

"I almost didn't call you," I admitted. The words felt heavy, but necessary.

"Why?"

"Because asking for help introduces a debt variable," I said, staring at the steam. "In the system—foster care—you learn fast that favors come with interest. Nothing is free. If someone gives you a ride, they want something. If they buy you dinner, you owe them."

I risked a glance up.

Luke looked angry. Not at me. His jaw was tight, a muscle jumping near his ear.

"I'm a person, not a bank," he said sharply.

I flinched.

He saw it and softened. He leaned forward, his massive shoulders blocking out the rest of the diner.

"In hockey," he said, "you get an assist if you pass the puck to the guy who scores. It doesn't mean you own the goal. It just means you helped get it there. That's it. No interest. No debt."

The waitress dropped our food. Steam rose from my soup.

I stared at it. "The assist," I repeated.

"Yeah. You set me up with the radiator noise the other day when I was... when I needed cover. That was an assist. This is just me passing the puck back."

I picked up my spoon. I looked at Luke. He wasn't keeping a ledger. He wasn't calculating ROI. He was playing the game.

The knot of anxiety in my chest loosened, just a fraction.

"The alternator is going to wipe out my savings for an apartment deposit, so I could live off campus next year," I said quietly. The most honest thing I'd said to anyone in years. "That's why I'm stressed. I've been saving for months."

"We'll figure it out," Luke said, dipping a fry in ketchup. "August is a long way off. Constants change."

I cracked a smile. "Variables change, Luke. Constants remain constant. That's the definition."

"Nerd," he said, grinning. "Eat your sandwich."

We ate. And for the first time in hours, I wasn't doing math. I was existing.

Midway through the meal, the waitress swung by with a milkshake. "On the house. Vanilla."

She dropped it in the center of the table with two straws.

I looked at the shake.

"I don't do dairy," Luke lied smoothly, sliding it toward me.

I narrowed my eyes. I had seen this man drink a quart of milk from the carton. "You drink protein shakes made of whey."

"Whey is different. It's... performance dairy."

I rolled my eyes, but I took a sip. The sugar hit my bloodstream like a drug. "It's good. Try it. Consider it extra fuel."

I pushed it back to the center.

Luke hesitated, then leaned in. He wrapped his lips around the straw—the straw right next to mine. I watched his throat work as he swallowed.

Heat flared in my stomach that had nothing to do with the soup.

"So," Luke said, pulling back. "Christmas break. You staying on campus?"

"Probably. Less travel cost."

"You should watch *Die Hard*," he said. "It's the ultimate Christmas movie."

I stopped mid-sip. I looked at him with genuine horror. "Excuse me?"

"You heard me. Bruce Willis. Nakatomi Plaza. Christmas Eve."

"It's a hostage situation in a corporate high-rise," I said, putting my spoon down. "The holiday is incidental. It provides a reason for the party, nothing more. You could set it on the Fourth of July or a retirement party and the plot remains functionally identical."

"False," Luke said, pointing a fry at me like a weapon. "The emotional core of the movie is John McClane trying to reconcile with his wife for the holidays. The music is Christmas music. There is literally a dead guy with a Santa hat on him."

"A corpse in festive wear does not a Christmas movie make," I countered. "A Christmas movie requires a theme of redemption, charity, or magical realism. *Die Hard* is about ballistics and glass shards."

"It has redemption! He realizes he was a jerk to his wife."

"He realizes he might die," I corrected. "That is survival instinct, not holiday spirit. If I am hanging off a building, I too would likely regret my marital disputes. That is adrenaline, not Santa Claus."

Luke laughed. A full, chest-deep sound that made heads turn in the diner. He looked delighted.

"Okay, Professor," he said. "What's a real Christmas movie then?"

"*The Muppet Christmas Carol*," I said instantly.

He blinked. "The Muppets?"

"It adheres to the source material while introducing a meta-commentary on the narrative structure via Gonzo the Great. It is statistically the most accurate adaptation of Dickens."

Luke stared at me. And he smiled. Not the polite smile he gave fans. The real one. The one that made his eyes crinkle at the corners.

"Fine," he said. "We'll watch both. We'll run a comparative analysis."

"Acceptable."

By the time we got back to Stony Creek Hall, the rain had stopped.

The dorm room was quiet. It smelled like lavender detergent and old books. It smelled like home.

I went to my desk. Picking up the puck,—the one Luke had given me after the shutout—I turned it over in my hands.

"Thanks for the ride," I said, not looking at him. "And the dinner."

"Don't worry about it." Luke sat on his bed, groaning as he stretched his back.

"Luke?"

"Yeah?"

I set the puck down, centering it perfectly under the lamp.

"If you ever need an assist..." I looked at him. "The stats say I owe you one."

Luke looked at me. His expression was unreadable, but his eyes were soft.

"That sounds more like a debt than an assist," he said. "But, if I ever need anything from you, I won't hesitate to ask. And you can do the same thing with me. I don't get what it had to have been like for you growing up in the system, but it sounds like it warped your perception of what friendship is."

"We're friends?" The words were out of my mouth before I consciously spent a second to ponder them.

"I hope so," Luke said, propping himself on the side of his bed looking at me.

"Besides Maya, I don't really have many friends. I have colleagues and acquaintances, but I've never really had friends. Growing up, I was rarely anywhere long enough to make them."

"That sounds horribly lonely."

"Maybe, but when it's all you've known, you really don't know any better. You adjust."

"Well, Mr. Lovell, I'm happy to call you a friend. And I'm happy that I 'stuck' with you as a roommate." He actually used air quotes.

I nodded. I opened my laptop. The blue light washed over my face. The repair bill was still a disaster, and I had no idea how this would impact my finances, but those were problems for tomorrow. But the room didn't feel cold anymore.

"And I'm happy to call you a friend," I whispered before turning my attention to my laptop. I wasn't a floating variable. I had a constant.

Chapter 9
Balancing the Ledger

LUKE

"Left post," I muttered, tapping the radiator valve with my knuckles like it was a goal frame I could square up against. The hiss leveled into a steady exhale—sixty-eight degrees, give or take. Acceptable.

I'd walked in three minutes earlier, fresh off a two-hour goalie clinic and a ten-minute snow-spit jog across campus. My hair was still damp under the beanie; sweat cooled fast in Stony Creek's hallway, but inside 317 the air felt clean with a hint of mint tea, fresh laundry, printer paper, and whatever soap Austen favored.

He sat cross-legged on his bed, laptop balanced on a pillow, earbuds in. I caught a line of numbers scrolling on the screen, stacked like apartment floors. His gaze flicked up, registered me, and slid back to the code without a word.

Normal, then.

I toed my sneakers onto the rug, lining them parallel with the mini-fridge. Hoodie followed, draped across the desk chair. The silence wasn't awkward; it was a safe space. Like between whistles when you're waiting on a faceoff—no crowd roar, just the hum of refrigeration units and the scratch of skates.

My stomach chimed louder than the radiator. Lunch still sat ninety minutes away, but that's why I kept protein shakes on standby. I snagged the coldest one I could find, strawberry banana.

The cap stuck. I twisted harder; the plastic squealed.

Across the room, Austen paused his typing, eyebrow tilting. He yanked an earbud free. "That cap giving you trouble?"

"I've got it." One more twist, cap surrendered. "How long have you been coding?"

"It's not really coding, not in the computer science sense. I am using advanced mathematical software to run calculations."

"Nerd," I said, giving him a half smile.

"Since eight-thirty." He rolled his wrist, checking the analog watch he thought I hadn't noticed. "But don't worry, I took a break for coffee at ten, then chaos resumed."

"Chaos sounds orderly." I nodded at the neat desk, papers stacked perpendicular.

He granted a small, dry smile. "Chaos with boundaries."

I gulped half the shake. *Hmm, fake fruit with a hint of a chalky aftertaste, my favorite.* "Heading to North Point after study hall. You want me to grab food?"

"I'm clear at thirteen-hundred." He tapped the screen once. "Hot food travels poorly."

"Blueberry oat bars travel fine."

"They do."

Agreement hung in the air for a beat. I replaced the shake, wiped condensation off the fridge door—habit or courtesy, not sure which—then went to my closet for a clean shirt. Shoulder twinged. The bruise flashed purple at the edge of my vision in the mirror shard taped above the dresser.

Austen's voice came, low. "Has Dalton cleared you?"

"Full range of motion," I said, rotating the joint in proof. "No missed practices."

He nodded once, like he'd logged it under *variables stable*, and slid the earbud back. The radiator ticked, satisfied.

I swapped shirts, grabbed the Intro to Financial Accounting notebook—yellow sticky notes bristling like caution flags—and headed for the door.

"Quiet hours expire at four," he said without looking up.

"Copy, roommate constitution." I hesitated, hand on the knob. "Say hi to the integrals."

"They rarely greet back."

"I know the type."

The hallway swallowed the reply.

North Point wound at half throttle—past breakfast rush, pre-lunch mobs. A line of hockey hoodies carved a path toward the grill station. Most nodded at me, some offered fist bumps in passing. Starting goalie perks. I ducked into a corner by the salad bar, set my tray, and thumbed a replay clip on my phone—last save drill, skate edge shaky. Correctable.

"Monk Carter, sighted in the wild," Ryan O'Connell announced, sliding his tray opposite mine. His grin could light an end board. "I thought you ate in cryogenic stasis between practices."

"Occasional solid food," I said. "Coach approved."

He pointed at my plate: grilled chicken, rice, spinach no dressing. "That's not food, that's an FDA-approved food diagram."

"Protein, carbs, greens." I stabbed the spinach. "Healthy diet. Ta-da."

"Healthy is overrated. You ever try fries?"

"What? And let something fried pass these lips?"

Ryan snorted, shook salt over his burger.

"And for the record, I had dinner out with Austen last week and ate a burger the size of a kettlebell and a basket of fries. I'm not perfect; I just try to balance the junk food with healthy food when I can."

"You and Austen?"

"My roommate."

"You're still together?" Ryan asked. "I thought you were supposed to get a single."

"Housing called, but I declined. I would have gotten a single, but Austen would have gotten stuck with a different roommate."

"You like him," Ryan said throwing a fry into his mouth. "He's a bit strange."

"Aren't we all?" I stabbed a piece of chicken and stuck it into my mouth. "He's actually a nice guy. Sure, he's awkward around the edges, but he's had a rough life. Makes my problems pale by comparison."

"How so?"

I looked around to see if anyone was hearing. In the back of my head, I knew I shouldn't be talking about Austen to anyone, but I needed to talk to someone, and Ryan seemed like a pretty decent guy.

"He was a foster kid. Grew up in all kinds of unstable environments. I think that's why everything has to be so organized now as an adult."

"Oh, dear God, your chaotic nature must be driving him into an early grave," Ryan joked. I stole one of his fries.

"I'm not that bad. And he's giving me some structure that I probably need in my own life. We balance each other. So, no, I stuck with Austen instead of getting a single. I couldn't ask for a better roommate."

"Does he know you're gay?" Ryan asked.

I'd been very open with my entire team before I even transferred here. I refused to play for a team that was homophobic or transphobic. The hockey world was masculine, and there's a ton of testosterone floating around, but save it for the ice.

"We haven't talked about that," I admitted. "Just not been a conversation that's come up."

"So, you're not lusting after the little math boy sleeping next to you at night?"

"Umm... No. He's totally not my type."

"Oh, so what is your type?"

"Are you hitting on me, O'Connell?" I asked, making my eyes go wide in faux shock. "If you are, I tend to go for more masculine guys."

"Fuck you!" he said, throwing a fry at me. I caught it in my mouth. "Good save!"

"But to answer the question. No, I am not dating anyone. No, I am not planning on dating anyone. No, I am not looking to date anyone. I have enough going on between classes and hockey. The last thing I need to do is add some needy guy on top of everything."

"Yeah, I get that. Last girl I dated didn't understand how much time hockey takes up during the season. She always complained about not seeing me enough. Finally ended up dumping me and dating some guy on the baseball team. She clearly had a type. You skipping Buckman again tomorrow night?"

"Probably. Gotta quiz the next day. Accounting. It's already kicking my ass."

"Brother, it's a Wednesday night." Bite, chew. "Live a little. You've got plenty of time to study between now and tomorrow."

I spun a pepper packet until the granules settled. "Living isn't the problem. Maintaining is."

"Translation: you're locked-in."

"Coach likes locked-in."

"Sure." He chewed thoughtfully, eyes narrowing enough to feel like x-ray specs. "Team also likes guys who show up for trivia night."

"I show up on the ice."

"Fair." He shoved the fries across the tray gap. "Come on, eat one more. Prove you won't combust."

I picked the smallest, crispy and over-salted. Ate it. Ryan saluted me with his paper cup.

"Miracle recorded," he said. "Seriously, you're allowed fun."

"Define fun that won't kill my reflexes."

"Watching Decker butcher pop-culture categories while we heckle him. Alcoholic hydration optional."

I huffed a laugh. "Tempting."

"Good. I'm texting you the time." He wiped ketchup on a napkin to unlock his phone. "Bring the math kid if you want. Lovell's brain might save us on the academic-y questions."

"He's got class."

"So do you." Ryan eyed me, softer. "You okay, Carter?"

"Fine."

"Fine means you're about to dive headfirst into goalie brain." He pointed a fry at me. "Remember, team's got your back."

The words pricked, not painful, unexpected—like skate lace biting skin where padding ends. I nodded, throat thick.

Ryan grinned again, tension gone. "Gotta roll. Film in ten." He stood, burger half demolished. "Don't monk out too hard."

"No promises."

He left, weaving through tables. A pack of freshmen parted like fish around him.

I finished the chicken, ignored the fries, and checked the time—12:41. My study group for accounting started at one. I grabbed two blueberry oat bars from the grab-n-go shelf, slid them into the hoodie pocket, and headed for the door.

It took me a few minutes to find the conference room the group had reserved inside the library, walls lined with motivational posters about synergy. Four athletes sat—soccer goalie I barely knew, two volleyball hitters, and the linebacker nobody called anything but Tank. The athletic department's tutor took attendance, then retreated behind a laptop.

Financial Accounting worksheet glared up—adjusting entries, deferred revenue. I filled columns, checked against examples. Numbers balanced, but only because I triple-counted. Exam next week weighed twenty-five percent. Borderline grades meant academic eligibility reviews. Reviews meant Coach Harper in your ear and, worse, Dad on the phone pretending not to panic.

I exhaled, leaned back. The overhead light buzzed like a wasp.

Two bars of phone signal—enough. I cleared notifications, answered a medical form email, ignored a message from Dad (voicemail length: forty-three seconds) and another from one of my ex-moms in New Jersey. *Was she number two or number four?* I couldn't remember anymore. No capacity.

Worksheet finished at 2:20. I packed up, nodded at Tank, and bolted before I got sucked not a conversation about eggs.

Snow sifted outside, fine and directionless. Practice ran at five. Lift after. The window between belonged to recovery and food—and whatever nonsense the dorm offered.

I quick-stepped across the quad, gripping the hoodie pocket to keep the bars from bouncing out. Heat rose under the beanie; breath fogged sideways.

In Stony Creek, I hoofed it up the three floors instead of waiting for the elevator. I opened the fire door, the third-floor carpet muffled my arrival. Room 317's door was cracked—Austen's standard setting when he was in. I nudged it open.

He sat at the desk now, hoodie draped over the chair back, earbuds dangling unused. Shoulders hunched, eyes on a screen full of red text. I could sense that something was amiss just by noticing how he slumped his body.

"Bad?" I asked.

"It keeps telling me I have an undefined variable," he said without turning. "Except I defined it twelve lines up."

"Ghost in the machine."

"Or in my logic." He scrubbed a hand through his hair, messing it worse. I walked over to him and placed a hand on his shoulder while I pulled out a bar. "You clearly need fuel."

He exhaled, tension bleeding enough to see. "Thanks." He grabbed the bar.

I kept my hand on his shoulder for a second longer than is strictly in the bro-code. I pulled it away quickly and walked to my side of the room as I peeled off my beanie. "How's the radiator?"

"Temperamental." He tapped the wrench beside the valve.

"I never asked, but where did that come from?"

"Facilities left it when they failed to fix the percussion concerto. And since it's still not fixed, I claimed the wrench for our room."

"You're a maintenance understudy now?"

"Pays zero, but the benefits are exact temperature."

I laughed before dropping onto my mattress. The springs protested; I eased back, pulling my phone out.

I opened the team portal. The assistant coach had uploaded the stats from the weekend scrimmage. I scrolled to the bottom, hoping the numbers looked better on a screen than they felt on the ice.

They didn't.

"Unbelievable," I muttered, tossing the phone onto the duvet.

Austen stopped typing. He spun his chair halfway around. "What's wrong?"

"Save percentage," I said, rubbing my eyes. "Point-eight-nine-two. Harper wants us above nine-hundred or we run suicides."

"Define the metric," Austen said.

"Shots on goal divided by saves. The only number that matters."

Austen frowned, looking at me like I'd said 2+2 equals a potato. "That is a statistically flawed metric."

I blinked. "It's the NHL standard."

"Then the NHL is bad at math." Austen turned fully toward me, resting his elbows on his knees. "Does the formula account for shot location?"

"No."

"Does it account for velocity or defensive screening?"

"No. A save is a save."

"So," Austen said, holding up a pen, "if a forward dumps the puck in from center ice—zero threat, floating at ten miles an hour—that counts as one shot?"

"Yeah."

"And if Morales comes in on a breakaway, dekes you out, and fires from the slot with three seconds of time—that's also one shot?"

"Yeah."

"Then the data is useless," Austen said flatly. "It treats a variable with a near-zero probability of success the same as a high-danger event. Lazy math."

I stared at him. For three days I'd been beating myself up over that .892. I'd watched the tape until my eyes bled. And Austen dismantled the entire premise in thirty seconds.

"Lazy math," I repeated.

"It's noise," he said, turning back to his screens. "You're measuring volume, not quality. Ignore it."

I picked up the phone again. I looked at the number. It still read .892, but for the first time, it didn't look like a judgment. It looked like a bad equation.

"You realize you invalidated the entire scouting combine," I said.

Austen shrugged. "Then the NHL should hire better statisticians."

We ate our bars in near silence after that, wrappers crackling.

I finished first, wadded the foil tight. "Ryan thinks you should join trivia night."

"Define trivia."

"Random facts plus heckling."

"Sample questions?"

"Last week's bonus round was naming states with only one major-league team."

"That's a horribly worded question. How does one define 'major-league' team?"

"You know, the NFL, NBA, MLB, NHL—"

"The MLS?"

"The what?" I asked.

"Major League Soccer," Austen replied, sounding offended on behalf of the sport. "You see, that question doesn't have enough parameters. If you exclude soccer, Oregon and Utah are correct answers because of the Trail Blazers and the Jazz. But if you acknowledge the MLS, which you should, given attendance metrics, they both have second teams. Oklahoma is the only state that remains a single-team answer regardless of the variable. It's not a geography question; it's a test of the host's bias against non-US-centric football."

I stared at him. He hadn't just answered the question; he'd dissected the methodology.

"Okay," I said. "We need exactly that energy. Tonight. Eight o'clock."

He considered. "Sounds tolerable."

I raised an eyebrow. "That's almost enthusiasm."

"Unverified."

"Tonight, eight. Can I let Ryan know we're in?"

Austen flicked his gaze toward the radiator, as if consulting the pipes. "We'll see."

Quiet resettled. Keys clacked under his fingers, code scrolling in new colors now—errors clearing. Shoulder twinge again; I swapped the empty wrapper for the L-bag peas, still frosted.

A chime pinged my phone—university email icon. I thumbed it without real focus, expecting a practice update.

SUBJECT: Academic Alert—Financial Accounting 221 Section 03

Carter, Lucas—Your current grade of 68 percent indicates a potential risk of course failure. Attendance at the graduate teaching assistant's tutoring sessions is strongly recommended. See attached schedule.

Blood flooded my ears. Sixty-eight. Passing but not by enough. I had to get at least a C- in the class for it to count toward my major. And I needed the C- to stay on the team. A string of expletives ran through my head. I sat straighter, screen inches from my face as if proximity could change digits. It didn't.

Across the room the keyboard stopped. "Everything okay?" Austen asked.

I flipped the phone screen-down on my thigh. "Yeah."

Pause. "Room rule—no lying about emergencies." His tone stayed even, not pushy.

"Not an emergency," I forced a slow breath through my nose. "Accounting grade."

"And?"

"Sixty-eight."

"Threshold for athletic eligibility?"

"I need at least a C- for it to count in the major and to keep eligibility." I hadn't meant to disclose the exact number; it slipped.

He spun his chair, elbows on knees. "Next quiz?"

"Tomorrow," I admitted.

"Study plan?" I shrugged. Austen looked at his watch. "We have time, let's get down to business."

"It's not calculus," I said. "And it's definitely not hockey stats."

"Numbers still obey rules." He opened a desk drawer, producing a yellow legal pad. "Show me the chapter."

"I—" My throat closed. No backup plan existed beyond white-knuckling the curve. "I don't want to drag you into—"

"Assist." He uncapped a pen. "I needed an assist, and you were there for me. You need an assist now; I am here for you."

The radiator clanged—two sharp beats, then a settling hush. Like punctuation.

I set the phone beside the puck on my nightstand, the alert still glowing. Couldn't change the score. Could change the variables.

"Okay," I said. "After dinner."

"Bring the syllabus," he replied, turning back to the screen. "And your patience. I'm available after nine."

Patience. Not my A-skill, but I nodded anyway.

I lay back, peas cold through the sleeve, eyes on the ceiling crack. The room didn't feel rearranged anymore. The math had changed, but so had the constants.

The radiator ticked, metronome steady, while Austen's keyboard resumed its measured cadence.

Chapter 10
Variable Shift

AUSTEN

Luke's phone chimed again—third time in ten minutes—and his jaw twitched like the muscle didn't know whether to lock or sprint. We sat at opposite ends of the dorm, him on his bed lacing up running shoes for weights, me at the desk debugging a freshman's horrendous MATLAB loop. From the angle of the screen, I couldn't read the alert, but whatever it said chased the color from his face.

He shoved the phone under his thigh, yanked the knot tight, and tried for casual. "Back by eight," he said.

"Mm-hmm." I kept eyes on my monitor, fingers still on the trackpad. The cursor blinked inside an if-statement I'd already fixed. "Have fun pushing iron."

He grunted acknowledgment, grabbed his backpack, then paused. "Need anything from North Point?"

"Blueberry oat bar. If civilization collapses, I'm building a fort out of them."

The smile he gave was automatic, not lived in. "One fort, coming up."

Door shut. Hallway swallowed his footsteps. The radiator hissed an exhale that sounded like *"don't buy it."*

I minimized the code window and opened a blank note.

VARIABLE: Luke OBSERVED DATA – Phone buzz x3 in 10 min – Pulse spike visible at temple – Left shoe double-knotted (stress habit) – Smile latency 0.5 s (not baseline)

Hypothesis wrote itself: something academic, probably ugly. Athletes didn't bother double-knotting for girlfriend drama.

Problem: No proof. Also, none of my business.

I closed the laptop before the note turned into a rescue plan, shoved it in my bag, and headed to Ridgeway. Numbers were safer when they belonged to other people.

The math lounge smelled like old carpet and burned Keurig pods. A cluster of sopho-mores argued over divergent series at the whiteboard. I claimed the far table, noise-can-celing earbuds in, and attacked stack two of tomorrow's quizzes. Twenty minutes and a dozen chain-rule misfires later, the door cracked.

"Austen," Maya sing-songed, sliding into the chair opposite me. Red beanie, fingerless gloves, eyes that missed nothing. "I have not seen you in the cafeteria in days, so I'm conducting a wellness check."

"Luke keeps bringing me nutrition bars, so I'm good."

Maya rolled her eyes. "You realize those are snacks and not meals? They're to tide you over until you eat actual food?"

"I know," I snapped.

"So, you're in a mood." She unzipped her coat. "Lay it on me."

"Nothing to lay." I flipped a quiz, red-penned a circled integral. "Roommate's busy, radiator at equilibrium, calculus kids mostly remembered their limits. Banner day."

She hummed. "Banner days don't make you talk in bullet points."

I kept pen moving. "Luke's phone had a small meltdown. That's all."

"Define meltdown."

"Trio of notifications, visible spike in heart rate, possible extra shoelace knot."

"Academic?"

"Statistically probable. I am tutoring him later in financial accounting." I dated the quiz margin, slid it aside. "Didn't ask."

"What do you know about financial accounting?"

"Nothing," I admitted. "But math is math. I can follow a formula with the best of them."

"So, what was wrong with Luke?"

"Didn't ask."

Maya leaned back until the chair squeaked. "Because asking would violate... what, subsection four of the Roommate Neutrality Pact?"

"Because he didn't offer." I lined up the next quiz square with the edge of the desk. "Data without consent is surveillance."

She snorted. "You're already surveilling; you want permission to analyze."

"Not the same."

"Sure." She stood, snagging my pen mid-stroke. "Break. Harbor Commons. You can buy me bubble tea with all the moral high ground you're saving up."

I opened my mouth to argue—saw the sophomore herd prepping to stampede my table—and closed the gradebook.

"Fine."

Harbor Commons never decided what it wanted to be—half café, half airport terminal, acoustics for neither. We wove through clusters of students and found two seats at the window bar. Outside, dusk bled pink across piles of plowed snow; inside, someone's Bluetooth speaker fought the house playlist and lost.

I ordered black tea, no tapioca; Maya went full unicorn—lavender milk, rainbow jellies, 150 percent sweetness. She watched me tap the debit pad.

"Want to talk now or after your annual sugar panic?"

"Now's good." I popped the lid on my drink, steam fogging my glasses. "Luke looks like he swallowed a hockey puck."

"Practice injury?"

"Phone injury." I told her the observable facts, stripped of speculation. She sipped purple sugar sludge and nodded like a clinician.

"What's your move?"

"Wait for him to say something."

Maya raised a brow. "And what if he doesn't?"

"Then I continue not violating room-rule confidentiality."

"You mean the rule only you follow."

I took a measured drink. "He's entitled to privacy."

"He's entitled to help, too."

I traced the moisture on the cup with a thumb. The condensation smear looked like a goal crease—semi-circle, chalky. "I am helping him, with math."

"You've got the academic recovery plan," Maya said, blowing on the steam rising from her cup. "But do you have the human plan?"

"Define human plan."

"Actually talking to him," she said. "You treat him like a broken equation. Maybe try treating him like a roommate. You know, ask a question that doesn't have a numerical answer."

Point, Chen.

I stared into the dark swirl of my black tea. I thought about earlier—Luke staring at his phone, the way his jaw had locked tight. I didn't know the sender, but I knew the reaction. It wasn't an academic failure; it was a personal one.

Risk assessment: Asking about his life might blur lines, but so did letting his problems become my problems. And they already were, whether I admitted it or not—the room felt off-balance when he left it unsettled.

Maya nudged my ankle with hers. "Your face is doing that linear-programming thing."

"Meaning?"

"Optimizing a solution while pretending it's hypothetical."

I cleared my throat. "He has weights until six. If he circles back before team film, I intend to... expand the inquiry parameters."

"In English?"

"I will ask him how he is. Qualitatively."

"Revolutionary." She poked a crumpled sugar packet at my forehead. "Proud of you, nerd."

I salvaged dignity by flicking the packet into the trash on the first try—two-point shot. The playful clap she gave echoed louder than I liked; heads turned, but no one cared.

Time check: 5:37 p.m. Enough to grade a few more quizzes, not enough to obsess.

"I should get these done," I said. Standing up and getting ready to head back Ridgeway. "You volunteering to double-check partial credits?"

"Tempting, but I have feminist lit at six." She picked up her bag. "Text me once you solve for x."

"x equals maybe."

"x equals yes," she called over her shoulder, disappearing into the quad.

I walked back alone now—tea cooling, and a variable I was done pretending to ignore.

Back at Ridgeway, I graded with the efficiency of a tax accountant on April fourteenth. Red pen flew. Exemplary answers got smiley slashes; sloppy ones, terse arrows. When the stack shrank to zero, my phone read 8:42.

I stuffed the papers, laptop, and emergency earplugs into my bag and made for Stony Creek. Snow squeaked under boots; vapor curled under my scarf. Every few steps I rehearsed neutral ways to open the conversation.

Hey, Luke, noticed you nearly cracked your phone in half with your quadriceps—need anything?

Too direct.

Radiator's holding steady at sixty-eight. You look twenty degrees lower—want to calibrate?

Too weird.

By the time I hit the third-floor carpet, I'd drafted nothing usable.

Our door was ajar—standard two-inch buffer. Light glowed. Inside, Luke sat at his desk, shoulders forward, textbook open but untouched. His phone lay screen-down on the keyboard. The rest of the room looked staged: bed made military-tight, gear bag zipped, even the stickhandling ball corralled in its pouch. I could see the shoulder taping under his tank top.

He glanced up. Relief crossed fast, like a flashcard flipped for half a second. "Hey."

"Evening." I closed the door, dropped my bag under the desk. Radiator check—valve perfect. Good. "How were weights?"

Luke spun the athletic-training ice cup in one hand, condensation dripping onto a towel he'd spread logically across his thigh. "Weights were fine. Coach didn't kill us."

"Pulse and respiration confirm survival." I toed off my boots. "Food acquired?"

He nodded toward the fridge. Two blueberry bars waited on my shelf spot, aligned like stalagmites. "Supply chain secured."

I peeled off my jacket and resisted the obvious stall. *Ask. Just ask.*

I opened the fridge instead, grabbed one bar, turned, and leaned against the door. "Phone quiet now?"

His gaze dropped to the device as if surprised to find it still there. "Sure."

Too fast. I unwrapped the bar, broke it in half, ate the smaller piece. "Quiet is an interesting metric. Three alerts earlier, then radio silence."

Luke's shoulders stiffened. He picked at the training-room tape around the cup lid. "Was nothing."

My turn to raise an eyebrow. "You ice your shoulder for nothing?"

"That's for practice." He forced a half-smile. The gesture carried the vibrancy of a wet firework.

"It wasn't just practice," he admitted, looking down at his knees. "We dropped the exhibition against Vermont last night. 4-3."

"I didn't see a score alert."

"Because we should have buried them. Instead, I lost the puck in traffic twice. Complete vision failure." He crushed the paper cup in his hand. "Coach is making sure I feel it."

"Statistical variance," I offered.

"Garbage goaltending," he corrected.

Silence chewed twenty seconds while the radiator ticked a metronome. Luke stared at the textbook page—statement of cash flows, bright blue heading. His finger traced the margin like reading Braille he didn't understand.

"You really don't have to help me," Luke said. "I've dug the hole, I can figure a way out."

I stepped away from the fridge, took the rolling chair opposite him. Kneecaps level. "Two data points." I held up fingers. "One: numbers obey structure. Two: we have structure."

"You're not in this class."

"Cash flow statements aren't sorcery."

He pinched the bridge of his nose. "Austen—"

"I said I was available to help after nine." I checked the watch he'd once teased me for polishing weekly. *9:03.* "Congratulations, it's after nine."

Relief flashed over his eyes, then vanished behind the same controlled mask he used in goal. The speed of it irritated me—like needing something for a fraction of a second was a crime.

I pulled his textbook closer, flipped to the quiz review. "Show me what tanked."

He opened a loose-leaf folder, slid out the graded paper. Red ink bled across margins: *Posting error, Wrong sign, Incomplete schedule.* I scanned line totals—he'd flipped debits and credits in three places. Simple inversion, compounding mistakes.

"Okay," I said. "These are sign errors."

"No, these are me-not-getting-it errors."

"Sign errors," I repeated calmly. "Systems don't care why your vector runs opposite. We correct direction, recalculate magnitude." I grabbed the legal pad from my desk drawer, drew a T-account. "Left side debit, right side credit. Mirror it in your head."

I drew a large T-account on the legal pad.

"Accounting isn't about money," I said, tapping the paper. "Money is emotional. This is a closed system. Like thermodynamics. Conservation of mass."

Luke squinted at the pad. "I'm pretty sure accountants don't do physics."

"They do. They call it 'balancing.' Inputs must equal outputs. Zero-sum game." I drew a line down the middle. "Left side is debit. Right side is credit. Think of it like goal differential."

I wrote HOME on the left and VISITOR on the right.

"Assets are your Home team," I explained. "When you gain cash or equipment, you debit the Home column. A goal for you. Positive differential."

Luke watched, elbow on knee, the training cup forgotten.

"Liabilities and Equity are the Visitors," I continued. "When you take out a loan, you credit the Visitor column. It balances the equation. The system stays at equilibrium."

I looked up. "If you score a goal (debit cash), you have to record where it came from (credit revenue). Action, reaction. Newton's third law applied to a ledger."

Luke's mouth twitched. He looked from the T-chart to me, his eyes narrowing as the logic clicked into place.

"So, a debit isn't 'subtraction,'" Luke said slowly. "It's... adding to the Home score."

"Exactly. And a credit isn't 'adding money'; it's acknowledging the Visitor's claim on that money."

Luke let out a short breath, shaking his head. "I spent three weeks trying to memorize acronyms, and you fixed it with a scoreboard analogy in thirty seconds."

"Systems are universal," I said. "Hockey is a system. Math is a system. Business is a system. You already speak the language; you were using the wrong vocabulary." I slid the quiz over, handed him my mechanical pencil. "Now re-enter this line. Ignore past mistakes. We forward-propagate corrections."

He hesitated, took the pencil. I saw him roll his shoulder a couple of times while he was working. I retrieved the spare bag of peas and pressed it to his shoulder without ceremony. He flinched, then settled beneath the cold.

"Peas are conditional incentive," I explained. "Balance the ledger, keep the ice."

"Cruel tutor."

"Effective." I hovered long enough to confirm the bruise blotch hadn't darkened, then returned to the desk.

Numbers scratched. Radiator punctuated. Outside, dorm hallway muffled a burst of laughter; quiet hours were still an hour off. Luke finished the line, handed the pencil back.

I checked: debits, credits, totals—perfect. "Good."

He exhaled, a small sound. "One line doesn't fix the exam."

"Lucky us, there are only"—I counted—"eight lines per problem. We iterate."

He started to nod, but the movement faltered halfway, like a glitch.

"What?" I asked, suddenly self-conscious of how close we were.

"Nothing." He pressed lips together. "Just—thanks."

"Just an assist," I reminded. "Besides, you brave North Point for my blueberry bar addiction."

"Not the same scale."

"Both hinder performance."

Luke stared at the legal pad, running his thumb over the graphite sums.

"Ryan says the team's got my back," he said quietly, not looking up. "But I didn't expect this. Not from the guy who got stuck with the overflow."

Stuck with.

The words hit a bruised spot I usually kept covered. Luke thought he was the burden? That was a miscalculation. *I* was the one who required noise-canceling headphones to survive a Tuesday. *I* was the one who alphabetized the pantry. People didn't get stuck with Luke Carter; they got stuck with me.

I recapped the pencil, the plastic click loud in the silence.

"You have your variables reversed," I said. "The Housing Office didn't stick you with me, Luke. They dumped you in the only room with a vacancy because nobody else wanted the guy who solves math problems for fun."

Luke looked up. The self-deprecation in his eyes vanished, replaced by genuine confusion. "You think I mind?"

"Most people do."

"I don't," he said. He leaned back, spinning the pencil I'd given him. "You're the only thing making sense in my life right now, Austen. I'm glad I'm here. Friends help friends, right?"

Friends.

He said it casually, like it was a given constant, not a variable he'd just introduced to the system. The word sat in the air between us, heavier than the textbook, but warmer.

"Right," I managed. My voice felt tight. "Friends help friends."

I cleared my throat, needing to shift the focus before the data overwhelmed me. "In that spirit... regarding your earlier inquiry about trivia night."

Luke's eyebrows shot up. "Yeah?"

"Ryan's harassment is becoming a disruption. I am willing to attend. As a counter-measure."

"A counter-measure," Luke repeated, a grin spreading slow and wide. "Thursday? Eight o'clock?"

"Conditional on this ledger balancing."

"It balances," he said, tapping the pad. "I checked it twice."

"Then the schedule is locked."

I checked my watch. "10:47. Quiet hours imminent."

Luke finished the last problem, tapped the eraser twice like sealing a deal. He offered the pencil back.

"Keep it," I said, opening my bottom drawer to reveal a pristine box of Ticonderogas. "Inventory redundancy."

He twirled it once, pocketed it. "Noted."

He stood to stretch, vertebrae popping, and paused, looking at the code scrolling on my open laptop screen—a mess of flocking simulations I'd been fighting with all week.

"What's that?" he asked. "Matrix code?"

"Thesis," I sighed, rubbing my temples. "Bird flocking behaviors. My advisor, Dr. Thorne, thinks the current model is too predictable. I need a new subject. Something with more chaotic variables."

Luke grinned. "You could study how fast I fall asleep reading this accounting textbook."

"Insufficient velocity," I said. But as I looked at him—sweatshirt rumpled, hair messy, vibrating with that restless athletic energy—the gears turned. *Chaotic variables. High speed. Unpredictable collisions.*

"Same time tomorrow?" he asked.

"If you're willing."

"Always."

He retrieved the ice pack, now room temperature, and exchanged it for a fresh one from the freezer. He thanked me with a nod, applying the cold like a ritual.

Lights dimmed at eleven on the dot. He crossed to his bed, peeled back covers and climbed under them. I powered down the desk lamp, but a slice of streetlight still found the puck on my shelf—centered, standing vigil.

Luke's voice drifted through the dark. "Austen?"

"Yeah?"

"Thanks. For not... you know. Treating me like overflow."

"We solve for the new perimeter," I answered.

"Yeah. We do."

Silence, then the soft rustle of sheets. If he smiled, I couldn't see it, but the room settled—puzzle edges aligned, picture not finished, yet recognizably ours.

I lay back, counting radiator ticks like metrical proof. Somewhere around tick twelve my phone buzzed—Maya: *x equals yes?*

I typed under the blanket: *System update in progress. Variable 'Friend' added to dataset.* Send.

Radiator ticked thirteen. The math held.

Chapter 11
The Lab

AUSTEN

Starlings are, statistically speaking, boring.

I sat in the library carrel, staring at a simulation of *Sturnus vulgaris* migration patterns. On my screen, thousands of digital dots swooped and swirled in a mesmerizing cloud. Efficient. Beautiful.

Putting me to sleep.

I checked my phone. No texts from Luke. He was at practice, likely stopping pucks or getting yelled at by Harper.

I minimized the birds and pulled up a different window—a pirated stream of the Merrimack game I'd found on a shady forum. I watched Luke move.

Shuffle. Post-tap. T-push. Freeze.

Technically, the players weren't a flock. Luke was a single point of data navigating a hostile geometric plane.

I typed *hockey as flock of birds* into a Google search to see if anyone had looked at flocking behavior of hockey players. All I found was an obscure reference to a pigeon. I read the result, *In hockey, a "pigeon" is a common slang term, usually a friendly jab, for a player who doesn't do a whole lot on their own but capitalizes on the work of others (e.g., scoring a goal off a lucky rebound after a teammate did all the hard work). Pigeons are often seen as "bench warmers" or not highly respected, much like the common perception of the bird itself.* This made no sense to me. If someone wasn't a working part of the system, why would they keep them. If a gear in a watch breaks down, you replace the gear with one that works. I made a mental note to ask Luke when I saw him.

The birds were random chaos masquerading as order. Luke was order imposed on chaos.

I closed the laptop. I couldn't write about birds. Not when I had a much more interesting variable sleeping five feet away from me every night.

I scribbled in my notebook, *"Flocking behavior?" Can we apply mathematical flocking behavior to hockey players? We already use the term to describe and analyze other forms of leadership. Can teamwork, positioning, and coordinated movement among players on the ice be evaluated in the same way? It is a metaphor for how individual players, without global control from a single leader (the goalie), follow simple local rules to achieve complex, collective movement, much like a flock of birds or a school of fish.*

But to prove it, I needed raw data.

The Audio-Visual Department lived in the sub-basement of the Arts building, a window-less dungeon that smelled of Doritos.

I walked up to the cage. Ben, the student manager—a guy who wore a beanie indoors and looked like he hadn't seen the sun since mid-June—was wrapping cables.

"We're closed, man," Ben said without looking up. "If you want a camera for a film project, fill out the form online."

"I don't want a camera," I said, leaning on the counter. "I want the login for the arena ceiling feeds."

Ben paused. He looked up, squinting. "The overheads? Those are for coaching staff only. Coach Harper locks that down tight."

"I know," I said. "But the server architecture for the Athletics Department shares a trunk with the AV archive. Which means you have an admin bypass?"

Ben crossed his arms. "And why would I give that to you?"

I reached into my bag and pulled out a sheaf of papers. "Math 304. Advanced Calculus."

Ben's eyes widened.

"I heard you're retaking it," I said. "I have the answer key for the midterm problem set. With proofs. And I'll throw in a tutorial on how to solve the partial derivatives, so you don't fail the class again."

Ben looked at the papers. He looked at me. A simple transaction: intellectual property for digital access.

"You're roommates with the goalie, right?" Ben asked.

"I am."

"Is he good? Like, actually good?"

"Statistically above average," I said.

Ben grinned. He grabbed a sticky note and scrawled a username and password. "Don't get caught. If anyone asks, you hacked it."

"Pleasure doing business."

The Theoretical Mathematics department was located in the basement of Ridgeway Hall, far from the flashy biology labs with their glass walls. We were in the "Bunker"—a corridor of whiteboards and humming servers.

I stood outside Office B-12. My heart rate was 98 BPM. High.

Dr. Aris Thorne did that to people.

"Enter if you understand the Fourier Transform," a voice called out from inside. "Leave if you're looking for the registrar."

I opened the door.

Dr. Thorne was standing on her desk—literally standing on it—adjusting a projector mounted to the ceiling. She was wearing a silk blouse tucked into high-waisted trousers, her heels abandoned on the floor. Six-foot-two in her stocking feet, a statuesque woman with sharp cheekbones and eyes that could dissect a theorem at fifty paces.

The smartest person I had ever met, and arguably the most terrifying.

"Dr. Thorne," I said.

"Lovell," she said, not looking down. "Hand me that screwdriver. Phillips head."

I grabbed the tool from her cluttered desk and handed it up. She tightened a screw on the mount, gave it a satisfied slap, and climbed down with the grace of a dancer. She slipped her feet back into her stilettos.

"Talk to me," she said, sitting behind her desk. "How are the birds? Have we solved the flocking algorithm?"

"Yes, but I'm dropping the birds," I said.

Thorne paused. She leaned back, tenting her fingers. "You're pivoting. Two months before the draft submission. That is either brilliance or suicide. Defend it."

"The birds are predictable," I said, clutching my laptop. "I found a new dataset. A closed system with high-velocity projectile variables. Specifically... the goaltender position in collegiate hockey."

Thorne stared at me. The silence stretched for five seconds.

"Hockey," she said flatly. "Men hitting each other with sticks? That is your muse?"

"It's not about violence," I said quickly. "It's about geometry. Look."

I connected my laptop to her monitor. I typed in Ben's stolen password.

The screen filled with a wide-angle, top-down view of the ice. Grayscale, grainy, and perfect. It showed the crease—the blue paint—and Luke.

"Where did you get this?" Thorne asked.

"I acquired it."

"Illegal acquisition. Good start." She leaned forward. "Just don't get caught."

I hit play.

On screen, the play developed. A pass from the corner. Luke didn't scramble. He didn't lunge. He rotated his hips and pushed—a sharp, clean vector—arriving at the post exactly as the puck arrived.

"Watch the efficiency," I said. "Most biological subjects in high-stress evasion scenarios exhibit panic—wasted energy, erratic movement. But Subject G..."

I pointed to Luke.

"He minimizes the hypotenuse," Thorne whispered.

She grabbed a dry-erase marker from her desk and drew directly on her monitor screen, tracing Luke's path in red.

"He doesn't track the object," she murmured, drawing a line from the shooter to the net. "He tracks the probable trajectory. Predictive topology."

"Exactly," I said, feeling the rush of validation. "I want to map his efficiency against the standard 'save percentage' model. Traditional stats reward volume. They don't account for difficulty. I want to build a model that quantifies positional success."

Thorne sat back, capping the marker. She looked at me, a small, knowing smile playing on her lips.

"Subject G," she said. "Does Subject G have a name?"

My face heated. "Luke. Carter. The transfer."

"I see." Thorne's eyes sparkled. "And does Mr. Carter know he is being reduced to a set of topological variables?"

"He... knows I'm helping him with accounting."

Thorne laughed, a rich, throaty sound that echoed in the small office. "Accounting. A tragic waste of bandwidth."

She stood and walked to a filing cabinet in the corner. She rummaged through a drawer marked *Confidential/Do Not Touch*, pulling out a dusty external hard drive.

"You're lucky, Lovell," she said. "I consulted for the Athletic Department three years ago on a biomechanics grant. They wanted to know if their conditioning program was working."

She tossed me the hard drive. I caught it with two hands.

"That drive contains the raw Catapult data," she said, sliding the sleek black rectangle across the mahogany.

"Catapult?"

"The GPS vests they wear under their jerseys," she explained. "It tracks heart rate, acceleration, metabolic load, and spatial positioning to within ten centimeters."

My mouth fell open. "You have his biometrics?"

"I have the *team's* data. I consult for the athletic department on performance analytics. If your Mr. Carter is wearing his vest, his data is in there."

She leaned against her desk, crossing her arms.

"Here is the deal. I am formally adding your name to the Kinetic Efficiency in Sport grant as a research assistant. That legitimizes your access to the video server and the biometric files. You aren't hacking anymore, Lovell. You're working."

I breathed out, a weight lifting off my chest. "Okay. What's the objective?"

"Overlay the GPS data with your video analysis and quantify Subject G's efficiency. Prove that his 'quiet' movement is statistically superior to 'active' movement."

"And if I do?"

"The Northeast Regional Symposium is in Boston in February," Thorne said. "I plan on attending to present a paper on fluid dynamics. If your work is good—and I mean *impeccable*, Lovell—I'll consider submitting this as a co-authored finding."

My stomach flipped. "Me? Presenting with you?"

"Don't look so terrified. It's not a done deal. It depends entirely on whether the math holds up against scrutiny." She winked. "But it would look excellent on a grad school application."

She pointed a manicured finger at me.

"But first, bring me the code. I want the preliminary script by next week. And Lovell?"

"Yes?"

"Do you have any conflicts of interest you need to disclose?"

"Yes, ma'am. Subject G is my roommate. We were thrown together this fall."

"Do you get along with the subject?"

"We have a working relationship. As for being a roommate, he's quiet and learning how to be organized. Though his math skills are subpar."

She arched one of her eyebrows. "Don't fall in love with your dataset," she said, her voice dropping to a warning tone. "It compromises the objectivity. If you fudge numbers to make him look good, I will scrub your name from the program completely."

I flushed, clutching the hard drive to my chest like gold bullion. "It's just geometry, Professor."

"Of course it is," she said, turning back to her whiteboard. "Get out of my office. Go calculate."

I walked out into the hallway, the hard drive heavy and cool in my hand.

I now had legitimate access to the video along with the GPS data. And who knows, maybe a potential ticket to Boston. At least Dr. Thorne hadn't laughed me out of her office; that's more than I had hoped for.

Now I just had to make sure the dataset didn't break my heart.

Chapter 12
Academic Probation

LUKE

The lecture hall for Business Psych 202 was clearing out. I shoved my notebook into my bag, wincing as the movement pulled at my shoulder.

"You okay, Carter?"

I looked up. Kayla was standing in the aisle, clutching a stack of flashcards. She looked tired—midterm season came for everyone—but her smile was sympathetic.

"Fine," I lied. "Stiffness from lifting."

"Right. Lifting." She adjusted her backpack straps. "Devon said he heard you pacing at three a.m. last night. He was going to write you up for a noise violation, but then he realized you were walking in circles."

Heat rose in my neck. "Sorry. Tell him I'll buy him earplugs."

"He's an RA, Luke. He normally sleeps like the dead. But you look like you're running on fumes." She hesitated, then tapped my arm. "If you need the notes from last week, let me know. You were staring at the wall for most of the lecture."

"I might take you up on that," I said, genuinely grateful.

"Do it. Don't fail. Devon hates doing the paperwork when athletes get academic suspensions."

She gave a little wave and headed for the door. I watched her go, the word suspension ringing in my ears louder than the dismissal bell.

I hoisted my bag and headed for the faculty wing, the dread in my stomach growing heavier with every step.

The hallway outside Professor Delvecchio's office was lined with still photos of last year's case-study champions—three deep rows of smiling undergrads in tailored blazers clutching fake oversize checks.

I resisted the urge to tug my Frost Demons hoodie lower. The Carver School of Business always made me feel like I'd walked into the wrong locker room: wrong gear, wrong game.

Eight of us waited on the bisected leather couch. Nobody spoke. Pages rustled; highlighters squeaked. A kid in a charcoal suit scrolled his phone, lips moving like he was rehearsing a pitch deck. Office hours, fifteen-minute slots, first-come first-served. The paper sign-up sheet on the door showed my name fourth. I checked my watch—3:07. Practice started at six. Plenty of time

The first kid was in and out in five minutes, almost in tears.

Suit Kid slid inside when Dr. Delvecchio called "next." I tried not to eavesdrop, but the walls weren't thick. Balance-sheet ratios, discounted cash flow, language I recognized but never heard from a goalie crease. My backpack felt heavier with every acronym.

Fifteen minutes, then the door cracked. Suit Kid emerged looking victorious, thanked the professor twice, and strode off like he'd closed seed funding. Delvecchio's voice followed: "Next."

I stood, shoulders doing an involuntary pre-game roll. The bruise protested, still purple under compression but manageable.

Dr. Delvecchio wore a tie patterned with tiny dollar signs, sleeves rolled. "Come in." He gestured to the chair opposite his desk, the kind that swallowed you lower than the interviewer. Power displacement in furniture form.

I sat in the hard plastic chair, my knee bouncing a nervous rhythm against the leg of the desk. I had the speech memorized in my head already: '*Student-athletes need to prioritize... maybe this major isn't a good fit... academic probation is looming.*'

Dr. Delvecchio didn't look up. He was grading, his red pen slashing through someone's work with violent efficiency.

Finally, he capped the pen. "Mr. Carter."

"Professor." I straightened up, bracing myself. "I know the midterm is coming up, and I know that sixty-eight last week was... below standard."

"It was," Delvecchio agreed, opening a folder. "It was lower than the average. Which is why I was surprised by this."

He slid a paper across the desk. Face down.

My stomach dropped. I reached out, expecting to see a fifty. Maybe a forty. I turned it over.

Eighty-two.

I stared at the number. Then I looked at Delvecchio. Then back at the number.

"Eighty-two?" I said.

"You got the entire section on adjusting entries correct," Delvecchio said, leaning back in his chair. "Last week, you didn't know a debit from a hole in the ground. This week, you balanced the ledger on the first try. That is a statistical anomaly."

"I... studied," I said, the word feeling inadequate.

"You didn't just study. You changed your method." He tapped the paper. "I see scratch work in the margins here. You're drawing out the flow of cash before you journalize it. You didn't do that before."

I looked at the margins. There were tiny, faint arrows drawn next to the accounts—Austen's "water flow" method. *Cash flows down, equity builds up.* I hadn't even realized I was drawing them until now.

"I found an excellent tutor," I admitted. "He... explains things differently. He makes it about logic, not just rules."

Delvecchio hummed, a low sound of approval. "Well, whatever he's charging you, pay it. I haven't seen a turnaround this clear in my section in a few years."

He pulled the quiz back to log the grade in the computer system.

"You're not out of the woods, Carter. One quiz doesn't erase a month of struggle. But this?" He gestured to the grade as he handed it back. "This keeps you on the ice."

"That's the plan, sir."

"Get out of here. And start studying for the midterm today. Don't make the mistake of waiting to the last minute."

"Yes, sir."

He made a shooing motion. I had been dismissed. The dread that had been sitting on my chest for a week suddenly gone, replaced by something lighter.

I looked at the quiz in my hand. *Eighty-two.*

I hadn't just survived. I'd understood it.

I pulled out my phone. I didn't text Ryan, Coach, or my dad. I opened the thread that had become the most active one on my phone.

Me: *82. The arrows worked.*

I hit send, grinning like an idiot in the middle of the business school hallway.

I slipped out of Carver Hall, notebook tighter under my arm than the blocker usually was on my hand. A snow-dusted quad funneled students to late afternoon classes.

Phone buzz—Dad again. Declined. Another buzz.

Ryan: Lift at 4:30, don't be late, Monk.

I thumbed back: on schedule.

Campus wind slapped the thought away. I tightened my parka hood and crossed toward the dorms, boots punching through crusted snow. Practice countdown: two hours, twenty-nine minutes. Enough time to eat and stretch.

Stony Creek Hall shimmered with radiator breath on the windows. I climbed to third, shoulder twinging from the notebook weight—even paper felt heavy now. Our door was ajar the regulation two inches.

Inside, Austen stood at the sink area rinsing a mug. His hair looked like he'd shoved a hand through it five times, then decided it was fine. He set the mug upside down on a towel, glanced over.

"Training room?" he asked.

"Office hours." I dropped my backpack, the thunk louder than intended.

"Action-packed. Congrats on the eighty-two, by the way."

I peeled off my parka, draped it on the bedpost. He didn't dig; he never did. Returned to his side of the room, shifting a stack of printouts to make space on the desk.

"Thanks, it was your tutoring that did it. I really can't thank you enough."

"Glad I could assist."

I opened the fridge, found two blueberry oat bars lined beside a Post-it note reading inventory: 3. Lifted one, offered it across the gap. "Trade?" I said.

"Accepted." He took the bar, slid a mechanical pencil and a yellow pad into the vacated space.

My pulse thudded in my ears. "I'm lifting at 4:30, practice at six." I unwrapped the bar with deliberate care. "Weights'll wreck me."

"We can continue with tutoring tomorrow then." He broke the bar in half, ate.

I chewed, swallowed chalk-sweetness. "I understand the theory. Execution still... leaks."

"An athlete complaining about execution feels ironic."

"Funny." I crumpled the wrapper, aimed for the trash. Rim, in. "No pointers besides 'reallocate ice time.'"

Austen made a noncommittal sound, spun the mechanical pencil between fingers. "Tonight, after practice?"

Practice would end at 8:15. Showers, media, maybe 8:45 back to dorm. "I'll be disgusting."

"Mathematics is odor-agnostic."

I almost laughed. "You sure?"

He met my eyes—steady, no sympathy gimmicks. "Yes."

Embarrassment prickled anyway, like forgetting a piece of gear before warm-up. "I don't want to drag you."

"Reciprocity," he answered, a word now so coded it skipped argument. "Nine-thirty? Gives you time to rotate the bruise and the laundry."

That precise. My chest loosened an inch. "Nine-thirty."

He tore a scrap of paper, wrote 21:30 – FAcct on it, stuck it atop his monitor. Then he reached into the freezer, retrieved the bag of peas. "Ice your shoulder. I saw you wince."

I nodded, throat tight. I ripped off my hoodie and T-shirt to let the peas sit on my skin.

Austen's eyes lingered on my six-pack before making their way up to my face. *Did he just blush?* He spun around, no longer looking at me.

"Thanks," I said, barely above normal volume.

He capped the pencil, clicked it twice. "We'll solve for direction. Magnitude follows."

I pulled out a book for my film class and learned about the history of documentary filmmaking. I kept getting distracted. The image of Austen's hazel eyes as they had raked up my torso flooded my mind and distracted me. I'm sure I'd imagined it, but for just a second, I swear there was longing there. But then, maybe I'm seeing things that don't exist because it's been so long since I had any man-on-man action that didn't involve the ice.

My phone chimed—Ryan's twenty-minute warning. I grabbed my gym bag, slung it over the opposite shoulder to spare the bruise.

At the door, I hesitated. Austen looked up.

"Radiator good?" I asked.

He angled a thumb toward the valve. "Posts aligned."

"Oh, Ryan wanted me to remind you that you are invited tomorrow night to trivia."

"As for right now, that sounds entirely probable."

Weights hammered every muscle fiber; practice finished the job. Harper barely spoke, but her stopwatch did, beep after merciless beep. By the time I limped into the dorm, the bruise sang in three languages. Clock read 9:22.

Room 317 glowed warm. Austen sat cross-legged on the floor, T-accounts sketched on the yellow pad, his mint tea sitting next to him. Next to him, he had a lime seltzer, a nutrition bar, and a bag of peas laid out waiting for me sitting beside my notebook.

He didn't say hurry or you're late. Looked up and patted the rug.

I dropped the gear bag, toed off shoes, and sat opposite him, shoulder loosening under the radiator's steady breath. Embarrassment lingered, but trust inched forward, enough to pick up the pencil and meet his eyes.

"Debit equipment," I started, voice steadier than I felt. "Credit cash."

"Show your work," he said, and the lesson began.

Chapter 13
Fact Check

AUSTEN

Going to a bar on a Thursday night violated at least three of my personal operating protocols:

1. Academic rigor requires sleep.

2. Crowds introduce uncontrollable variables.

3. I don't fit in with people who wear jerseys as formal wear.

Yet, at 7:45 p.m., I was standing in front of the mirror in Room 317, adjusting the collar of a button-down shirt I hoped said "casual but competent."

Luke was leaning against his dresser, arms crossed, watching me. He wore a gray henley that fit arguably too well and a beanie pulled low, his navy wool peacoat in his arms.

"You look like you're heading to a court date," he observed.

"I am attempting to blend in," I corrected, smoothing a wrinkle. "Social camouflage is vital in high-density environments."

"It's Buckman Grill, Austen. Not a jungle." He pushed off the dresser, grinning. "Lose the top button. You'll suffocate."

I undid the button. He was right; the air intake improved by four percent.

"Ryan says there's a category on 80s rock," Luke said, grabbing his keys. "He's convinced he's going to sweep it. I need you to fact-check him, so he doesn't embarrass the program."

"I am not a repository of hair-band trivia."

"No, but you're a walking encyclopedia for everything else. Consider yourself the special teams unit." He opened the door, bowing slightly to gesture me through. "After you, Professor."

I rolled my eyes but walked through. The hallway smelled of popcorn and floor wax. "If we lose, I'm giving you more financial accounting problems."

"Fair stakes." He joked as he casually slung an arm across my shoulder.

We walked across campus in the crisp November dark. The wind had teeth, but I barely felt it. Walking next to Luke made me feel safe. We fell into step effortlessly, his long stride matching my quicker pace.

"Shoulder holding up?" I asked, glancing at his left side.

"Dalton says I'm cleared for contact tomorrow. Pain's a two."

"Keep it a two. If you spike to a five because you tried to lift a pitcher of beer, I'm resigning as your tutor."

"Understood." He bumped my shoulder with his—gentle, controlled. "You're bossy when you're right."

"I'm always right. It saves time."

He laughed, a warm sound that heated the air between us.

The Buckman Grill was a sensory assault.

The noise hit first—a wall of bass, shouting, and clinking glass. Then the smell: fryer grease, stale hops, and too much cologne.

I hesitated in the doorway. This was a mistake. I should be in Ridgeway, grading quizzes. I felt the rise of a panic attack welling from inside me.

Luke's hand settled on the small of my back. Light, barely there, but it anchored me instantly, all sense of anxiety fleeting with his touch.

"Table's in the back," he said, his voice low near my ear. I could feel his warm breath. "Follow me."

He moved forward, using his size to carve a path through the mob. I tucked into his wake, drafting like a goose.

We emerged at a large booth in the corner. Ryan O'Connell was standing on the bench, waving a basket of onion rings like a scepter. Javier Morales sat opposite him, looking bored but intense. Two other guys I recognized from the roster—Decker and a freshman defenseman—were cramming into the far side.

"The brain trust has arrived!" Ryan yelled, jumping down. He pointed a finger at me. "Math! Tell me you know state capitals."

"I know all of them," I said, sliding into the booth.

"Yes!" Ryan slammed the table. "We're winning the pitcher. Carter, sit. You're blocked by the fry basket."

Luke slid in next to me. The booth was designed for four; with six hockey players and me, it was tight. Luke's thigh pressed against mine from hip to knee. Heat radiated through the denim.

"Also," Ryan announced to the table, pouring cheap lager into a plastic cup, "we are celebrating the fact that we beat Merrimack 7–6 last night, even though Carter tried to give me a heart attack in the third period."

Luke's jaw tightened. He didn't reach for the pitcher. "It wasn't a heart attack. It was a collapse. Three soft goals in ten minutes."

"We won, didn't we?" Ryan grinned, foam spilling over his hand. "Offense carried you. You're welcome. That's how teams work. You can't be the golden boy every game."

"I shouldn't need carrying," Luke muttered, staring at the scarred laminate table. "My job is to stop pucks. I can't be giving up three soft goals in the third period."

"Define 'soft,'" I said.

The table went quiet. Ryan lowered his pitcher. Javier blinked, looking at me like I'd spoken in binary.

Luke turned to me. "Soft. Easy. Shots I should have had."

"I watched the game feed," I said, adjusting my glasses. I pulled my phone out, tapping the screen. "Goal number four was a rebound from the low slot. Statistical shooting percentage on rebounds is over twenty percent higher than a direct shot."

I scrolled down.

"Goal number five was a cross-ice pass. It crossed the Royal Road—the line dividing the offensive zone." I turned the phone so Luke could see the heat map. "When the puck moves laterally across that line, the goaltender has to reset his angle. Save percentage on Royal Road shots drops by almost thirty percent."

"So?" Ryan asked, looking confused.

"So," I continued, my voice gaining edge, "they weren't soft. They were high-danger chances. The defense allowed the pass; Luke was dealing with the mathematical fallout."

I looked at Luke.

"I calculated your GSAx—Goals Saved Above Expected. Based on the shot quality Merrimack generated, an average goalie would have let in eight goals. You let in six."

I set my phone down on the table with a click.

"You didn't collapse, Luke. You were a plus-two. You stole a game the defense tried to give away."

Luke stared at me. Something shifted in his expression—the tightness around his jaw eased, his shoulders dropped an inch. Not reassurance. Proof.

Ryan whistled low. "Damn, Monk. You brought a human calculator to a knife fight."

Javier laughed, shaking his head. "I like him. He makes me feel better about my blown coverage."

"For those of you who haven't met him, this is Austen, my roommate," Luke said, looking around the circle. "He's fixing my GPA. And as you can see, he knows more about our team stats than anyone. Treat him like a starter."

"Nice to meet you," Decker said around a mouthful of burger.

Javier looked me up and down, his gaze sharp. "Luke says you understand angles."

"Geometry is universal," I said, meeting his stare. "Pucks follow physics, mostly."

Javier smirked. "Mostly. Wait until you see O'Connell skate. He defies physics."

"Hey!" Ryan threw an onion ring at him.

Javier caught it midair, not even looking. He chewed it slowly, watching me. "So, Austen. You play?"

"Musical instruments? No."

"Sports," Javier clarified. "Anything with a ball or a puck?"

"I ran cross-country in high school," I said. "It requires zero hand-eye coordination, only the willingness to suffer."

Ryan laughed. "Respect. Running sucks."

"Why math?" Decker asked, leaning over the table. "Like, you do it for fun? Or because you hate yourself?"

"Math is predictable," I said, taking a sip of the club soda Luke had slid toward me. "Unlike humanities, the answer doesn't depend on how the professor is feeling that day. X is always X."

"Unless X is O'Connell," Javier muttered. "Then X is usually in the penalty box."

"I have a ninety-percent pass completion rate!" Ryan protested.

"Eighty-two," I corrected automatically.

The table went silent.

Ryan blinked. "What?"

"Your pass completion rate," I said. "It's eighty-two percent. I updated your stats after the Caribou game. Your faceoff win percentage is fifty-eight, which is elite, but your pass completion drops to sixty-four in the third period. Likely fatigue-related."

Ryan stared at me, mouth open. Javier looked from me to Luke, eyebrows raised, and busted out laughing.

"Damn!" Javier said. "He just put you in your place, O'Connell."

"He did the math," Luke said, grinning into his water glass.

"You memorized my stats?" Ryan asked, sounding awed.

"I analyzed the dataset," I said, shrugging. "Patterns are easy to spot. Morales shoots blocker side seventy percent of the time on breakaway attempts. Decker drifts left on the backcheck."

Decker dropped his burger. "Dude. Is he a spy?"

"He's my secret weapon," Luke said, nudging my shoulder with his.

Javier leaned forward, resting his chin on his fist. The boredom was gone from his eyes. "Okay, Math. What's Carter's tell?"

I hesitated. Luke went still beside me.

"He doesn't have one," I lied. "His save percentage is purely reactive. He waits for the shooter to commit."

It wasn't true. Luke dropped his left shoulder a fraction of an inch before he went into the butterfly. But I wasn't about to tell Javier Morales that.

Luke looked at me, surprise and gratitude flashing in his eyes.

"Damn," Ryan said. "We really are winning this pitcher."

The trivia thing was chaos, but somehow slightly organized.

Ryan dominated the Sitcoms category, writing answers before the emcee finished reading the questions. Javier surprised everyone by sweeping Geography, naming the capital of Burkina Faso—Ouagadougou—without blinking.

Then came Quantum Mechanics.

"Question four," the emcee droned. "What is the principle that states you cannot simultaneously know the position and momentum of a particle with perfect accuracy?"

The table went silent. Ryan looked at his beer. Decker looked at the ceiling.

I picked up the answer slip.

"Heisenberg Uncertainty Principle," I wrote in block letters.

"Wait," Ryan said. "Are you sure? Maybe it's the... Schrödinger thing? The cat?"

"The cat is a thought experiment about superposition," I said, not looking up. "Uncertainty is position and momentum. Trust me."

I handed the slip to Luke. He looked at it, then at me, grinning.

"Running it to the judge," Luke said.

We swept the category.

By Round 3, the dynamic had shifted. I wasn't the outsider; I was the asset. Ryan was high-fiving me after every correct answer. Even Javier nodded approvingly when I calculated the conversion of kilometers to miles in my head for a travel question.

I was sipping my club soda, feeling a strange, warm buzz that had nothing to do with alcohol, when a shadow fell over the table.

Three guys stood there. They wore polos with popped collars—lacrosse team, if I recalled the campus hierarchy correctly.

"Carter," the lead guy sneered. He was holding a pitcher of cheap beer. "Didn't know the hockey team allowed tutors at the varsity table."

The noise at our table died instantly.

"Beat it, Kyle," Ryan said, his voice dropping an octave.

"Just asking," Kyle said, eyes sliding to me. "Heard you needed help counting to ten, Carter. Brought the babysitter?"

My stomach twisted. I gripped my glass. This was the variable I hated—the one where I became a prop in someone else's status game.

I started to slide out of the booth. "I should go get a refill."

Luke's hand clamped onto my thigh under the table. Firm. Immovable.

"Stay," he said.

He didn't look at me. He looked at Kyle. His expression hadn't changed much—he still looked calm—but the air around him dropped ten degrees. The same look he had in the crease right before a penalty kill.

"Austen isn't *the tutor*," Luke said, his voice carrying over the bar noise. "He's my roommate and probably the smartest guy in the room. Which puts him about one-hundred IQ points north of you, Kyle."

The table went dead silent.

Kyle flushed. "Whatever, man. Just saying it looks weird."

"What looks weird," Luke continued, standing up slowly, "is you interrupting my team's dinner. We're celebrating. You're blocking the view."

Javier stood up too. Then Ryan. The booth became a wall of Frost Demons.

Kyle looked at the three of them, did the math, and realized his probability of winning was zero.

"Whatever," Kyle muttered. He turned and shoved his way back into the crowd.

Luke sat down. He didn't make a big deal of it. He looked at me.

"You okay?"

"I'm fine," I said, though my pulse was hammering. "He wasn't entirely wrong. I am a tutor."

"You're the MVP of Round 3," Ryan declared, slamming his drink down. "To Austen!"

"To Austen!" the table roared.

Luke raised his glass, clinking it against my soda. "To constants," he murmured, for me alone.

I looked at him—the way the bar lights caught his eyes, the set of his jaw, the protective weight of his hand resting on my thigh.

We won second place—a twenty-dollar gift card and a pitcher of lukewarm beer that Ryan claimed as a "moral victory." The team that won first place was a group of graduate students, so they had the deck stacked in their favor.

Returning to the dorms, the group dwindled to just Luke and me. The wind had died down, leaving the campus silent and frozen.

"Thanks," I said after we crossed the quad.

"For what?"

"For sticking up for me when that Kyle asshole came to the table."

Luke shrugged, hands deep in his pockets. "Defensemen protect the goalie. Goalies protect the house. You're in the house, Austen."

You're in the house.

It was a hockey metaphor. It meant territory. It meant team.

But the way he said it made it sound like something else.

"I had fun," I admitted. "Javier is... a lot. But fun. And Ryan seems like a genuinely nice person."

"Both of them like you. Ryan agreed that you're a highly underutilized 'weapon.'" Luke chuckled. "High praise."

We reached the door of Stony Creek Hall. Luke held it open, and as I brushed past him, the smell of cold air and him filled my lungs.

"We iterate," I said softly.

Luke smiled, tired but easy. "Yeah. We iterate."

We walked up the stairs to the third floor, shoulder to shoulder.

Chapter 14
Empty Net

AUSTEN

The acoustic properties of an empty dormitory are haunting. Without the dampening effect of five hundred bodies, music, and slamming doors, Stony Creek Hall echoed like a tomb.

It was eleven a.m. on Thanksgiving Thursday. Campus was a ghost town. The cafeteria was closed. The library was locked. Even the EDM guy next door had packed up his bass and gone home to Long Island.

As far as I could tell, I was the only person left in the building. I know the complex director was around somewhere, since I couldn't be in the building without some official university presence, but I wouldn't know how to find them if there was an emergency. I sat at my desk, staring at a blank terminal window. My original plan for the day had been to spend the it refactoring a neural network for my thesis, but the silence was distracting. Sure, I love quiet, but this was unnerving. It pressed against the windows like the gray November sky outside. Every creak of the building settling felt like a gunshot.

Technically, I had options. Maya had invited me to her aunt's house in Vermont (*"There will be wine and arguments, come shield me!"*). My former foster family in New Jersey had sent a generic text: *Thinking of you, hope school is good*. Not an invitation to come visit.

But holidays in the system are performative. You sit at tables where you don't quite fit, eat food you didn't help cook, wait for the polite timeline to expire so you can leave, and hope desperately to avoid small talk that involves politics, religion, or your sexual orientation. You are a guest in a family portrait, blurring the edges.

I preferred the dorm. Here, the loneliness was a variable I controlled.

I stood up, stretching my back, and decided to execute Plan B: The Vending Machine Feast. I had twelve dollars in quarters and a hunger for anything that wasn't a blueberry oat bar.

I grabbed my key, opened the door, and walked face first into a massive wall of muscle.

Luke stood in the hallway, key in hand, looking like he'd been caught breaking and entering. A beanie pulled low and a thick wool coat suggested the cold, but the lack of a duffel bag made it clear he wasn't traveling. Instead of luggage, a plastic grocery sack from the 24-hour convenience store on Route 9 dangled from his grip.

We stared at each other for a second. The hallway lights flickered overhead, buzzing in the silence.

"You're supposed to be in Glen Rock," I said. My brain scrambled to recalculate. Luke had left yesterday. I'd heard him pack. I'd watched him walk out the door with a "See you Sunday" that felt too casual.

"Travel issues," Luke said, not meeting my eyes.

"You drive a giant truck."

"It was making a noise, I think it's the transmission."

"You had that repaired in August," I said. "What's going on?"

"I told my dad that the truck was making noises, and since it was Thanksgiving, I was stranded here," Luke admitted.

"You lied to him."

Luke sighed, his shoulders dropping two inches. He looked exhausted—not physical fatigue, but the bone-deep weariness that comes from holding up a ceiling that keeps trying to collapse.

"I didn't want to go," he admitted, voice low.

"I can see that. Why?"

He looked down at the plastic bag in his hand. "Because if I go home, I have to sit at a mahogany table for four hours while my dad critiques my save percentage between courses. And I decided..." He looked up, meeting my eyes. "I decided I'd rather eat gas station nachos in a hallway than do that again."

The admission hung in the cold air.

I stepped back, opening the door wider. "Get in here. It's freezing." The university had reduced the temperature in the dorm's communal areas. We had heat in our room, but the rest of the building was just warm enough to ensure no pipes burst.

Luke stepped inside. The room felt instantly smaller, warmer. He set the bag on his desk.

"Honestly, I didn't think you'd be here," he admitted, unwinding his scarf. "Didn't Maya invite you to Vermont?"

"She did, but I wasn't in the mood to be around a large group of strangers pretending to be thankful," I said, sitting on the edge of my bed. "Holidays are chaotic variables."

"So, we're both hiding."

"Strategically retreating."

He grinned—a flash of the real Luke, the one who emerged when the pressure gauge dropped. "Well, strategic retreat requires supplies."

He upended the bag. A tragedy of nutrition: two boxes of generic macaroni and cheese, a can of Spam, a bag of frozen peas (ironic, given their usual medical application), and a carton of milk that expired tomorrow.

"I panicked," he said, looking at the pile. "The store was picked clean."

"We can work with this," I said, standing up. "But not in the microwave. We need the communal kitchen."

"The basement kitchen? The one the freshmen used for a failed candle-making experiment?"

"It has a stove. And I have a pot." I grabbed the single saucepan I kept for tea emergencies. "Grab the milk. Let's go."

The basement of Stony Creek was a concrete bunker that smelled of mildew and industrial-strength cleaning supplies. The kitchen was a windowless alcove with a stove from the 1970s and a refrigerator that hummed in the key of G minor. Fluorescent lights overhead had a distinct yellow tint, casting us both in a jaundice-like glow.

But for today, it was completely ours, even if it was only a few degrees above the average temperature inside an igloo.

I set the water to boil. Luke hopped onto the counter, his legs swinging, watching me measure milk and butter powder.

"You have good technique," he noted.

"Chemistry is cooking with higher stakes. Macaroni is forgiving."

I dumped the noodles into the boiling water. They hit the surface with a splash that echoed off the tile walls.

"My dad has a chef," Luke said. He was staring at the blue flame of the burner. "Every Thanksgiving. Catered. Perfect turkey, perfect sides. We eat in the formal dining room. It's quiet. You can hear the silverware hit the china."

I stirred the pasta. It was turning a translucent, gummy white. "Sounds expensive."

"It was a performance review," he corrected. "Last year he brought a tablet to the table to show me a breakdown of goalie stats for the incoming freshman class. Told me I needed to 'eat hungry' because they were coming for my spot."

He laughed, but it was a hollow sound. "I realized yesterday... I'm the starter. I'm posting shutouts. And I became physically ill just thinking about walking through his front door."

I turned down the heat. The steam rose between us, smelling of processed cheese and comfort. I dumped the powdered cheese packet in. It exploded in a cloud of neon orange dust.

"My eighth-grade foster home," I offered, staring into the pot as the sauce turned a nuclear shade of tangerine. "They forgot to set a place for me. Everyone sat down, and there wasn't a chair. The dad had to go to the garage to get a folding chair. I ate off a TV tray at the corner of the table."

Luke went still. "Austen."

"It's fine. It was a learning experience," I said, shrugging. "Taught me not to rely on assigned seating."

Luke slid off the counter. He walked over to the stove, standing next to me. Close—close enough that I could feel the heat radiating off him through his sweater.

"You have a seat here," he said quietly.

I looked up. His eyes were dark and serious. No sarcasm, no deflection. Steady, terrifying sincerity.

"Here," he repeated, gesturing to the grim basement kitchen, the bubbling pot of orange sludge, the empty dorm above us. "With me."

My heart stuttered against my ribs. "The mac and cheese is ready."

"Good." He grabbed two plastic bowls from the drying rack. "Because I'm starving."

We ate on the floor of Room 317, sitting cross-legged with our bowls. I had added the peas and cubed the Spam (pan-fried first, I'm not a savage).

It was, objectively, a sodium bomb of questionable texture. The sauce was too thick, gluey, and coated the roof of my mouth. The peas were mushy, and the Spam was salty enough to pickle a tongue.

"This," Luke said around a mouthful, "is the best meal I've had in months."

"Your palate is broken."

"No. It's..." He pointed his fork at me. "Quiet. No expectations. No school, no hockey."

"Just mushy goo?"

He chuckled, scraping the bottom of his bowl. We finished eating and set the dishes aside, but neither of us moved. The radiator hissed—our third roommate, keeping time.

Luke stretched his legs out, leaning back on his hands. He looked relaxed in a way I rarely saw—shoulders loose, jaw unclenched. The silence wasn't heavy anymore. It felt safe.

"What are you doing for the rest of the break?" he asked.

"Working. Reading. Maybe sleeping more than four hours."

"Want company?"

I looked at him. "You're staying? The whole weekend?"

"Yeah. Unless you kick me out." He shifted, his knee brushing mine. He didn't pull back. "Maybe you can help me understand financial accounting better. Or play chess. Or... exist."

Exist. It sounded like a luxury I couldn't afford, and yet, here it was.

"I could use a chess opponent," I said. "My computer beats me too fast."

Luke smiled. He shifted again, sliding down until he was lying on the rug, looking up at the cracked ceiling.

"Hey, Austen?"

"Yeah?"

"Thanks for not prying."

I looked down at him. His eyes were closed, his lashes casting long shadows on his cheeks. He looked young. Not the star goalie, not the disappointment son. Just Luke.

"You came back because the dorm has better heating than sleeping in your car," I said softly.

He huffed a laugh, eyes still closed. "Yeah. That's it. The heating."

I lay down next to him. Not touching, but close enough that I could hear his breathing sync with the radiator's rhythm.

The room grew darker as the afternoon sun faded. We didn't turn on the lights. The streetlamp outside the window cast striped shadows across the floor. We lay there in the silence, the ghost of powdered cheese hovering between us.

"My mom used to make stuffing with apples," Luke said into the dark. His voice was soft, barely a whisper. "Before she left. She said the sweetness cut the sage."

"Left?" I asked. I turned my head on the rug. I could make out his profile in the shadows—the sharp line of his nose, the eyelashes resting on his cheek.

"She lives in Scottsdale now," he said. "Owns a yoga studio. She sends me a card on my birthday, usually filled with mindfulness quotations that make no sense."

He let out a short, dry laugh.

"She didn't leave me, technically. She left the show. The Rick Carter Experience." He shifted, staring up at the ceiling. "I was fourteen. Dad was intense. He was already mapping out my high school career, talking about prep schools, dietitians. Mom wanted to eat dinner without analyzing protein intake."

"So, she ran."

"She asked me to come," Luke whispered. The confession hung heavy in the air. "She had the car packed. She said, *'Lucas, get in. We're going to Arizona.'* I looked at her, then I looked at my goalie pads drying in the mudroom, and I stayed."

My heart ached for the twelve-year-old boy forced to choose between a parent and a dream.

"You chose the net," I said.

"I chose the approval," he corrected. "I thought if I stayed, if I became what he wanted, it would be worth it. But she drives a Prius and teaches breathing exercises, and I think maybe she's the one who actually won."

He turned his head to look at me. "What about you?"

"My mom passed when I was ten."

"Who took you in?"

"The State of Massachusetts," I said. "Department of Children and Families."

"No family?"

"No viable options," I said, slipping into math speak to keep the sting away. "My father was an unknown quantity. No siblings. So... the system."

"What was it like?"

"Efficient in its cruelty," I said honestly. "I lost count of the number of placements I had between ten and eighteen. You learn to spot the 'Return to Sender' signals early."

Luke propped himself up on one elbow. "Signals?"

"The trash bags," I said. "That's the first rule of foster care: never buy luggage. Luggage implies you're staying. Luggage takes up space. If you keep everything in a trash bag, you can be ready to leave in five minutes."

"Austen..."

"And the food," I continued, needing him to understand why I hoarded oat bars, why I panicked about my car. "My third home—the Millers. They were nice. They bought me a bike. But two weeks before they called the caseworker to come get me, Mrs. Miller stopped buying the family-sized cereal. She started buying the small boxes. The variety pack."

"Why?"

"Because the family size implies a long-term commitment. The small boxes? Those are finite. Those ran out exactly when the placement did."

Luke's hand moved across the rug. His fingers brushed against my wrist, hot and rough.

"I'm sorry," he whispered. "That sucks, Austen."

"It taught me that permanence is a myth," I said, trying to sound nonchalant, though my voice trembled. "People keep you as long as you fit the equation. When you become an outlier... they solve for X, and X is you leaving."

Luke's hand closed over mine. He didn't squeeze. He held on, anchoring me to the floor, to the room, to the moment.

"I'm not going to solve for X," he said fiercely. "I'm not the Millers."

"Everyone is a Miller eventually, Luke. It's a matter of time."

"No," he insisted. "My mom left because she couldn't handle the pressure. You've seen the pressure. You've seen my dad. And you're still here. You're eating Spam on a rug with me."

"The Spam is arguably the breaking point," I joked weakly.

He didn't laugh. He moved his thumb over my knuckles, a slow, deliberate rhythm.

"Do you think she'd like me?" Luke asked. "Your mom?"

I thought about it. My mom, who laughed too loud and loved too hard and never understood math but always checked my homework. Who made lemon meringue pie for breakfast on my birthday because nutrition was secondary to joy.

"She would have liked that you label the pea bags," I said. "She liked order, even if she couldn't keep it herself."

Luke smiled in the dark. I could feel it.

"My mom would like you," he said. "She hated hockey. She liked people who read books. She used to tell me, *'Lucas, be a person, not a position.'* She'd like that you force me to be a person."

"I force you to be an accountant," I corrected. "Distinct difference."

"Close enough."

His finger hooked around mine. The tip. A tentative anchor.

"Go to sleep, Austen," he whispered. "We iterate tomorrow."

"Okay," I whispered back.

"And Austen?"

"Yeah?"

"I bought the family-sized mac and cheese," he said. "We have leftovers."

I smiled into the pillow, a small, painful cracking in my chest. It wasn't a promise of forever. But for tonight, it was enough.

Outside, the wind howled around the empty brick corners of Stony Creek Hall. Inside, on a cheap rug between two twin beds, the variables settled.

We were the only two people in the world. And for the first time in my life, the math worked out perfectly.

Chapter 15
Road Grade

LUKE

The team bus smelled like diesel, stale coffee, and twenty-five guys trying to sleep in upright positions.

We were somewhere on I-91, heading toward UMass Amherst for a Friday night tilt that Coach Harper had circled in red ink on the schedule three weeks ago. "*Conference points,*" she'd said. "*Must-haves.*"

I pressed my forehead against the cold glass of the window. Outside, the Massachusetts landscape was a blur of gray trees and dirty snowbanks.

My phone buzzed in my lap.

Austen: *Radiator is making a sound like a dying bagpipe. Have initiated percussive maintenance.*

I smiled, the tension in my chest loosening a fraction.

Me: *Don't dent the valve. I need heat when I get back.*

Austen: *Heat is preserved. Also, I've been reviewing Amherst's game tape against Merrimack.*

I frowned. He was watching tape?

Me: *Why?*

Austen: *Data collection. Sending you a heatmap. Look at the Green Line.*

An image loaded on my screen. A diagram of the offensive zone, but Austen had drawn a bright green line straight down the center, splitting the ice into two vertical halves.

Austen: *This is the "Royal Road." It's the line dividing the ice. Amherst's entire offense is predicated on crossing it.*

I had to grin. Getting nerd-splained hockey gave me the giggles. Across the aisle, Ryan opened one eye and looked at me. "Austen's nerd-splaining again." Ryan grunted and closed his eyes again.

Me: *It's called a cross-ice pass, Austen.*

Austen: *It's geometry. When the puck crosses that line laterally, the goalie must change his angle and depth simultaneously. The save percentage on shots following a Royal Road crossing drops by 28 percent.*

I stared at the screen. Twenty-eight percent. Massive.

Austen: *Do not let them cross the Green Line. If they pass across it, move early. Beat the angle.*

Me: *You're such a nerd.*

Austen: *I'm a nerd who wants you to win. Defy the physics.*

I locked the phone and slid it into my pocket.

"So, what did Lovell have to say?" Ryan asked.

"The usual," I said, staring at the seat back in front of me. "Still trying to get me to employ mathematical reasoning to defend the crease."

I closed my eyes and visualized the rink, seeing the glowing green line running down the center of the ice.

"Well, if it stops one puck from getting past you tomorrow, follow the nerd." Ryan spat a shell into a paper cup. "Amherst's a grinder game, Monk. Small rink, lively boards. Their student section sits right on top of the visiting goalie. They're gonna chirp you about everything from your pads to your mother."

"Let them chirp."

"That's the spirit." Ryan kicked my boot. "Lock it in. We need you to be a wall. Javier's got the flu or a hangover, I saw him skating slow in morning practice. Maybe he'll be at one-hundred percent tomorrow, but who knows."

I looked back two rows. Javier was asleep, his face pale, a hoodie pulled tight over his head.

Great. Our top scorer was out of commission. That meant a low-scoring game. That meant one mistake would kill us.

I put my headphones back on, but I didn't play music. I turned on the noise-canceling and listened to the low hum of the bus and tried to find the zone.

The Tsongas Center was loud.

Even for morning skate, the building hummed with HVAC noise and the echo of pucks hitting glass. The rink had hard ice, which was a godsend.

I spent twenty minutes working the crease, testing the angles. Ryan was right; the arena was loud, and there weren't even people in the stands. A puck fired wide of the net ricocheted back out into the slot like a grenade.

Geometry, I told myself. *Geometry.*

"Carter!" Harper barked from the bench. "Rebound control! Stop kicking it back into traffic!"

"Yes, Coach."

I reset. I focused. But my mind felt crowded.

In the locker room before the game, Javier sat in his stall, looking green. He was taping his stick with slow, miserable movements.

"You alive?" I asked him.

"Fluids," he muttered. "Need fluids."

Ryan stood in the center of the room, playing air guitar with a composite stick to a track only he liked. "Let's go, boys! We steal two points, we own the bus ride home! Who wants it?"

"We want it!" a few rookies yelled back, nervous energy spiking.

I sat in my corner, the noise of the room fading into a dull hum. Time for the ritual.

In the book of goaltending, equipment isn't protection; it's an extension of the skeleton. If the gear fails, the goalie fails.

I started with the foundation. Base layer, then the knee pads.

A lot of guys taped their knees to death, terrified of them slipping, but I never had an issue. I trusted the friction. I slid the knee stacks in place, pulled the heavy knit hockey socks over the top, and let the fabric lock them down.

Next, the cup. Essential. Keep the vitals covered.

Then, the pants.

I stepped into the breezers and cinched the internal belt. No suspenders—I didn't like the restriction on my shoulders. I tightened the waist until it sat flush.

Then, and only then, did I reach for my skates.

I knew guys who put their skates on before their pants. I couldn't trust people like that. There was something fishy about the mechanics of it, fighting to pull nylon over a sharpened blade. It was, in Austen's words, inefficient and illogical.

I pulled the left skate on. I ran my thumbnail across the inside edge of the blade. It scraped a thin curl of nail—sharp. Good. I liked a 3/8-inch hollow, deeper than most guys, because I needed that bite to push across the crease instantly. I tightened the laces until my circulation throbbed.

Now, the leg pads.

Strapping them on wasn't enough; they needed calibration. Toe ties were fastened with shock cord, not lace, to relieve the strain on the ankles. Rotation was the priority: too tight, and the five-hole stayed open; too loose, and the landing gear failed.

Fully armored from the waist down, the upper base layer came next, followed by the chest protector. The unit slid over my head, carrying the metallic tang of the drying room. Side buckles cinched tight. Next came the neck guard. Hated or not, the NCAA mandated the restrictive collar, even if it choked me every time I dropped into the Reverse-VH to look for pucks.

Finally, the helmet. Chin cup checked, but the throat dangler stayed off. The constant *ching, ching, ching* of plastic hitting the cage was a distraction I couldn't afford. Silence was the only option.

Finally, the gloves and the stick.

Everything was a constant.

Singular. That's what my dad always said. *Be singular. Nothing exists but the puck.*

But as I snapped my helmet straps, I wasn't thinking about being singular.

I was thinking about how much I missed the constants I couldn't tape or strap down. The radiator. The tea. The guy who told me I didn't have to be a robot.

Coach Harper walked in. The room died.

"Amherst plays heavy," she said, her eyes scanning us. "They dump and chase. They crash the net. They want to make it ugly. We don't play ugly. We play fast."

She looked at me.

"Carter. You're the backstop. Clean sights, no soft ones. Give us a chance to win 1-0 if we have to."

"Got it," I said.

"Let's go."

The first period was a war of attrition.

Amherst came out flying, hitting everything that moved. They didn't try to finesse plays; they threw pucks at the net from everywhere to generate chaos.

My job was to kill the chaos.

A defenseman wound up at the point. I fought through the screen, looking over the shoulder of their massive center. I found the release point.

Thud.

The puck hit my chest protector dead center. I collapsed my upper body, smothering the rebound against my jersey before it could drop to the ice. Whistle.

"Nice pillow," Ryan muttered, giving me a tap on the pads.

Two minutes later, a shot from the half-wall. I didn't block it; I punched it with my blocker, directing the rebound into the corner, away from the slot. *Control the chaos.*

I was busy. I liked busy. It kept the brain off.

We escaped the first period 0-0. My shot count was fourteen. Decker's count on the bench was probably zero, lucky guy.

In the second, the game opened up. Ryan sprung Javier on a breakaway. Javier, looking like death warmed over, managed a weak deke that the Amherst goalie bit on. Javier tucked it five-hole.

1-0 Frost Demons.

Amherst answered three minutes later. They were on the power play. They set up the umbrella formation.

Their point man had the puck. He faked a shot.

My instinct—my training—said to challenge him. To telescope out and cut down the angle.

I saw his eyes shift. He wasn't looking at the net. He was looking cross-ice. To the winger waiting in the left circle.

The pass was coming. It was going to cross the center line.

The Royal Road.

Austen's text flashed in my mind: *Save percentage drops by 28 percent. Move early.*

I didn't wait for the release. I pushed off my right skate—hard. I slid across the crease in a butterfly slide, arriving at the far post a split second before the pass connected.

The Amherst winger one-timed it. A perfect shot, destined for the open net.

Thud.

The puck slammed into the NRU logo on my chest. I was already square.

The crowd gasped. The winger looked at the ceiling in disbelief.

"How did you get there?" their center muttered as he skated by.

I flipped the puck to the ref. "I took the Green Line."

I tapped my posts.

Constant.

Amherst eventually scored on a scramble goal that bounced off three skates—physics is cruel like that—but that cross-ice save? That stayed with me.

Third period. 1-1. Four minutes left.

My legs were burning. My shoulder was starting to throb with a dull, persistent ache every time I lifted my glove.

Amherst was pressing. They sensed blood.

Our defenseman took a tripping penalty. Two minutes in the box.

Thirty seconds later, Ryan slashed a guy's stick in half. Broken stick, automatic penalty.

5-on-3. Two minutes left in the game.

The Amherst coach called a timeout.

I skated to the bench. Coach looked intense, drawing lines on her whiteboard with violent strokes.

"Kill box," she ordered. "Collapse the triangle. Let them shoot from the outside. Carter sees everything. Do not screen your goalie."

"We got you, Monk," Ryan said, breathless, sweat dripping off his nose.

"Clear the garbage," I said. "If I make the first save, you have to win the battle for the second."

I skated back to the net. The crowd was deafening. It felt like the roof was coming down.

Faceoff won by Amherst.

They set up the umbrella. Pass to the point. Pass to the wing.

One-timer—bam.

I didn't have time to react. I squared up. I took it off the mask. My ears rang, a high-pitched whine, but the puck dropped straight down into my glove. Whistle.

"Nice face save," the ref muttered.

"Thanks. I use it for modeling."

Faceoff again. Amherst won it.

They worked it low. Pass across the Royal Road—the imaginary line down the center of the ice. That forces the goalie to move laterally.

I slid across—butterfly slide, digging my edge in to stop momentum. I sealed the post.

The shot came. Blocked by our defenseman.

The puck careened wildly into the air. It hit the glass behind the net and bounced back over the top of the goal—a chaotic, impossible bounce off a stanchion.

It landed in the crease behind me.

I heard the crowd gasp before I saw it.

I was down in the butterfly, facing out. The puck was behind me. The net was open.

A Amherst forward lunged for it.

The textbook said: *Push off the post, rotate hips, square up.*

The textbook was too slow.

I abandoned the manual. I didn't think. I didn't calculate.

I threw my body backward. I twisted my torso, flinging my stick arm back like I was trying to swim through the ice, engaging "paddle down" desperation mode.

Ugly. A scramble. Exactly the kind of chaos my dad hated.

The Amherst player swiped at the puck.

My stick blade slammed down on the ice, covering the goal line, a split second before the puck hit it.

Clack.

Rubber met composite.

I smothered it with my blocker, curling my body around the puck like a grenade.

The whistle blew.

For a second, silence. Then, my teammates were on me.

"No way!" Ryan screamed, hauling me up by my jersey. "No way you got that!"

The ref was reviewing it on the overhead camera.

I stood there, chest heaving, sweat stinging my eyes. I looked up at the Jumbotron.

They showed the replay. The chaotic bounce. The desperate lunge. The paddle of my stick slamming down as the puck crossed the red line.

No goal.

The crowd groaned. The "Sieve" chant died.

We killed the rest of the penalty. Regulation ended.

Shootout.

I hated shootouts. They reduced the game to a coin flip.

Coach tapped my helmet. "Patient, Carter. Wait them out. Don't bite on the first move."

I skated to the crease.

First shooter: Forehand, backhand, trying to open my legs. I kept the five-hole locked. Save.

Second shooter: Tried to go high glove. I flashed the leather. Save.

Third shooter: Their captain. He came in slow, weaving. He faked a shot, froze me, and tried to tuck it around my pad.

I stretched out, extending my leg in a split, the toe of my skate catching the puck enough to deflect it into the post.

Ping. Out.

Javier, miraculously, scored on his turn—an ugly, wobbling shot that fooled their goalie purely by accident.

Final: 2-1 NRU.

The locker room was a sensory overload.

Music blasted—something with a bass line that shook the benches. Equipment was everywhere: skates scattered on the rubber floor, wet jerseys hanging from hooks, tape balls flying through the air.

"Three stars!" Ryan yelled, standing on a bench in his compression shorts. "Third star, me, for the moral support. Second star, Morales, for scoring while technically dead. First star..."

He pointed a composite stick at me.

"The Monk! For robbing that kid of his dignity in the third!"

The guys roared, throwing towels and empty water bottles at me.

I sat in my stall, exhausted. My shoulder throbbed. My knees ached. I started the process of peeling off the gear.

Leg pads first. My hands shook as I undid the buckles.

"Hey," Javier said, slumping down next to me. He looked better now that the adrenaline had peaked. "That save? The paddle down?"

"Yeah?"

"That was filth. Pure filth."

"It was lucky," I said, unlacing my skates. "Bounce was weird."

"Luck is preparation meeting opportunity," Ryan said, sliding down next to me. "Or whatever the hell your math boyfriend would say."

I froze. The room was loud, but I heard that clearly.

"My what?"

Ryan grinned, unrepentant. "Please. You check your phone every thirty seconds. You're quoting him in the intermission. You guys are vibrating on a frequency only dogs can hear."

I looked down at my skate, heat rising in my neck. "He's helping me with accounting."

"Uh-huh," Ryan said. He clapped my shoulder. "Well, tell the accountant that his variables worked tonight. We got the dub."

I pulled my phone out of my bag.

One text waiting.

Austen: *Data confirms victory. 38 saves?*

I smiled, and this time, I didn't try to hide it from the room.

"Yeah," I said to Ryan. "We got the dub."

The bus ride home was a party.

Ryan had smuggled a speaker on board. The rookies were singing. Even Coach Harper was smiling in the front row.

I sat in my seat, icing my shoulder with a bag Dalton had given me. I was exhausted. Every muscle felt like it had been pulled apart and put back together wrong.

But I felt light.

I pulled out my phone. One a.m.

Me: *Geometry held up.*

Me: *Nice call on the green line. Win is on you.*

Austen: *Glad I could assist.*

Austen: *Rest required. Room is quiet. Valve is silent.*

Me: *See you in the morning.*

Austen: *I'll be here.*

I smiled at the screen, letting the blue light wash over me in the dark bus.

I looked out the window. The highway was empty, a ribbon of road leading back to Cold Harbor. I closed my eyes and let the bus carry me home.

Chapter 16
Ice and Elevation

Austen

The email notification pinged at 7:04 p.m., cutting through the silence of the dorm room like a gavel strike.

SUBJECT: Submission Update – Northeast Regional Mathematics Symposium

My heart did a traitorous double-time rhythm against my ribs. I hovered the cursor over the subject line. This was it. The verdict on three months of sleepless nights, pirated game footage, and Dr. Thorne's red-pen massacres.

I clicked.

Dear Mr. Lovell, We are pleased to inform you that your abstract, "Quantifying the Crease: A Geometric Analysis of Goaltender Efficiency," has been accepted for presentation...

I let out a breath I'd been holding since October.

"Bad news?" Luke asked from his bed. He was nursing his shoulder again, ice pack strapped tight.

"The preliminary work for my thesis," I said, turning my chair. "The paper was accepted for presentation at a pretty prestigious math conference."

Luke sat up, the ice pack sliding a fraction. A slow, genuine grin spread across his face. "You're presenting? On the main stage?"

"Breakout session B," I corrected. "But yes. I have to build a slide deck. I have to defend the methodology in front of a room full of people who think sports analytics is a pseudoscience."

"You're going to crush them," Luke said. "You've got the best dataset in the league."

"I have you," I said, realizing too late how soft that sounded.

"Exactly." He leaned back. "So, does this mean you're famous?"

"It means I'm presenting," I said, trying to keep my voice level. "Fame—or at least tenure-track viability—comes later. If the presentation goes well, Thorne thinks we can submit for publication in the *Journal of Quantitative Analysis in Sports*. That's the real goal. That's the Stanley Cup."

"I'm sure you'll get that, too," Luke said, with the easy confidence of a man who stopped pucks for a living. "But for now, we iterate, right?"

"We iterate," I agreed.

I closed the laptop, letting the glow of the screen fade. The acceptance email was safe in my inbox, a problem solved. Now, I had to solve the one sitting on the bed with an ice pack strapped to his shoulder.

I spun my chair around and slid to the floor, grabbing the yellow legal pad.

"But first," I said, tapping the paper with the end of a pen, "we have to keep you eligible long enough to see it. Back to the grind."

Luke groaned, the celebration in his eyes dimming into concentration. He adjusted his posture, wincing as the movement pulled at his bruise, and focused on the first problem of the practice set.

"Debit cash, credit accounts payable."

Luke spoke the line like it cost him years off his life. He braced the pencil an inch above the yellow pad, then dropped the words onto paper—block letters, no hesitation.

"Show your work," I said.

He added a tidy arrow from cash to AP, plus the date. No red pen, no slashes. Balance held: seven hundred left, seven hundred right. Good enough to satisfy both accountants and goalies.

"Sign error risk?" he asked.

"Zero. You'd have to try to flip it."

He exhaled hard, like the steam valve on the radiator. The pea bag slid off his shoulder with a muted thud. Twenty minutes in, condensation had soaked the towel beneath it; cold water darkened the cotton like a bruise echo.

I retrieved the backup peas from the freezer, traded them out without ceremony. "Swap that." I reclaimed my spot on the rug.

Clock on my desk: 22:14.

Luke flexed the shoulder under fresh cold. "Dalton would say limit to fifteen."

"Room rule five: ignore Dalton after nine p.m." I flipped the quiz sheet. "Next, transaction: prepaid rent. Asset or liability?"

"Asset." Pencil scratched. "Debit prepaid rent, credit cash."

"Offset timeline?"

"Expense recognition in March, assuming monthly accrual." He looked up, waiting for judgment.

I didn't give him words; I raised two thumbs. His grin snuck out, lopsided and unguarded, then disappeared like he remembered who was watching.

Outside, somebody burst into drunken song. The hallway muffled it; radiator muttered a low reply. Luke's eyes twitched toward the door but he didn't flinch.

He lined up the next blank T. "We doing the whole set tonight?"

"Depends if your brain is still frost-shelled."

"Memory's good." He rolled the pencil across his knuckles—surgeon-level dexterity, wasted on bean-counting. "Confidence is... loading."

"Confidence is an output variable," I said. "Get the mechanism right, the metric stabilizes."

He huffed. "Speak slower for the business major?"

"Fine. Do enough reps, and confidence joins automatically." I slid a fresh worksheet into his orbit. "Reps start here."

He bent over the pad; hair fell forward, dark strands breaking formation. I resisted the uninvited urge to tuck it back—my fingers didn't have clearance for that maneuver. Instead, I uncapped a red pen and watched numbers appear.

Debit Supplies 450

Credit Cash 450

"Explain," I prompted.

"Used team card for stick tape and skate laces." He underlined supplies. "Assets up, cash down."

"Acceptable. Next."

The pace settled: problem, explanation, micro-nod from me. Every correct entry shaved tension off his shoulders; each slip—rare and minor—added only seconds of recalibration before he tried again. The bruise under his shirt never quite sat still, but the peas kept inflammation honest.

Half an hour in, he capped the pencil. "Ledger balances."

"Verify." I traced columns with a fingertip. Totals matched like mirror images. "Ledger balances."

Luke leaned back on both hands, careful not to jostle the pea bag. "First clean run all week."

"You're starting to get this."

He looked at me, really looked, pupils dilated from effort or relief. "You might be a terrifying tutor."

"Terrifying or effective?"

"Both." He angled the pencil at me like a pointer stick. "Weirdly comforting."

The radiator pinged—metal cooling. Heat cycle ended; silence grew dense enough to measure.

I reached toward the desk for the mint-green highlighter. "Time to lock the memory." I flicked a neon band across each correct transaction. "Visual reinforcement."

"Color coding," he mused. "Thought you were anti-frills."

"Highlighter isn't a frill. It's metadata." I recapped the pen. "Next step: sample quiz."

He blinked at the pad. "Tonight? It's almost eleven."

"Brain's warm. Strike while the neurons fire."

"Coach Harper would approve." He squared his posture. "Hit me."

I covered the pad with a spare sheet. "Journal entry: University bookstore buys six laptops on thirty-day credit."

"Debit Equipment." Quick scribble. "Credit accounts payable."

"Follow-up: Record the payment ten days later."

He grinned—cocky now. "Debit accounts payable, credit cash."

"Attach dates."

He did. Totals: fifteen grand each.

I lifted the overlay sheet. "Glove save."

"No rebound," he said.

Something in my chest twisted—not unpleasant, but unfamiliar. I shifted, cross-legged and tingling from circulation loss.

Luke set the pencil down, both pointer fingers tipped against the floor. "So utility expense?"

"Variable. If prepaid, asset; if due, liability."

He opened his mouth, closed it, nodded—taking the concept like a puck to the chest protector, letting it absorb.

"You done?" I asked.

"For tonight, yeah." He rubbed the back of his neck. "Exam's still a cliff, but at least I can see the trail."

"Trails iterate." I stacked the worksheets, squared the edges. "Tomorrow, we drill adjusting entries."

Luke groaned and threw back his head. "I won't survive that."

"You will." I placed the stack on my desk, centered. "Now off with the ice. Fifteen minutes elapsed."

He lifted the pea bag; water beaded off the plastic. "You timing?"

"Sort of." My watch had been quietly counting down while we worked. I didn't mention that.

He stood, rotated the arm, winced but less than earlier. "Pain scale?"

"Three if I don't poke it."

"Maybe Dalton knows what he's talking about," I said.

"He's a good trainer." He smiled, sheepish, reached for the towel, and patted the floor dry where droplets landed. Muscles in his back stretched under the T-shirt. I looked away before observation registered as staring.

He disappeared into the sink alcove, wringing the water, returned with the towel slung over one shoulder. The room felt bigger with him up, yet more crowded.

"Need anything else?" I asked, voice too even.

"Hot shower, eight hours of sleep, and one miracle midterm curve." He opened the mini-fridge, grabbed two seltzers, tossed me one.

"Seltzer covers none of those."

"Hydration's a miracle in hockey." He cracked the tab; hiss echoed the radiator's last gasp. "Thanks, by the way."

"For carbonated water?"

"For... all of it." He gestured to the pad, the peas, maybe the space between us. "Nobody's done that before."

"Everybody has study groups."

"Study groups don't provide individualized tutoring and write twelve-point room constitutions."

I sipped lime fizz. "Normal is relative."

He laughed under his breath. "Relative to what?"

"Chaos with boundaries."

He toasted the air. "I can live with that." He drained half the can, then set it on the windowsill, condensation halo already forming.

"Trivia on Thursday?" he asked.

"Conditional yes." I lifted my can.

His eyes crinkled. "Ryan said he'll buy you fries."

"Bribe rejected until after the exam."

"Blueberry bar? Trade staple for staple."

"Maybe." My lips twitched. "I'll run inventory."

He leaned a hip against the desk, closer than before, but casual, like proximity was background noise now. His gaze landed on the puck centered under the desk lamp: black disk, NRU logo scratched from game collisions.

"Article five still stands," he murmured.

"It's weight-tested." I reached out, spun the puck a quarter-turn so the gouge faced outward. "Constant."

He didn't reply. Watched my hand retreat, expression unreadable. In goalie gear, he hid behind fiberglass. Here, no mask, but still layers.

He picked up the legal pad, flipped through neon-striped pages. "Can I keep this?"

"Of course." I slid a fresh pad from the drawer. "I have extras. Boundaries need paper."

He tucked the used pad into his backpack. "Makes the cliff look climbable."

"Cliffs are slopes with poor marketing."

He huffed out a laugh so genuine it surprised both of us. The radiator thunked, restarting, benign percussion.

Quiet settled, softer now. Same silence as before, different charge.

Luke tipped his head toward the clock. 22:47. "Lights in thirteen?"

"Quiet hours, yes."

He bent, collected stray pencil shavings in his palm, deposited them in the trash. Each motion neat, absorbed, as if he found calm in closure tasks. The discipline made sense—crease cleanup in human form.

I wiped the desk surface with a microfiber cloth—fingerprint smudges gone. When I finished, he stood beside my chair, hands empty.

"Can I ask something?" he said.

"Within reason."

He glanced at the door, the puck, then me. "You're spending a lot of hours on this. With me. You could be picking up paid tutoring shifts. Or working on your thesis."

Not the question I expected. "My thesis is two weeks ahead of schedule. And my finances are solvent. Even after that alternator issue."

"Humor me," he pressed. "You're burning prime hours on basic accounting. What's *your* ROI?"

I capped the highlighter, setting it in its slot with a precise click. "Return on Investment isn't always monetary, Luke. Sometimes it's environmental."

He frowned. "Meaning?"

"Meaning that when you are stressed, the room is chaotic. When you are failing, the ambient anxiety in here increases. Helping you stabilize your GPA stabilizes my living environment."

"So, I'm a noise reduction project?"

"You're a variable," I corrected. "And I prefer my variables controlled."

"That sounds cold."

"It's efficient."

He shook his head, looking down at his hands. "It feels lopsided, Austen. You're saving my ass, and I'm just... here. Reciprocity shouldn't mean you're working for free."

I clicked off the desk lamp, leaving only the blue glow of his computer screen between us.

"Your math is off," I said softly. "Helping you is not a cost center."

"Feels like one."

"I don't always understand feelings. I have no problem admitting that. But I do know that feelings aren't ledger entries."

He opened his mouth, closed it, and exhaled. "I just don't want to be the reason you fall behind."

"I don't fall behind," I said, meeting his eyes. "And honestly? Dealing with your logic puzzles is... a relief. It's better than arguing with Dr. Thorne about vectors."

"So, I'm a distraction," Luke said, a small smile touching his lips.

"You're a necessary deviation from the mean." I rose, brushing past him to hang the microfiber cloth on its hook. "Now, sleep. You have practice before the crack of dawn."

His lips parted like he might argue, but instead he nodded. A simple, wordless *okay* that folded itself into the space between our beds.

Lights-out time. He moved first, flicking the overhead. Darkness swallowed the corners; streetlamp glow striped the ceiling.

I crossed to my bed, peeled back the blanket. Mattress dipped beneath me. He mirrored, sitting on his own, positioning the shoulder carefully. Springs sighed.

Silence again.

I turned to my side, facing away from Luke. Cold leaked in; radiator compensated. Behind me, Luke adjusted the blanket, springs creaked once more, then stilled.

Five ticks of the radiator.

"Austen."

"Mm?" I kept eyes on streetlight glare.

"Thanks for making the rink smaller."

I didn't correct the metaphor. "Thanks for making the classroom quieter."

No reply, but the mattress opposite rustled, like he'd turned to face me across eight feet of half-dark.

More radiator ticks. Nine, ten, eleven.

Outside, drunk freshmen launched into an off-key fight song. Luke huffed a soft laugh. "Vectors misfiring," he whispered.

I answered without thinking. "Ignore amplitude, track trajectory."

He chuckled, low. The mattresses quieted; breathing leveled under the radiator's hiss.

Tick.

Tick.

Somewhere beyond the hallway, a door slammed, feet pounded stairs. None of it breached the room's new equilibrium.

Luke spoke again, words feather-soft. "We iterate tomorrow?"

"We iterate."

Tick.

Tick.

I closed my eyes, counted another cycle, waited for sleep.

Before drift, his voice slipped across the dark one last time—barely audible:

"Good night, constant."

Heat shot through me, unexpected as a power surge. I swallowed, answer stuck half a beat.

"Good night, goalie."

Silence took the rest.

Chapter 17
Crossing the Blue Line

LUKE

I stared at the hairline crack in the ceiling until the dark went grainy.

Twelve radiator ticks, then the pipe sighed. Outside, somebody in the stairwell stumbled through the fight song—again, flatter this time, like the beer had quit halfway down.

I should have been asleep. Practice rolled at six-thirty, alarm at five-forty. But every time I closed my eyes the ledger lines from Austen's pad drifted across my eyelids, neon from his highlighter. Debit Equipment, credit cash. Balance. Simple. Except my pulse wouldn't copy the math.

Across the room his mattress creaked, faint, like he'd shifted an inch. Streetlight slipped past the blinds and penciled his outline—shoulder, hip, knee under the blanket. No movement after that. I told myself he was out cold, that waking him for no reason would violate at least two roommate articles.

Another tick. I tested a deep breath; the bruise in my shoulder answered with a dull complaint. Good excuse to get up, shake it off. Noise might yank him from sleep, but the pain wasn't letting me stay still, so the excuse felt legal enough.

I eased upright, feet landing on the rug without sound. The pea bag was lukewarm. I crossed to the fridge, door hinge squeaking enough to swear at facilities in my head. New bag, colder. When I turned, Austen's eyes were open, catching the street-glow.

"Sorry," I whispered. "Pea rotation."

He nodded once, no irritation, but he didn't look away. His hair stuck up on the left where he'd flattened it against the pillow. Somehow, that detail felt louder than the hallway singer.

"You, okay?" he asked, voice rough with sleep.

"Restless." I pressed the cold against the bruise.

He hummed acknowledgment but still didn't shut his eyes. I managed two steps toward my bed before the silence filled with things I hadn't said all week.

"If the peas aren't working," he murmured, "I have ibuprofen."

"I'm good." Not a lie—shoulder was background noise compared to the static in my head. "I can't get my brain to shut up."

"Perseverating?"

"*Gesundheit.*"

"Perseverating, when a thought keeps running around in your head."

He pushed up on an elbow. The blanket slid, revealing the worn Frost Demons T-shirt he'd borrowed from my drawer after laundry day. It hung loose on him; I'd pretended not to notice how much I enjoyed seeing him in it.

Austen ran a hand through his hair, smoothing nothing. "You want the chessboard?"

Midnight chess once helped after the starter announcement. This felt different, but I latched on anyway. "Could work."

He swung legs over the side, stood, and the mattress springs squealed like sneakers on wet ice. He froze, then relaxed when no one banged on the wall. The board lived on his desk—magnet travel set, size of a paperback. He grabbed it, hesitated, glanced at my bed, then his.

Less distance if we use one mattress. The thought arrived uninvited, vivid, and my throat tightened around it.

"Floor?" he offered.

"Beds are warmer." I cleared mine with an elbow sweep. Shoulder protested; peas slipped. He noticed—of course—and crossed the small room.

"Let me." He set the chessboard on the pillow, flipped the towel open, and positioned it under my arm so condensation wouldn't soak the sheet. I didn't stop him. My fingers brushed his wrist by accident—or maybe not; I wasn't sure anymore.

Pieces snapped onto magnets. He sat cross-legged near the foot, leaving half the mattress between us. Close enough to feel the shift every time I breathed.

"You're white," he said, sliding the board my way.

I nudged a pawn forward. He mirrored. Two moves each, nothing fancy. The radiator hissed through the space. I tried to focus, but my attention kept skidding to the hollow of his throat, the way shadows dipped there when he leaned over the board.

"How's your brain?" he asked after I blundered a knight.

"Improving." My voice came out tight. "Still some interference."

He studied me, not the pieces. "Want to reframe the problem?"

"Please."

"Okay." He tapped the knight I'd misplaced, moved it back, and set my pawn upright again—reset the variables. Then he surprised me: closed the board entirely and set it aside.

No distraction now. The narrow mattress, the radiator, and him looking at me like the next move wasn't on the board at all.

A dozen possible words lined up in my head; none cleared grammar check. I settled for honesty. "Don't know how to shut it off."

"Your brain?"

"Check," Austen said, sliding his rook across the duvet.

I ignored the board. My shoulder was throbbing—a dull, rhythmic ache that timed perfectly with my anxiety.

"Yeah." I swallowed, staring at the white and black pieces. "If I screw up the exam, eligibility's gone. If eligibility's gone, starter spot follows. Scholarships get reviewed. That's the whole net, Austen."

He nodded slowly, watching me rub the joint. "And if you pass?"

"We celebrate with fries at trivia."

"Reasonable incentive."

I grabbed the tube of muscle cream from the nightstand. The smell of menthol cut through the room instantly. I squeezed a glob onto my fingers and tried to reach back over my left shoulder to the scapula, but the angle was impossible. My deltoid seized up, and I hissed through my teeth, dropping my hand.

"You are mechanically compromising the joint you are attempting to heal," Austen observed.

"I can reach it," I lied. I tried again, contorting my arm. Pain shot down my triceps.

Austen sighed—not annoyed, just practical. He reached out. "Give it here."

I hesitated. "It smells like a locker room."

"I've smelled your gear after a game. This is an improvement. Turn around."

I let out a shaky breath, handed him the tube, and shifted my legs, turning my back to him.

The mattress dipped as he shifted closer.

"Shirt," he commanded.

I pulled my T-shirt up over my head, bunching it at my neck.

The air was cool, but the gel was freezing. I flinched when he applied it. His hand followed—warm, firm, and shockingly strong.

"Relax," he murmured.

He worked the cream into the muscle with efficient, circular motions. The sensation of his thumb digging into the knot near my spine made my eyes flutter shut.

"What's the actual probability you fail now?" he asked, his voice vibrating slightly against my back. The heat of his breath on my bare skin made me shudder.

I ran the numbers out loud—quiz weight, assignments, projection of midterm scoring distribution. Came up with a range. Low, but not zero.

"So, not catastrophic," he said, pressing harder on a trigger point. "Noisy."

"Noise can still ruin the play."

"True."

He shifted his weight. His knee bumped against my lower back. He didn't pull away. He stayed there, a solid anchor while his hand moved from my shoulder to the tense cord of my neck.

"Is the amplitude lower?" he asked. "The noise?"

"Lower," I whispered. Truth. Every exhale from him felt like closing a gate against the crowd.

"Good."

He didn't stop. The cream was absorbed, but his hand lingered, thumb resting against the vertebrae of my neck.

I should move. I should say thanks for the help, pull my shirt back on, and go to sleep. That was the safe play.

Instead, I turned my head.

He was right there.

I hadn't realized how close he'd gotten to get better leverage. His face was inches from mine. He wasn't looking at my shoulder anymore; he was looking at me. His pupils were blown wide behind his glasses.

My heart hammered—hard enough to hurt.

"Luke," he said.

We were close. Closer than during tutoring, closer than the stands.

It was hard to misread the data.

"You good with this?" I asked, voice low.

"Yes." No hesitation, fact.

I shifted, turning my body until I was facing him fully, knees tangled between us. I froze.

The alarm bells in my head were screaming. *Bad idea. Don't do it. Don't complicate the season. Don't be the distraction.*

I looked at his mouth. Then his eyes. He wasn't pushing. He was waiting.

If I crossed this line, I couldn't uncross it. I couldn't go back to being the roommate who borrowed his highlighters.

I waited, giving him space to retreat if the variables changed. Giving *myself* space to retreat.

He didn't retreat.

Fingers brushed my wrist, tentative, feather-light. I twitched, my instinct to pull away fighting the magnetic pull to lean in.

He paused. When I didn't pull back, his touch grew firmer. His thumb traced one slow line over my pulse.

It was racing. If he'd rattled off my BPM, I'd have believed him.

The radiator clicked off, abrupt quiet.

His gaze flicked to my mouth, back to my eyes—confirmation request.

Do it, the impulse whispered. *Risk it.*

Don't, the discipline warned. *You'll lose everything.*

I looked at him—messy hair, steady eyes, the guy who labeled my frozen vegetables and argued about *Die Hard*.

With a jolt of panic and clarity, I realized I didn't care about the risk. I wanted the noise to stop, and he was the only thing that could make the noise stop.

I closed the gap.

I stopped an inch from his lips, giving him one last chance to shove me away, to tell me I'd misread the signals.

He didn't shove. He exhaled, a soft, broken sound, and tilted his head.

Lips touched once, soft, experimental.

I pulled back a fraction, terrified I'd done it wrong, terrified I'd broken the friendship.

But Austen chased me. He leaned forward, closing the distance I'd tried to leave, and the second kiss wasn't experimental. It was magnetic like the chess pieces, pulling until both sides clicked.

First kiss should have felt like fireworks; instead, it felt like life locking into place. In that one kiss, Austen solved a problem in me I didn't even know existed. He exhaled against my mouth, the lime seltzer taste hung on his breath.

We broke apart a fraction, foreheads close, breath mixing. I expected awkward, got gravity.

"Still noisy?" he whispered.

"Only in a good way." My hand found the hem of his T-shirt where it draped loose. I tugged. He shifted forward, answering.

A second kiss, deeper, and the mattress answered with a soft groan. Somewhere in the hallway a toilet flushed—thin walls, potential audience. He didn't pull back; neither did I. The risk buzzed under my skin, adrenaline without the crash.

I slid my hand to the base of his neck, fingers threading the hair that never stayed down. He shivered—small, involuntary. His palm settled on my waist, light, like contact itself was the variable he was testing.

"Shoulder?" he asked between breaths.

"Fine." Honest—pain drowned under chemistry.

Another kiss tipped us sideways until we lay parallel, his head on my arm, noses almost touching. I memorized the scene: his lashes, the furrow easing from his brow, the way his hand splayed over my ribs as if measuring distance. I laughed—quiet, but real.

"What?" he murmured.

"Ice melted all over your towel experiment."

He huffed a soft chuckle. "Acceptable collateral."

The pea bag had indeed warmed to lukewarm, leaking. I retrieved it, tossed it onto the desk tray, wiped stray droplets with the edge of the blanket. He watched, amusement flickering.

"Rule breach," I said. "Produce misuse after 23:00."

"We'll amend the constitution." His thumb stroked a slow arc at my waist. "Article six: exceptions for emergent variables."

"Draft it tomorrow." My eyelids felt heavy, weight surrendering.

He brushed hair off my forehead—not a grand gesture, tidying data noise. "Sleep, goalie."

"Stay?"

His eyes softened, like the request surprised him; like leaving had never crossed his mind. "Planned on it."

The dorm clock blinked 1:03. I shifted onto my back; he draped half over my chest, head tucked near the bruise he'd iced all week. Comfortable enough. Risky enough. I removed his glasses and sat them on the desk; mine lived somewhere in the gear pile—obstacles for dawn.

I threaded fingers through his, anchored them on my stomach. His breathing synced to mine by degrees. The radiator cycled on, warm against the window glaze. The hallway settled into late-night hush: elevator ding, distant door, nothing else.

I waited for the panic. Instead, there was only the steady proof of his weight against me.

"Luke?" he said into the fabric of my shirt.

"Yeah."

"Promise me you won't regret this in the morning."

"Promise." I squeezed his hand.

A hum of agreement, then his body relaxed. Twenty seconds later his breaths evened—soft, rhythmic.

I let my eyes close. The math of the day collapsed into simple integers: two bodies, one mattress, zero distance.

I slept.

Morning slapped me with the metallic ring of my phone alarm. I jerked, disoriented, until the warm shape against my side crystallized. Austen blinked up, hair worse than midnight, pillow crease on his cheek. No panic in his eyes, slow awareness. My alarm buzzed again; I silenced it.

"Time?" he croaked.

"Five-forty."

He processed that, then made to roll away. I tightened my arm. "You're good."

"Practice?"

"Starts at six-thirty. Need campus shuttle by six." My shoulder twinged but held. "We have ten."

He sat up, rubbing his face. Blanket pooled at his waist; Frost Demons logo distorted across his chest. He caught me staring, color touched his ears. "Still no regrets?"

"None." I grinned. Couldn't stop.

He returned the smile. His gaze swept the room.

"You're thinking," I said.

"Trying not to overthink this." His voice was still sandpaper from sleep. "Outcome appears positive."

"I concur."

I swung my legs over the side, stood, and stretched. The floor was colder than expected. He followed, toes curling on the rug.

"What's your morning like?" Austen asked.

"Skate edges."

"Coffee for you after?"

"I would love that." My hand hovered at his waist. Habit said stop. New data said don't. I let my fingers brush his hip through the shirt; he leaned into it.

Quiet intimacy lasted three heartbeats before the radiator clanged, reminding us somebody, somewhere, still existed. We stepped apart, but the distance felt pretend now.

I gathered practice gear, shoulder test—twinge, tolerable. As I laced my runners, he climbed back into my bed.

At the door, I paused. Sun hadn't climbed yet; the hallway fluorescents flickered half power. I looked back.

"Later, roommate," I said—habit.

He met my eyes, brow quirked. "We may need a new noun."

I swallowed a grin big enough to betray us in public. "Work on it. We iterate."

I walked back over to him, leaned down, and kissed him on the forehead. He smiled up at me. No words. I turned and left.

The hallway smelled like bleach and someone else's stale pizza. I tapped both door-posts—left, right—before jogging toward the stairs.

Somewhere between ticks of the radiator and the first cool breath outside, I realized the net I'd been protecting hadn't been the crease.

And "roommate" definitely wasn't the right word.

Chapter 18
Controlled
Variables

Austen

I woke to an empty bed and the smell of soap.

The pillow beside me still held the impression of Luke's head. I pressed my palm into it, feeling residual warmth that might have been real or imagined. The clock read 7:14—he'd been gone for over an hour.

Chess pieces littered the floor. The bishop had rolled under my desk. The pea bag sat in a puddle on the towel, forgotten casualties of whatever had happened at 1:03 a.m.

I replayed the data: his lips, the radiator click, the way his hand had found mine in the dark. I'd kissed Luke Carter. Luke Carter had kissed me back. These were facts now, entered into the permanent record.

My phone buzzed on the nightstand.

Luke: *Edges felt good. Shoulder at 1.5. Ryan asked why I was smiling during bag skate.*

I read it three times before I typed back.

Me: *What did you tell him?*

Luke: *Podcast.*

Me: *You don't listen to podcasts.*

Luke: *He doesn't know that.*

I smiled at the ceiling. The crack was still there, same as always. But the room felt different—recalibrated, like someone had adjusted the variables without telling me.

I got up, collected the chess pieces, threw away the pea bag, and hung the towel to dry. Now I was the one perseverating. My entire operating system had been rewritten overnight.

The next three days existed on two parallel planes.

In public, nothing changed. Luke sat with the team at meals. I sat with Maya or alone. We passed each other in hallways with the careful neutrality of acquaintances. In class, I took notes. In Ridgeway Hall, I helped students prepare for finals. The surface held.

In private, everything changed.

Luke came back from practice at 4:47 each afternoon. I learned his schedule like a theorem—shower by five, protein shake by 5:15, homework spread across his bed by 5:30. I learned to listen for his key in the lock, the specific weight of his footsteps.

The first night after the kiss, he'd hesitated at the threshold between our beds.

He gestured to my bed, "Can I?—"

"Yes."

He grabbed his pillow, crossed the room in three steps, and kissed me against the desk. My laptop rattled. I didn't care.

We developed protocols. Door locked during contact. No visible evidence—no marks, no borrowed clothes left in obvious places, no lingering looks that lasted longer than roommate-appropriate.

It was exhausting. It was exhilarating. It was like running a constant simulation in the back of my mind: *if person enters, then separate; if text arrives, check sender before reacting; if proximity exceeds threshold, then recalibrate.*

On Wednesday, Ryan knocked without warning.

Luke and I had been on his bed, my back against the wall, his hand on my knee, textbook open between us as plausible cover. The knock sent us apart like magnets reversed—me to my desk, him to the door, textbook sliding to the floor with a thud.

"Monk!" Ryan's voice carried through the wood. "Lift in ten. Harper's orders."

"Coming," Luke called back, voice steady.

I heard Ryan's footsteps retreat. Luke turned to look at me, chest heaving.

"Close," I said.

"Too close." He ran a hand through his hair. "We need better protocols."

"Agreed."

He grabbed his gym bag, then paused at the door. Glanced back. The look on his face—half frustration, half something softer—made my chest tight.

"Later," he said.

"Later."

The door closed. Then it opened again, and Luke crossed the room to me and kissed me before heading out again. I exhaled and pressed my palms flat against the desk until my heartbeat normalized.

Finals week arrived like a freight train.

Luke's accounting exam loomed on Thursday—twenty-five percent of his grade, the number that would determine whether seventy-two became seventy-three or whether everything collapsed. I watched the stress accumulate in his shoulders, in the way he stopped sleeping through the night, in the frequency of ignored calls from a contact labeled simply "Dad."

We studied every evening. I drilled him on journal entries until the words lost meaning, until *debit* and *credit* became pure sound. He improved. The practice problems came faster, the errors less frequent. But the margin was razor-thin, and we both knew it.

"What if I choke?" he asked on Tuesday night, staring at a trial balance that had finally come out even.

"You won't."

"But if I do."

I set down my pencil. "We find another path. But you won't."

He looked at me—really looked, the way he did when the goalie mask was off and there was nowhere to hide. "How do you know?"

"Because I've seen you block shots that defied physics. Because you memorized adjusting entries in two days when it should have taken you two weeks. Because—" I stopped myself.

"Because what?"

"Because I believe in your ability to perform under pressure."

He was quiet for a moment. He leaned across the desk and kissed me, soft and quick, and went back to his practice problems.

I didn't tell him what I'd almost said: *Because I can't imagine a version of this where you fail.*

Thursday morning, I walked him to the business building.

We kept appropriate distance—two feet, hands in pockets, nothing that would register as unusual. But at the door, he paused.

"Wait here?" he asked.

"I need to go to Ridgeway Hall and get some grading done."

"After. Will you wait?"

I nodded. "I'll be in the east carrels. Third floor."

He took a breath. Squared his shoulders. Walked inside.

I spent the next two hours marking papers I couldn't remember touching. The clock moved like it was dragging weights. At 11:15, I positioned myself at a carrel with a clear view of the stairwell.

At 11:47, Luke appeared at the top of the stairs.

His face was blank—the game face, the one that gave nothing away. I stood, heart hammering, trying to read the data in his posture, his gait, the set of his jaw.

He stopped in front of my carrel. Said nothing.

"Well?" I whispered.

"Seventy-three."

The number landed like a puck in an empty net.

"Seventy-three," I repeated. "Cumulative?"

"Point four." The game face cracked. Underneath it was something bright and stunned. "I passed, Austen. I actually passed."

I wanted to kiss him. I wanted him to lift me off the ground and spin me around and shout the number until the whole building heard.

"Statistically inevitable," I said, my voice dropping an octave. "Given sufficient preparation."

He laughed—quiet, breathless, the sound of a weight being lifted. "You're impossible."

"I'm correct. There's a difference."

He stared at me, his eyes bright, the adrenaline of the exam still flushing his skin. He stepped closer. Then closer again. The air between us evaporated.

"Austen," he breathed.

He didn't wait for a response. He reached out, curled a hand around the back of my neck, and pulled me in.

It wasn't a tentative test of the waters. It was a collision.

I made a noise in my throat—half surprise, half surrender—and grabbed the lapels of his coat. His mouth was hot, tasting of mint gum. For three seconds, the building around us ceased to exist. The glass walls all dissolved into the friction of his stubble against my chin and the desperate, solid pressure of his body against mine.

My mind emptied as I held on to him like a life preserver during a hurricane.

Then, reality rebooted.

We broke apart, gasping, chests heaving.

The silence of the third floor rushed back in, deafening.

Panic spiked. I whipped my head around, heart hammering against my ribs. Glass walls. We were in a fishbowl.

I scanned the perimeter. The graduate student three rows down was still hunched over her laptop, oversized headphones firmly in place. The rest of the floor was empty.

"Clear," I whispered, the word shaky.

Luke was looking around too, eyes wide, hand still hovering near my shoulder. He looked back at me, his mouth swollen, his cheeks bright red.

"Did anyone see?" he asked, though he didn't look sorry.

"Negative," I exhaled, adjusting my glasses, which had been knocked askew.

Luke grinned—a reckless, blinding thing.

"Good," he said. "Because I really needed to do that."

"Reciprocity established," I managed, my pulse still racing. "But we should probably de-escalate. Before any professors round the corner."

That night, we went to trivia.

Ryan had been asking for weeks to come back. Luke had been deflecting, citing study obligations, shoulder maintenance, early practice. But with the exam behind him and eligibility secured, the excuses evaporated.

"One hour," Luke said as we walked to Buckman Grill. "Show face. Collect on the fries. Leave."

"Agreed."

The bar was at crush capacity, vibrating with the chaotic energy of students celebrating the end of finals. It was warm, loud, and smelled of spilled beer—a sensory nightmare I had somehow grown to moderately tolerate.

Ryan had commandeered our usual corner booth, waving a pitcher in the air when he saw us.

"Thank God," he yelled over the bass. "The brain trust has arrived."

I guided Maya through the crowd. "I brought reinforcements," I said, sliding into the booth. "Ryan, this is Maya. She's a Humanities major, which means she actually reads books."

"You are a lifesaver," Ryan said, shaking Maya's hand enthusiastically. "Miller and Johnson bailed early for their flights home, so we're down two men. And Javier is useless with anything that isn't sports or geography."

"Hey," Javier protested, mouth full of pretzel.

"I have a near-eidetic memory for celebrity scandals and literary awards," Maya offered, stealing a fry from the center basket.

Ryan looked at me. "I like her. She stays."

Luke squeezed in next to me, his knee finding mine, which caused everyone else to move around the table a bit to give us room. Feeling his warmth next to me was a familiar signal now—a secret, constant pressure that grounded me. He looked tired but happy, the weight of the financial accounting exam finally gone from his shoulders.

"Beer?" Luke asked, already pouring.

"Please."

"Round one starts in two minutes," Ryan announced. "Categories are 90s Music, organic chemistry—which is a gift from the gods for you, Austen—and current events. We need a win to close out the semester."

We didn't get the win, but we salvaged respectability. We came in third, mostly because Maya single-handedly swept the music category while Ryan and Javier stared blankly at the speakers. Luke laughed more than I'd seen in weeks, the tension in his jaw finally loose, and every time the table cheered, his leg pressed harder against mine. At one point, we held hands under the table.

At 9:30, Luke caught my eye. The subtle nod. The protocol.

"No early practice tomorrow, but I still need to hit the weight room before my last final," he announced, standing up and grabbing his coat.

"Gross," Javier sympathized.

"Austen, you heading out?" Luke asked, the script practiced.

"The library closes at ten," I lied smoothly. "I need to return a reference book before the break."

"Weak," Ryan jeered, but he bumped fists with me anyway. "Good game, Lovell. Maya, you're officially on the roster for next semester."

"I'll have my agent call you," she deadpanned. "Actually, if you two don't mind, I'll hang out here for a little longer."

"Cool," Ryan said. "Be our guest."

We said our goodbyes—casual, appropriate, nothing that would linger in anyone's memory.

Outside, the December air was a shock, biting through my jacket and turning our breath into white plumes. The noise of the bar faded behind us. We walked in silence, maintaining a respectable distance until the shadows of Stony Creek Hall rose in the distance.

Only then, when we hit the blind spot beneath the old oak tree, did Luke's hand find mine in the dark. His fingers laced through mine, warm and rough.

"That was fun. We had a good night," he said, his voice dropping to that low register reserved for the dorm room.

"Acceptable night," I corrected. "We could have performed better. Without Maya, we would have been far below average."

He pulled me into the deeper shadow of the trunk, cutting off my analysis.

"Shut up about the math," he murmured, and kissed me until I forgot about the statistics entirely.

Friday brought the question I'd been avoiding.

"Christmas break," Luke said, tossing clothes into a duffel. "What's your plan?"

I was at my desk, organizing notes for a January syllabus I didn't need to review yet. "Stay here. Catch up on reading. The dining hall runs a reduced schedule, but there's a microwave in the basement."

He paused mid-fold. "You're staying on campus. Alone. For three weeks."

"It's cost-effective."

"It's depressing."

"I don't celebrate Christmas. The isolation is irrelevant."

He set down the duffel. Walked over. Sat on the edge of my desk, close enough that his knee pressed against my arm.

"Austen."

"The room is already paid. A plane ticket to anywhere else would be—"

"I'm not asking about logistics." His voice was soft. "I'm asking if you're okay."

I stared at my notes. The words blurred. "I've spent holidays alone before. It's fine."

"Fine isn't okay."

My phone buzzed before I could respond. Maya's name on the screen.

Maya: *Vermont. Christmas. My parents have a guest room. Say yes.*

I read it twice. Luke read it over my shoulder.

"Say yes," he said.

"I can't just—"

"Yes, you can." He took the phone from my hand, typed a response, and handed it back. *Yes. Thank you.*

"That was presumptuous," I said.

"That was efficient." He kissed my temple, quick and light. "You deserve an actual holiday. With people. And probably a fireplace."

"Maya's family has a fireplace?"

"I'm guessing... it's Vermont." He returned to his duffel. "Point is, you're not sitting in an empty dorm eating microwave oatmeal or mushy mac-n-cheese while I'm in Jersey pretending my dad isn't disappointed in everything I do. At least one of us should get a chance at being happy."

I watched him pack. The tension had crept back into his shoulders at the mention of Jersey, the familiar armor reassembling.

"You could stay too," I said. "Skip the trip."

"Can't. If I avoid him through another holiday, the voicemails will get worse." He zipped the bag with more force than necessary. "Three weeks. We text. We call. We survive. If you're lucky, maybe I'll send you some shirtless pics."

"Only if they're headless. Aren't all sexy pictures sent by gay men headless? But honestly, survival seems like a low threshold."

He looked at me, and the armor slipped just enough to show what was underneath. "It's the only one I've got."

Saturday morning, we said goodbye.

His bus left at seven. Maya wasn't picking me up until noon, but I woke with him anyway, watching him move through the dark room by muscle memory. Toothbrush, deodorant, phone charger.

At 6:40, he stood by the door with his duffel over one shoulder.

"Three weeks," he said.

"Twenty-one days. Five hundred four hours. Thirty thousand—"

He crossed the room and kissed me. Not quick this time. Not careful.

When he pulled back, his forehead rested against mine.

"I'll miss you," he said. "You have no idea how much I'll miss you."

"I'll miss you too." The words felt strange in my mouth—too simple for the weight they carried. "Text when you arrive."

"Promise."

One more kiss, briefer, then he was gone. The door clicked shut. His footsteps faded down the hall.

I sat on his bed. It still smelled like him. The chess set was packed in my bag for Vermont, and the pea bags were restocked in the freezer. The room was exactly as he'd left it except for the absence that filled every corner.

I pulled out my phone. No messages yet—he probably wasn't even out of the building yet.

I typed anyway.

Me: *Safe travels. The probability of bus-related incidents is statistically negligible, but I wanted to note that I hope you arrive without complications.*

Three dots appeared.

Luke: *That might be the nerdiest "I love you" I've ever seen.*

I stared at the screen. My heart stopped, restarted, stopped again.

Me: *That is not what I said.*

Luke: *Close enough.*

Another pause.

Luke: *I'll text when I land. Don't let Maya's family feed you too much turkey.*

Me: *No promises. And, I do love you.*

Luke: *I love you more.*

I set the phone down. Pressed my palm against the mattress where he'd slept. We'd just said our first '*I love you*'s' through text messages. I closed my eyes and let out a long breath. Twenty-one days. Five hundred four hours.

Chapter 19
Slapshots and Holidays

LUKE

The drive down I-87 had been a straight shot, the kind of autopilot fugue state where you lose three hours to the rhythm of the tires.

I pulled into the driveway of the Glen Rock house at 2:47 p.m.

Dad's truck was already there, parked dead center in front of the three-car garage. It was an F-150, same make and model as mine, but while mine was road-weary black, his was candy-apple red. Flashy. Polished to a shine.

I pulled up alongside it, killing the engine. The silence of the suburbs rushed in—no dorm noise, no locker room bass, just the ticking of the cooling engine.

The front door opened before I even unbuckled.

Dad walked out. He looked the same—silver at the temples now, jaw set in that permanent, game-ready clench. He wasn't wearing a coat, just a cashmere sweater that cost more than my semester of books.

I grabbed my duffel from the passenger seat and stepped out.

"Made good time," he said, coming down the steps.

He didn't hug me. He extended a hand.

I took it. His grip was firm.

"Traffic was light," I said.

"Good. Saves daylight." He nodded at my truck, then at my left arm. "Shoulder holding up on the drive?"

"It's fine."

"Saw the tape of the Amherst game," he said, turning back toward the house without waiting for me. "You're dropping your glove on the blocker side when you butterfly. You're exposing the top corner."

"I'm aware."

"Awareness doesn't stop goals, Lucas. Correction does." He held the door open, ushering me into the foyer that smelled of lemon polish and expensive coffee. "Put your bag in the room. We're eating at six."

I stepped inside. Three weeks of this. Twenty-one days of unsolicited coaching advice and the constant, crushing weight of being the only investment in the portfolio.

My phone buzzed in my pocket.

Austen: *Arrived in Vermont. The Chen family has a Labrador named Calculus. I am not making this up.*

I smiled before I could stop myself.

"What's funny?" Dad asked.

"Nothing." I locked the screen. "Just a friend."

The house hadn't changed.

Same split-level in the same subdivision, same dead lawn waiting for spring, same garage where Dad kept his workout equipment and the trophies he never threw away. I dropped my duffel in my old bedroom—twin bed, faded posters, desk I hadn't used since high school—and stood at the window watching the neighbor's Christmas lights blink on and off in an arrhythmic pattern that would have driven Austen insane.

Me: *My childhood room.*

Austen: *The color distribution on those string lights in the background is mathematically offensive. Two reds, one green, three blues?*

Me: *It's random.*

Austen: *That's not random, that's just ugly.*

I laughed, then caught myself. The walls here were thin. Dad was downstairs, probably already queuing up game film, ready to dissect every save I'd made since September.

Me: *How's Vermont?*

Austen: *Cold. The Chens have strong opinions about board games. Maya's mother asked if I have a girlfriend. I said no, which is technically accurate.*

Me: *Smooth.*

Austen: *I panicked. She asked if I have a boyfriend. I froze.*

I read the message twice. Something warm spread through my chest, counteracting the chill of being back in this house.

Me: *What did Maya do?*

Austen: *Choked on her hot chocolate. But got me out of answering the question. I believe she suspects something.*

Me: *You think?*

Austen: *Probability increasing by the hour.*

I heard Dad's footsteps on the stairs. I pocketed my phone and opened my duffel, pretending to unpack.

"Dinner's at six," Dad said from the doorway. "I made the brisket."

"Thanks."

He lingered. I could feel him cataloging the room—the unmade bed, the duffel I'd barely touched, the phone-shaped bulge in my pocket.

"You talk to Coach Harper lately?" he asked.

"Before I left. She's happy with the first half."

"Happy doesn't win championships."

"I'm aware."

Another silence. The Christmas lights blinked. Springsteen drifted up from the kitchen, muffled but persistent.

"Good to have you home, Luke."

"Yeah," I said. "Good to be here."

We were both lying.

The first week crawled.

Dad and I existed in parallel orbits—breakfast at different times, dinners eaten in front of game tape, conversations that circled endlessly back to hockey. He had opinions about my butterfly technique. He had opinions about my rebound control. He had opinions about Harper's line combinations and the freshman defenseman who kept screening me on point shots.

I nodded. I deflected. I escaped to my room as often as I could justify.

Austen became my lifeline.

We texted constantly—a running commentary that made the hours bearable. He sent photos of Vermont: snow-covered pines, Calculus the Labrador asleep on his feet, Maya's younger brother attempting to explain TikTok trends with the fervor of a missionary. I sent photos of New Jersey: my high school, the diner where I'd eaten post-game pancakes as a kid, the sunset over the turnpike that looked like bruised fruit, and maybe one or two shirtless selfies to keep him interested.

Austen: *The Chens play Settlers of Catan with alarming intensity. Mrs. Chen has won four games in a row. I suspect card counting.*

Me: *Can you card count in Catan?*

Austen: *I'm developing a theory.*

Me: *You would.*

On Wednesday, we FaceTimed for the first time.

I waited until Dad was asleep, then locked my door and propped my phone against the pillow. Austen's face appeared, pixelated at first before sharpening into focus. He was in what looked like a guest room—floral wallpaper, a quilt that was probably made by someone in the Chen family, and soft lamplight.

"Hi," I said.

"Hello." He adjusted his glasses. "You look tired."

"Dad's been running me through film sessions. Four hours today."

"That seems excessive."

"That's his love language." I shifted on the bed, trying to find an angle that didn't make me look like a corpse. "How's the Chen family circus?"

"Chaotic. Warm." He paused. "I'm not used to this much... togetherness."

"Bad togetherness?"

"No. Just unfamiliar." He was quiet for a moment. "They included me in the family photo. For the Christmas card. Mrs. Chen insisted."

Something in my chest cracked open a little. "That's good, Austen."

"Is it? I'm not family. I'm Maya's strange friend who showed up with a suitcase and opinions about optimal dishwasher loading."

"You're their guest. They want you to feel included."

"The concept is... taking time to process."

I wished I could reach through the screen. Touch his face, smooth the furrow between his brows. Instead, I just looked at him, memorizing the details I'd been missing—the way his hair fell across his forehead, the precise angle of his jaw, the small scar above his eyebrow I'd never asked about.

"I miss you," I said.

"I miss you too." He said it like a fact, clinical and certain. "The bed here is objectively comfortable, but I keep reaching for a body that isn't there."

"Same."

We sat in silence for a while. Not awkward—just present. His breathing through the speaker, mine loud in the quiet room. The distance between Vermont and New Jersey collapsed into the space of a phone screen.

"Luke?"

"Yeah."

"Thank you. For making me go."

"You would have been miserable in that dorm."

"Probably. But I would have been miserable while saving money and maintaining my routine." He almost smiled. "This is better. Even if Mrs. Chen keeps asking about my love life."

"Tell her your love life is classified."

"I told her it was 'under development.' She seemed satisfied."

I laughed, quiet enough not to wake Dad. "Under development. I like that."

"It's accurate." His eyes met mine through the screen. "We are still developing, aren't we?"

"Yeah," I said. "We are."

Maya figured it out on December twenty-third.

Austen told me about it in a text that arrived at 11:47 p.m., long enough that I had to scroll.

Austen: *Incident report. Maya walked up behind me in the kitchen while I was reviewing your last attachment. She achieved full visual contact with the screen.*

Me: *Which attachment?*

Austen: *The mirror selfie. The shirtless one from the locker room.*

I groaned, dropping my head back against the bus seat. I had sent that twenty minutes ago—a flexing joke that was definitely forty percent vanity.

Me: *Oh God.*

Austen: *She studied the image for a full four seconds. She asked if I was switching my major to Anatomy.*

Austen: *She also asked if the "study materials" were available for checkout. She has drawn conclusions.*

Me: *I am never looking her in the eye again.*

Austen: *Too late. She says your obliques are "statistically significant."*

Austen: *She said, and I quote: "Oh my GOD, Austen. How long has THIS been happening?"*

Me: *And you said?*

Austen: *I attempted to deny. She was not convinced. I attempted to redirect. Also unsuccessful. Finally, I confirmed that we are "involved" and requested her discretion.*

Me: *How'd she take it?*

Austen: *She hugged me. Made hot chocolate. Then she asked seventeen questions about timeline, physical compatibility, and whether you are good to me. Her words.*

Me: *Am I?*

Austen: *I told her yes. She seemed satisfied. She has promised not to tell anyone, including Ryan, which she emphasized would require "significant willpower" given their apparent ongoing communication.*

I read the message three times. Someone else knew now. Someone outside the two of us. The secret had expanded, and with it the risk—but also, maybe, the reality. If Maya knew, then this was something that existed in the world, not just in the space between our beds.

Me: *You okay?*

Austen: *Unexpectedly relieved. The cognitive load of maintaining complete secrecy was harder than I expected. Having one person who knows... it helps.*

Me: *Yeah. It does.*

Austen: *She also informed me that she "called it" weeks ago and that we are "disgustingly cute." I am not sure how to process that feedback.*

Me: *Accept it. We're disgustingly cute.*

Austen: *If you say so.*

Me: *I say so. Now, go to bed. It's almost midnight.*

Austen: *Fine. But only because your imperative aligns with my circadian preferences.*

Me: *That's the nerdiest "good night" I've ever seen.*

Austen: *I learned from the best.*

Me: *Love you.*

Austen: *I love you, too.*

Christmas Day arrived gray and cold.

Dad and I exchanged gifts with the enthusiasm of a hockey line change—him to me: new gloves, top of the line, already broken in the way I liked. Me to him: a frame for the photo from my first varsity start, something I'd found in a box in my closet and figured he'd want displayed.

"Good gloves," I said.

"Good frame," he said.

We ate ham in front of the TV, watching an NHL game neither of us cared about. The house was too quiet. Mom had been gone since I was fourteen—not dead, just relocated, remarried, living in Arizona with a man who sold insurance and didn't understand hockey. She'd sent a card. I hadn't opened it. And dad was currently single after going through a string of wives.

At two p.m., I escaped to my room and called Austen.

"Merry Christmas," I said when he answered.

"Merry Christmas." He was wearing a sweater I didn't recognize—chunky knit, forest green, probably borrowed from Maya's dad. "The Chens are doing a puzzle. A one-thousand-piece rendering of the Milky Way. I have been assigned the edge pieces."

"Sounds intense."

"It requires focus." He shifted the phone, and I glimpsed the living room behind him—fireplace, tree, people moving in the background. "How's New Jersey?"

"Quiet. Dad gave me gloves."

"That's... practical."

"It's his way." I leaned against the headboard. "I got you something. It's back at the dorm. I'll give it to you when we get back."

"You didn't have to—"

"I wanted to." I'd found it at a used bookstore in town—a first edition of some math text he'd mentioned once, spine cracked but intact. Probably too sentimental. I didn't care.

"I have something for you as well," he said. "Also, at the dorm. It's not... significant. Just something I saw."

"I'm sure it's perfect."

"You haven't seen it yet."

"Doesn't matter."

He was quiet for a moment. Through the phone, I heard laughter—the Chens, probably, celebrating something puzzle-related. Austen glanced toward the sound, then back at the screen.

"I wish you were here," he said.

"I wish I was there too."

"Only five more days."

"Five more days."

We stayed on the phone for another hour, not talking much, just existing in the same digital space. He worked on edge pieces. I stared at the ceiling. Sometimes presence didn't require words. I had more fun staring at the Chen's ceiling than I had since getting back home.

New Year's Eve, Dad tried.

He bought sparkling cider and made his famous seven-layer dip and put on the countdown coverage like we were a normal family who did normal things. We sat on opposite ends of the couch, watching the ball drop in Times Square, surrounded by the ghosts of holidays that had gone differently.

"You're playing well this season," he said at 11:58.

I looked at him. It was the first compliment he'd offered all break.

"Thanks."

"Harper knows what she's doing. The team's got structure." He paused, jaw working like he was chewing on words he couldn't quite swallow. "I'm proud of you, Luke."

The ball dropped. The crowd roared. Dad raised his cider glass, and I raised mine, and we clinked them together in the flickering TV light.

"Happy New Year, son," he said.

"Happy New Year, Dad."

It wasn't enough. It was never enough. But it was something—a crack in the wall he'd built, a glimpse of the father I remembered from before the injury ended his career and turned him into a man made entirely of regret.

I texted Austen at 12:01.

Me: *Happy New Year. Dad said he's proud of me.*

Austen: *That's significant.*

Me: *Maybe. I don't know what to do with it.*

Austen: *You don't have to do anything with it. You can just let it exist.*

Me: *Oh, is that how feelings work?*

Austen: *I'm learning that they might.*

I smiled at my phone. Across the room, Dad was cleaning up the dip, moving with the careful economy of a man who'd spent his life protecting his body from damage.

"I'm heading to bed," I said. "Early drive tomorrow."

"You're leaving tomorrow?"

"Day after. But I want to check the truck, make sure it's road-ready."

He nodded. "I'll look at it with you. In the morning."

"Okay."

Another silence. He crossed to the couch and did something he hadn't done in years—put a hand on my shoulder, brief and heavy, and squeezed.

"Good night," he said. "And keep your glove up."

"I will."

He went upstairs. I stayed on the couch, staring at the TV as the celebrations continued in cities I'd never visit. My phone buzzed.

Austen: *The Chens have started singing karaoke. I am hiding in the bathroom.*

Me: *Coward.*

Austen: *Strategic retreat.*

Me: *Same thing.*

Austen: *Agree to disagree. Happy New Year, Luke.*

Me: *Happy New Year, Austen.*

On January third, I drove back to campus.

The truck handled the I-95 corridor without complaint, heater blasting, radio playing the same classic rock Dad had raised me on. I'd left at dawn, watched the sun rise over the Delaware Water Gap, and felt the tension drain from my shoulders with every mile north.

Austen was waiting.

I knew because he'd texted his arrival time—4:47 p.m., precise to the minute—and I'd calculated my own to match. When I pulled into the campus lot at 4:52, his Camry was already there, engine off, a figure visible through the driver's side window.

I parked two spaces away. Got out. The January air bit at my face, sharp and clean.

Austen emerged from his car. He was wearing the green sweater—he'd kept it, or bought one like it—and his hair was longer than I remembered, curling at his temples.

We stood there, two spaces apart, breath fogging between us.

"Hi," I said.

"Hello."

"Good drive?"

"Acceptable. Yours?"

"Long."

The distance felt unbearable. Three weeks of screens and texts and the phantom weight of his absence, and now he was here, real, solid, close enough to touch.

I closed the gap in four steps and kissed him against his car.

He made a sound—surprised, pleased—and his hands fisted in my jacket, pulling me closer. The cold vanished. The parking lot vanished. Everything vanished except the pressure of his mouth and the proof that he was here, he was real, the separation was over.

When we finally broke apart, his glasses were fogged.

"That was—" he started.

"Yeah."

"We're in public."

"I don't care."

"Someone could see."

"Still don't care."

He looked at me, eyes bright behind the foggy lenses. "I missed you."

"I missed you too." I pressed my forehead to his. "Let's go inside."

"Yes. Let's."

The next six weeks existed in a haze.

We fell into a rhythm—classes, practice, study sessions that turned into something else, nights tangled together in Luke's narrow bed. The secret held, mostly. Maya covered for us when she could, deflecting Ryan's questions with the skill of a veteran diplomat.

We went on a date. A real one—off-campus, a Thai place twenty minutes away where no one knew us. I ordered pad Thai. Austen ordered something with a heat level that made my eyes water just looking at it. We argued about probability theory and whether pineapple belonged on pizza and what constituted a "real" date versus "just eating."

"This is a real date," Austen insisted. "We traveled. There's atmosphere. You're not wearing a jersey."

"It's a flannel."

"Exactly. Effort was made."

I laughed and stole a bite of his curry before thinking better of it as my mouth suddenly burst into flames and I thought a baby dragon was hatching on my tongue. I scrambled for the water. My mouth settling as one of Dante's lesser levels of hell.

"How do you eat that?" I asked between gasps.

"I put it in my mouth and chew."

"Dear God, Austen. How do you have any tastebuds left after eating that stuff."

He shrugged.

February arrived with a cold snap and a schedule that made my head spin.

"Boston," Harper announced at Monday practice. "Northeastern. Saturday. This is the big one, people. Scouts confirmed. I want everyone sharp."

I tapped my posts and tried to focus. The game mattered. The scouts mattered. Everything I'd worked for was converging on one weekend in a city I'd never much liked.

That night, Austen mentioned his own news.

"I got accepted," he said, not looking up from his laptop. "The symposium. Northeast Regional Mathematics."

"That's great." I set down my protein shake. "When is it?"

"February fourteenth through sixteenth. In Boston."

I stared at him. "We're playing Northeastern on the fifteenth. In Boston."

He finally looked up. "That's... coincidental."

"We'll both be in the same city."

"It appears so." He pushed his glasses up. "I doubt our schedules will align, though. You'll have the game, and I'll be presenting, and—"

"But we'll be there. At the same time."

"Theoretically."

I grinned. The idea was absurd—both of us in Boston, moving through the same streets, breathing the same air.

"We should try to meet up," I said. "After the game. Or before your presentation. Something."

"The logistics seem complicated."

"When has that stopped us?"

He considered this. Then, slowly, he smiled. "Fair point."

"Valentine's Day weekend in Boston," I said. "Could be worse."

"Could be significantly better if we were in the same location for more than five minutes."

"We'll figure it out." I crossed the room and kissed the top of his head. "We always do."

He leaned into me, laptop forgotten. "Your optimism is statistically unfounded."

"And yet."

"And yet," he agreed.

Chapter 20
Away Game

LUKE

Road trips usually followed a strict pattern: bus, headphones, hotel, meal, sleep. I liked the rhythm. It left no room for anything extraneous.

But this trip to Boston in mid-February was different.

We were playing Northeastern on Saturday. A huge game—scouts were confirmed, the alumni association was throwing a mixer, and Harper was vibrating with intensity.

I sat in the fourth row of the bus, headphones on but playing nothing. I wished I was driving myself. Leaving my truck sitting in the campus lot while I rode on a coach bus felt like a waste of horsepower.

The engine hummed beneath my feet, a low vibration that usually put me to sleep. Today, I was wired.

My phone buzzed in my lap. I shielded the screen with my hand, glancing around. Ryan was two rows up, arguing with Javier about fantasy football stats.

Austen: *Entering Massachusetts airspace. Traffic density increasing.*

I smiled, thumbing a reply.

Me: *You flying the Camry or driving it?*

Austen: *Low altitude flight. ETA 45 minutes.*

I pictured him in his beat-up sedan, NPR probably playing, his hands at ten and two. He was driving three hours to present a paper at a math symposium, but we both knew that wasn't the only reason he was coming.

Me: *We're twenty out. Coach is in a mood. She made the freshmen carry her espresso machine.*

Austen: *Power move. I respect that.*

I huffed a laugh, then caught myself. I looked up. Ryan had turned around in his seat and was watching me with narrow eyes.

"What's funny, Monk?"

"Nothing," I said, locking my phone screen. "Podcast."

"You're listening to a comedy podcast?" Ryan asked skeptically. "You usually listen to, like, thunder sounds."

"It's a new one. About... goaltending bloopers."

Ryan stared at me for a long second. "Right. Listening to bloopers. Hilarious."

He turned back around. I let out a breath I didn't know I was holding. Ryan had said nothing, but I was suspecting that he'd figured out Austen and I had become more than roommates. We'd been secretly—or not so secretly—dating for two months. I don't know why we hadn't announced it publicly. Apparently, we were both out, we'd just never been out to each other before that kiss.

I looked out the window. The Boston skyline was rising in the distance, gray and steel against the winter sky. Usually, this view made my stomach tight—another city, another arena, another sixty minutes where I had to be perfect.

Today, looking at the Prudential Tower, all I could think was that Austen would be somewhere in that grid of streets. I couldn't believe my game and his conference put us in the same city at the same time. But the distance already felt like we were millions of miles away.

We hit Matthews Arena first for a practice skate.

Matthews was old school—the oldest indoor ice arena still in use. The rafters were dark wood, the seating steep, the ice hard and fast. It smelled of eighty years of sweat, beer, and popcorn.

I loved it.

I tapped my posts, settling into the crease. Harper blew the whistle.

"Flow drill! Keep the feet moving! Carter, I want you aggressive on the angles!"

I pushed out to the top of the paint. Shot from the point—*snap*. Glove save.

I dropped the puck, reset.

Shot from the slot—*thud*. Blocker.

I was in the zone. The puck looked like a beach ball. My edges were biting perfectly into the ice.

"Looking sharp, Monk!" Ryan yelled, skating by.

I felt good. Fast. Singular.

But in the back of my mind, a clock was ticking. *Austen is in the city. Austen is close.*

The team bus smelled like stale coffee and nervous energy as we pulled up to the Marriott Copley Place.

I grabbed my gear bag, slinging it over my good shoulder. My bad shoulder was at a steady two—manageable.

"Carter, listen up!" Ryan yelled from the front of the bus, waving a clipboard. "Odd numbers on the travel roster this weekend. You drew the short straw. You're in a single."

"Does that mean I get the king-size bed?" I asked, stepping onto the sidewalk.

"It means you have no one to talk to. Try not to cry."

"I'll manage," I muttered, suppressing a smile. A single room. Silence. No listening to Morales grind his teeth or Miller play video games until two a.m.

The Boston wind cut through my tracksuit as we exited the bus. We flooded the lobby—a sea of navy tracksuits and massive hockey bags.

I picked up my key card from the manager, enjoying the weight of a solo room key in my pocket. I turned to head toward the elevators, scanning the crowd for the team.

That's when I saw him.

Austen was standing at the far end of the reception desk, looking smaller than usual in his oversized wool coat. He had a rolling suitcase that looked like it had survived a war and a conference lanyard around his neck.

He was also arguing with the front desk clerk. Or, rather, he was politely stating facts while the clerk looked bored. How had we not put two-and-two together and realized we were staying in the same hotel? I headed his direction to see if I could help. I dropped my gear bag next to Javier. "Cover me."

"Where you going?" Javier asked.

I ignored him and cut through the lobby, dodging a luggage cart.

"I have a confirmation number," Austen was saying, tapping his phone screen. "Reserved three months ago. Standard king."

"I see the reservation, sir," the clerk sighed, typing loudly. "But the system shows it as canceled yesterday."

"I didn't cancel it." Austen's voice pitched up—a frequency I recognized. Distress. "I have a presentation at eight a.m. tomorrow. I need a room."

"We're fully booked. There's a hockey tournament and the math convention. I can try to find you something at our sister property near the airport."

"The airport is forty minutes away," Austen said, his hand gripping the counter. "My presentation is—"

I slid up to the counter next to Austen.

"Problem?" I asked.

Austen jumped, turning to face me. Relief washed over his face so fast it almost made my knees buckle.

"Luke. Hi. What are you doing here?"

"Apparently, the school booked us in the same hotel as your conference."

"Lucky you. I guess I'm not staying here because the system ate my reservation. He says it was canceled," Austen added, looking back at the clerk. "It's an error."

"It's not an error, it's a lack of inventory," the clerk said, not looking up. "Like I said, the airport Hilton might—"

"He's with me," I said.

The clerk paused. Austen froze.

"Excuse me?" the clerk asked.

"He's with the team," I lied smoothly. "Administrative support. Tutor. He's supposed to be on the rooming list."

I pulled out my wallet and slapped my team per diem card on the counter—which wouldn't help, but it looked official. I looked at the clerk with my best *I stare down ninety miles per hour slapshots* expression.

"Put him in my room," I said. "Carter. Room 412."

The clerk blinked. He looked at the line of hockey players behind me, then at Austen's desperate face, and decided he didn't get paid enough to argue.

"I can add him as a guest," the clerk muttered. "Here's a key."

He slid a plastic card across the marble.

I grabbed it and handed it to Austen. His fingers brushed mine—electric.

"Go up," I said, voice low. "Wait for me."

"Carter!" Coach Harper's voice cut through the lobby noise.

I winced. I turned around.

Harper was standing by the elevators, holding her clipboard. "Bag drop in five. Conference Room B in ten. We have tape on Northeastern's power play."

Austen looked at me, eyes wide.

"Go," I whispered to him. "I have to do this. Order room service. I'm starving."

"Room service," Austen repeated, clutching the key card. "Okay."

"Don't wait up," I joked, though I desperately hoped he would.

Austen nodded and hurried toward the elevators. I watched him drag his rolling bag behind him, then turned back to the team.

Ryan was watching me, eyebrows raised so high they were practically in his hairline. Javier was leaning on his stick, looking back and forth between me and the empty space where Austen had been.

"So," Ryan drawled. "Since when does the math department travel with the team?"

"Coincidence," I said quickly. Too quickly. "Symposium."

"Right. A symposium. At the exact same hotel where we're staying." Ryan smirked. "What are the odds?"

"Don't start with the math," I muttered, hoisting my bag higher on my shoulder. "The hotel lost his reservation. He was going to spend the night in the lobby."

"Tragic," Ryan said, deadpan. "Let me guess. You, being the benevolent soul you are, offered to help your *roommate*."

"I couldn't leave him there. I told him he could crash in my room."

Javier's eyes went wide. The lightbulb finally flickered on. "Wait. That's who you're always texting on the bus?"

I felt my ears burn. "You know he helps me study, Javy. And I help him understand hockey."

"You text him a lot for 'studying,'" Ryan said, a grin spreading across his face. "Bro, you lit up like a Christmas tree when you saw him."

"I did not."

"You absolutely did," Ryan confirmed. "But here's the logistical issue, Carter. You drew the single with the king-sized bed." Ryan was enjoying this way too much.

My brain stalled.

"I'll take the floor," I said, keeping my voice flat. "Or the chair. It's one night."

Ryan hummed, a sound that showed he believed zero percent of that statement.

"Right. The floor. Excellent for the bad shoulder. Coach will love that."

"I'll manage. Drop it."

"Dropped," Ryan said, patting my good shoulder. "Just... do us a favor. If you guys decide to do any late-night 'geometry,' put the Do Not Disturb sign up. We have an early skate."

"Go to hell, Ryan."

"Love you too, buddy. Just... put a sock on the door if you're 'tutoring,' okay?"

I ignored him and marched toward Conference Room B.

The conference room was airless and hot.

Harper killed the lights. The projector whirred to life, throwing grainy footage of Northeastern's last game against Boston University onto the screen.

"Watch the cycle," Harper said, laser pointer circling a blur of movement. "They overload the half-wall. Carter, look at this entry."

I stared at the screen trying to focus. I analyzed the skater's hips, the release point, the traffic in front.

But my phone vibrated in my pocket.

I checked it under the table.

Austen: *Room 412 secured. It is... excessively large. There is a robe.*

Me: *Put it on. I'm trapped in a dark room watching power plays.*

Austen: *I ordered a burger. And a salad. And something called 'Truffle Fries' which cost $35.*

Me: *Worth it. Eat. I'll be there soon.*

"Carter!" Harper snapped. "Eyes up."

I shoved the phone away. "Sorry, Coach."

"What did I say about their point man?"

"He fakes the slap shot and slides it to the bumper," I recited automatically.

"Good. Don't bite on the fake."

The meeting dragged on. Thirty minutes. Forty-five.

I felt like I was vibrating out of my skin. Austen was upstairs. In a robe. Waiting for me.

And I was watching slow-motion replays of a guy missing the net.

Harper clicked off the projector.

"Curfew at eleven," she said. "Hydrate. Visualize. Win."

"Win," the team mumbled.

I was out of my chair before the lights came fully up.

"Where's the fire, Monk?" Ryan asked, stretching, a grin spreading across his face.

"Sleep," I said. "Need the rest."

"Right. Rest." Ryan winked. "Say hi to Math for me. Don't do too much cardio tonight."

I walked out of the conference room my face turning who knows how many shades of crimson. I hit the elevator button. I tapped my foot against the carpet until the doors slid open.

I rode up to the fourth floor alone.

I walked down the long, beige hallway. Room 408. Room 410.

Room 412.

I stopped, took a breath, smoothed my hair, pulled the keycard out of my pocket, and entered.

Chapter 21
Variable Crash

AUSTEN

The algorithm for a successful academic conference trip is simple: Arrive early, verify reservation, review notes, sleep.

My trip to Boston was failing on step one.

I was somewhere on the Mass Pike, gripping the steering wheel of my 2014 Camry as if it were the only thing keeping me tethered to the earth. Traffic was a snarl of brake lights and aggressive lane changes.

My GPS claimed I would arrive at the Marriott Copley Place in forty-five minutes. My anxiety claimed I would be stuck here until the next ice age.

I turned up the volume on the podcast—*Topology and the Shape of Space*—but the host's soothing voice couldn't drown out the variables bouncing around my skull.

Variable A: The Northeast Regional Mathematics Symposium. I was presenting a paper on "Quantifying the Crease: A Geometric Analysis of Goaltender Efficiency and High-Danger Probability." It was a good paper. It deserved my full attention.

Variable B: The Frost Demons were playing Northeastern tomorrow.

Variable C: Luke.

I wasn't going to a conference. I was chasing a bus. I was driving three hours into a snowstorm to be in the same zip code as a goalie who had started signing his texts with *we iterate.*

Everything about our relationship defied logic. Yet, it was the most exciting thing I'd done... ever.

I checked my phone at a standstill.

Luke: *You flying the Camry or driving it?*

I smiled, typing back a retort about low-altitude flight.

He was thinking about me. He was on a bus full of teammates, heading into a high-pressure game, and he was thinking about my beat-up sedan.

I merged onto the off-ramp, the city skyline rising like a circuit board of light and steel in the distance.

Get to the hotel, I told myself. *Check in. Go from there.*

The lobby of the Marriott was chaos.

A collision of two distinct ecosystems: the frantic, caffeine-fueled energy of the math symposium and the loud, sprawling confidence of a hockey tournament.

I wove through a group of track-suited athletes, my rolling suitcase bumping over the marble floor. My wool coat wore me instead of the other way around. I clutched my confirmation printout like a shield.

I reached the front desk. The clerk, a man named Todd with tired eyes, tapped at his keyboard.

"Name?"

"Lovell. Austen."

Tap. Tap. Tap.

Todd frowned. "I don't see a reservation."

My stomach dropped. "I have a confirmation number." I held up the paper. "Booked last month. Standard king."

"I see the record," Todd sighed, not looking at the paper. "But the system shows it as canceled yesterday."

"I didn't cancel it." My voice pitched up—a frequency I recognized. Distress. "I have a presentation at eight a.m. tomorrow. I need a room."

"We're fully booked, sir. There's a hockey tournament and the math convention. I can try to find you something at our sister property near the airport."

"The airport is forty minutes away," I said, my hand gripping the counter edge until my knuckles turned white. "My presentation is—"

"Problem?" Luke's voice asked.

I exhaled, the breath rushing out so fast I went dizzy. I spun and my knight in goalie armor stood before me. "Luke. Hi. The system ate my reservation." I gestured helplessly at Todd. "He says it's canceled. It's an error."

"It's not an error, it's a lack of inventory," Todd droned. "Like I said, the airport Hilton might—"

"He's with me," Luke said.

The clerk paused. I froze.

"Excuse me?" Todd asked.

"He's with the team," Luke lied. His voice was smooth, bored, utterly convincing. "Administrative support. Tutor. He's supposed to be on the rooming list."

He pulled out his wallet and slapped a team per diem card on the counter. Meaningless plastic for this transaction, but the gesture carried the weight of authority.

Luke looked at the clerk with his game face—the one that stared down slapshots.

"Put him in my room," Luke said. "Carter. Room 412."

Todd blinked. He looked at the line of hockey players forming behind Luke—Ryan, Javier, a wall of navy blue. He looked at my desperate face.

He decided the math wasn't worth the argument.

"I can add him as a guest," Todd muttered, typing furiously. "Here's a key."

He slid a plastic card across the marble.

Luke grabbed it. He handed it to me. His fingers brushed mine—electric, grounding.

"Go up," he said, his voice dropping to a low rumble meant only for me. "Wait for me."

I nodded, clutching the key card like a lifeline. "Thank you."

"Go."

"Carter!" Coach Harper's voice cut through the lobby noise.

Luke winced. And turned turned around.

Coach Harper stood by the elevators, holding her clipboard. "Bag drop in five. Conference Room B in ten. We have tape on Northeastern's power play."

"Go," Luke whispered to me. "I have to do this. Order room service. I'm starving."

"Room service," I repeated, clutching the key card. "Okay."

"Don't wait up," he joked.

Of course, I would be awake when he got to the room. That wasn't even a question. I hurried toward the elevators, heart hammering against my ribs.

I glanced back once. Luke was standing with his team, looking calm. Ryan was watching me go, eyebrows raised high enough to clear the ceiling.

I stepped into the elevator and let the doors close behind me.

Room 412 was excessive.

Not a room; a suite. A massive king bed dominated the center, flanked by mahogany nightstands. There was a sitting area with a velvet sofa. A minibar. A view of the city that probably cost more per night than my car was worth.

I stood in the center of the beige carpet, feeling like an intruder.

I took off my coat and the conference lanyard.

I checked my phone.

Me: *Room 412 secured. It is… excessively large. There is a robe.*

Luke: *Put it on. I'm trapped in a dark room watching power plays.*

Me: *I ordered a burger. And a salad. And something called 'Truffle Fries' which cost $35.*

Luke: *Worth it. Eat. I'll be there soon.*

I smiled at the screen. The panic of the lobby was fading, replaced by a humming anticipation.

I was in his room. He had publicly claimed me.

About twenty minutes later, there was a small knock on the door. "Room service," a voice said through the door. I walked over to the door and opened it. A guy in his mid-twenties wheeled in a cart and asked, "Where would you like it?"

"Anywhere works for me."

"How about the desk by the window?"

"Sounds perfect."

The man wheeled my food over and set it up for me. Then had me sign for the food, and I made sure to add what I thought was a good tip. I'm not exactly used to this environment. Sure, I've stayed in hotels before, but this was different. This place was nice.

I ate at the small desk by the window, watching the city lights blink on through the snow.

I finished. And wasn't quite sure what to do next. *Do I call them to let them know I'm done? Do I just leave this here and they come get it later? I'll ask Luke when he gets here.*

I graded three quizzes, but the numbers wouldn't stick.

At 9:45 p.m., I heard the keycard followed by the opening of the room door.

I was across the room in two seconds. Luke stood there. He looked exhausted. His hair was messy, his eyes shadowed, but when he saw me, his whole posture loosened.

"Hey," he breathed.

"Hey."

He stepped inside carrying his equipment. I closed the door. I locked it.

The click of the deadbolt was the loudest sound in the world.

"The guys gave me a hard time about this room only having a single bed," Luke said, dropping his bag by the closet. "It appears they are right."

"If you're worried about someone walking in, I can sleep on the floor. I mean it's your room, and you've got a game tomorrow. You need spinal alignment. And..."

"Don't be ridiculous," Luke said, looking at me, wrapping me in his arms for the first time. "The only difference between this place and the dorm is that we have a lot more pillows and more room to spread out."

Luke went still. He looked at me and informed me, "Ryan knows, or at least he suspects."

"He knows?" I asked. "Are you okay with that?"

"I'm okay with the truth. Even if we aren't screaming it from the rooftops."

I looked up into his eyes. "I'm okay with anything as long as I'm in your arms." He reached touched the collar of my shirt.

"I missed you," he said. "On the bus. I kept wish you were with me."

"I was in a Camry on I-90 listening to a podcast on topology," I said, my voice shaky. "I would have preferred the bus."

He laughed, a low sound that vibrated in my chest. He stepped closer, closing the gap until the toes of his sneakers touched my socks.

"Presentation tomorrow?" he asked.

"Eight a.m. Have to wear a tie and everything."

"Sounds sexy."

"It's incredibly dry," I whispered, tilting my head back to look at him. "Distract me."

He reached up and cupped my face. His hands were warm, rough with calluses.

He kissed me.

It wasn't the tentative, careful kiss from the dorm room. This was hungry. It was the relief of being three hundred miles away from campus, behind a deadbolted door.

He backed me up until my legs hit the edge of the mattress.

I sat down heavily, pulling him with me. He landed on his knees, pinning me between his thighs, his hands tangling in my hair.

I made a noise—a low hum in my throat—that I didn't recognize.

"Luke," I breathed, gripping his shoulders. "Game tomorrow."

"I know."

"Energy conservation."

"I'm conserving," he lied, biting lightly at my collarbone.

I shivered. "This... this is not conservation."

He pulled back, breathing hard. His forehead rested against mine. We were a mess of tangled limbs and heavy breaths.

"We stop whenever you want," he said. "I mean it."

I looked at him. His eyes were blown wide, pupils swallowing the iris. He looked wrecked. He looked beautiful.

"I don't want to stop," I admitted. "But if you play tired tomorrow and let in a soft goal, I'll statistically analyze your failure until you cry."

He laughed, collapsing onto the mattress beside me. "Cruel."

"Effective."

He rolled onto his side, facing me. He traced the line of my jaw with his thumb.

"We have to be careful," he whispered. "I don't want this to get out until you're ready."

"I don't care about Ryan," I said. "I only care about you and what you think. I want this. Here. Now. We're in a suite in a fancy hotel in Boston on Valentine's Day. We need to make the most of it."

He smiled. "Shut up and come here."

We slept in the middle of the king bed.

We didn't need the space. We gravitated to the center, limbs tangled, creating our own gravity.

I woke up once in the middle of the night. The room was pitch black, save for the red light of the smoke detector.

Luke's arm was heavy over my waist. His breath was warm on the back of my neck.

I lay there, listening to the hum of the hotel, and realized that for the first time in my life, I wasn't calculating an exit strategy.

I just was. *Best Valentine's Day ever.* I closed my eyes and let sleep take me under again.

Morning came too fast.

The alarm on my phone blared at 6:30 a.m.

Luke groaned, burying his face in the pillow. "Five more minutes."

"No," I said, sliding out of bed. The room was cold. "I have to shower. I have to present a paper on geometry in ninety minutes."

"Geometry," Luke mumbled. "Angles."

"Exactly."

I showered quickly, trying not to think about the fact that Luke was just feet away from me.

When I came out, dressed in my presentation clothes—slacks, button-down, the blazer I only wore twice a year—Luke was sitting on the edge of the bed.

He was wearing his team tracksuit. He looked like a goalie again.

"You look smart," he said.

"I am smart." I checked my watch. "I have to go. The symposium breakfast starts at seven."

"I have team breakfast at seven-thirty," he said.

He stood up. He walked over to me. He pressed his forehead against mine for a long second.

"Good luck," he whispered.

"Good luck," I said, grabbing my bag and lanyard.

I walked to the door.

"Austen?"

I turned.

"I love you," he said.

"I love you, too."

I opened the door. The hallway was empty.

I walked out, leaving the sanctuary of Room 412 behind.

Down in the lobby, the chaos had returned. Math students were drinking coffee in one corner; hockey players were stretching in another.

I saw Ryan O'Connell by the elevators. He waved at me.

"Hey, Math!" he yelled across the lobby. "How was the floor?"

I adjusted my glasses. I channeled every ounce of academic detachment I possessed.

"Adequate," I called back. "Spinal alignment maintained."

Ryan laughed.

I walked toward the ballroom, my heart still beating in time with the goalie upstairs.

Chapter 22
Quiet Study

AUSTEN

The fourth floor of the university library was designated as the "Deep Quiet" zone. No talking, no headphones with bleed, no snacks louder than a marshmallow.

My natural habitat.

Or, at least, it had been. Usually, I came here to escape variables. Tonight, I was here waiting for one.

I sat at a corner carrel tucked behind the Slavic Literature stacks, a location I had selected for its optimal obscurity. My thesis draft was open on the screen, cursor blinking at the end of a sentence I had written twenty minutes ago.

In a system with multiple unknown factors, the hidden variable often exerts the most force on the trajectory.

I stared at the words. The irony was heavy-handed, even for me.

My phone buzzed against the wood of the desk. One short vibration.

Luke: *Elevator.*

My pulse did a traitorous little jump. I turned my phone face down and forced myself to look at the screen. Focus. You are a scholar. He is a guy.

He wasn't a guy. He was the guy who had kissed me senseless in a Marriott king bed thirty-six hours ago.

Soft footsteps on the carpet. Not the heavy, cleat-stomping walk of an athlete, but the quiet, deliberate tread of someone trying not to disturb the peace.

I looked up.

Luke rounded the corner of the stack. He wasn't wearing team gear—no logo, no Frost Demons branding. Jeans and a dark-green sweater that made his eyes look unfair.

He saw me. The "media smile"—the polite, guarded one he gave reporters—didn't appear. Instead, his face softened into something private. Something for me.

He didn't walk to the empty chair across from me. He walked to the one right next to me.

He pulled it out, wincing as the wood scraped the floor, and sat.

"Hey," he mouthed, no sound.

"Hey," I mouthed back.

He smelled like the cold outside and the peppermint soap from our shower. He unpacked his bag with slow, deliberate movements—playbook, notebook, a black pen.

He shifted.

His leg pressed against mine. Not a brush. A lean. Solid, heavy warmth running from hip to knee.

I froze, instinct screaming *people will see.* I glanced at the aisle. Empty.

Luke didn't look at me. He opened his playbook to a diagram of a penalty kill, clicked his pen, and began making notes. His hand drifted down and settled on my thigh.

His thumb rubbed a slow, calming circle against the denim.

My brain short-circuited. The thesis draft might as well have been written in Wingdings.

I looked at him. He was staring at the playbook, expression perfectly serious, while his hand claimed me in the middle of a public building.

He slid his notebook toward me.

Focus, Professor, he had written in the margin.

I grabbed my pen. *You are violating my personal space.*

He read it, smirked, and wrote back: *Yeah, but you like it.*

I fought a smile. I turned back to my screen, but I didn't type. I was too busy feeling the heat of his palm. Terrifying. Exhilarating.

We worked like that for twenty minutes—a silent, secret circuit connected by the touch of his hand. It felt like getting away with a heist.

Then, footsteps. Fast ones.

"Austen?"

The whisper was loud, cutting through the silence.

I jumped. My heart hammered against my ribs.

Luke didn't jump. His hand vanished from my leg instantly—smooth, controlled, no guilt-jerk—and reappeared on his own neck, rubbing a knot as he turned his head.

Kayla, Devon's girlfriend, stood at the end of the aisle. She was holding a stack of psych textbooks.

"Oh, hey," she whispered, stepping closer. "Devon said you guys might be here. Is Luke—oh, hi Luke!"

I couldn't speak. My throat was locked. I was convinced there was a neon sign above my head flashing *WE ARE SLEEPING TOGETHER.*

Luke smiled at her. Easy. Calm. "Hey, Kayla. Cramming?"

"Midterm research paper," she groaned. "I'm looking for the abnormal psych section. Numbers 600?"

"Two aisles over," Luke said, pointing with his pen. "Left side."

"Lifesaver. Thanks." She looked between us, her gaze lingering a fraction of a second too long. "You guys studying together?"

Panic spiked. *Here it comes.*

"Austen's walking me through accounting," Luke said smoothly. He tapped his notebook. "I'm hopeless."

"Wait, I thought that was last semester," she laughed.

"Busted," Luke said with a shrug. "He's studying and I'm going over strategy notes for the next game." He gestured to his open playbook, which had a hockey rink clearly drawn in it.

"Well, you two have fun." She waved and disappeared into the stacks.

I let out a breath that shook. My hands were trembling on the keyboard.

"We're going to get caught," I whispered, barely audible. "She looked at us. She knows."

Luke turned to me. The easy smile was gone, replaced by that intense focus he used when tracking a puck through traffic.

He leaned in, pretending to look at my screen. His shoulder pressed against mine.

"She doesn't know," he whispered back. "She saw two roommates studying. That's it."

"I jumped," I hissed. "I looked guilty."

"You looked startled in a quiet zone."

He moved his hand back. He didn't put it on my leg this time; he gripped the edge of my chair, his fingers brushing my hip. Grounding me.

"I hate hiding," he admitted, his voice rumbled low near my ear. "I hate that I can't hold your hand while we walk here. But I will not stop touching you when I can."

Luke was out, but his personal life wasn't public. That was his line, and I respected it.

I looked at him. His eyes were dark, defiant.

"Let them look," he whispered. "They don't know what they're seeing. Only we know what's going on between us."

The panic receded, replaced by a strange, fierce thrill. We were a secret world. A pocket universe existing in the middle of the library.

"Okay," I breathed.

"Okay."

He squeezed my knee once, then let go. He went back to his playbook.

I looked at my screen. I deleted the sentence about hidden variables.

In a closed system, I typed, *stability is achieved when internal forces balance external pressure.*

We left at closing.

Outside, the campus was a snow globe. Fat, wet flakes drifted down, coating the sidewalks in fresh white.

The quad was empty.

We walked side by side, hands deep in our pockets. We didn't hold hands—too open, too risky under the streetlights—but we walked close enough that our arms bumped with every step.

Bump. Bump. Bump.

A Morse code of contact. *I'm here. I'm here. I'm here.*

"I think I learned something tonight," Luke said, kicking a drift of snow.

"What?"

"That the stacks are incredibly hot."

I laughed, the sound puffing out in a white cloud. "They are temperature controlled at sixty-eight degrees."

"That's not what I meant, Math."

He looked at me, grinning, snowflakes catching in his eyelashes.

We reached Stony Creek Hall. Luke swiped his card, held the door.

We walked up the stairs, down the hall, past the RA's door, past the EDM guy.

We reached Room 317.

I unlocked it. We stepped inside.

The door clicked shut. The lock engaged.

The public world vanished.

Luke didn't wait. He dropped his bag and pulled me in, his icy hands framing my face, his mouth finding mine with a hunger that had been building for three hours of silence.

I gripped his sweater, pulling him closer, safe in the only variable that mattered.

Chapter 23
Duplication Error

AUSTEN

"What's the error probability if I double-side these?"

I asked out loud so I wouldn't think about Luke's hand on my waist six hours earlier. The Ridgeway copier chugged, indifferent. Curling steam from the exit slot fogged my glasses; I pushed them up with a knuckle and kept feeding the tray.

Seventy-two Calc II quizzes, duplex. My left thumb had a new paper cut—evidence I still lived in a world where toner mattered.

Luke's hoodie hung around my shoulders, long enough that the cuffs swallowed my wrists. I'd grabbed it by accident—or muscle memory—when I left the room. Smelled like detergent and faint eucalyptus from his shower gel. I'd tried not to notice.

Packet forty-three caught, jam icon blinked. I popped the front panel, rescued the crimped sheet, smoothed the crease on my thigh. The machine spat a scolding beep.

"Live," I muttered, closing the panel. Copy cycle resumed.

Someone cleared a throat behind me. I turned, half expecting Maya's raised eyebrow, but it was Luke—sweats, beanie, backpack slung single-strap. Fresh from weights, probably en route to business psych. Normal schedule. Normal roommate. No big deal that I'd fallen asleep with my face tucked against his collarbone.

He held two coffees, the campus-brand cardboard sleeves aligned like they'd passed inspection. "Printer coffee," he said. "Black, two sugars."

I took the closer cup; heat stung the paper cut. "Quality control?"

"Barista owed me for spotting her rink-side tickets." He gestured at the copier. "Jam day?"

"Inevitable." I stepped aside so he could watch the pages stack. His shoulder brushed mine—fractional contact that shouldn't register. It registered anyway.

"You good?" he asked, like last night existed in a sealed envelope we could reference but not open here.

"Running on caffeine and stress." I sipped. Too sweet; he'd remembered. "You?"

"Bench presses and motivational screaming." His smile reached one eye, not both. "Harper moved film to four, so I'm clear tonight if we're still iterating."

Iterating. The word flashed warm. "Ledger practice after dinner?"

"Works." He tapped his cup against mine—quiet clink of cardboard. "Text me room temp; the radiator sounded petulant this morning."

"Valve stabilized at sixty-eight point four." I tried to be casual. It came out earnest; he grinned wider.

Machine dinged; stack complete. I pulled the tray, slapped the pages against the table. "Go learn about synergy."

"Go terrorize quiz averages." He backed away. He disappeared down the stairwell, sneakers squeaking.

I sent Maya a text.

Me: *Forgot to ask earlier, Lunch?*

Maya: *Sounds good. I'm heading to North Point around 12:15.*

Me: *See you soon. Save me a seat.*

I exhaled, counted to eight, then slid the quizzes into my bag. The hoodie sleeves still covered my hands. I cuffed them twice.

North Point smelled like fryer oil and cinnamon waffles—two things the human brain shouldn't process simultaneously. I threaded through noon traffic, acquired soup and saltines, then scoped for Maya.

She waved from a corner booth, laptop open, highlighter between teeth. Red beanie today—signal flare. I slid in opposite her, balancing the tray on sticky laminate.

"Your text said, 'emergency caloric intake.'" I unwrapped a cracker. "I brought sodium."

"You're a prince." She set the highlighter down. "You sleep?"

"Define sleep."

"REM cycles where your face looks less haunted."

"Then no."

She eyed the hoodie. "Wardrobe change?"

"Laundry backlog." I stirred the soup. Broccoli cheddar clung to the spoon.

Maya flipped her laptop shut, attention fully mine—terrifying upgrade. "You're humming."

"I don't hum."

"You are today—that guy from *Frozen* in the sauna scene."

"I don't know the reference."

"Sure." She rested her chin on both fists. "Something happened."

"Many things happen every day."

"Specific thing." She tapped the hoodie cuff. "Spill."

Heat flooded my ears. I focused on aligning crackers. "Not classroom appropriate."

"North Point is a cafeteria, not a confessional."

Exactly. Too many ears, none caring until one word lit their gossip receptors. I shook pepper into the soup.

Maya waited—a talent forged over years of me stalling. She said, "Did you do the thing you're terrified to want?"

I swallowed broth. "Maybe adjacent to the thing."

"And you're... what? Happy? Panicked?"

"Quantifying." I broke a cracker, shards sinking. "System variables shifted. Observation window too small for conclusions."

Her stare softened. "You like him."

"Don't psychoanalyze."

"Math-analyzing then: is wanting this inside the margin of error?"

I opened my mouth, closed it. The honest answer tasted like the soup—thick, too hot. "I'd need a bigger sample."

"Then gather data." She nudged my foot. "Don't pretend you're running a double-blind when he clearly sees you."

I flicked soup off the spoon. "He acts normal. That's... disorienting."

"Maybe normal is good."

"Or maybe normal means temporary." The words escaped before I could reroute them.

Maya's expression went gentle; she didn't pounce. "Temporary like every foster placement?"

I kept my eyes on the bowl. "Past is prologue as they say."

She sighed. "Austen, he clearly likes you and you clearly like him. The hard part is over."

I snorted. "Hallmark called; they want the slogan back."

"Fine. I'll keep the royalties." She pushed her tray aside, elbows on table like a coach in a timeout. "Question: are you still *tutoring* him?"

"Of course not, he passed financial accounting last semester. He doesn't need me anymore."

"Whoa, that sounded loaded," Maya said. She looked around and lowered her voice. "Just because you're not tutoring him doesn't mean he doesn't need you anymore. You have a lot more to offer than strategic tutoring. And from what I know about gay men in their early twenties, tutoring is the last thing on their minds when they're together."

I hesitated half a beat too long.

Maya's smile was small, satisfied. "Run your study. Remember the null hypothesis: you deserve constants too."

I hated how much that landed. I drained the rest of the soup to have something to do.

She gathered her backpack. "Office hours. Text if you need a pep talk."

"I hope that's code for something."

"It's exactly what it sounds like." She stood, squeezed my shoulder—short, not pitying—and vanished into the press of students.

Across the room, the TVs looped Luke's glove save from Caribou State. The caption read *CARTER WALL*. My chest tightened—not pride, not fear, something between.

I dumped the tray, hoodie sleeves brushing the trash rim, and headed back to Ridgeway.

My afternoon tutoring session was horrible. I was on complete autopilot. My pulse raced, I almost hyperventilated at one point. One student asked me if I was coming down with the flu. I half expected her to pull out a surgical mask. I promised her I was just sleep deprived.

Hoodie pocket buzzed—text.

Luke: *Radiator 69.4. Intro to Management at 4:45. Available after 8?*

Me: *I'll be there.*

Luke: *Nice. Need anything?*

Need. Dangerous prompt. I considered answers—pens, coffee, certainty.

Me: *Just you and maybe a couple of oat bars. Probability of survival improves with carbs.*

Luke: *Copy. See you.*

I slid the phone away, stared at the board until the letters blurred. Want wasn't the problem. Trusting that want had a half-life longer than one semester—that was the variable singing off-key.

Clock ticked toward four. Students trickled in and out of my office hours.

Chapter 24
Too Many Men

LUKE

The room was dark except for the streetlamp glow slicing through the blinds, painting stripes across Austen's bare back.

My hands were on his waist, skin warm under my palms. He was straddling my lap, his forehead resting against mine, breathing a rhythm that matched my own.

"We should stop," Austen whispered, though he made zero move to do so.

"Why?" I murmured, pressing a kiss to the pulse point under his jaw.

"Because you have a seven a.m. lifting block. And you need sleep."

"I'm resting," I lied. "This is active recovery."

Austen huffed a laugh—a vibration I felt in my chest. He shifted, friction sparking a heat that had nothing to do with the radiator.

It had been three days since the library. Three days of this—stealing hours in the dorm, locking the deadbolt, pretending the rest of the world stopped at the threshold of Room 317.

It felt safe. It felt like we'd hacked the system.

I ran my hands up his bare spine, feeling the tension leave his muscles. For a guy who lived in his head, Austen was present when we were like this. No math. No variables. Weight and touch.

He leaned back, breaking the kiss with a contented sigh.

BOOM. BOOM. BOOM.

The pounding on the door shook the frame.

"Carter! I know you're in there! Open up!"

Ryan.

The sound was like a gunshot in a library.

Austen froze. His eyes went wide, panic flashing white-hot.

"Shit," I hissed.

I shoved him.

It wasn't gentle. Pure, reactive instinct. I pushed him off my lap. He stumbled back, catching himself on the edge of his own bed.

"Shirt," I whispered, frantic. "Shirt."

Austen scrambled. He grabbed his T-shirt from the floor, yanking it over his head inside out. He dove for his desk chair, grabbing a pen, spinning around to face his laptop screen—currently black.

BOOM. BOOM.

"Carter! Don't tell me you're asleep, I can hear the radiator clanking!"

"Coming!" I yelled, my voice cracking.

I looked down. Shirtless. Jeans unbuttoned.

I scrambled off the bed, buttoning the fly with shaking fingers. I grabbed my hoodie from the floor—smelling of sex and sweat—and yanked it on.

I ran a hand through my hair, trying to tame the mess.

I looked at Austen. He was hunched over his desk, typing furiously on a computer that wasn't on.

"Turn it on," I hissed.

He hit the power button. The Apple logo glowed.

I took a breath. I forced my heart rate down—goalie mode. *Calm. Square to the shooter.*

I unlocked the deadbolt and opened the door four inches. I planted my foot behind it as a stop.

Ryan was standing there, grinning, holding a greasy cardboard box.

"Pizza," Ryan announced. "Meat lovers. And Morales is arguing that *Die Hard* isn't a Christmas movie. We need a tiebreaker."

He tried to push the door open. "Let me in, it's freezing out here."

I braced my shoulder against the wood. "Can't, man."

Ryan stopped, blinking. "Why? You decent?"

"I'm... sick," I lied. Weak save. "Stomach thing. Ate bad sushi."

Ryan peered through the crack. He looked past my shoulder.

"Math?" he yelled. "You sick too?"

Austen turned in his chair. His face was pale, his glasses crooked. "I... am maintaining a safe distance." He sounded like a robot from a bad 50's show.

Ryan looked back at me. He sniffed the air. The room smelled like peppermint soap, stale heat, and... us.

"You look flushed, Monk," Ryan said, his grin fading. "You got a fever?"

"Yeah," I said. "Fever. Need to sleep it off."

"Alright." Ryan looked at the pizza, then back at me. "Well, if you hurl, aim for the trash can, not the floor. Devon gets pissy about the carpet."

"Thanks."

"Feel better."

He turned and walked down the hall.

I waited until he rounded the corner. I slammed the door and threw the deadbolt.

I slumped against the wood, my legs water.

The silence in the room was deafening.

Austen sat at his desk, staring at the blank wall. He reached up and fixed his glasses.

"That was..." he started, voice trembling. "That was close."

He tried to laugh. It came out as a jagged exhale.

I didn't laugh.

I pushed off the door and walked to my bed. I sat down heavily.

My hands were shaking. Not from the adrenaline of almost getting caught, but from the realization of what would have happened if Ryan had pushed harder. If I hadn't locked the door.

He would have seen us.

And by morning, the locker room would know. Harper would know. My dad would know. Sure, I think Ryan and Javier suspected something, but they didn't have proof.

"Luke?"

Austen was looking at me. He had turned his chair around. The fear was gone from his face, replaced by tentative concern.

"He's gone," Austen said softly. "We're good."

"Are we?"

The words hung there.

I looked at him—hair messy, shirt inside out, lips swollen from my mouth. Ten minutes ago, that sight made me want to lock us in forever.

Now, it made my stomach turn. Not because of him. Because of the target it put on my back.

"I shoved you," I said.

"Reflex," Austen said quickly.

"I panicked." I rubbed my face with my hands. "If he had seen..."

"He didn't." Austen stood up. He took a step toward me. "We handled it."

He reached for me.

I flinched.

I didn't mean to. The wall was back up. The mask was back on.

Austen stopped. His hand hovered in the air for a second, then dropped to his side.

"Okay," he whispered.

He stepped back. He walked over to his side of the room. He took off his glasses and set them on the desk, next to the puck.

"Lights out?" he asked.

"Yeah," I said. "Lights out."

He flicked the switch.

In the dark, I listened to him get into bed. I listened to the radiator hiss.

I touched my chest, right over the Frost Demons logo. My heart was still hammering, loud and frantic.

Entanglements.

The word floated up from the dark, heavy and cold.

We hadn't almost been caught. It's not like the team didn't know I was gay. But it's one thing to know someone is gay and something completely different to know who that guy is gay with. That's why I'd avoided relationships at my last school. I can't let them distract from the game.

Chapter 25
Scouting Report

AUSTEN

The decay rate of a relationship is rarely linear.

In my experience, it doesn't follow a steady downward slope. It follows a step function. You are on one level—stable, constant, safe—and then a single event occurs, a variable shifts, and you drop instantaneously to a lower plateau.

The event was the knock on the door. The variable was fear.

It had been forty-eight hours since Ryan pounded on Room 317, forty-eight hours since Luke shoved me off his lap with enough force to bruise, forty-eight hours since I started feeling like Luke's dirty little secret.

I sat at my desk, my back to the room. five a.m.

Usually, this was our "quiet friction" time. Luke would be waking up, grumbling about the cold floor, making his way to the coffeemaker. I would be reviewing my schedule for the day. We would exist in a comfortable, shared orbit until he went off to practice.

Today, the silence was sterile.

Rustle of sheets. Heavy thud of feet hitting the floor. Zip of a gear bag.

"I'm heading out," Luke said. His voice was rough, tight.

I turned in my chair. He was dressed—hoodie up, hat low. He wasn't looking at me. He was looking at the door, his hand on the knob.

"You have a lift block at six," I said. "It's only five."

"Going early. Need to stretch."

"I made coffee."

"I'll grab some on the way."

He opened the door. The hallway air rushed in, cold and smelling of floor wax.

"Luke?"

He paused, but he didn't turn. His knuckles were white on the door handle.

"We iterate," I said, offering the phrase that had become our shorthand for *we keep going, we fix this.*

He stood frozen for a second. Tension in his shoulders, the way his head dipped. For a moment, I thought he might turn around. I thought he might drop the bag and come back to me and apologize for the thousandth time for the shove, for the panic, for the hiding.

"Sure," he said to the doorframe. He walked out. The latch clicked shut.

I looked at the coffee pot. Full. Hot. Useless.

I opened my laptop and pulled up our text history.

- Last Month Average Response Latency: 4 minutes.

- Last Forty-Eight Hours Average Response Latency: 3 hours, 12 minutes.

- Word Count Average (Sent): 15.

- Word Count Average (Received): 4.

The data screamed. The trend line plummeted toward zero.

A familiar, cold sensation in my gut. It wasn't heartbreak—heartbreak is a hot, sharp thing. This was old. This was the dull, heavy ache of recognition.

I knew this pattern.

I had lived in seven foster homes between the ages of six and sixteen. I considered myself an expert in the signs of "Placement Termination."

It never happened all at once. The adults didn't wake up one day and tell the caseworker to come get you. There was always a lead-up. A shift in the atmosphere.

I looked at Luke's side of the room. Neat. Too neat. He hadn't left his books on his desk. His gear bag was gone. His bed was made with military precision.

He was packing up his emotional investment. He hadn't told me yet.

I dressed and fled the room.

Ridgeway Hall was my fortress of solitude, but today, the equations on my screen refused to resolve. I was staring at a complex manifold, but my brain was running a different simulation.

Simulation A: Luke stays. Probability: Low. The pressure from his father is a constant force. The fear of exposure is an escalating variable.

Simulation B: Luke leaves. Probability: High. The path of least resistance is to cut the tether. To be "singular."

"You're doing it again," a voice said.

I looked up. Maya dropped her bag onto the table next to mine. She didn't ask if the seat was taken. She sat down, unwound her scarf, and fixed me with a look that was equal parts pity and annoyance.

"Doing what?" I asked, closing my laptop.

"Calculating the end of the world." She pointed at my face. "You have your 'doomsday actuary' expression on."

"I am merely analyzing behavioral trends."

"You mean Luke."

I flinched. "He is... distant. Since the interruption."

"Austen," Maya sighed. She reached across the table and put her hand over mine. Her fingers were warm, stained with ink. "He's a hockey player. He's the starter. He's a transfer student with a dad who treats him like a racehorse."

"I know the variables, Maya."

"Do you?" She squeezed my hand. "Because you're looking at him like he's a math problem you can solve if you find the right formula. But he's not a proof. He's a person. And people like Luke... they have trajectories."

"Trajectory implies a predetermined path. He has agency."

"Does he?" Maya challenged. "Look at him. Look at his life. His dad maps out his diet. His coach maps out his sleep schedule. The scouts map out his future. Where exactly does his agency live, Austen? Because from where I'm sitting, the only time he exercises it is when he's with you. And that realization probably terrifies him."

I pulled my hand away. "He loves me. He said it."

"I know he does. I believe him." Maya softened. "But love is an emotion. Self-preservation is an instinct. And right now, you are the biggest risk to his trajectory."

She wasn't telling me anything I didn't know. That was the worst part. She was vocalizing the data points I had been trying to suppress.

"So, what is your hypothesis?" I asked, my voice thin. "That he will terminate the relationship to secure the asset?"

"I think," Maya said carefully, "that you need to protect yourself. You have a scholarship to keep. You have a thesis to write. You have a life that matters, Austen. Don't let him burn it all down because he's afraid of the dark."

I looked out the window. The sky was the color of a bruised plum.

"I don't have a life without him," I whispered. "Not a constant one."

"That," Maya said, her voice hard, "is the scariest thing you've ever said to me."

I left the library at four p.m.

I needed to walk. I needed the cold air to numb the panic rising in my chest like floodwater.

I walked the perimeter of the campus. I counted my steps. *One, two, three, four.* I forced my breathing to match the count. *In, two, three, four. Out, two, three, four.*

I found myself near the athletic complex. It wasn't a conscious decision. My feet knew the vector.

The parking lot was full. It was a Tuesday, but the lot was packed with team trucks, student beaters, and faculty sedans.

I scanned the rows. Luke's truck was parked in the back row, isolated, like him.

But then I saw something else.

Parked near the entrance to the rink, in a spot reserved for "VIP/Administration," was a black Lincoln Navigator.

Sleek. Clean. It looked like a shark swimming in a pool of minnows.

The license plate wasn't Massachusetts. It wasn't New York or New Jersey.

It was Minnesota. Land of 10,000 Lakes.

I stopped walking. I stood on the sidewalk, the wind whipping my coat around my legs, and stared at the plate.

Minnesota.

The Wild. The team his dad played for. The team that was rumored to be looking at goalies for their development camp.

The door of the rink opened.

Two men walked out.

One was Coach Harper. She looked serious, pointing at a clipboard.

The other man was tall, wearing a camel-hair coat that cost more than my entire tuition. He had silver hair and the kind of posture that comes from never having to wait in line. He was nodding, listening to Harper, but his eyes were scanning the campus like he was appraising real estate.

He stopped at the Navigator, shook Harper's hand, and got in.

The car pulled away, sliding silently past me.

I watched it go.

It wasn't a car. It was the future. It was the variable that solved the equation of Luke's life.

If that car was here, the offer was coming. And if the offer was coming, the timeline had accelerated.

I turned and walked back to the dorm. I didn't count my steps this time. There was no point. The math was done.

I texted him from the sidewalk.

Me: *You okay?*

The reply came forty minutes later, while I was sitting in the dark.

Luke: *Long day. Talk tomorrow.*

Four words. No iteration. The trend line didn't lie.

By eleven p.m. Luke still wasn't back. His practice had ended hours ago. He should be here. He should be icing his shoulder.

I sat on my bed. I didn't turn on the lights.

I took out my notebook. Not my class notebook. My scratch pad.

I wrote: *Minnesota.*

I started doing the math.

- Distance: Cold Harbor to St. Paul. 1,248 miles.

- Travel Time: 19 hours driving. 4 hours flying.

- Cost of Flight: $350 avg. (Unaffordable on my stipend).

- Duration of Development Camp: 6 weeks (July–August).

- Likelihood of Rookie Contract: High (based on current stats).

If he signed, he would leave in June. He would go to St. Paul. He would be surrounded by press, by scouts, by teammates fighting for a roster spot.

He would be under a microscope.

And me?

I would be here. In Cold Harbor. In graduate school, probably. Living in a beige apartment we talked about renting together.

I looked at the variables.

- Luke in Minnesota: Closeted again. Scared. High pressure.

- Austen in Cold Harbor: Secret. Liability. Distraction.

A long-distance relationship requires transparency. It requires communication. It requires a foundation of trust that can withstand the silence.

We didn't have that. We had panic attacks in hotel rooms. We had "just a friend." We had silence that stretched for hours because he was afraid his father might hear him breathing on the phone.

If he went to Minnesota, he wouldn't take me with him. Not really. He couldn't.

He would pack me away. He would put me in a box marked *College* and leave me on the shelf, intending to come back for me when it was safe.

But I knew about shelves. I knew about storage.

Foster kids know that once you go into storage, you rarely come back out. You gather dust. You get forgotten. You get replaced by something newer, shinier, less complicated.

I closed the notebook.

The door opened.

Luke walked in. He looked exhausted. His eyes were red-rimmed. He smelled of sweat and the cheap deodorant he kept in his locker.

He saw me sitting in the dark. He paused, hand on the light switch.

"Hey," he said.

"Hey."

He flicked the light on. The brightness made me squint.

"You're still up," he said, walking to his side of the room. He didn't look at me. He started unzipping his jacket.

"I saw a car today," I said.

Luke froze. His jacket was half off. He didn't turn around.

"What kind of car?"

"A black Navigator. Minnesota plates. Parked at the rink."

The silence that followed was heavy.

Luke finished pulling his jacket off. He hung it on the back of his chair.

"Yeah," he said quietly. "That was Gulliver Vane. The head scout."

"He was here."

"He watched practice."

"And?"

Luke turned around. He looked wretched. He looked like a man who was drowning and trying to pretend he was swimming laps.

"And he wants to meet," Luke said. "Tomorrow. With my dad."

"Your dad is coming?"

"He's driving up tonight."

I nodded. A strange, cold calm. The data was verified. The simulation was running exactly as predicted.

"So, it's happening," I said.

"It's a meeting, Austen. It's... talking."

"Talking about the future."

"Yeah."

"Does that future include variables?" I asked. "Or is it singular?"

Luke flinched. He walked over to me. He sat on the edge of my bed, close enough to touch, but he didn't reach out.

"I don't know what they're going to say," he whispered. "But I know what I want."

"Do you?"

"I want the net," he said. "And I want you."

"In that order?"

He looked at me, his eyes pleading. "It's not that simple."

"It is," I said. "It's math, Luke. It's finite resources. You have a finite amount of courage. You have to decide where you're going to spend it."

"I'm spending it," he insisted. "I'm here, aren't I?"

"You're here physically. But you're packing, Luke. I can see it."

"I'm not packing."

"You are. You're pulling away. You're checking the exits. You're getting ready to leave before you've even signed the paper."

"That's not true."

"It is," I said, my voice trembling. "I know the signs. I've lived them."

I stood up. I couldn't be this close to him. It hurt too much.

"My third foster home," I said, walking to the window. "The Millers. They were nice. They bought me a bike. They took me to the movies. But two weeks before they sent me back, Mrs. Miller stopped making eye contact. She stopped asking about my day. She stopped shopping for me."

I turned to face him.

"You're buying the small cereal, Luke."

Luke looked stricken. He stood up. "Austen, no. That's not—I'm stressed. It's the playoffs. It's my dad. It's not you."

"It's always me," I said. "I am the complication. I am the thing that doesn't fit in the suitcase."

"Stop it." He crossed the room. He grabbed my shoulders. His hands were shaking. "You are not a complication. You are the only thing that makes sense."

"Then tell them," I said.

"What?"

"Tomorrow. When you meet Vane. When you see your dad. Tell them. Tell them you have a boyfriend. Tell them you're not going to live in a closet in St. Paul."

Luke dropped his hands. He stepped back. The fear was back in his eyes, shutting down the light.

"I can't," he whispered. "Not yet. I need the contract first. Once I sign... once I'm valuable... I can have leverage."

"Leverage," I repeated.

"Yes. That's how it works. You play the game until you win, then you change the rules."

"And in the meantime?"

"In the meantime... we iterate," he said, his voice weak. "We make it work. We find a way."

I looked at him. I saw the desperation. I saw the love. But mostly, I saw the fear.

And I knew, with the cold certainty of a mathematical proof, that the fear was winning.

"Okay," I said softly. "We iterate."

It was a lie. We both knew it.

Chapter 26
Draft Prospects

LUKE

Coach Harper didn't look up from her clipboard when I skated to the bench.

"Carter. Stick in the rack. Office. Five minutes."

She didn't shout, which was worse. Harper shouting meant she was coaching you. Harper speaking in that flat, library voice meant something was happening off the ice.

My stomach dropped. *Ryan.*

Had he figured it out? Had he realized that "stomach flu" was a lie and seen two pairs of shoes by the bed? Or worse, had he heard us before he knocked?

"Copy," I said, my voice tight.

Ryan skated by, tapping my pads with his stick. "Principal's office?"

I searched his face for a sign—judgment, disgust, a smirk. Nothing but the usual chirping grin. If he knew he'd almost walked in on me hooking up with my roommate, he was hiding it well.

"Probably film review," I lied, though my pulse was hammering against my neck protector. "I was late on the post-seal during the penalty kill."

Ryan didn't look convinced, but he let me go.

I showered in record time—three minutes, cold water, no soap—and threw on my team tracksuit. I ran a hand through my wet hair as I walked down the concrete tunnel toward the admin offices.

My phone buzzed in my pocket. A text from Austen: *Ledger review at 8? I have snacks.*

I looked at the screen. For the last month, that text would have been the highlight of my day. *Ledger review* was code. It meant locking the door. It meant the quiet heat of his skin against mine.

But now, looking at the words, all I could think about was the sound of Ryan's fist pounding on the wood. *Boom. Boom. Boom.*

How fast the air had left the room. Austen scrambling for a shirt, his eyes wide with a panic that I had put there.

I slid the phone back into my pocket without replying and knocked on Harper's door. "Enter."

I stepped inside. The office was small, smelling of dry-erase markers and stale coffee. But today, the air was heavier.

Harper wasn't alone.

Sitting in the folding metal chair opposite her desk was a man who looked like he'd been ironed into existence. Navy suit, gray tie, haircut that cost more than my tuition. He held a tablet like a weapon.

"Have a seat, Luke," Harper said. She didn't smile.

I sat. My knee started bouncing instantly. I forced it to stop.

"As you know, this is Gulliver Vane," Harper said. "He's with the Minnesota organization."

The air left the room. The Minnesota Wilds. The team my dad had played on for two seasons before his knee exploded. The team that was practically a religion in my house.

"Mr. Carter," Vane said. His voice was smooth, polished. He didn't offer a hand. "I've been watching your lateral movement. Your recovery time is... elite."

"Thank you, sir."

"We're looking at our roster for the summer Development Camp in St. Paul," Vane continued. "It's an invite-only camp. Eight goalies. Two contracts at the end of it."

My heart hammered against my ribs. This was it. The conversation I'd played in my head since I was four years old, strapping pillows to my legs in the driveway.

"I'd be honored," I said, my voice sounding thin.

"We think you're ready," Vane said. He tapped the tablet. "We like your numbers. We like your size." He paused, his eyes narrowing. "And we appreciate the context your father provided."

The room went dead silent.

"My father?" I asked.

Vane smiled, but it didn't reach his eyes. "Rick has been very... proactive. He's been sending us tapes since October. Every shutout. Every save percentage update. He's been very clear that you are one hundred percent committed to the path. No distractions."

I felt sick. The breakfast burrito I'd eaten churned.

I wasn't here because I'd posted a .930 save percentage. I was here because Rick Carter was calling in favors, selling me like a used car to his old buddies.

Before I could process that, the door behind me opened.

"Sorry I'm late," a voice boomed. "Traffic on I-90 is a killer."

I froze. I knew that voice. It was the voice that narrated every mistake I'd ever made on the ice.

Rick Carter walked in. He was wearing a leather jacket over a cashmere sweater, looking every inch the retired pro. He filled the small office instantly—not with his size, but with his gravity.

"Dad?" I whispered.

He grinned, clapping a hand on my shoulder. His grip was heavy. "Hey, kid."

He looked at Vane. "Gulliver. Good to see you. How's the knee?"

"Better than yours, Rick," Vane said, actually chuckling.

My dad laughed—a loud, charming bark that made people want to lean in. He sat in the empty chair next to me, dragging it closer until our elbows touched.

"So," Dad said, leaning back. "We talking contracts? Or is my boy still on probation?"

"We were discussing the camp," Vane said. "And the expectations."

Dad nodded, his expression shifting from jovial to serious. He looked at me. It was the look. The one he used when I let in a soft goal in pee-wee. The one that said, *I love you, but only if you're worth it.*

"Luke knows the expectations," Dad said softly. "Focus. Discipline. He knows what happens when you take your eye off the puck."

He tapped his own bad knee. It was a joke, but it wasn't funny.

"He wants what's best for me," I said to Vane, the words tasting like ash.

"He wants a return on investment," Vane corrected. He leaned forward. "And so do we. If we offer you this slot, Luke, we need to know you are the player he says you are. Disciplined. Focused. Singular."

He let the word hang there. *Singular.*

"We don't want campus drama," Vane said, his gaze flicking to Harper and back to me. "We don't want grades slipping. We don't want... entanglements."

Entanglements.

The word hit me like a physical blow.

Austen's shirt inside out. The way I'd shoved him off my lap when Ryan knocked. The lie I'd told through the crack in the door.

If Ryan had pushed that door open...

If Vane knew what I was doing in Room 317...

My dad leaned in closer. "Luke doesn't have entanglements," he said smoothly. "He knows the drill. Hockey first. Everything else is noise." He squeezed my shoulder. "Right, Luke?"

I looked at him. I saw the pride in his eyes—pride that was entirely conditional on me being the version of his son that played for the Wild. The version that wasn't gay. The version that wasn't in love with his roommate.

If I told him the truth, that pride would vanish. It wouldn't be anger. It would be worse. It would be indifference. He would look at me like a bad investment he needed to liquidate.

"Right," I whispered. "Hockey first."

"The camp starts July first," Vane said. "But the vetting starts now. We'll be watching."

He stood up. The meeting was over.

"Think about it," Vane said. "We need confirmation by Monday."

I stood up, shaking his hand. His grip was dry and hard.

"Thank you," I said.

Dad stood up too. He hugged me—a quick, hard embrace that smelled of expensive cologne and expectations.

"Proud of you, kid," he murmured in my ear. "Don't blow it."

He walked out with Vane, laughing about old times.

I walked out of the office. I walked down the tunnel, past the locker room, past the weight room. I didn't stop until I hit the exit doors and burst out into the cold morning air.

I sucked in a breath, but it felt like breathing through a straw.

My phone buzzed again.

Austen: *Update: I bought the good pretzels. The ones with the peanut butter.*

I stared at the screen.

The vetting starts now.

Ryan bought the lie. But luck is a variable you can't control.

If I took this spot, I was gone in July. If I took this spot, I had to live up to my monk nickname. I had to be exactly what everyone wanted, but Austen.

In hockey culture, "distraction" was code for anything that didn't help you win. And being queer in a development camp full of guys fighting for two contracts? That was a target on my back the size of a barn door.

I looked at the text. *The ones with the peanut butter.*

So small. So kind. Exactly the kind of "entanglement" Vane warned me against.

I realized I couldn't protect Austen. The closer we got, the more likely I was to drag him down with me when the hammer dropped.

I typed three dots. Then I deleted them.

I turned my phone off.

I started walking. Not toward the dorm. Toward the gym.

I needed to lift until I couldn't feel anything else.

Chapter 27
Defensive Zone Coverage

LUKE

The laptop screen flickered in the dark room, casting a blue pallor over my unmade bed.

I hit the left arrow key. Rewind. Space bar. Play.

On screen, the Cornell forward dragged the puck. My on-screen self dropped into the butterfly, sliding right. The forward stopped, pulled it back left, and roofed it.

I looked like I was having a seizure. My arms flailed. My head snapped back and forth.

"Swimming," Harper had called it. *You're drowning in open air, Carter.*

Rewind. Play.

"You've watched that frame forty times," Austen said from his desk.

"Forty-two," I muttered. "I'm looking for the tell. He dipped his shoulder. I should have frozen."

"It's not his shoulder," Austen said. The chair squeaked as he spun around. "It's your eyes."

I paused the video. "My eyes are fine. 20/20. I get them checked every preseason."

"Not acuity. Stability."

Austen stood up. He walked over to my bed, invading the space I'd been trying to keep empty for days. He pointed a slender finger at the frozen image of my face inside the helmet.

"Look at your head position," he said. "In the first ten games, your gaze was fixed for an average of three-hundred milliseconds before you moved. You were locking on."

He tapped the screen.

"Here? You're tracking three different variables in under a second. The stick blade, the skater's hips, the traffic in front. Your eyes are darting. It's called saccadic suppression."

I stared at him. "English, Austen."

"When your eyes move that fast, your brain goes blind for a fraction of a second to prevent motion blur. You aren't seeing the puck. You're guessing where it will be."

He sat on the edge of the mattress. Too close. I could smell his laundry detergent—the same lavender stuff I used now.

"It's the Quiet Eye theory," he said, his voice soft, reasonable. "Elite athletes fixate their gaze on a single target—the release point—for more than one-hundred milliseconds before initiating movement. It quiets the neural noise."

He reached out, his hand hovering near my knee.

"You're panicking, Luke. Your brain is noisy, so your eyes are noisy. You need to slow down the input."

I looked at his hand. Then I looked at the screen, where I looked like a desperate amateur.

He was right. I knew he was right. The math checked out. The biology checked out.

But I couldn't take it.

I couldn't take the fact that he saw me so clearly when I was trying so hard to hide. I couldn't handle his patience when I was planning to betray him for a contract.

"Stop," I snapped, pulling my leg away.

Austen froze. "I'm trying to help."

"I don't need a lecture on optics," I said, my voice harsh in the quiet room. "I need to stop the puck. This isn't a thesis project, Austen. It's my career."

"I know it's your career. That's why I'm telling you that you're physiologically choking."

"Choking?" I slammed the laptop shut. The room plunged into darkness. "Is that the official diagnosis? Did you run a regression analysis on how much I suck right now?"

"Luke—"

"I have a goalie coach," I said, standing up and grabbing my towel. I needed to get out. I needed air. "I have a head coach. I have a scout breathing down my neck and a dad who thinks I'm soft. I don't need some random undergraduate math major telling me I'm blinking wrong."

Austen stood up, too. He didn't flinch at my tone, which made it worse. He looked hurt.

"I'm random?" he whispered.

"You know what I mean," I said, dismissively opening the door. "Because this," I gestured between me and him, "it's too much. I can't do the variables right now, Austen. I can't."

I walked out.

I didn't look back to see if he was watching. I knew he was.

I kept my eyes on Javier's blade—visual attachment locked-in. I didn't look at his eyes or his shoulders; liars, both of them. I focused on the black edge feathering the puck at the near-side hash marks.

"Go!" Harper barked.

The drill was a modified Breakaway Relay. High speed, zero passing, pure isolation.

Morales drove inside, protecting the puck on his forehand.

I telescoped out to the top of the crease, cutting down his angle, challenging him to find net that wasn't there. I stayed low, knees bent, chest up—"big in the net," like my years of training taught me.

He opened the blade, faking a high blocker snapshot.

I held my ground—patience.

He dragged the puck across his body, trying to freeze me. I bit. I dropped into the butterfly a fraction of a second too early.

He pulled it to his backhand, trying to tuck it short-side.

Panic flared, but muscle memory took over. I pushed off my outside edge, sliding hard into the post. I slammed my skate blade against the iron and leaned my shoulder into the vertical bar—textbook RVH technique.

Thunk.

The rubber hit my leg pad right on the knee stack. The vibration rattled up my shin, but the seal held.

"Reset!" Harper yelled. She didn't raise her voice; she never had to. One word landed like a bench-press bar on the sternum. "Carter, you're swimming. Quiet that upper body."

I scrambled up, my edges carving deep ruts in the blue paint.

"Again," Harper ordered. "Morales, stop dusting it off. Shoot to score."

Javier circled out, collected a new feed from the corner. This time he came in with speed, no dekes. He looked low, dropped his shoulder—a classic tell for a five-hole shot—but at the last second, he snapped his wrists.

The puck elevated. Backhand roof.

I reacted late. I threw my arm up, abandoning the compact box structure I was supposed to maintain. The puck clipped the cuff of my glove—*sting*—and skittered into the corner.

Not pretty. Still alive. But technically garbage.

The whistle blew long. Harper skated toward me, her edges whispering on the ice.

"You're chasing the hands, Carter," she said, tapping my pads with her stick. "You're reacting to his twitch instead of reading the release. Read the hips."

Her expression didn't change, but the message was plain: *dial in or sit.*

She turned to Javier. "Make him work. If he cheats the pass, bury it."

Great.

I reset. I tapped my posts—left, right—centering myself. The frost burned my lungs. My shoulder throbbed under the chest protector, a dull ache I pushed into the background.

Javier smirked. Nothing personal, predator-prey physics.

Next rep. He came in wide. He leaned like he was going blocker side again, hips flat, looking for the far post.

Exactly what Coach had warned.

I waited. I held my edge. I didn't drop.

I watched his hips turn. He wasn't shooting far side; he was trying to open me up for the near side.

I saw the real lane open glove side.

He released.

I pushed—a hard, explosive T-push across the crease. I snapped my glove hand out, tracking the puck all the way into the pocket.

Snap.

Clean. No rebound. I held the catch for a full second, proving possession.

"Better," Harper muttered. Her approval measured.

We ran the drill until the Zamboni gate creaked. By the final rep, my calves quivered from holding the stance, and every heartbeat thudded against last night's short sleep.

Doesn't matter. Net still mine.

Locker room steam fogged every mirror. I peeled sweat-stiff undershirt, bruise on the shoulder blooming red-violet again. Ryan tossed a towel over the stall wall.

"You good, Monk?" he asked, voice muffled by his jersey half over his head.

"Fine." Standard lie. I shoved the towel against the bruise like a mute button.

He dropped onto the bench, gear half off, energy still bouncing. "Coach was in murder-hobo mode."

"Playoffs in three weeks," I said. "Not murder, prep."

"Prep with machetes." Ryan bumped my knee. "Come to Buckman tonight? Team's grabbing burgers."

"Need to study."

Ryan eyed me. "Study hall or Lovell private tutorial?"

"Study Hall. Grades don't fix themselves."

"Neither does fun." He shoved my helmet into the cage bag for me. "Don't let your brain gridlock, Carter."

Easy for him to say. He hadn't watched his dad couch-surf after one blown ACL.

Across the row, Javier snapped his tape roll shut. "Head in the crease tomorrow, Carter. Not in the spread*sheets*."

I met his stare. "Copy that."

He nodded once—agreement or warning, impossible to tell—then left.

Ryan followed, humming off-key. I lingered, packing slow. Helmet, pads, glove. My phone buzzed in the stall shelf.

Austen: *Should be in the room by 19:45.*

My chest squeezed. Want flooded so quick it felt like weakness.

Me: *Probably be back late—lift got extended. Keep options open?*

Three gray dots blinked, then stopped. No reply.

Good. Space.

The athletic center smelled like rubber and chlorine. Team hour in the weight pit officially ended at six, but I dug in for an extra circuit—deadlifts, rows, whatever punished thought into silence. Headphones blared nothing; I'd forgotten to hit play.

Fourth set, 225 on the bar, grip slipping. Shoulder barked. I added chalk, ignored the voice saying *enough.*

On rep six, Ryan's hand closed on the bar sleeve mid-lift. "Rack it."

I let go; metal slammed rails. "What?"

"You're tilting left. Gonna tweak something."

"Need the volume."

"Need the arm attached." He folded his arms, sweat darkening the Frost Demons on his tee. "Talk to me."

I wiped chalk on my shorts. "Earning ice time."

"Coach wrote your name on the board, red marker. Stop acting like it's penciled."

"It is." The words came out harsher than planned.

Ryan's brows pinched, then he softened. "Look—whatever noise is chewing you, skate it out, don't bench-press it. Okay?"

"Copy." Automatic. He clapped my shoulder—wrong one—pain flared. He felt me flinch; eyes narrowed. He didn't push, nodded at the exit. "Ice it. And if you don't talk to Dalton, I will."

He left. I stared at the bar, hands itching for another pull. Instead, I stripped plates, returned them to racks. Thirty-minute bike cooldown, heart rate at the top of zone three until it blurred into zone four.

Sweat drowned the worry for exactly eleven minutes. After that, Austen slid back in, uninvited: the hoodie he'd borrowed, the way his pulse had steadied under my hand when he fell asleep against me.

Focus. I upped the resistance.

Twilight iced the pavement on the walk to Stony Creek. My phone buzzed twice—Dad; voicemail. I swiped ignore. Another buzz.

Austen: *All good to hang tonight?*

My thumb hovered. I typed, erased, typed again.

Me: *Need extra film, might rain-check. Sorry.*

Three dots blinked, vanished. Nothing else.

My sweat drenched T-shirt started to freeze next to my body. I ran a hand through my crunch hair, ice crystals already forming.

Distance.

Third floor hallway smelled like microwave popcorn. Our door sat cracked two inches per rule. Light on. I palmed it open.

Room empty. Desk lamp on Austen's side was off. Two blueberry bars centered on my chair, note on top: *We iterate.*

Guilt punched first, then relief. Distance easier if he wasn't here to watch me manufacture it.

I set the bars on his shelf, unopened. After a quick shower, I swapped my sweat-drenched practice tee for a fresh one, then grabbed the shoulder peas.

I parked at my desk, opened SynergyStats film. Replay after replay of glove-side goals I'd already seen. Shoulder throbbed under cold. Brain still perseverating: Javier's release time, Harper's stopwatch, Ryan's questioning, my father's sixth call this week, my grades, Minnesota.

Somewhere across campus, Austen was probably recalculating the sample quiz, wondering if I still loved him. He'd call it data. I called it distraction. Distraction tanks careers.

Clock read 20:17. Quiet hours in three. I killed my lamp, crawled onto bed fully dressed, laptop flickering against the ceiling texture. Film kept playing; I watched pucks beat alternate versions of me until my eyes sanded over.

In the dark, radiator hissed its steady percussion. Usually, I matched its rhythm to calm down. Tonight, every tick underlined the distance I'd shoved between two beds.

Until things settle.

I repeated it like a pregame mantra. Until the grade climbs, until Harper stops dissecting each rebound, until Dad quits calling.

The room answered with heat pipes and silence.

Careful felt like safety. Safety felt like alone.

I rolled onto the good shoulder, stared at the sliver of hallway light beneath the door, and waited for the math to make sense again.

Chapter 28
Impact Warning

AUSTEN

I had initiated the disconnect protocol forty-eight hours ago. It was simple game theory: if the variable is going to become unstable, you remove it from the equation before it ruins the entire dataset. I would abandon him before he could abandon me. It was the only way to keep the control on my side of the ledger.

Sitting at my desk, back rigidly turned to his empty bed, staring at a paragraph I hadn't processed in twenty minutes, I assured myself I wasn't waiting for him. I deleted him. I was singular.

BOOM. BOOM. BOOM.

I turned and stared at the door. That familiar knock brought back dread. A key in the door lock. The door flung open. Ryan filled the frame like an off-duty bouncer—hood up, cheeks raw from cold.

"Special delivery," he announced.

Luke followed, slower. His right hand clamped the doorjamb; his left arm hung stiff at his side, glove still on. He tried for a smile and missed by yards.

I'd been at my desk pretending to read eigenfunction drafts, but the sight yanked me to my feet. The defensive logic evaporated. My heart gave a singular, painful thud against my ribs.

"What happened?" I asked, too sharp.

"Bad angle drill," Ryan said. "Morales tried to turn him into modern art. Shoulder caught the post weird."

Luke's gaze cut sideways—*shut up, O'Connell*—but he didn't argue. Sweat darkened his undershirt straight through the pads. His face was a shade of gray I usually associated with old snow.

I stepped back, making space between the beds. Ryan edged Luke inside, gear bag bumping his leg.

"Why is he wearing gear?" I asked.

"I couldn't carry him and his gear, so he had to wear it or leave it the locker room. And you know how he is," Ryan told me as he helped Luke onto his bed.

"You need anything?" Ryan asked him.

Luke shook his head. "I'm good. Thanks for the escort."

Ryan frowned at the word *escort* but didn't correct it. I could practically see the quip sitting on Ryan's tongue, but instead of going for the joke he looked to me instead. "You've got him?"

"Yeah," I said. "I can manage him."

He hesitated, eyes flicking from Luke's shoulder to my face. Whatever confirmation he needed, he must've found it; he slapped Luke's good arm once and left without another word. The hallway swallowed his footsteps.

Silence dropped—only the radiator wheezing and Luke's uneven breathing.

I shut and locked the door two inches. "Sit," I said, nodding at his bed.

He tried to unclip his blocker with one hand and failed. I crossed the gap, unfastened straps, slid it off. His fingers trembled, whether from pain or adrenaline I couldn't tell.

"I can undress myself," he muttered.

"Eventually." I tugged the Velcro on his chest protector. "But we'll both die of old age before that happens."

He didn't fight me after that. Pads hit the floor in slow sequence: chest, elbow, helmet, glove. Each drop landed like a punctuation mark to the week he'd spent backing away from me.

Using all the detachment of running integers, I had him in his boxer briefs in under a minute. The bruise—formerly violet—had spread like spilled ink down his triceps. New mottled red and eggplant radiated from the center.

I kept my voice level. "Scale?"

"Four." He sat, winced. "Okay, seven."

"Horizontal or vertical?"

"Moves to six if I lift anything heavier than my phone."

"Phone's banned for the next hour."

He huffed—half-laugh, half-exhale—but didn't argue.

I fetched the labeled pea bags—two this time—and the towel. When I turned, he was untying his shoelaces with his right hand, clumsy and slow. "Stop that," I grumbled. I placed the towel and peas on his shoulder before kneeling to finish untying the double knots and helping him out of his shoes. Old habit from early childhood placements: help first, talk later.

I guided him to sit cross-legged against the headboard, radiator heat at his side. He followed every nudge like he'd forgotten how to decide for himself.

"Hydration?" I asked.

He nodded. I opened the fridge, grabbed a can of lime soda, popped the top, and pressed it into his good hand.

Only then did I step back.

"What are we going to do with you?" I kept it casual, examining the bruise instead of his eyes.

He hissed a breath as I probed the deltoid. "You could start by not pressing on the hematoma."

"I'm checking for structural damage," I said, keeping my voice flat. "Unlike you, I don't ignore the warning signs."

The double meaning hung there. I felt his good shoulder tense under my hand. He knew I wasn't talking about the injury.

"I wasn't ignoring you," he said quietly.

"Could have fooled me."

"Needed to refocus," he said.

"On getting destroyed by your own post?"

"On keeping the net." He flexed fingers on the injured side; they barely moved. "Guess that worked out."

The sarcasm tried for levity and drowned.

I folded my arms. "Luke, you can't play if your arm stops lifting."

He stared past me, somewhere near the dent in our drywall. "I'll tape it and load ibuprofen."

"Great plan. Very 1990s."

He closed his eyes, chin tipping to his chest. Exhaustion blanketed him. I saw it land—the moment adrenaline quit and pain surged.

Instinct shoved irritation aside. I crossed, sat on the edge of the mattress, careful not to jostle him.

"Hey," I said, quiet. "Let me provide the assist."

His eyelids lifted halfway. Whatever he read in my face cracked something; his shoulders slumped. "I'm screwing everything up."

"Which part? Hockey, school, or human interaction?"

"All of it." He tried a sigh; it got stuck halfway, became a wince. "I thought if I pulled back, I could think straight. Instead, I can't think at all."

"And you tanked your shoulder."

"Bonus miscalculation." A faint attempt at humor, gone as quickly as it came.

I reached for the fresh pea bag, swapped it onto the bruise, rotated the melty one onto the towel. "Dalton should look at this again."

"Tomorrow." His voice frayed. "I need tonight to not be a disaster."

"Define disaster."

"Losing the crease. Losing…" He cut himself off, teeth caught his lower lip as his eyes looked up and caught mine.

Me, I almost filled in. The word landed between us, anyway.

I focused on practicalities. "Rule change. No work tonight. Quiet hours start now; you need sleep."

"I have film to review."

"Film will exist tomorrow." I stood. "But, we need to get you showered first; blood flow helps muscles. Can you manage?"

He shot me a look—*seriously?*—but the effect was ruined by the way he cradled his arm. "May take a bit."

"What do you need, Luke?"

Red crept up his neck. "Assist, please."

I pretended not to notice embarrassment.

"You smell like a locker room," I noted. "And you have an abrasion on your elbow that needs disinfectant."

Luke looked down at his boxers, then at his useless left arm. "I can't lift it past my hip, Austen. I can't wash my hair."

"Understood." I stood up, rolling up the sleeves of my button-down. "Let's do this. Grab your caddy. We're going down the hall."

He hesitated, red creeping up his neck. "You're going to…?"

"I am going to facilitate the process. Unless you want to ask Ryan?"

"God, no."

"Then move."

I checked the hallway—clear—and ushered him toward the communal bathroom at the end of the wing. It was empty, thankfully. The fluorescent lights hummed over the damp tile. I locked the main door.

"Stall three," I commanded. "It has a handheld nozzle."

Luke shuffled into the stall. He looked small in the tiled space, shivering slightly despite the heat of the room. I reached in and turned the water on, testing the temperature with my wrist until it was hot enough to soothe the muscle but not scald.

"Boxers," I said.

He hooked his thumb into the waistband and shimmied them down with one hand, kicking them into the corner. He turned away from me instantly, facing the tile wall.

"I've seen it all before. Step in."

He stepped under the spray, hissing as the water hit the bruise.

"Keep the shoulder out of the direct stream," I instructed, my voice flat, professional. "Turn thirty degrees to the right."

He adjusted. I grabbed the bottle of 2-in-1 from his caddy. I poured a measure into my palm and stepped into the spray, ignoring the water soaking the front of my shirt.

"Head down."

He tipped his head forward. I worked the lather into his hair, fingers digging into his scalp. It was mechanical—scrub, rinse, repeat—but the sound of his breath hitching in the echoey stall betrayed the tension.

"Eyes closed," I murmured.

I rinsed the suds away, shielding his face with my hand. I moved to his back.

I soaped the sponge. I washed his neck, the broad expanse of his scapula, the curve of his spine. I treated his skin like a topographic map—terrain to be navigated. But it was impossible not to feel. The muscle under my hand was hard and hot.

"Turn," I said.

He turned slowly. He kept his eyes closed, water streaming down his lashes.

I washed his chest, careful to avoid the angry purple blooming on his shoulder. My knuckles brushed his sternum. He sucked in a breath.

"Steady," I warned. "Almost done."

I washed his good arm. I washed his stomach, my hand moving in efficient, quick circles, refusing to linger on the V of his hips. I handed him the sponge.

"Can you manage the rest?"

He nodded, not opening his eyes. "Yeah."

"I'll wait outside the curtain."

I stepped back, my shirt clinging damply to my chest, and leaned against the sink. My heart hammered a frantic rhythm against my ribs, but I forced my breathing to match the steady drum of the water.

Two minutes later, the water cut off.

"Towel," he called.

I handed it around the curtain. He emerged a moment later, wrapped at the waist, skin pink and scrubbed clean.

"Efficient," I said, handing him his clean boxers.

"Humiliating," he corrected, though there was no heat in it.

"Medical necessity." I unlocked the main door, checking the corridor again. "Coast is clear. Move."

We made the walk back in silence. Once inside the safety of our room, the energy shifted. The clinical detachment frayed at the edges.

I helped him into a soft T-shirt, guiding the injured arm through the sleeve with the precision of a bomb disposal unit. He sat on the edge of the bed, damp hair plastered to his forehead, looking exhausted.

"Better?" I asked.

"Clean," he whispered. "Thanks."

"Don't mention it," I said, turning away to hide hands that were shaking just a little. "Variable stabilized."

He sat, back hitting the headboard like his strings had been cut.

"Pain level?" I asked.

"Hovering at five, flirting with six."

"Means we swap ice every quarter-hour until it stays below five."

"Dictator."

"Efficient dictator." I arranged the pack. "Food?"

"Stomach's on strike."

"Oat bar?"

He shook his head. "Later."

I opened his nightstand drawer, retrieved the bottle of over-the-counter painkillers. "Two now."

He swallowed them dry.

When I straightened, his gaze followed me—uncertain, apologetic. "I'm sorry," he said, voice low. "For everything."

The words nudged every nerve that had hummed all week. I perched on the mattress edge again, leaving inches between us but no more.

"I'm not mad," I said. "I'm... confused."

"I thought keeping distance would stabilize things."

"Constants by subtraction?"

He grimaced. "Right. You warned me math jokes are dangerous."

I shrugged. "Dangerous only if misapplied."

Silence stretched. I picked at a loose thread on the blanket.

He cleared his throat. "The shoulder isn't the only thing that hurts."

I waited.

"Every time I tried to pull back, it felt like I was dimming the rink lights on myself. Thought that meant I was weak."

I traced the stitching, kept my tone neutral. "Maybe it means you're human."

His mouth twitched. "Terrifying prospect."

I looked up. He wasn't hiding behind sarcasm; the line was simple truth and it rattled me more than the bruise.

"Why do you do it?" I asked. "The extra lifts. The hours. You're the starter. You're good."

Luke looked away, toward the dark window. "Good isn't safe."

"Safe from what?"

"From becoming average." He said the word like a slur. "My dad... he was great. For two seasons. Then he got hurt, and he became an average guy. Then he got bitter." He turned back to me, his eyes dark. "I can't be average, Austen. Average gets cut. Average ends up sitting in a big house with nothing but old trophies and a bad knee."

My heart ached for him. For the little boy who must have learned that love was conditional on performance stats.

"Luke, you're not average," I said. "And you're not him." I touched the blanket near his knee, not him. "If you need space, say it. Don't vanish."

"Don't want space." He swallowed. "I need balance. I don't know how to skate that angle."

"Trial and error." My finger hooked the thread again, tugged until it snapped. "We iterate."

His shoulders dropped as though those two syllables loosened a ratchet. He shifted, inching his leg until his knee touched mine. Contact light, deliberate.

I let my hand stay on his good shoulder. My heart pounded like a mis-set metronome, out of sync with the quiet room.

"I should thank Ryan," I said, mostly to fill the silence. "I'm glad he knew to bring you here."

"He threatened to tape me to the bench if I didn't let him walk me back," Luke said. He offered a smile—weak, but real. "He knows, Austen. He knows I've been avoiding you."

"Great. So, the entire roster knows."

"They're not gossip hounds. But Ryan... he sees the ice better than anyone. He noticed I was drifting. And he knows why I was drifting."

Luke closed his eyes for a moment, leaning into my touch. "I don't know if I ever mentioned it, but the team knows I'm gay. I was very clear about that when I agreed to transfer here. I don't hide that."

"Why hide us?" I asked, the question slipping out sharper than I intended. "If they know, why not just tell them we're dating? Why the secrecy?"

"Because once it's public, it's a thing. It's a topic. It makes it... real."

I pulled my hand back. "So, you're ashamed of the reality of me?"

Luke's eyes snapped open. He reached out, grabbing my wrist with his good hand. His grip was desperate.

"No. Never think that. You are the best thing that has happened to me in this school. But that's the problem."

"I don't follow the logic."

"My dad," Luke said, the word heavy. "He's known for years that I'm gay. Honestly, doesn't care about who I sleep with. What he cares about is where my head is."

Luke let go of my wrist, rubbing his face with his palm.

"Since I was six, it's been drilled into me that the only thing that matters is the ice. Anything outside the rink is noise. Friends, parties, relationships—they're all just distractions. Leaks in the system where the focus drains out."

Luke looked up at me, his expression miserable.

"My dad wouldn't care if you were a guy, a girl, or an extraterrestrial. He'd see you as a liability. And as much as I hate it... I still hear his voice in the back of my head. Every time I want to spend time with you, I feel like I'm failing him."

The radiator hissed, steam filling the pause. The equation finally balanced. He wasn't fighting me; he was fighting a ghost.

"Your father's data is flawed. Trust me, I've spent my entire life trying not to depend on anyone. It doesn't work. If it worked, I would have figured out a way to do it by now," I said quietly. "But I understand the conditioning."

I looked at him and saw the soggy peas drooping against his shoulder. "Time for another bag." I stood, removed the bag from his shoulder, and swapped it for one that was frozen. He flinched, then settled.

"Lie down before you fall over," I ordered. "We can debug the rest of the programming later."

He complied, sliding to his side, good arm tucked under the pillow. The hoodie bunched; I straightened the hem, pulling the blanket over him. He watched, expression unreadable but soft around the edges.

"You don't have to stay," he murmured.

"I wasn't planning to." I grinned. I dragged my desk chair closer anyway, angled so I could time the ice rotations. Phone timer set to fifteen.

Luke exhaled, long. "If Coach benches me tomorrow—"

"She won't."

"You can't know that."

"True." I leaned back, folded arms. "Admittedly, probability favors people who can lift their glove. Sleep helps that."

His eyelids drooped. "Constant?"

That word again—so small, so unsteady. My chest tightened.

"Still here," I said.

Timer ticked down. I watched the steady rise and fall of his back. The whole building felt like it was breathing with us, radiators syncing to Luke's slower inhales.

At the next ice change, he was half asleep. I eased the peas away, dabbed condensation, and laid a dry towel before swapping out the bag. He mumbled something—maybe thanks, maybe nothing—and drifted before I answered.

Twenty minutes later the pack slid off; I replaced it without starting the timer, then stayed seated. Desk lamp dimmed; outside, frozen rain tapped the pane. My calculus notes lay forgotten, highlighters drying open.

I should have crawled into my own bed. Instead I sat, ankles crossed, counting the seconds between his breaths, telling myself it was to monitor pain levels.

A half-snore escaped him. At least, if Coach asked tomorrow why he was late on the glove side, he could blame me and sleep deprivation instead of reckless lifting.

My gaze landed on the puck under the lamp—still centered, still article five. Constant. Maya's voice echoed—*constants aren't found, they're named.* Had we named this yet? No. Did that stop me from wanting it? Also no.

Luke shifted, face relaxing into deeper rest. He trusted me with unconsciousness; that counted for something.

Chapter 29
Bench Boss

LUKE

Coach Harper didn't waste time with hello.

"Sit."

I dropped onto the plastic chair across her desk. My left shoulder barked; I kept the wince small. The office was the size of a broom closet, all metal filing cabinets and a single framed photo of her hoisting a championship trophy. No yelling in here—verdicts.

She flipped a tablet around so the screen faced me—slow-motion of last night's collision. Morales, sharp angle, me lunging glove side, shoulder slamming the post. She froze the frame on impact.

"Walk me through this," she said.

"Bad read," I answered. "Over-rotated."

"And the extra lifts after team block?"

I kept my stare on the photo behind her head. "Needed volume."

"You needed recovery." She tapped the tablet, changed to a still image: my arm, purple spreading under tape. "Dalton logged a pain score of six. You told him four."

"Numbers drifted."

Her silence felt heavier than shouting. She slid the tablet aside. "Carter, injury happens. Lying about it is optional."

I knotted my fingers together so she wouldn't see them shake. "Shoulder's functional."

"Functional isn't the bar." She leaned back, arms crossed. "You're our starter. That means availability. It also means you model process—fitness check-ins, study hall, sleep." She opened a drawer, removed a folded sheet of paper—the roster for Friday at Stonehill. My name sat in red beside *STARTER*. She laid it between us. "I wrote this before I saw the film or the report from Dalton. That trust can move, Carter. Don't make me move it."

"Yes, Coach." My voice sounded steady; inside everything rattled.

She studied me another second, then softened a fraction. "You're good at your job. Act like it off the ice too. See Dalton twice a day until he's satisfied."

I nodded.

"And Carter?"

"Yeah?"

"Control is useful. Isolation isn't. I don't delve into my player's personal lives, but I'm not oblivious."

The sentence landed like a puck to the mask—loud, harmless, unforgettable. I stood when she gestured. "You're clear for limited practice tomorrow," she said. "No contact. Prove you can follow orders."

"Copy."

Dalton taped the joint, strapped on a compression wrap, and told me the bruise was "borderline charming." I managed a grin. He handed over two ice packs and a schedule: cold at noon, stim at sixteen-hundred, follow-up after weights—lower body only. Orders, signed and timestamped. Easy—compared to the mess in my head.

Locker room traffic thinned; teammates drifted toward class and breakfast. Ryan lingered by the exit, phone in hand. When I passed he lifted his brows: *you alive?* I answered with a thumbs-up too fast to look sincere.

He didn't chase me.

Campus noon rush smelled like wet wool and burned espresso. I cut through it, keeping my bad arm tucked close. The plan—new plan, better plan—formed with every step: tighter schedule, no dead minutes, no off-script distractions. Dalton, class, early bed. Minimum variables, maximum control.

Stony Creek's hallway felt hotter than usual; maybe the radiator, maybe my pulse. Our door stood ajar the habitual two inches. I pushed in.

Austen sat cross-legged on the rug, laptop beside him, three-color ledger grid chalked across a legal pad. He looked up the second the door clicked.

"Dalton clear you?" he asked.

"Conditionally." I nudged the door closed with my foot, dropped my gear bag next to the dresser.

His gaze skimmed the wrap peeking from my sleeve. "Pain level?"

"Manageable." I crossed to the fridge, stowed the professional-grade ice packs.

He set the pad aside, unfolded from the floor. "Coach meeting?"

I shrugged—tight movement. "Standard accountability talk."

He waited. When nothing more came, he dusted chalk from his palm and pointed at the desk where two fresh oat bars sat.

"Thought you might want fuel," he said, tone light.

"Thanks." I didn't move toward them.

Quiet filled the room, not the easy kind. The radiator hissed like it noticed.

Austen tapped a finger on the legal pad. "I'm free after eight if you want to, you know, hang out or something."

Eight meant two hours after stim, perfectly inside the no-excuse window. I opened my mouth to say yes. What came out was, "Might run film instead. Need to tighten angles before Stonehill."

His posture didn't change, but something in his face did—a small shift around the eyes, like he'd taken a breath and held it. "Okay," he said after a beat. "Tomorrow?"

"Maybe. Depends on how the shoulder tracks."

A nod—neutral, professional. He reached for the pad, flipped the top sheet, began uncapping highlighters. Yellow, blue, green, precise clicks. "Let me know."

The colors blurred. I turned to my dresser, yanked out a clean T-shirt—smelled like his detergent because we'd mixed laundry last week. I shoved it back, grabbed another.

"You should eat something," he said, still not looking up.

"Later." I cinched the drawer shut, harder than necessary.

Another silence. This one throbbed.

He capped the markers, lined them edge to edge. "How limited is limited practice?"

"No contact, no extra sets." I quoted Dalton before he could ask. "Harper's orders."

"Harper is sensible."

I barked a humorless laugh. I looked up. He met my stare head on.

The urge to step closer, apologize, crawl back into last night's calm scraped at my ribs. Control first, softness later. That was the rule. A rule I'd invented ten minutes ago, sure, but it felt safe.

I bent to retie a lace I hadn't undone. "I'll eat after stim."

"Copy," he said, echoing my earlier deflection. He swiveled to his laptop and typed. Keys clacked, steady.

I stood, shoulder complaining. "Heading to library. See you." I grabbed my backpack, ignoring the oat bars on the desk. Door shut behind me with a soft latch.

The library's business stacks were near empty at mid-afternoon. Perfect. I commandeered a cubicle, spread my management textbook on the table and read. Shoulder ached; I popped Dalton-approved acetaminophen, skipped water—water meant breaks.

Every ten minutes my phone flashed: Dad calling, then Dad again from a different number. I muted the screen, face down. Another notification—Austen, one line:

Don't forget to ice.

I stared until the bubbles stopped. No reply.

Focus.

I shoved the textbook aside and queued the Stonehill film on my laptop. Left winger loved blocker side; nothing I didn't know. Shoulder tight. I muted the commentary, let the images run until they meant nothing.

At eighteen-hundred my stomach complained. I ignored it—fifteen more minutes, then stim. Numbers said routine mattered.

Training room fluorescence buzzed above Dalton's head. He strapped electrodes around the bruise; the current made the muscle twitch like an eel under skin.

"Pain?" he asked.

"Four."

He didn't look impressed. "Coach gave me leeway to bench you if you inflate numbers. Try again."

I exhaled. "Five... maybe a five-point-five."

"That I believe." He adjusted the dial, watched my face. "After this, ice it for twenty minutes."

"Got it."

"And Carter?" He dropped his voice. "If you try to BS your way through this, Harper will notice. If there's a problem, talk to her before she talks to you. Remember, missing a single game is better than a career-ending injury. Of all the guys in this program, you should understand that."

I offered half a nod.

Back in Stony Creek the corridor smelled like overcooked ramen. Our door was shut. I pulled out my key, unlocked the door, and stepped in.

The desk lamp glowed, illuminating a single sheet of paper on my pillow next to the chessboard: *White to move. Mate in three. We iterate.*

There were also two unopened oat bars.

I sat, shoulder throbbing in time with my pulse. The quiet felt different—less shared, more vacant. My fault.

I picked up the page. First move: *Knight to F6 check.* Obvious. Aggressive.

I looked for the follow-up. *Bishop takes...*

My brain stalled.

Across the room his bedspread lay smooth, corners hospital tight. His hoodie—the one he'd worn to Ridgeway—hung on my chair, sleeves folded. I rested a hand on it before I caught myself, jerking back like it was on fire.

Control first.

I pulled out my phone, thumbed a text:

Film until late. Don't wait up. Shoulder better.

Sent. Three dots blinked, disappeared. No answer.

I dropped the phone face down, shoved both oat bars into my backpack, and shrugged on my jacket.

Quit being weak. Move.

The arena sat mostly dark, lights on only over the far crease where the maintenance guy ran drills with his kid. I settled in the bleachers, laptop on knees, cold bleeding through the bench.

Stonehill's winger scored blocker side four times last season. I replayed every frame until movement fused into noise. Shoulder cramped; I shifted, stubborn.

Phone vibrated. Unknown number—Dad again. Voicemail. I deleted it without opening.

Another buzz—Austen.

Understood. Be safe.

That was all. I read it twice, hunting for anger, couldn't find any.

Lights overhead clicked off one by one. Maintenance guy whistled for closing. I packed up, shoulder stiff, blood sluggish. The walk back felt longer than a regulation game.

Dorm hall quiet hour had started; doors muted TV sounds. Ours was shut but unlocked. Inside, Austen sat at his desk, hoodie traded for flannel. He turned when I entered, eyes tracking me like a puck.

"Stim help?" he whispered.

"Yeah." I toed off shoes, shrugged the jacket carefully.

"You ate?" He nodded toward the backpack.

"I had an oat bar." I tossed the bag under my bed.

His mouth tightened; he didn't press. "Ice pack's in the freezer. Timer's set."

"Thanks." I opened the fridge, retrieved the professional ice pack, pressed it against the bruise. Cold shocked the skin.

Austen closed his laptop, folded glasses, stood. "I'm gonna crash."

"Copy." My voice scratched.

He moved toward the light switch, paused. "My next move is on your pillow. No penalty if you tackle it tomorrow."

"Got it."

He nodded once, flipped the switch. Darkness swallowed him, then the rustle of his blanket. I sat in the glow from my desk lamp, ice numbing half my chest.

After a minute he spoke into the dark. "Luke?"

"Yeah?"

"Good luck Friday."

The words were soft, not sweet—a fact, like ice melts at zero Celsius. Somehow that hurt more than sarcasm would have.

"Thanks," I said. I waited, hoping for something else—a joke, a rule update, anything. Silence.

I swapped the ice, dried condensation on my jeans, and reached for the chess game. I stared at the diagram. *Knight to f6 check.* The black King was cornered, but I couldn't see the kill shot.

"Black is forced to h8," a voice murmured from the other side of the room.

I jumped, the pen slipping in my sweat-slick fingers. I looked over. Austen hadn't moved; his back was still to me, the duvet pulled up to his ear.

"You're awake," I whispered.

"Hard to sleep when you're thinking that loudly."

I looked back at the paper. *King to h8.* That put the King in the corner, blocked by his own pawns.

Suddenly, the line snapped into focus. It wasn't about brute force; it was about removal. To clear the lane for the mate, I had to throw away the most valuable piece on the board.

My hand shook slightly, but I wrote it down.

Queen to g8 check.

"Sacrifice the Queen," I said aloud, testing the logic.

"Bold," Austen replied, his voice thick with sleep but approving. "I'll respond tomorrow."

Across the room his breathing steadied into sleep—slow, even. My chest tightened with something I refused to name.

Chapter 30
The Rumor Mill

AUSTEN

North Point always ran hot at lunch—lines three deep at the stir-fry station, trays clattering, freshmen yelling across booths like distance was a dare. I kept my headphones in without music, noise reduction on.

No luck. Two days since we'd spoken more than eight syllables. I told myself hockey made the schedule brutal, nothing personal, variable not constant. My chest disagreed.

Maya slid into the seat across from me, ponytail damp. She clocked the untouched chickpea salad on my tray, then the way my gaze kept lifting over her shoulder.

"Looking for Mr. Radiator?" she asked, tearing open a granola bar.

"Scanning for statistical anomalies." I stabbed a tomato. "Cafeteria's overdue for a foodborne outbreak."

"Mm-hmm." She leaned on her elbows. "Heard anything from your favorite anomaly?"

"He's busy. Playoffs."

"And you're... fine." She said it like marking false on a test.

"Define *fine.*"

"Not rearranging your pencils alphabetically at three a.m. by their pet names."

"I don't name my pencils."

Over her shoulder, the hockey table erupted—Ryan, Javier, a tangle of parkas and backward caps. Luke wasn't with them.

Ryan's voice cut over the din. "—agent thinks Carter's got a real shot if he keeps numbers steady."

Javier answered, lower. "Pro camp in August, right? Dude could bounce."

Ryan laughed. "Development camp, rookie tourney. Could be Minnesota if the scout calls back."

The words threaded through clatter, too clear. *Could be Minnesota. Bounce.*

My fork paused midair. Sweat prickled under my collar despite North Point's relentless air-con.

Maya followed my stare. "What?"

"Nothing." I forced a chew, nearly gagged on acid dressing.

Across the room Ryan kept talking—stats, glove side percentages, something about "next year."

Maya's hand settled on the table, palm up. "Austen."

I shook my head, swallowed hard. "Noise."

She didn't push, closed her palm like tucking the question away. "Need to get out of here? Fresh air?"

"I'm heading to Harbor Commons after this. I promised a calc kid review."

"Then let's go."

Outside, wind knifed off the quad, cold enough to numb ears. Might've helped, except every step clanged with Ryan's words. *Could be Minnesota.*

Temporary, my brain whispered. *Placement ending. Math proof solved: constants don't transfer conferences.*

Maya nudged my elbow. "Dinner later? Text me."

"Sure." My voice cracked on the s. She frowned but let it drop.

Harbor Commons smelled like stale pastries and caramel lattes. I claimed a two-top near the windows, laptop open, derivative problems queued. Students drifted past in Frost Demons jerseys—game-week energy humming. Every so often someone mentioned Carter: insane glove, Stonewall Friday, starter's locked.

Locked—for now, I thought.

I pushed through proofs, red pen marking corrections, but decimals slithered. My phone facedown vibrated twice: campus push alert, *FROST DEMONS READY FOR STONEHILL.* I flipped it, screen full of Luke's save against Caribou, glove hand frozen midair.

Pressure behind my eyes pulsed. I clicked the phone dark, slid it under the laptop and kept grading.

My phone buzzed as another text popped.

Luke: *Weights till five. Sanity check status?*

I stared at the bubble. Simple, almost caring—proof he remembered I existed. My thumb hovered.

All variables stable, I typed, then deleted.

Me: *Good luck in lift. Still have the peanut butter-filled pretzels lying around.*
Message read, no response.

I returned to my room after having dinner with Maya and spending some much needed time editing my thesis in Stone Ridge. By the time I got home a little after eight, the evening painted the dorm hall in sodium orange. The door to 317 stood cracked. I pushed in.

Luke kneeled by the gear rack, one-handed, hanging his chest protector with slow precision. Shoulder wrap peeked from under a practice tee. He didn't look up.

"Time for ice?" I asked.

He flinched at my voice like I'd snapped tape near his ear. "Thanks, I got it."

"Okay." I set my backpack on my desk. Books there looked wrong now, intimate as toothbrushes. I gathered the legal pads, highlighters, and pencils one by one and set about reorganizing, stacking them perpendicular to the puck.

He watched the relocation in silence, eyes dark, unreadable.

"Reconfiguring workspace," I said, aiming for casual.

"Right." He unlaced his shoes with his good hand, slower than any six-year-old. "Less clutter."

I shrugged.

Gear shed, he sat on his bed, phone glowing. I heard the faint whine of voicemail playback—male voice, too muffled to parse. Luke hit delete before it finished and dropped the phone face down.

Before the screen went dark, I caught a glimpse of his notifications. Three missed calls from *Dad*. One text from a contact labeled simply *Mom*—no photo, no emoji, just the name. He hadn't opened it.

I didn't ask. Some variables weren't mine to solve.

I tugged my chair under the desk—territory established.

"They finally fixed the heater in the lobby," I mentioned, testing the airwaves.

"That's good." Short. Distracted.

I hesitated. "Forecast says snow for the game this weekend."

Luke didn't look up from his phone.

"I saw."

"Might make it hard for the the team to get here," I added.

"Yeah." He swiped his thumb across the screen, scrolling past content he clearly wasn't reading. "I know Harper has already been in contact with their Coach."

That was it. Just polite, empty noise.

The radiator hissed. Eight feet never sounded so loud.

I opened a topology article, pretended the symbols held my focus. Luke swapped one ice pack for another before setting the timer on his watch. Precision man bleeding under control.

Twenty minutes crawled. I didn't read past page one. Finally, I gave up and capped my pen. "I'm heading to Ridgeway early tomorrow. Calc reviews."

He nodded without lifting his head. "Sleep's smart."

No goodnight joke, no constant check. Bare data.

I stood, hesitated. The puck's surface caught lamplight—the night he handed it to me, glove-save grin bright. I turned it upside down. The weight felt the same; the meaning flipped.

His breath hitched, soft sound I almost missed. When I faced him, his gaze was on the inverted puck. Something like regret flickered, gone before measurement.

I clicked off my lamp, crawled into bed under stiff sheets. Facing the wall, I listened to him swap ice packs one last time.

After lights-out he whispered, "Night, Austen."

I let two breaths pass, then answered, "Night."

Chapter 31
Home Team Pressure

LUKE

The puck clanged off the far post and ricocheted straight back at my mask.

I tracked it—visual attachment locked—caught the rebound with the top of my blocker, and swallowed the sting that jumped down my taped shoulder.

"Reset," Harper called from the blue line.

No praise, no critique—the next rep already waiting. That was fine. I didn't want praise. Praise meant she'd seen the wince.

I shuffled back to the center of the crease—short, choppy strides to keep my legs loaded. *Left skate, right skate, square to the puck.* The ice smelled like scraped tin; my breath fogged inside the cage.

Morales cued up at the hash marks again, stick blade on its heel, reading me like a textbook he'd already highlighted.

Whistle.

He snapped high glove.

I dropped into the butterfly, flaring my knees wide to seal the ice. I threw my glove hand up. My shoulder screamed on the extension—a hot, tearing sensation under the deltoid.

Thunk.

The puck hit the pocket, popped loose, and died in the blue paint. I hadn't absorbed it; I'd blocked it. Sloppy.

I covered, froze, waited for Harper's second whistle before I breathed.

Four reps later, the fatigue set in. I started losing the timing—half a beat behind, chasing the release instead of reading the body.

"Go!" Harper barked.

Javier came in with speed. He opened his blade—fake shot.

My brain said *push*. I needed a hard T-push to get across to the far post. But my body hesitated, protecting the shoulder. Instead of driving with my legs, I reached with my upper body.

I broke my stance. I opened up holes.

Javier saw it; predators always do. He dragged the puck to his backhand, changing the angle in a split second.

I tried to recover, desperate, lunging.

He tucked it softly inside the far post.

The net light blinked red behind me.

Groan from the benches; freshman forwards thumped sticks on the boards. Harper's whistle cut the noise.

"Carter," she said, voice level. "Crease. Now."

I pushed up from the ice, sliding to her skates. The pain in my shoulder jackhammered, but I gave it a three on the internal meter. Three was functional.

She kept her tone calm, almost quiet. "Postseason in fourteen days. Your reads are late by half a frame. You're swimming out there."

"Yes, Coach."

She pointed her stick at my chest. "You're reaching. You're trying to make glove saves because you don't want to move your body behind the puck. That's lazy goaltending, Carter."

It wasn't lazy. It was agony. But I couldn't say that.

She glanced at the black tape peeking out from my sleeve. "Pain score?"

"Three."

Her eyes narrowed. "Honest three?"

A beat. "Four when I reach."

"Then stop reaching." She tapped her stick on the ice once. "Economy of movement, Carter. If you're square, the puck hits you. If you reach, you open the armpit. Smart angles cost less than hero saves."

"Coach?"

"The net doesn't need you to bleed for it. It needs you to be here Friday."

She pivoted away. The conversation had lasted maybe eight seconds, but my pulse was sprinting.

Practice cycled through breakouts, two-on-zeros, and the dreaded Screen Drill.

Ryan parked his massive frame right in my vision. The point man fired. I couldn't see the release. I had to fight through the screen, looking over Ryan's shoulder, trying to find the puck through the forest of legs.

Down. Up. Shuffle. Down.

I ran the lane work like a robot, blocking out the feedback from my shoulder, counting pucks: 112 shots, three goals against, one bad rebound.

Numbers were a life raft.

The Zamboni horn sent us off. I coasted to the bench, legs rubber, my edges barely biting the ice.

Ryan met me at the gate. He didn't offer a fist bump today. He looked grim.

"Good grind," he said, but his eyes were tracking something over my shoulder in the stands.

"What?" I asked, following his gaze. The stands were empty except for the student manager collecting pucks.

"Check your phone when you get inside," Ryan said, voice low. "And maybe skip the Buckman Grill tonight."

"Why?"

"Trust me, Monk." He patted the back of my helmet—right side, merciful—and skated off.

Locker room benches creaked under damp gear. I stripped slower than usual, one strap at a time. The bruise had spread ugly yellow under the tape; Dalton's handiwork crunched when I peeled it off.

I checked my phone.

Ryan: *Heads up, I think your dad's here. Saw a red Ford F-150 with Jersey plates in the visitors lot.*

My stomach dropped out. Dad.

He wasn't supposed to be here. He'd said he was coming for the Friday game, driving up game day. It was Wednesday.

I shoved the phone deep into my bag, under the dirty laundry, as if burying it could block the signal.

Across the row, Javier snapped his tape roll shut. "Keep your head in practice tomorrow, Carter. Not in la la land."

I met his stare. He knew. Everyone knew Rick Carter's truck.

"Copy that," I said.

I showered and dressed in record time—jeans, hoodie, beanie pulled low. I bolted. I needed to be somewhere he couldn't find me. The gym was obvious. The rink was obvious.

That left the dorm.

The walk back to Stony Creek was a blur of paranoia. Every engine revving made me flinch. I kept my head down, cutting through the science quad to avoid the main road.

I hit the third floor of the dorm breathing hard, shoulder throbbing.

Our door was cracked the standard two inches.

I pushed it open the security door, desperate for the quiet of our room, for the smell of mint tea and the click of Austen's keyboard. I needed to answer the note he'd left yesterday. I needed to explain why I'd ghosted him for forty-eight hours.

I'm done doing this wrong, he'd written.

Me too.

But when I stepped inside, the room was dark.

The blinds were drawn tight against the afternoon gray. Austen was in bed, face turned to the wall, blanket pulled up to his ears.

I froze. It was 4:30 p.m. Austen didn't nap.

I stepped closer, quiet on the rug. The oat bar I'd left on his desk yesterday was gone, but the wrapper wasn't in the trash. He'd cleared his desk completely—laptop, papers, highlighters all put away.

It looked sterile.

On the nightstand, under the lamp, the puck sat upside down.

The message was clear: *Closed.*

"Austen?" I whispered.

He didn't move. His breathing was too even, too controlled. He was awake. He didn't want to talk to me.

I stood there, hand hovering over his shoulder, wanting to shake him, to beg him to wake up and tell me the probability of us surviving my dad's arrival. If I forced him to talk to me, with my dad prowling campus and my shoulder on fire, I'd bring the chaos right to his bed.

I pulled my hand back.

I went to my desk, sat down, and didn't turn on the lamp. I sat in the dark, listening to the radiator hiss, waiting for my phone to buzz.

It took ten minutes.

Buzz.

I pulled it out of my pocket. It wasn't Ryan. It wasn't Javier.

Dad: *I'm outside. Bring your playbook.*

I stared at the screen until the backlight timed out, plunging the room back into gray.

I looked at Austen's back one last time.

"I'm sorry," I whispered to the silence.

I grabbed my playbook and walked out the door.

Chapter 32
The Handshake Line

LUKE

The rink lights dropped to half-dark for introductions, and the student section roared hard enough to vibrate the aluminum bleachers.

I stood in the tunnel, the concrete cold seeping through my skates. My dad was out there. Section 104, probably critiquing my posture during the anthem. Gulliver Vane was with him.

The roster in my pocket felt like a lead weight.

I skated out last, mask tilted back. I tapped each post once—left, right—no extra flourish, then settled into a compact ready stance.

I scanned the north end. Habit. I didn't expect him to be there. I'd basically avoided him for a week, and two days ago I'd walked out of the dorm while he lay facing the wall.

But he was there.

Three rows higher than his usual spot. No Maya today. Austen, arms crossed, face unreadable behind his glasses. He was wearing his own coat, not my hoodie.

My heart hammered a rhythm that had nothing to do with hockey. He showed up. Even after I failed every variable, he showed up.

Show me tomorrow, he'd said.

I pulled my mask down. *Okay. Watch this.*

Puck drop.

Stonehill came out flying, a swirl of white and navy flooding the zone. They were fast, desperate for a playoff spot, and they knew I was playing injured. They tested the shoulder immediately.

First shift: A dump-in chased down by their forecheck. The puck cycled to the point.

My heart hammered against my ribs—the old panic, the noise. I wanted to crouch lower. I wanted to tense up.

Austen's voice drifted through the static in my head. *"Quiet the eye. Slow the input."*

I took a breath and stopped scanning the chaos of legs and sticks. I locked my gaze on the puck carrier's blade.

Visual attachment.

The defenseman walked the blue line and fired.

Old Luke would have lunged. Old Luke would have tried to punch the puck into the netting to look dominant.

New Luke did less. I didn't reach. I didn't lunge. I made a six-inch shuffle to the right. Economy of movement. Distance equals time. If I moved less, I had more time to react.

Thud.

Blocker save. I didn't punch at it; I angled the board, steering the puck gently into the corner, away from the danger zone.

Controlled. Quiet.

"Nice steer, Monk," Ryan called, collecting the rebound.

Another shot thirty seconds later—low glove. I dropped into the butterfly, sealing the ice, and swallowed the puck. No rebound.

The crowd noise spiked, a wall of sound, but inside the helmet, it was silent.

I exhaled. The period blurred into an Austen math lesson: shot vectors, clearance angles, probability trees folding down to one outcome at a time. I counted thirteen shots before Stonehill registered a real danger chance.

Power play. They set up the umbrella.

The pass snapped cross-ice, finding a seam through our penalty kill box. It was a one-timer set up for their sniper in the circle.

Old Luke—panic Luke—would have slid early, opening the five-hole.

This Luke waited.

I pushed off my post—a hard, explosive T-push. I arrived at the top of the crease exactly as the stick met the puck. I was square. I was set.

Whap.

The puck hit the NRU logo on my chest protector dead center. I collapsed my shoulders, trapping it against my body like a precious stone.

No rebound. No drama.

The crowd erupted like I'd roofed a breakaway, but I barely nodded. I dropped the puck to the ref's hand and tapped my posts.

Boring, Harper had said. *Make it boring.*

I realized what she meant. "Exciting" meant you were out of position. "Exciting" meant you were recovering from a mistake. "Boring" meant you had already solved the equation.

Second period.

We generated offense. Ryan deflected a point shot for a goal, ugly but effective. Morales scored on a wrap-around, stuffing it past their goalie's skate.

2–0.

Students pounded on the plexiglass behind me, screaming my name.

I ignored them. I used the stoppage to smooth the snow in my crease, scraping the blue paint clean. *Calm eye of the storm.*

Stonehill answered late.

They set a screen—a massive forward parked right in my vision.

My instinct screamed: *Look around him! Bob your head! Find the puck!*

I tried to look around. I shifted my head left, then right, trying to find the release point.

Mistake.

Austen's voice: *Saccadic suppression. If you move your eyes fast, you go blind.*

Because I was moving my head, I missed the release frame. The shot came from the point. I never saw it.

I heard the *clack* of the stick, the *ping* of the crossbar, then the roar of the Stonehill bench.

2–1.

I didn't smash my stick. I didn't yell at my defenseman for the screen. I knew exactly why that puck went in. My eyes had been too noisy.

I took a drink of water. I reset my stance. I tapped both posts—left, right. *Constants.*

Intermission.

The tunnel smelled of rubber mats and adrenaline. I walked with my head down, conserving energy.

Dalton met me outside the locker room. He checked the tape tension on my shoulder.

"Shoulder?" he asked.

"Functional."

"Keep it that way. Don't be a hero in the third. Be a mechanic."

I sat in my stall and didn't look at my phone. I closed my eyes and visualized the north end. The gray coat, the glasses, the guy who calculated vectors to keep me calm.

He's there, I told myself. *He showed up.*

Third period.

Stonehill sensed the equalizer. They forechecked like hornets, crashing the blue paint, slashing at my pads after the whistle.

I stayed narrow. I stayed deep.

At 12:14, their winger broke loose on the left side. He wound up for a slap shot.

I telescoped out, cutting the angle. He fired—high glove, aiming for the ear hole.

I watched the puck all the way in. I forced my eyes to lock on the rotation of the rubber. Quiet eye.

My glove hand flashed out—not a windmill, a precise snare.

Snap.

I caught it clean. I held it for a beat, freezing the play, then flicked the puck to the ref with unnecessary spin.

I glanced up at Section 104 in time to see the scout make a note on his tablet. My dad leaned over and said something to him, looking satisfied.

See? I thought. *Singular.*

But I wasn't doing it for them.

Time bled out. The clock ticked down: 2:00... 1:30... 1:00.

Stonehill pulled their goalie. Six skaters against our five.

"Empty net!" Ryan yelled. "Heads up!"

The chaos increased. Bodies everywhere. Sticks hacking.

The puck came back to the point. Shot—blocked by Ryan. Rebound. Shot again—wide.

It bounced off the backboard and came out the other side. A Stonehill forward jumped on it. He had a half-open net.

I pushed across—RVH. I slammed my skate into the post and sealed the ice, leaning my shoulder into the iron.

I didn't dive. I didn't swim. I let the geometry do the work. I became a wall.

The shot jammed into my pad stack. I held the seal. I didn't give an inch.

The buzzer sounded.

3–1 Demons. Postseason alive.

The team mobbed me. Ryan slammed his helmet against my chest protector, screaming. "That's a statement, Monk! That is a statement!"

Javier punched my glove. "Stone. Cold."

I tapped both posts one last time.

I looked up to the north end.

The crowd was filtering out, a sea of navy blue. But he was still there.

Austen was standing. He wasn't cheering. He wasn't jumping up and down. He was watching me, his hands deep in his coat pockets.

He had been right about the eyes and the math. Most importantly, he was right about me not needing to be a hero; I needed to be a constant.

He raised a hand—a small, tentative wave.

I raised my blocker. *I see you.*

He smiled. Then left.

The locker room was a riot of towel snaps and victory playlist bass. I showered fast, skipping the beer Ryan offered.

I needed to get to the lobby. I needed to find Austen and explain everything—the dad, the pressure, the fear. I needed to tell him he was the only constant I actually cared about.

Grabbing my bag, hair still wet, I pushed through the double doors.

The lobby was packed. I scanned the edges.

There.

Austen was waiting by the trophy case, hands in his pockets, looking out of place in the sea of jerseys. He saw me and straightened. He took a half-step forward.

I started toward him. "Austen!"

"Luke!"

The voice boomed from my right. A heavy hand clamped onto my shoulder—the bad one. I flinched.

Rick Carter stood there, grinning like he'd shut out Stonehill himself. He was wearing his old NHL leather jacket, smelling of expensive cologne and stadium beer.

"Hell of a game, kid," he said, shaking my shoulder. "That glove hand? That's the money maker."

"Dad," I said, trying to pull away. "My shoulder—"

"Is fine. Adrenaline handles it." He didn't let go. He turned, gesturing to the man beside him. "You remember Gulliver Vane."

The Minnesota scout nodded, slick and polished. "Good to see you again, Luke. Your father was right about your recovery time. Impressive."

"Thank you," I said, my eyes darting past them.

Austen had stopped moving. He was standing ten feet away, watching.

"We're going to dinner," Dad announced. "The Steakhouse on Main. Gulliver wants to talk about the summer schedule. Development camp starts July first, but they want you in St. Paul by mid-June for conditioning."

"Dad, I can't tonight. I—"

"Nonsense. This is the offer, Luke. This is the next step." Dad's grip tightened. His smile didn't waver, but his eyes went hard. "Don't fumble the handoff."

I looked at Austen. He was watching the scene with that analytical detachment he used when the variables weren't adding up.

"I have plans," I said weakly.

Dad followed my gaze. He looked at Austen who started walking toward us—scruffy hair, worn coat, nobody special.

"With whom?" Dad asked, loud enough for Vane to hear. "Your roommate?"

The word hung there. *Roommate.*

Austen's chin lifted, waiting to see how I would respond.

I looked at Vane, watching me for signs of "entanglements." I looked at my dad, whose approval I'd been chasing since I was five years old.

I froze.

"He's... yeah," I muttered, "my roommate."

Austen flinched. It was small—a blink, a slight recoil—but I saw it.

My dad laughed, clapping me on the back. "Well, tell him you're busy. We're celebrating. Big leagues, Luke. Focus."

He steered me around. He physically turned me away from Austen.

"Come on," Dad said. "Car's out front."

I took a step. I let him move me.

I glanced back over my shoulder.

Austen wasn't looking at me anymore. He was looking at the floor, at the trophy case, at anything but me. He turned around.

He pushed through the exit doors and walked out into the cold.

I didn't chase him.

I got in my father's car.

Chapter 33
Game Misconduct

AUSTEN

I didn't go back to the dorm immediately.

I walked. I walked until the cold numbed my face and the wind off the creek dried the humiliating dampness in my eyes. I walked until I could treat the last hour as an error message rather than a memory.

Fact: Luke had played a perfect game.

Fact: His father had arrived with a scout.

Fact: When presented with the choice between his father's approval and my dignity, Luke had chosen the former. Fast.

Without a flinch.

I'm only his roommate.

The variables were run repeatedly in a search for a different outcome, a mitigating factor. None were found. The equation was balanced, and the result was zero.

Stony Creek Hall accepted my keycard at 11:15 p.m., the beep echoing in the deserted lobby.

Upstairs, Room 317 sat dark and silent. A relief.

The overhead light clicked on, washing the space in harsh artificial brightness.

Me: I need to get out of here. Can I stay with you?

Maya: Of course, what's going on?

Me: I'll explain when I see you. Be there in thirty.

From the closet, the duffel bag was retrieved. Essentials were packed with mechanical efficiency: toiletry bag, chargers, clothes for a few days. The zipper hissed shut just as the door opened.

Luke stumbled in. He was still wearing the nice jeans and the button-down shirt he'd worn to dinner, but he looked wrecked. His hair was wind-blown, his eyes wild. He smelled of expensive steakhouse and alcohol.

He saw the bag on my bed and froze.

"Austen," he breathed. "Don't."

I didn't look at him. I picked up the laptop power cord and coiled it. Loop, tuck, secure. "I'm staying at Maya's tonight."

"Please." He stepped into the room, reaching for me, then stopping short when I took a sharp step back. "Let me explain."

"There's no need for an explanation, Luke."

"It wasn't real," he rushed out, the words tumbling over each other. "What I said to them—it wasn't real. It was Vane. It was my dad. I froze. I needed to get them off my back so I could get out of there."

"You succeeded." I zipped the side pocket of the duffel. "You successfully erased me."

"I didn't erase you. I—I protected the offer." He ran a hand through his hair, frantic. "Vane is old school. My dad is... you know how he is. If they thought I was distracted, if they thought I was—"

"Queer?" I supplied.

He flinched. "Complicated. If they thought I was complicated."

"I am complicated," I said, finally looking at him. "I am a foster kid with a complex history and a scholarship I can't afford to lose. I am a male math major dating the male hockey goalie. That is the definition of complicated."

"I know. And I want that. I want us."

"No," I said calmly. "You want the *idea* of us. In this room. With the door locked and the blinds drawn. You want a constant you can keep on a shelf like a puck."

I walked over to the desk. The puck was there, sitting on the roster sheet.

I picked it up.

"You looked at me," I said, voice trembling for the first time. "He called me 'the roommate,' and you looked right at me, and you agreed."

"I panicked!"

"You calculated," I corrected. "You ran a risk assessment. Weighed the Minnesota contract against me, and I lost. That's fine. That's rational. Don't lie and say it was an accident."

Luke leaned back against the closed door, looking defeated. "They want me in St. Paul in June. Mid-June."

The timeline clicked into place. "So, you're leaving right after the semester ends and never coming back."

"I have to. It's the development camp. If I don't go, I lose the spot."

"And when were you going to tell me that?"

"Tonight. I was going to tell you tonight."

"After you introduced me as your roommate? After you let your dad laugh at me?"

He squeezed his eyes shut. "I screwed up. I know I screwed up. But I can fix it. I'll call Vane tomorrow. I'll tell my dad to back off. Don't leave."

"You're the one leaving, Luke."

I held out the puck. The NRU logo caught the overhead light.

He stared at it like it was radioactive. "No. I gave that to you. It's yours."

"Article five," I whispered, my voice trembling for the first time. "Constants keep us honest."

"Screw the articles."

"Take it." I grabbed his hand—his clammy, shaking hand—and forced the hard rubber disk into his palm. Curling his fingers over it, I said, "I'm not your constant anymore. You made sure of that."

I pulled my hand away. The loss of contact felt like a physical blow.

"Austen, please." His voice cracked, fracturing under the weight of the room. Tears pooled in his eyes, spilling over before he could blink them back. "I love you."

The words hung in the air, suspended in the fluorescent hum.

It should have been a victory. It should have been the solution to the equation. Instead, it felt like a casualty.

"I know," I said. And I did. That was the worst part. He loved me, but he feared his father more. "But love isn't enough to fix this."

I shouldered my duffel bag. The strap dug into my shoulder.

"I won't be your secret," I said, my voice thick. "I won't be the thing you hide in the dark. And I won't stay here and watch you lose this dream, Luke. Because if you miss the draft... if you fail... you will look at me one day and you will hate me for being the distraction."

"I could never hate you," he choked out.

"You would," I said gently. "And I love you too much to let that happen."

He stood there, clutching the puck so hard his knuckles turned white. He looked young. Terrified. Not the big star goalie people stare at on the Jumbotron, just a boy who'd been told his whole life that he had to be alone to be great.

"If you walk out," he whispered, "I don't know how to do this. The shoulder, the scouts, the pressure... I can't do it without you."

"You have to," I said. "It's the only way you'll know if the dream is actually yours, or just your father's."

I waited.

Slowly, painfully, he stepped aside.

I opened the door. The hallway air hit me, cooler, smelling of the same old floor wax and silence.

"Austen?"

I paused, hand on the frame. I squeezed my eyes shut, fighting the urge to turn around, to drop the bag, to fix him one last time.

"I'm sorry," he sobbed.

"I know."

I walked out, letting the door close gently behind me. The latch clicked into place like a bone breaking.

I walked down the hall, down the stairs, and out into the night.

I didn't look back at the window, knowing if I saw him standing there I would cave and go running back to him.

I just walked, letting the freezing air burn the tears off my face.

Chapter 34
Goals Against Average

LUKE

The room froze. This wasn't the productive calm of a Tuesday night. It was a void—a hollowed-out space where air and life used to be.

Austen's side of the room was empty. The desk was cleared—no highlighters, no laptop, no sticky notes color-coded by urgency. At some point, he'd even stripped his bed. There was no evidence that I'd ever had a roommate. I finally got the single I had thought I desperately wanted.

It had been three days. Ninety-six hours of dead air.

I sat on the edge of my bed, staring at the spot where the puck used to sit on his shelf. It was gone.

It was currently weighing down the front pocket of my hoodie. I kept reaching for it, running my thumb over the edge, terrified to let go of the only piece of him I had left.

I'm not your constant anymore.

My phone buzzed on the mattress.

Dad: *Gulliver sent the contract revisions. I'm at the hotel. Come by after practice.*

I let the screen go dark. Pushing myself off the bed, I stepped over a pile of laundry I hadn't bothered to sort just sitting in the middle of the floor. The room smelled wrong. The scent of Austen and his peppermint tea was gone. Instead, the room smelled like a locker room that had been cleaned out after a loss.

I grabbed my gear bag. Practice in twenty minutes.

I walked out, leaving the door unlocked. I didn't care who got in. There was nothing left to steal.

Practice was a disaster from the first whistle.

My legs were heavy, like I was skating in mud. My reaction time was off by milliseconds—an eternity in the crease.

Morales came down the wing, winding up for a slap shot. I saw it coming. I knew the angle. But when I tried to drop into the butterfly, my left knee caught an edge. I stumbled. The puck sailed over my shoulder, hitting the water bottle on top of the net with a hollow *ping*.

"Wake up, Carter!" Ryan yelled from the point. Half-joking, half-serious.

I fished the puck out of the net. "Bad edge," I muttered.

Next drill: Three-on-two rush.

The freshmen forwards were buzzing. Fast, hungry, and they could smell blood. They knew I was off.

A rookie named Miller carried the puck across the blue line. He telegraphed a pass to the slot. I cheated left, anticipating the one-timer.

Miller didn't pass. He snapped a wrist shot short-side.

I wasn't even close. The puck hit the back of the net before I'd fully squared up.

"That's two!" Coach Harper barked from center ice. "Move your feet, Carter!"

I slammed my stick against the post. The vibration rattled up my arms, a dull ache that settled in my bad shoulder.

Focus.

But I couldn't focus. All I could see was Austen's back as he walked out the door. All I could hear was my dad's voice saying *a friend*.

Third drill: Screen shots.

Ryan parked himself in front of me, his big frame blocking my view. The defenseman wound up at the point.

I tried to look around Ryan. I tried to find the release point.

Thwack.

The puck hit my chest protector, but I didn't squeeze it. It dropped to the ice—a juicy rebound sitting right in the paint.

Ryan spun around and tapped it in. Easy.

"Rebound control!" Harper shouted. "Where is your head, Carter?"

My head was in a hotel room with a contract I didn't want to sign. My head was in an empty dorm room where my life had imploded.

The fourth goal was the worst.

It was a dump-in from center ice. A floater. A nothing shot meant to get the puck deep.

I went out to play it, putting my stick down to stop the rim.

I missed.

The puck hopped over my blade, hit the boards at a weird angle, and ricocheted back toward the empty net.

I scrambled back, diving, desperate.

It crossed the line a split second before my glove covered it.

The rink went silent.

"Carter! Wake up!"

Coach Harper's voice cracked like a whip.

I was on my knees in the blue paint, staring at the puck inside the net.

"Sorry," I muttered, fishing it out.

"That's four," Harper said, skating over. She stopped at the top of the crease, looming over me. "Four soft goals in twenty minutes. You're playing like you've never seen rubber before."

"Bad bounce," I lied.

"Bad head," she corrected. She leaned down, voice dropping to a low, dangerous register. "I don't care what happened with the scouts. I don't care what happened with your boyfriend. You step into this crease, you lock it down. Or you sit."

Boyfriend. I almost laughed. Of course, she knew.

"I'm here," I said, gripping my stick until my gloves creaked.

"Physically, maybe. Mentally, you're in the parking lot." She pointed to the gate. "Get off the ice."

The rink went silent. Ryan froze in the faceoff circle. Javier stopped chewing his mouthguard.

"Coach?" I asked, stunned.

"You're a liability today, Carter. Go shower. Go sleep. Don't come back until you remember who you are."

She blew the whistle. "Decker! Net!"

Humiliation burned hot under my mask, paralyzing me for a heartbeat. Then I turned. Skating off, I kept my eyes locked on the ice—ignoring Ryan, ignoring the team.

The gate gave way under a frustrated kick. The tunnel swallowed me whole, the sound of Decker's pads hitting the ice echoing behind me like an accusation.

I didn't go to the showers. I didn't go to the dorm.

My feet carried me straight to Ridgeway Hall.

His schedule was burned into my memory: Tuesday, four p.m., Calculus tutoring.

Leaning against the lockers with my hoodie pulled up, I waited. Seeing him was the only priority. I needed to verify the variable still existed.

At 2:50, the door opened. Students filed out, complaining about proofs.

Austen came out last.

He looked tired. He was wearing his own coat, the collar turned up. He wasn't carrying his usual coffee. He looked smaller, somehow. Less distinct.

He turned toward the stairs and saw me.

He stopped. His hand tightened on the strap of his bag.

"Austen," I said. My voice sounded wrecked.

He looked at me—really looked at me—with an expression that wasn't anger. It was exhaustion.

"You're supposed to be at practice," he said.

"Coach kicked me off the ice."

He didn't blink. "That's statistically unlikely."

"I let in four soft goals. I can't focus." I took a step toward him. "Austen, please. The room is... I can't be in there without you."

"Then move," he said flatly. "Oh wait, you'll be moving soon, so it really doesn't matter."

"I'm trying to fix this."

"There's nothing to fix, Luke. You made a choice." He adjusted his bag. "And your choice had consequences for... both of us. Now, if you don't mind, I have a shift at the tutoring center. Excuse me."

He walked past me. He didn't speed up, and he didn't slow down.

"I haven't signed it!" I yelled after him.

He paused at the top of the stairs. He didn't turn around.

"That's between you and your investors," he said, before walking down the stairs and out of sight.

I drove to the Marriott on Route 9.

My dad was staying in a suite on the top floor—of course he was. Rick Carter didn't do standard rooms.

I banged on the door.

He opened it, wearing a hotel robe and holding a tumbler.

"Lucas! Early. Good. Gulliver emailed the conditioning schedule."

He waved me in. The room smelled of room service steak and scotch.

Papers were spread out on the coffee table—contracts, schedules, flight itineraries to St. Paul.

"Sit down," Dad said, gesturing to the sofa. "We need to go over the signing bonus structure. I got them to bump the housing stipend."

I didn't sit. I stood in the middle of the room, still wearing my practice sweats, my hair still a bird's nest on top of my head from sweat I hadn't washed off.

"I'm not going," I said.

Dad paused, glass halfway to his mouth. He laughed. "Cold feet? That's normal. Big league jitters."

"No," I said. "I mean I'm not going to St. Paul in June. And I'm not signing with Minnesota if you're the one holding the pen."

Dad set the glass down. The smile vanished. "Excuse me?"

"You came here," I said, my voice shaking but getting louder. "You came here and you embarrassed me. You humiliated the person who matters most to me."

"The roommate?" Dad scoffed. "Luke, grow up. That boy was a distraction. I did you a favor. You need focus. There will be plenty of guys for you mess around with in Minnesota. You need to get your singular focus back."

"I don't want to be singular!" I shouted.

The silence rang in the hotel room.

"I don't want to be you," I said, quieter now. "I don't want to sit in a big empty house with a trophy case and no one to talk to. I don't want to look at my stats and realize they're the only thing that loves me back."

Dad's face turned a mottled red. "Now listen here, you little shit."

The back of his hand slammed into my face, violent and heavy, snapping my neck back so hard I felt something pop. The room spun. I had to grab the dresser just to stay upright.

"I gave you everything. I built this path for you."

"You built it for yourself," I corrected. "You had an injury and it took you out of the game forever. But I'm not your second chance, Dad."

Walking to the coffee table, I looked at the contract—Minnesota Wild logo at the top, thick paper, life-changing money.

"I'm staying at Northern Ridge," I said, my voice steady for the first time in my life. "I'm finishing my degree. I'm playing my senior year here. If Minnesota still wants me after that, they can call *me*. Not you."

"You're throwing it away," Dad hissed, stepping into my space. "You walk out that door, you're on your own. You are cut off. No stipend. No rent. No support. You'll starve."

I looked at him. Really looked at him. I didn't see a safety net. I saw a cage.

I thought about the empty dorm room. I thought about the beige apartment with the maple tree Austen and I had looked at. I thought about the ledger sheets and the frozen peas and the way the quiet burned inside me when we lay together—not a terrifying silence, but a stabilized one.

"I don't need your stipend," I said.

I turned around and walked to the door.

"Luke!" Dad yelled, desperation cracking his voice. "Don't be an idiot! You're nothing without this!"

I opened the door; just turned the handle.

"No," I said, looking back one last time. He looked small standing there, red-faced and shaking, but I didn't feel the old fear. Just exhaustion. "I'm just done being your investment."

I stepped out and pulled the door shut. It clicked into place—a soft, final sound.

I didn't bother with the elevator. I raced down the ten flights of stairs, cutting off my dad's string of curses behind me. When I hit ground level, I exited a side door, catching my breath in the biting wind.

My truck was parked in the back row. I reached for the door handle, but my hands were shaking so violently the keys slipped through my fingers. They hit a pile of dirty slush and skittered underneath the chassis.

"Come on," I hissed, dropping to my knees. The freezing wet soaked through my.

I swept my hand blindly through the muck until my fingers brushed cold metal. I snatched the keys up, wiped them on my hoodie, and threw the door open. I fell into the driver's seat, jamming the key into the ignition before the door was even closed.

The engine roared to life—a rough, familiar rumble that usually calmed me. Not tonight. I gripped the steering wheel, squeezing until my knuckles turned white, trying to force the tremors to stop. The adrenaline crash—the physical cost of telling Rick Carter "no" for the first time in twenty-one years. My chest heaved, lungs burning as if I'd played a triple-overtime period.

I pulled out of the parking lot, tires spinning on a patch of black ice before gripping the pavement.

I didn't go back to the dorm. The dorm was a dead end.

I drove toward the bridge.

The windshield wipers slapped back and forth, clearing a fresh layer of wet, heavy snow. The heater blasted air that smelled like burned dust, but I couldn't stop shivering.

What do I say?

I rehearsed the opening line a dozen times as I sped down Route 9.

I'm sorry. No, too small.

I love you. I'd said that in Ridgeway, and he'd walked away. Words weren't enough. Austen dealt in proofs. He needed evidence.

I didn't sign it, I whispered to the empty cab. *I walked away. I chose my constant.*

The wipers slapped back and forth, hypnotic and useless against the wet April snow. The truck fishtailed slightly on a patch of slush, and my heart didn't even jump.

That was the problem. I was numb. My hands were gripping the wheel so hard my forearms ached, but my brain was somewhere back in that hallway, screaming at my father.

I blew through a red light and heard car horns blaring at me.

Pull over, I told myself. *You're a hazard.*

I couldn't drive like this. My adrenaline was spiking, looking for a physical outlet that wasn't there. I needed to hit something. I needed to sprint until I tasted copper.

I saw the sign for the access road. There was a running trail that looped under the bridge and followed the creek—a three-mile circuit I used for conditioning in the off-season. I didn't care if it meant running in six inches of snow, I needed to move.

I wrenched the wheel to the right, tires crunching over the gravel of the maintenance lot. A sign read, *No Parking After Dusk.* I didn't care about the parking ban. I killed the engine, the sudden silence ringing in my ears.

Air. I just needed air. The urge to run until my legs gave out and the static in my head cleared was overwhelming.

The door flew open with a shove, dumping me out into the cold. The wind cut through my hoodie, biting and real. Sucking in a sharp, freezing breath, I scanned the darkness for the trailhead.

The path ran parallel to the bridge structure before ducking under it. I glanced up at the steel span above me, just checking the distance, checking the terrain.

I froze.

The bridge should have been empty. No one stood on a wind-blasted overpass in a snowstorm.

But there was a silhouette at the midpoint of the span. A figure in a gray wool coat, standing perfectly still, looking down at the frozen creek like he was calculating the drop.

My breath hitched.

I didn't run because I needed the exercise. I didn't run to clear my head.

I ran because I knew that coat.

"Austen!" I screamed, the sound torn away by the wind.

I scrambled up the embankment, boots slipping in the mud, and sprinted toward him.

Chapter 35
Undefined Variable

AUSTEN

Maya's apartment was a study in entropy.

Her living room was a riot of clashing textiles, half-finished art projects, and the lingering scent of chai and acrylic paint. Warm. Welcoming. Objectively a safe harbor.

But for the last four nights, I had been sleeping on her lumpy velvet sofa, and my spine was a crooked integral sign.

I sat up, pushing off the heavy knit blanket. Eight p.m. on Tuesday.

On the coffee table, my laptop sat open to the NHL prospect tracker. I hadn't meant to load the Catapult data. Muscle memory. A glitch in the algorithm.

I stared at the data from the team. Carter's data stopped about half-way through practice. I clicked open the notes section, where the assistant coach took diligent notes about qualitative player behavior that could be balanced against the quantitative.

Goals Against Average (GAA, Trending): 3.45 (Last three sessions).

The numbers didn't make sense. Luke's baseline GAA was 1.95. A deviation of this magnitude suggested mechanical failure. Or, more likely, a processor error.

"Stop looking at the stats," Maya said.

I jumped. She was standing in the kitchenette doorway, holding two mugs. She wasn't wearing her usual bright colors; she wore a gray sweater, mirroring the mood that had settled over the apartment since I arrived.

"I am merely observing data trends," I lied, closing the tab.

"You're pain-shopping." She set a mug of mint tea down on a coaster for me—the only orderly thing in the room. "He's tanking, Austen. Everyone knows it. Ryan texted me Harper kicked him off the ice today."

My chest gave a painful, traitorous squeeze. "That is his problem to solve. He prioritized the Minnesota contract."

"He hasn't signed it."

I looked up. "What?"

"Ryan said the scout sent it to Luke's dad. Luke hasn't actually signed it yet." Maya sat on the armchair, pulling her knees up. "Data. Thought you should know."

I picked up the tea. Hot, scalding my fingers.

Unsigned.

Why? He had the offer.

The equation should be balanced.

Unless the variable he removed—me—had been bearing more structural load than he calculated.

"I can't stay here tonight," I said.

Maya frowned. "Austen, you're welcome as long as you need. The couch isn't great, but—"

"It's not the couch." I stood up, the restlessness that had been vibrating under my skin for ninety-six hours finally peaking. "It's the... I can't... I can't think here."

"So where are you going? The dorm?"

"No." I couldn't go back to the dorm. Not while he was there. That would be worse.

"The library," I said. "Ridgeway Hall. I just need to go somewhere and get lost in my work."

Maya looked at me with sad, knowing eyes. "Work isn't going to fix it, Austen."

"Probably not. But work is..." My voice trailed off as I grabbed my coat. "Work is predictable."

"Okay," she said softly. "Go work. Take the spare key. If something changes, just text me so I don't call the police and have them send a search party."

I nodded and walked out into the cold night. The wind whipped around the corners of the academic buildings, stinging my face, but I welcomed it. The cold was a known quantity.

A curt nod ended the interaction, and the cold night took over. The wind whipped around the corners of the academic buildings, stinging my face, but the sensation was welcome. The cold was a known quantity.

Ridgeway Hall was the only logical destination. The ID scanner beeped me in, and the stairs led straight to the fourth floor—the Deep Quiet zone.

My usual carrel was empty. Secluded. Silent. Exactly the controlled environment needed to re-establish a baseline.

The laptop came out. The thesis draft loaded on the screen. My hands found the home row, ready to sink into the comforting logic of higher mathematics.

But the cursor blinked.

It pulsed rhythmically against the white page. Attempts to define a manifold failed; every thought kept looping back to a Boston lobby. To a secluded dorm room. To a game-day puck sitting on a desk.

The blinking line on the screen didn't stop. It was waiting for a value I couldn't provide.

In programming, an undefined variable is an error. A symbol that has been referenced but holds no value. It breaks the code. It stops the execution.

For the last five days, I had been living as a syntax error.

I took a breath and got to work.

My laptop screen was a blur of code and thesis revisions, but I hadn't typed a character in twenty minutes.

I pulled out a legal pad and sketched out a formula for my life. I attempted to calculate the efficiency (E) of the routine:

$E = (A+B)/C$

Where:

A (Solitude) = 1

B (Academic Focus) = ∞

C (Emotional Stability) = 0

Result: Calculation failed. Divide by zero error.

I closed the laptop. The magnetic latch snapped shut—a sharp, final sound that echoed in the empty room.

It was exactly what I had asked for. I had asked for no secrets. I had asked for clarity.

Luke had given it to me. He had chosen the contract, his dad, and the "singular" path that led him to Minnesota. I had given him back the puck.

So, why did it feel less like clarity and more like amputation?

The equation wasn't making sense. I couldn't solve for E. I needed another change of venue. Maybe fresh air would help me come up with a logical solution. I packed my bag. I put on my coat and walked out into the corridor.

Ridgeway smelled like chalk and floor wax. It used to smell like a sanctuary. Now, it smelled like an empty building where people came to work alone.

I walked back to Stony Creek Hall.

The wind was biting, cutting through my scarf. I kept my head down, avoiding eye contact with the groups of students heading toward the bars.

I swiped into the dorm. The lobby was deserted.

The elevator ride to the third floor took seventeen seconds. I counted them.

I walked down the hall. I passed the RA's door. I passed the EDM guy's door (silent for once).

I reached Room 317.

I unlocked it and stepped inside.

The room was dark. I flicked the switch.

The light flooded the space, revealing the architecture of absence.

Luke's side of the room was still there, physically. His bed was made—hastily, the blanket crooked. His desk was cluttered with the debris of a student athlete: a roll of black tape, a half-empty water bottle, a stack of flashcards for his business ethics class.

But the *presence* was gone.

The air was stale. It lacked the scent of his body wash and the faint, cold smell of his gear bag.

I walked to my desk. I set my bag down.

I looked at the spot on the shelf where the game-day puck used to sit.

Wood now. A dusty circle in the laminate.

I sat down in my chair. I spun it around to face the room.

We had signed a constitution. We had established rules. *Quiet hours. Guest protocols. Radiator management.*

Now, the silence was absolute.

The radiator clanked—one sharp, metallic bang.

I didn't flinch. I didn't grab the wrench. I stared at it.

A sharp knock on the door made me jump.

"RA on rounds," a voice called.

The door pushed open. Devon stood there, holding a clipboard. He looked bored, scanning the room for fire hazards or illegal hot plates.

His eyes landed on me, then swept to my side of the room. He took in the empty bed, the vacant desk.

Devon frowned, tapping his pen against the clipboard. He looked at Luke's side of the room—posters still up, dirty laundry overflowing the hamper, hockey bag shoved in the corner.

He looked at mine: stripped mattress, bare desk, two duffel bags sitting by the door. "You moving out?"

"Temporarily," I lied, hoisting the strap of the heavier bag onto my shoulder. "I'm staying at Maya's. Need a quiet environment for the thesis."

Devon let out a low, sympathetic whistle. "Damn. Kayla owes me ten bucks. She bet Carter would be the one to bail first."

I froze, my hand hovering over the light switch. "Bail on the room?"

"On the relationship," Devon said, casual as if discussing the cafeteria menu. "We figured the draft pressure would make him snap. Didn't think you'd be the one to walk."

"Relationship," I repeated.

"Yeah. Team 'Lusten' is taking a huge hit in the polls today." Devon smirked, checking a box on his form. "Kayla wanted 'Ausuke,' but I told her that sounded like a sneeze."

"You... knew."

"Lovell, you guys share a twelve-by-twelve room and you look at him like he hung the moon. The walls are thin. It hasn't been a secret since the semester started. Kayla had it pegged last October."

My stomach dropped. The "secret" we'd been destroying ourselves to protect—the potential scandal I was removing so he could have his shot—hadn't been a secret at all. It was a campus-wide spectator sport.

"Right," Devon said, oblivious to the fact that he had just dismantled my entire logic for leaving. "Well. Hang in there, man. If you ever need to talk, that's what I'm here for."

He closed the door.

I stood in the silence, staring at Luke's unmade bed. I was leaving to save him from a liability that apparently didn't exist.

I hit the light switch, plunging his mess and my emptiness into the dark, and walked out.

Maya: *I'm at Buckman Grill. Come eat. You can't photosynthesize despair.*

I stared at the text. Maya was a good friend. She was trying to force a variable change.

Me: *Not hungry. Working.*

Maya: *Liar. I saw your light go on. Open the door or I'm picking the lock.*

I sighed. I stood up and opened the door.

Maya was there, hand raised to knock. She lowered it, looking me up and down.

"You look like a Victorian widow," she said, stepping inside without asking. She was holding a paper bag from the bagel shop.

"I am tired," I said, closing the door.

"You're miserable." She sat on Luke's bed—a violation of territory I didn't have the energy to police. She opened the bag and pulled out a bagel with cream cheese. "Eat."

I took it. I wasn't hungry, but arguing with Maya was an energy expenditure I couldn't afford.

"You're still spiraling," Maya said, watching me dismantle the bagel instead of eating it.

"I am processing."

"Is this about practice this afternoon? I told you, everyone has a bad day. Getting pulled from a scrimmage doesn't mean his career is over."

"It wasn't a scrimmage," I corrected, staring at the small pieces of bagel. "It was a fundamental drill. He shouldn't be missing those."

"Well, he did. Because he's miserable." She took a sip of coffee. "But that's not why you look like you're about to throw up."

"Devon dropped by," I said. Maya's face blanked. "Our RA."

"And?"

"He asked if 'Lusten' was breaking up. Apparently, Kayla had money on us making it to finals."

Maya choked on her coffee. "Excuse me?"

"The whole campus knew, Maya. Devon said we weren't exactly stealth. They had a pool going. They even had team names."

I looked out the window at the dark quad, feeling a bitter laugh building in my chest.

"Did you know about this?" I asked her.

"God, no," Maya said. "I would have told you if someone had ever mentioned that to me. Honestly, now I'm a little peeved no one talked to me so I could have gotten in on the action. And for the record, I would have bet on you."

"We calculated every angle," I whispered. "We expended so much energy, so much anxiety, trying to control the narrative. We were terrified of the fallout if we were exposed. And the whole time... the variable was already out of the equation. It was public domain."

"Austen..."

"I left to protect a secret that didn't exist," I said, my voice hardening. "I broke my own heart to save him from a scandal that was already just... campus gossip."

"You didn't leave just for the scandal," Maya said softly.

"I left because I was a distraction. And clearly, based on his performance at practice, I was right."

"You're an idiot," she said, but without heat.

I turned back to her. "Excuse me?"

"You think you were the distraction? You were the support structure. You were the only thing keeping him vertical under his dad's pressure. And now you're both falling apart."

"I am not falling apart," I insisted. "I am maintaining a 4.0 GPA and proceeding with my thesis."

"You're tearing a bagel into subatomic particles and analyzing a breakup like it's a math problem," she pointed out.

I looked at the decimated bagel. I hated that she was right.

"He was ashamed, Maya. That wasn't about the team knowing. That was about him knowing. He couldn't look at his dad and choose me."

"I know," she said, standing up and brushing crumbs off her jeans. "And that sucks. He panicked. But don't sit here and pretend you left for *his* good. You left because it hurt too much to stay."

She grabbed her backpack.

"I'm going to the library. If you want to come be grumpy in public, you're welcome."

"I'll stay," I said.

She nodded. "Okay. But check your equation again, Austen. I think you're solving for the wrong outcome."

She left.

The door clicked shut, leaving me alone with the silence and the cold, hard realization that I couldn't calculate my way out of this.

Solving for the right outcome.

The outcome I wanted was stability. Safety. A life where I didn't have to wonder if I was a temporary placement.

But looking at the empty room, I realized something terrifying.

Stability without him felt exactly like the foster homes. Safe. Clean. Ordered.

And completely, devastatingly lonely.

I couldn't stay my former room. The walls pressed in. The silence was too loud.

I grabbed my coat.

I didn't go to the library or Ridgeway.

I walked toward the edge of campus. I walked past the science buildings, past the darkened arena.

I walked until the pavement turned into the steel grating of the footbridge.

The wind was brutal out here, whipping off the frozen creek below. It stung my face. It made my eyes water.

I stopped at the midpoint.

I gripped the railing, the cold metal biting through my gloves.

I closed my eyes.

Constants are named.

I had named him. Even if he hadn't named me back, I had named him.

Standing in the wind, I realized that I couldn't un-name a constant. You can remove it from the equation, but the math will never balance again.

I stood there, shivering, waiting for a logic that would fix this.

But there was no logic. There was the wind, the dark, and the crushing realization that I was waiting for a variable that wasn't coming back.

Headlights swept across the far end of the bridge.

A large, gas-guzzling monstrosity pulled up to the curb—illegally parking in the maintenance zone.

The engine cut.

I turned, my breath catching in my throat.

The door opened.

A figure stumbled out. No coat. A gray hoodie and jeans.

He started running.

Chapter 36
Overtime

AUSTEN

Not a jog—a frantic, slipping sprint. His sneakers skidded on a patch of ice; he caught himself on the railing, knuckles white, and kept coming.

My heart stopped, then restarted at double speed.

Luke.

He reached me, chest heaving, his breath exploding in white clouds. He looked frantic. His hair was a mess, blown wild by the wind. His face was flushed from the cold or the run, his eyes wide and dark and terrified.

He stopped two feet away, gripping the railing as if he might fall off the earth if he let go. He stared at me like I was a ghost he hadn't expected to find haunting the machine.

"You're here," he choked out.

"I'm here," I said, my voice flat. I didn't move toward him. I kept my hands in my pockets, protecting myself from the cold and from the gravity of him. "Maya said the contract came through. Ryan told her it was a done deal, you just needed to sign it."

"It was," Luke said.

"Why are you here? You should be celebrating. You should be with the scouts. Or your father."

"I left them."

"For a breather? Before you sign your life away?"

"I didn't sign it."

The words hung between us, suspended in the swirling snow.

I stared at him, the data not computing. "What?"

"I didn't sign it," he repeated, louder this time, shouting over a gust of wind. He let go of the railing and stepped closer, invading my personal space, radiating heat and desperation. "I told my father I wasn't going to St. Paul. I told him I was finishing my degree."

He took another step, his boots crunching on the frozen grit.

"And I told my dad to go to hell."

My brain stalled. The variables weren't adding up. "Luke. The camp. The contract. That is the optimal path."

"I don't care," he said violently. "I don't care about the camp if it means I have to be... *singular*. I don't want to be singular. I hate being singular."

He reached for me, his hands hovering, shaking slightly.

"I tried, Austen. For four days, I tried to do it the way he wanted. I shut everything out. And you know what happened? I let in four goals today. Harper kicked me off the ice."

"I heard," I whispered.

"How?"

"Ryan by way of Maya. And I may have looked at the Catapult data."

"Those two are the best gossip machine on campus, I swear."

"You might be surprised," I said with a roll of my eyes, but I doubted he could see it in the dark.

"What do you mean?"

"Well, let's just say it's been brought to my attention that people have been placing bets on our relationship."

"What?" Luke stood there not saying anything for a minute. "Ohh, Coach made an offhanded comment about my 'boyfriend.' I just thought it was a slip of the tongue." We stood in silence, as the air whipped around us.

"So, you turned down Minnesota," I said, testing the weight of the sentence. "You risked your career."

"I postponed it. If they want me next year, they can call me. Me. Not Rick Carter's son." He swallowed hard. "But I can't do next year without you. I can't do *tomorrow* without you."

"I'm not a variable you can plug back in, Luke," I said, my voice trembling. "You erased me. In that lobby, you looked right at me and you erased me."

"I know," he whispered. "I know I did."

"Why?" I demanded. "Why was it so easy?"

"It wasn't easy," he said, his voice breaking. "It was reflex. It was twenty years of conditioning. My dad... he doesn't get angry, Austen. He dismisses. He liquidates. If you aren't useful to the goal, you don't exist."

He tightened his grip on my coat, pulling me a fraction of an inch closer.

"When he saw you... when he looked at you like you were nothing... I froze. I thought if I claimed you, he'd destroy you. He'd find a way to hurt your scholarship, or your placement, or make you feel small. And I couldn't watch that. So, I hid you."

"You didn't hide me to protect me," I said, tears spilling over, hot against the icy wind. "You hid me to protect yourself. To protect the approval."

Luke flinched. He looked down, then back up, his eyes wet.

"You're right," he admitted. "I wanted him to look at me and see a winner. Once. I wanted to be the son he bragged about."

He took a ragged breath.

"But I got it. Tonight. I was standing there getting ready to sign my life away and I felt... nothing. I realized his pride weighs nothing. It's hollow. But when you look at me? When you tell me I made a good save? That has weight."

He stepped closer, pressing his forehead against mine. His skin was freezing, but his breath was hot.

"I'm sorry," he whispered. "I am so sorry I was a coward. I am sorry I made you feel like a secret. You aren't a secret, Austen. You're the headline." He turned and yelled, "Austen Lovell, I love you!" The echoes reverberated out across the frozen creek.

I closed my eyes. The cold wind bit at my cheeks, but the heat from his hands was grounding.

Constants aren't found, Maya had said. *They're named.*

He had named it. He had chosen it over the biggest variable in his life.

"You shouted?" I asked softly.

"I shouted." A ghost of a smile touched his lips

I let the words settle. "Your dad's going to make your life difficult."

"He's been making my life difficult since I was six." Luke's voice was steady now, certain. "At least this time it's for something I chose. He promised to cut me off, but I don't care. I'd rather work three jobs and go to college without hockey if it means I get to stay here with you."

"You froze your career."

"I have time."

"You froze your ears," I whispered, brushing my thumb over his cheekbone. Ice cold. "Where's your hat?"

Luke ignored the question. He reached into his hoodie pocket, his hand trembling as it pulled out something.

"I carried this for four days," he whispered, his voice rough. "I didn't want to look at it, but I couldn't put it down."

He reached out and pressed the puck into my gloved hand.

"It belongs on your shelf, Austen. Nowhere else."

He turned his face into my palm. "Take me home, Austen. Please."

Home.

Not the dorm. Home.

"Okay," I said.

He kissed me.

It wasn't like the first time in the dark, tentative and testing. And it wasn't like the desperate, hidden kisses in the hotel room.

This was an anchor. Heavy and sure and claimed everything. He kissed me like he was trying to breathe for both of us. He kissed me like he was rewriting the last four days.

I buried my hands in his wind-tangled hair, pulling him down. His arms wrapped around me, crushing the air out of my lungs, lifting me off my toes. Messy and desperate and cold—teeth clashing, noses bumping—but the heat radiating between us was enough to melt the ice on the creek below.

I tasted the salt of his tears and the coffee on his breath. I felt the shudder run through him as he let go.

When we broke apart, he was shivering violently. Adrenaline crash.

We stood there, foreheads pressed together, breathing clouds into the frozen air. "I thought you were gone," I whispered. "I thought I'd calculated it all wrong."

"You calculated it right," he said. "I was just too scared to run the proof."

I pulled back enough to look at him. His face was red from cold and crying, his hair a disaster. He looked terrible. He looked like everything I wanted.

"I need you to understand something," I said. "I'm not going to be a secret anymore. If we do this—if we iterate—it has to be real. Public. Named."

"I know." He didn't hesitate. "I'm done hiding. Even if it costs me."

"It might."

"You're worth more than the cost."

"Car's over there," he chattered, jerking a thumb toward the curb.

"You parked in a tow zone."

"I didn't care."

I grabbed his hand—intertwining fingers. "Let's get you out of the wind before you get frostbite and I have to explain to Harper why her starter is compromised."

We reached the truck. I pushed him into the passenger seat because his hands were shaking too hard to drive.

I got in the driver's side. The engine was still warm. I started the truck and the heater blasted, slowly thawing us. Luke had his head back against the seat, eyes closed, but his hand was on my thigh—anchoring, not hiding.

"What happens tomorrow?" I asked.

"I call Vane and tell him I'll reconsider next year. On my terms." He opened his eyes. "And I tell Harper I'm staying. And then..."

"Then?"

"Then we get breakfast at Harbor Commons, hold hands in public, and make everyone jealous. And tomorrow we look at that apartment on Elm Street." He squeezed my leg. "If you still want to."

"I still want to."

"Where to?" I asked, putting it in gear.

Luke looked at me, his eyes heavy with exhaustion but clear for the first time in weeks.

"Maya's," I said. "I need to move my stuff back."

I smiled, putting the truck in drive.

Chapter 37
Final Score

LUKE

Two weeks later, the hallway outside the rink smelled like damp tape and the distinct, stale air of the end of a season.

We'd lost in the conference semifinals—a double-overtime heartbreaker that still stung—but the locker room didn't feel heavy. It felt finished.

I slung my gear bag over my good shoulder—a solid zero on the pain scale for three days running—and pushed through the double doors into the lobby.

Coach Harper was waiting by the trophy case, arms folded, jacket draped over one arm.

I stopped. "Coach."

She lifted her chin. "Got a minute, Carter?"

"Sure." I set the bag down.

Her expression stayed even. "Exit interviews start Monday, but I didn't want this to sit. You came here to keep pucks out and steady the room. You did both."

She jerked her head toward the rink. "That net's yours to lose next fall."

The words settled behind my sternum, warm and heavy. "Thank you, Coach."

"Don't make me regret the marker color," she said, almost smiling. "Grades solid?"

"Everything's As and Bs this semester... despite all the drama."

"Miracles happen." She offered her hand; I shook it, grip firm. "Enjoy the off-season, Carter. You earned it."

She walked off. I stood there for a second, listening to the silence of the rink. I hadn't signed with Minnesota. I hadn't gone to the development camp. But I had the net, I had the grades, and I had a summer in Cold Harbor that belonged entirely to me.

Footsteps clattered behind me. Ryan jogged up, winter coat flapping. "Coach give you the speech?"

"Short version."

He grinned and flicked my ear. "You still owe me fries for making you less of a robot."

"Joint account handles debts now."

Ryan's laugh echoed down the vestibule. "Text me when you're free. We'll celebrate nobody turning into a pumpkin. Tell Austen I said hi."

"Will do."

Ryan headed for the parking lot.

I shouldered my bag again—lighter now—and stepped into the late afternoon chill.

North Point at 8:30 p.m. was a different world—lights dimmed, only one grill open.

I spotted Austen at our regular table. Maya sat across from him, headphones in, laptop haloing her face.

Austen's eyes tracked me from the moment I cleared the sneeze guard. No guarded tilt, no calculation. Recognition.

I slid into the chair beside him. "Made good on fries," I said, dropping a cardboard boat of sweet potato wedges between us.

He nudged a cup my way. "Extra milk, one sugar."

I stole a fry. "Coach told me the crease is mine next season."

"Variable promoted to constant," he said, soft enough that only I heard.

Maya peeled off her headphones. "Is that math flirting? Because I'm officially charging a finder's fee."

Austen handed her half the fries. "Consulting fee paid."

She accepted with a grin. "You two signing the lease agreement tomorrow?"

I glanced at Austen. "Eleven, right?"

"Landlord confirmed." He opened his planner—actual paper, color-coded tabs—and circled the slot in green.

Ryan banged through the doors, Javier in tow. They spotted us and detoured, dropping a slice of plain pizza onto our table like tribute.

"O-kay, nerd conclave," Ryan announced. "Who's grading me for calories?"

"Three hundred sixty," Austen said without looking up.

Javier clapped my shoulder. "Coach said you're stone next season if you don't break."

"Planning on neither," I answered.

He tilted his head at Austen. "You're the contingency."

"I prefer 'statistical safeguard,'" Austen countered, mouth twitching.

We ate until the trays were empty. When the room emptied out, Austen stacked our trash with clinical precision.

"Home?" he asked.

"Yeah." I brushed my knuckles against his. He didn't pull away.

The apartment building sat three blocks off campus, beige siding and a couple of stubborn snow piles along the curb that just wouldn't melt.

The landlord—an older woman named Nora—met us on the porch at 11:02 holding a manila envelope.

"You boys have the cashier's check?" she asked, cutting straight to the chase.

"Bank certified," I confirmed, patting my pocket.

"Good. Top-floor walk-up, heat included, utilities extra. I cleaned the carpets yesterday, so take your shoes off."

We climbed narrow stairs that creaked like honest admissions.

Inside, the place smelled of damp shampoo and fresh paint. Living room: twelve by fourteen. Kitchen: galley style. Bedrooms identical. It was empty, echoing, and waiting.

Austen did one last sweep. He opened every cabinet door, tested the water pressure in the kitchen sink, and checked the window locks.

"Upper bound acceptable," he concluded, wiping his hands on his jeans.

"Meaning?" Nora asked, squinting at him.

"It means the structural integrity passes his baseline tolerances," I translated. "And the bedroom walls share no direct line with the bathroom pipes. He hates midnight plumbing noises."

Nora looked at me. "He's thorough."

"He's got math brain; I've got goalie ears. We're a high-maintenance pair."

I walked to the living room window. A maple tree scratched the glass. There was space for my stickhandling mat and his desk. Beige walls, beige carpet—nothing special. Yet the thought that this space was ours—paid for with our savings, signed for with our names.

Nora spread the paperwork out on the laminate counter. "Standard twelve-month lease. Sign at the X, initial at the bottom. Since the unit is vacant, pro-rated rent starts today."

We signed. The scratching of the pen sounded louder than anything I'd heard in days.

I pulled the envelope from my pocket and handed over the check. Deposit plus first month. It was a decent chunk of change, but I didn't feel the loss. I felt the gain.

Nora checked the amount, nodded, and dropped two silver keys into my palm. The metal was cold and heavy.

"Welcome home," she said. "The place is yours. You can start moving in right now if you want."

Austen looked at the keys in my hand, then at the empty room.

"Variable secured," he said, a small, genuine smile breaking through. "I'll go get the bags from the truck."

Back at Stony Creek Hall, the adrenaline faded into a quiet, steady hum. Austen spread our carbon copy of the lease on the communal table, highlighters fanned out like surgical tools.

Even though he'd read it and reread it and we'd signed it an hour ago—he was now categorizing it.

"Rent schedule is codified," he said, capping a neon yellow pen. "I've set up a shared calendar alert for the twenty-eighth of every month."

"We good on the utilities?" I asked, leaning against the desk.

"Projected costs are within variance. I will pick up extra TA hours in April to cover the internet installation. And I've made it clear I'm available all summer."

"I've got backup fund money," I reminded him. "Since I'm not spending it on a one-way flight to St. Paul anymore, it's going into the rent fund. And I was asked to help with the hockey campus run on campus this summer, so I'll be bringing in cash there, too."

He hesitated, looking at the spreadsheet he was building, then nodded. "Acceptable."

I reached into my pocket and pulled out the second silver key Nora had given me.

"Here," I said. "Yours."

I held it out. It wasn't a grand gesture, but it felt heavier than a championship ring.

Austen didn't just take it. He closed his fingers over mine, pressing the jagged metal into my palm for a second before sliding it free.

"Access granted," he whispered.

We both exhaled, the tension of the last week finally unspooling.

My phone buzzed on the desk, vibrating against the wood. I glanced down.

A number I didn't recognize. Arizona area code.

Mom: *Your father called. Said you turned down Minnesota. I just wanted to say I'm proud of you, Lucas. It takes courage to choose yourself.*

I stared at the screen. Thirteen years of birthday cards with no money and mindfulness quotes, and this was the most she'd ever said.

Me: *Thanks, Mom.*

I almost left it there. But something made me add

Me: *Maybe I could visit this summer. If you want.*

The reply came faster than I expected.

Mom: *I'd like that. Bring your friend.*

I showed Austen the screen. He read it twice. "She called me your friend," he said carefully.

"She'll learn." I pocketed the phone. "We iterate, right?"

He smiled—that rare, open one. "We iterate."

Austen reached into his bag with his free hand.

"One more thing," he said, pulling out a thin, glossy booklet. "Mail came to Ridgeway yesterday."

He slid it across the communal table, right on top of the lease.

Journal of Quantitative Analysis in Sports—Spring Edition.

I picked it up. I flipped it open to the bookmarked page. There, on page forty-two, was the title: "Quantifying the Crease."

And below it: *By A. Lovell and A. R. Thorne.*

"You got published," I said, running my thumb over his name.

"Peer-reviewed and in print," Austen said, adjusting his glasses, though I could see the flush of pride on his neck. "Dr. Thorne sent a bottle of champagne. I'm saving it for move-in night."

I scanned the abstract. Charts. Graphs. And there, Figure 1A, was a wireframe diagram of a goalie in the butterfly.

Me.

"Subject G," I read aloud. "Anonymized for data integrity."

"Obviously," Austen said. "Can't have the academic community knowing I'm sleeping with the data set. It introduces bias."

"Bias?" I laughed, tossing the journal back onto the table next to our signed lease. "I think you mean 'competitive advantage.'" I wrapped my arms around his waist and drew him to me.

Austen smiled—that rare, open smile he saved for us. "Statistically speaking," he said, "it appears to be both."

I kissed him.

"Lunch before you grade the derivative apocalypse?" I asked, when we finally pulled away from air.

"Omelets. You're paying. Roommate initiation tax."

"Future roommate."

He locked the door to 317—habit, though we were moving out in three weeks.

As we turned toward the stairwell, the door across the hall opened. Devon stepped out, looking groggy, wearing a bathrobe and holding a shower caddy.

He stopped when he saw us. He looked at the lease paperwork sticking out of my jacket pocket. He looked at my hand, inches from Austen's.

Devon grinned. It wasn't the polite RA smile. It was real.

"Finally escaping the radiator?" he asked.

"Found a place on Elm," I said. "Top floor. No pipes."

"Nice." Devon shifted his caddy. "Glad you two figured things out. Kayla owes me twenty. Firmly betted on team "Auluk" (*Aw, look!*). You guys were the quietest room on the floor. I'm gonna miss the lack of drama."

"Oh, God, No." Luke said. "That's worse than Lusten or Carvell."

"It could have been Ausuke, but that just sounded indecent."

Austen snorted. "We had plenty of drama, Devon. We kept the amplitude low."

"Whatever you say, Math." Devon jerked his chin at us. "Good luck. Don't fail the finals."

"We won't," I said.

Devon headed for the showers. We walked side by side down the hall.

At the stairwell landing Austen stopped, fumbling with something in his coat.

The puck emerged.

"Choose a pocket," he said.

I held out the inside breast pocket of my jacket—right over the heart.

He slid the puck in, tapped it once like sealing a vault. "Keep us honest."

I grinned. "Post on the left, post on the right."

"Constant in the middle," he finished.

We descended the stairs, winter sun bouncing off salt-streaked windows. The future didn't feel like a scouting report anymore. It felt like overtime—manageable, familiar, and still up for grabs.

Outside, the spring breeze cut, but it wasn't cruel. Austen linked his fingers with mine. No checking the hallway for witnesses this time.

"Ready?" I asked.

He squeezed my hand once. "Direction pending," he said, smiling. "But yes."

About the author

Jason Wrench

Jason Wrench is the author of *12 Days of Murder* (November 2021) and *Till Death Do Us Wed* (February 2022); the Up on the Farm series: *Finding a Farmer* (August 2022), *Bewitched by the Barista* (September 2022), *Sanctuary for the Surgeon* (January, 2023), and *Catching the Composer* (May 2023); *Wolf Island* (October, 2022); and the Love and Liquidation Series: *Boy Bands and Bullets* (November 2023), *A Choreographed Coup* (April 2024), and *Rhythmic Reclamation* (June 2024) all with Pride Publishing. He's also the author of *The Veil, Jekyll/Hyde, Life on the Naughty List, or What the Elf!* (November 2024), and Shattering Securities (June 2025). And translated *Manor: A Novella by Karl Heinrich Ulrichs* (August 2024). And he's the man behind the cozy mystery pen name, J. J. Justice.

When he's not writing novels, he's a college professor at SUNY New Paltz in the Department of Communication. In that capacity, he's authored or edited twenty academic books, thirty-five plus research articles, and numerous chapters in other books.

In his downtime, he loves reading/writing, Broadway, coffee, and his puggle, Max (7-year-old) and Branch (6-year-old).

He's a member of the Authors Guild, Romance Writers of America, and the Textbook and Academic Author Association.

You can find his other works on his website: https://jasonwrench.com/

Romancing the Rookie

Book 2 - Tales from the Crease

Get Ready for Book Two: Romancing the Rookie
Coming March 2026

Romancing the Rookie Cover

Chapter 1: The Cold Read

Rowan

The air in the visitor's locker room tasted of old sweat and cold cement. Not a bad smell—familiar, an anchor in a world that had felt untethered too long. I dragged it in deep, letting the family smell of a locker room fill my lungs as I taped the blade of my stick. New team, new barn, same ritual. One full wrap around the toe, overlapping strips down the blade, a final pass of wax to keep the snow from building up.

Control what you can control.

My gear was a mismatched collection. Skates from a clearance sale, pants I'd had since juniors that somehow still fit, and a helmet—one good knock away from retirement—I'd found at a garage sale over the weekend. Everything black. Unbranded. Anonymous. Blending in was the whole point. For years, I'd been a walking billboard, every piece of equipment dictated by contract and color-coded for the camera. Now, for the first time in a decade, I wasn't Chase St. Clair, the kid from the cereal box and the front man for a hockey movie franchise. I wasn't number seventy-three, I was just a walk-on hopeful with a transfer transcript and a prayer.

Oakridge University had lost a player at the end of the fall semester. They needed a body to fill the roster. When the call went out for walk-ons, I thought, *might as well.*

I'd chosen Oakridge for a reason. Six hundred miles from Los Angeles, buried in the Northern California redwoods, small enough to stay invisible but still close to the ocean. That's what I needed. A place where I could finish my degree. Playing a sport I'd once before the industry hollowed it out, would be the icing on the cake.

A guy a few stalls down, younger and built like a vending machine, was re-taping his stick for the third time, hands trembling. The sound of ripping cloth echoed off the low ceiling. A freshman. He had that particular brand of terror in his eyes that only came from having your entire identity wrapped up in a game you weren't sure you were good enough to play at the collegiate level. I knew the feeling. I'd had a five-year head start on it.

"You Calloway?"

The voice came from my left. I glanced over. A player with 'Maddox' stitched onto his gloves was leaning against the lockers, already dressed. He wasn't a walk-on; his gear was pristine, all matching Oakridge University Ospreys navy blue and orange. A junior, maybe a senior, here to help run the tryout drills and size up the new meat.

I smoothed the wax on my blade. "Yeah."

"Great." He placed a mark next to my name on the clipboard. "I'm Reece Maddox, team captain." He didn't extend his hand. His eyes did a quick, dismissive scan of my equipment—the mismatched black, the worn padding, and the garage-sale helmet. I watched him file it away: *nobody.*

He flipped through a few pages on his clipboard. "So, it says here you've played a little before."

"A little." The truest and most dishonest thing I could say. The league I'd played in before going to Hollywood had been dismantled, my stats scrubbed from the internet along with my career. All that was left were the ghost-ship fan sites and the grainy YouTube clips from *Ice Kings 3: Dynasty's End.*

Maddox grunted, a sound that wasn't quite a welcome. "You seem a bit old for this."

"I'm not that old," I said. Twenty-three felt ancient in this room, but I'd seen thirty-year-old rookies grind their way onto NHL rosters. Age was just a number if your body cooperated.

Maddox grunted again. "So, why? Why do you want to be a walk-on?"

"Just transferred. Finished my associate's degree in December at Alpine County Community College. Finishing my BA in journalism here."

"Yeah, I don't really care about your life story. Why do you think you're better than the six other guys trying out for the same position?"

"I have experience. I know how to handle myself on the ice. I want to be a team player."

Maddox rolled his eyes like I'd given the worst answer on a job interview. Turning to the freshman. "That means you're Davies."

"Yes, sir. Captain, sir." The hulking kid's voice cracked on the second *sir*.

The guy seemed way out of his depth. Maddox was a shark, and the tank was about to become his chum. I'd skated with guys like Maddox before—alpha dogs who needed to rub others' faces in it to feel big. I wanted to stick up for the young kid, but that would go against keeping my head down. I finished waxing my blade and ignored the rest of their conversation.

"Coach expects you on the ice in five. Don't be late," Maddox said after finishing up with the tank. Maddox pushed off the lockers and headed for the tunnel, his new skates leaving clean white slices on the rubber matting.

I pulled on my helmet, the worn foam compressing against my temples. I fastened the cage, and the world snapped into a grid.

I stood, my knees protesting the shift from a crouch. At twenty-three, I was the old man in the room. Most of these kids were coming straight from juniors or high-level U-18s, their whole lives still ahead of them.

The walk down the tunnel was short. Concrete walls gave way to padded boards, and the muffled sounds of the locker room were replaced by the vast, hollow echo of the arena. I stepped through the gap in the boards and onto the ice.

For a second, I stood there.

The cold hit my face like a baptism—clean, mineral-sharp, almost sweet. The arena wasn't a pro barn. I'd grown up in those, with their Jumbotrons and endless tiers of seats that climbed into darkness, the roar of fifteen thousand strangers who thought they knew me. Oakridge's rink was different. Smaller. The opposite of wide, it was *tall*. The stands rose from the glass at a steep angle, like the walls of a canyon carved by some ancient glacier. When this place filled with bodies, they'd be right on top of you, breathing down your neck, close enough to hear the scrape of every edge and the grunt of every check. The effect was borderline claustrophobic.

I loved it immediately.

Half a dozen other walk-ons were skating tentative laps. The ice was freshly flooded, a perfect, unbroken sheet of white under the bright lights. No logos yet—just pure, clean surface waiting to be marked. My blades bit in with that first stride, the sound a crisp tear that echoed off the high ceiling. I pushed off, gliding, letting my legs remember the rhythm. Left, right, crossover, glide. The knot in my stomach loosened with every stride.

This was why I was here. Not for the degree, not really. Not even for the anonymity, though that mattered. I was here because the ice was the one place I'd ever felt like myself. Before the cameras, before Chet Finlay turned me into a brand, before the *Ice Kings* franchise made my face into something that belonged to everyone but me—there had been this. Just this. The cold air, the smooth surface, the physics of blade and momentum. On the ice, I wasn't a product or a disappointment or a cautionary tale. I was my movement. My edges, my speed, my choices.

The head coach, a man named Sterling with a face like a worn catcher's mitt, blew a whistle that cut through the murmur of skates and sticks. We converged at the center circle.

"Welcome to Oakridge." His voice was a low gravel that carried without effort. "For the next two hours, you're not freshmen or transfers. You're hockey players. We need skaters who are smart, disciplined, and relentless. We're a defense-first program. If you want to be a hero, you're in the wrong barn. We win games in the corners and in front of our own net."

His gaze swept over us. I kept my eyes forward, my posture neutral—just another hopeful, just another number.

"We're watching everything. How you skate, how you listen, how you finish a drill. Show us you belong here. First up: laps. On the whistle."

The whistle blew, sharp, and we were off.

A test. Not of speed, but of conditioning and control. Forward, backward, crossovers, pivots. My lungs burned, the cold air scraping my throat. I settled into a rhythm, keeping my strides clean and efficient, my upper body still. I wasn't the fastest guy out there. A few of the younger kids shot out like they were spring-loaded, all frantic energy, burning themselves out in the first five minutes. I let them go. I found a pace in the middle of the pack, focused on the skater in front of me, on the clean, rhythmic scrape of my own blades.

Don't stand out. Don't disappear. Just be solid.

After the skating drills came puck handling. Weaving through cones, stickhandling in tight spaces. My hands felt good—too good. The puck snapped to my blade like it was magnetized, responding to the smallest adjustments of my wrists. Muscle memory buried deep, a language I hadn't spoken in years but hadn't forgotten. On one sequence through the cones, I felt my body wanting to add a flourish—a quick toe-drag, a behind-the-back pull—the kind of flashy move great cinematic closeups. I caught myself, forced my hands to stay simple, and finished the drill clean but unremarkable.

Control what you can control.

I kept my head up, eyes scanning the ice even when there was nothing to see. Habit. Or maybe self-preservation.

Always know where your exits are.

It was during a one-on-one drill that I felt it.

A shift in the air. The low-grade hum of being observed sharpened into a single, focused point. I wrote it off at first. Of course, we were being watched—that was the whole point of a tryout. Coach Sterling and his assistants stood by the boards, clipboards in hand, faces unreadable. A few assistant coaches were scattered in the first rows behind the bench, men in team jackets with stoic expressions.

I was skating back to the line, heart pounding from the drill. I'd made a decent play—didn't score, but I'd protected the puck, maneuvered around the defenseman with a sharp cut to my forehand, and put a hard, low shot on net that the goalie had to scramble for. A good, solid, unremarkable play. The kind of play that kept you employed but didn't get you noticed.

As I came to a stop, I chanced a look up into the stands.

The seats were mostly empty, a sea of dark blue plastic rising into shadow. But halfway up, right on the center line, a single figure sat alone.

He wasn't wearing a team jacket or holding a clipboard. Just a guy in a gray hoodie, leaning forward with his elbows on his knees, hands steepled in front of his face. The steep angle of the canyon walls made it feel like he was hovering directly above me, a gargoyle perched on a cathedral ledge. Even from this distance, I could feel the weight of his stillness. He wasn't scanning the group. He wasn't watching the drill.

He was watching *me*.

A cold spike of adrenaline, entirely separate from the athletic burn in my muscles, shot through me. My stomach clenched. Old instincts—ones I'd thought years of therapy and six hundred miles had buried—flared to life. The reflexive cataloging of a face. The assessment of a threat. *Is that a camera? A phone? Does he recognize me? How did he find me here?*

He was just some student, bored, killing time between classes. Maybe a friend of one of the other players. Nothing to do with me. I was in a helmet, hiding behind a cage.

The whistle blew. Another drill. Three-on-twos, rushing the net. I fell back into the rhythm, my mind screamed at me to focus. *Read the play. Find the open man. Backcheck.*

My body went through the motions, but a part of my awareness stayed snagged on that figure in the stands. Like skating with a burr in my sock—a constant, irritating point of pressure.

On the rush, I found myself with the puck in the high slot. Open ice ahead. The goalie cheating to his glove side, leaving the five-hole vulnerable. My hands knew what to do—a quick fake, a snap shot low—but my brain screamed *don't.* Don't make a highlight. Don't give anyone a reason to look twice.

I dumped the puck into the corner and peeled off for a line change.

Sterling blew his whistle. "Water break. Two minutes."

We skated to the bench in a loose cluster. I grabbed a bottle from the rack, tilted my head back, and lifted the bottom of my cage just enough to get the nozzle underneath. The water hit the back of my throat. For those few seconds, the world narrowed to just breath and hydration and the burn in my legs.

I squeezed the bottle, sending a stream of water across my overheated face, then lowered the cage back into place. The grid snapped over my vision—steel bars sectioning the world into manageable pieces.

I tossed the bottle back and pushed off toward center ice.

The scrimmage was the last part of the tryout. Full ice, two teams of cobbled-together hopefuls. I was on the 'skins' team, the cold arena air biting through my base layer. I played my game. Kept it simple. Dumped the puck in deep, finished my checks, got back on defense. I focused on being a 200-foot player—pressuring the puck carrier, clogging the passing lanes, backchecking like my roster spot depended on it.

Solid. Dependable. Forgettable.

Maddox slid a pass to me as we crossed the blue line, too hard, too far in front. I stretched, my stick tipping the puck, redirecting it. I chased it down, a defenseman hot on my heels.

I checked my shoulder, mapping the ice in a split second. I saw the defenseman over-committing to the body hit, eyes on my numbers rather than the puck. Instead of trying to force a play to the net, I saw our third man, Davies, streaking toward the far post.

I stopped hard, my edges biting deep to spray up a wall of ice, and feathered a backhand pass—using just the right amount of soft hands to ensure it landed flat on his tape.

He had a wide-open net. He buried it. And I got slammed into the glass.

A good play. A smart play. The kind of play that won teams games. 'An assist is better than a selfish shot'—the words of one of my peewee coaches shot through my memory. I peeled off toward the boards, and despite every cell in my body screaming not to, my eyes flicked up to the stands again.

The guy was still there. Still leaning forward. But now his hands were down, and I could see his face more. He hadn't moved a muscle. Who the hell was he?

Maddox skated past, bumping my shoulder. "You ever gonna shoot the puck, Calloway? Or just donate it?"

"I made the smart play," I said, without glancing at him.

"You dumped it." His voice dripped with condescension. "There's a difference."

He was right. And the fact that he was right—that this cocky college kid could see what I'd done, could see the fear dressed up as strategy—made my skin crawl.

The coach's whistle blew. Over.

A wave of exhaustion so profound it was almost peaceful washed over me. We skated to center ice, gathering around Coach Sterling one last time. My thighs screamed. My lungs felt scraped raw.

"Good work today." Sterling's eyes were dark chips of granite, his expression giving nothing away. "We saw some things we liked. We saw some things we didn't. The roster will be posted outside the locker room tomorrow morning at eight. If your name is on it, practice is at three. If it's not, thank you for coming out."

That was it. No feedback. No encouragement. A clean, brutal cut. I appreciated the efficiency.

We tapped our sticks on the ice in a ragged salute and drifted toward the exit. As I skated off, legs like lead, I couldn't help it.

One last look.

The figure in the gray hoodie was moving. Arms stretched overhead as he stood—taller than I'd thought, lanky, with a mess of dark hair visible even from this distance. No longer watching the ice. Turned toward the exit at the top of the aisle.

A student. Just a student who'd wandered in, watched for a bit, and left when he got bored. I felt a wave of relief so strong it made me lightheaded. I'd built the whole thing up in my head—a phantom from my past projected onto a stranger. The pressure I'd felt wasn't his. It was mine. A ghost I'd brought with me to Oakridge.

I shook my head, disgusted with myself, and stepped off the ice onto the rubber mats, the familiar clomp of my skates grounding me. First the vending-machine kid, now me. Everyone was terrified of their own shadow today.

***

In the locker room, no one talked much. We were all rivals, but we'd shared something—a two-hour trial by fire. We stripped off our gear in near silence, the only sounds the rip of Velcro and the clatter of equipment being tossed into bags.

I worked methodically, reversing my earlier ritual. Wiping down my blades. Stowing my helmet. The smell of sweat was stronger now, mixed with the damp chill of the ice. I was one of the last to the showers, the hot water a blessed relief on my aching muscles. I stood under the spray for a long time, forehead pressed against the cool tile, letting the water wash away the grime and, I hoped, the lingering paranoia.

By the time I was dressed—jeans, black T-shirt, old Bruins hoodie—the locker room was almost empty. The vending-machine freshman was sitting on a bench, staring at his phone, face pale. I slung my bag over my shoulder.

"Calloway, right?" His voice was quiet.

"Yeah."

"Jayceon Davies." He extended his hand. I gripped it and immediately regretted it—the guy's grip could pulverize concrete. He seemed oblivious to his own strength. "You played well. That pass on the three-on-two was sick."

"You finished it. That's the part that matters."

He offered a small, grateful smile. "Hope I see you tomorrow, man."

"You too." I meant it.

I pushed through the door and walked out into the main corridor of the arena. Empty now, the lights dimmed to a pale amber glow. My footsteps echoed off the concrete. My beat-up hockey bag felt like it weighed a thousand pounds. All I wanted was my apartment, a microwaved burrito, and twelve hours of sleep. The anxiety from the tryout had been replaced by a deep, physical weariness that was almost peaceful.

I'd done it. I'd survived.

I rounded the corner toward the main exit, already thinking about the walk across the quad, the chilly January air, my empty apartment waiting with its blank walls and careful absence of anything personal—

And stopped dead.

Leaning against the wall, right beside the doors, was the guy from the stands.

My relief evaporated. The exhaustion vanished, replaced by a sharp, cold clarity. He was *waiting*. He'd come down from the stands, found the exit, and positioned himself where I'd have to pass.

Up close, he was all sharp angles and deliberate presence. Tall—maybe six feet—and lean in the way of runners or dancers, people who used their bodies as instruments. The gray hoodie said OAKRIDGE THEATRE in faded letters across the chest. His hair was a chaotic mess of wavy black. His face was the kind you'd call interesting before you'd call it handsome—strong nose, defined jaw, dark eyes that caught the dim light and held it.

Those eyes were fixed on me. Had been fixed on me since I'd stepped into the corridor.

He pushed off the wall. A slow, deliberate movement. Controlled. The way an actor moves when they want you to watch them move.

"Seventy-three." His voice was a low tenor. "I was wondering when you'd be done."